She clearly had no idea how powerful lust could be. Her first experience would hit her like a tidal wave.

It would be so easy to seduce her, Kasimir thought. One kiss, one stroke. Josie would be totally unprepared for the fire. But she would be an apt student. He felt that in the tremble of her hand, as he slid the ten-carat diamond ring on her finger. In the rosy blush on her cheeks as she placed the plain gold band on his. All he would have to do was kiss her, touch her, and she'd be lost in a maelstrom of pleasure she would not know how to defend against. She'd fall like a ripe peach into his hands.

Except he couldn't. Wouldn't.

S0-ABB-207

Dear Reader,

We know how much you love Harlequin® Presents®, so this month we wanted to treat you to something extra special—a second classic story by the same author for free!

Once you have finished reading *A Reputation for Revenge,* just turn the page for another sinfully sensual tale of revenge from Jennie Lucas.

This month, indulge yourself with double the reading pleasure!

With love,

The Presents Editors

Jennie Lucas

A REPUTATION FOR REVENGE

PRINCES
Untamed

HARLEQUIN PRESENTS®

If you purchased this book without a cover you should be aware that this book is stolen property. It was reported as "unsold and destroyed" to the publisher, and neither the author nor the publisher has received any payment for this "stripped book."

ISBN-13: 978-0-373-13130-3

A REPUTATION FOR REVENGE

Copyright © 2013 by Harlequin Books S.A.

The publisher acknowledges the copyright holder of the individual works as follows:

A REPUTATION FOR REVENGE
Copyright © 2013 by Jennie Lucas

THE GREEK BILLIONAIRE'S BABY REVENGE
Copyright © 2007 by Jennie Lucas

Recycling programs for this product may not exist in your area.

All rights reserved. Except for use in any review, the reproduction or utilization of this work in whole or in part in any form by any electronic, mechanical or other means, now known or hereafter invented, including xerography, photocopying and recording, or in any information storage or retrieval system, is forbidden without the written permission of the publisher, Harlequin Enterprises Limited, 225 Duncan Mill Road, Don Mills, Ontario M3B 3K9, Canada.

This is a work of fiction. Names, characters, places and incidents are either the product of the author's imagination or are used fictitiously, and any resemblance to actual persons, living or dead, business establishments, events or locales is entirely coincidental.

This edition published by arrangement with Harlequin Books S.A.

For questions and comments about the quality of this book, please contact us at CustomerService@Harlequin.com.

® and TM are trademarks of Harlequin Enterprises Limited or its corporate affiliates. Trademarks indicated with ® are registered in the United States Patent and Trademark Office, the Canadian Trade Marks Office and in other countries.

Printed in U.S.A.

CONTENTS

PRINCES *Untamed*

Only the most innocent touch can melt their ice-cold hearts

Introducing the notoriously ruthless and devilishly sexy Princes Kasimir and Vladimir Xendov: two brothers torn apart by the past, bitter rivals in the present.

Vladimir's enemy is most definitely in his sight—he can't take his eyes off her! But she's played her final card…and he knows he's going to win.

DEALING HER FINAL CARD

February 2013

Kasimir will consume everything in his path on his road to revenge…even if the obstacle standing in his way is 5 feet 5 inches of pure desire.

A REPUTATION FOR REVENGE

March 2013

Other titles by Jennie Lucas available in ebook:

Harlequin Presents®

A REPUTATION FOR REVENGE

CHAPTER ONE

TWO DAYS AFTER Christmas, in the soft pink Honolulu dawn, Josie Dalton stood alone on a deserted sidewalk and tilted her head to look up, up, up to the top of the skyscraper across the street, all the way to his penthouse in the clouds.

She exhaled. She couldn't do this. *Couldn't.* Marry him? Impossible.

Except she had to.

I'm not scared, Josie repeated to herself, hitching her tattered backpack higher on her shoulder. *I'd marry the devil himself to save my sister.*

But the truth was she'd never really thought it would come to this. She'd assumed the police would ride in and save the day. Instead, the police in Seattle, then Honolulu, had laughed in her face.

"Your older sister wagered her virginity in a poker game?" the first said incredulously. "In some kind of lovers' game?"

"Let me get this straight. Your sister's billionaire ex-boyfriend *won* her?" The second scowled. "I have real crimes to deal with, Miss Dalton. Get out of here before I decide to arrest *you* for illegal gambling."

Now, Josie shivered in the cool, wet dawn. No one was coming to save Bree. Just her.

She narrowed her eyes. Fine. She should take responsibility. She was the one who'd gotten Bree into trouble in the first place. If Josie hadn't stupidly accepted her boss's invitation to the poker game, her sister wouldn't have had to step in and save her.

Clever Bree, six years older, had been a childhood card prodigy and a con artist in her teens. But after a decade away from that dangerous life, working instead as an honest, impoverished housekeeper, her sister's card skills had become rusty. How else to explain the fact that, instead of winning, Bree had lost everything to her hated ex-boyfriend with the turn of a single card?

Vladimir Xendzov had separated the sisters, forcibly sending Josie back to the mainland on his private jet. She'd spent her last paycheck to fly back, desperate to get Bree out of his clutches. For forty-four hours now, since the dreadful night of the game, Josie had only managed to hold it together because she knew that, should everything else fail, she had one guaranteed fallback plan.

But now she actually had to fall back on the plan, it felt like falling on a sword.

Josie looked up again at the top of the skyscraper. The windows of the penthouse gleamed red, like fire, above the low-hanging clouds of Honolulu.

She'd caused her sister to lose her freedom. She would save her—by selling herself in marriage to Vladimir Xendzov's greatest enemy.

His younger brother.

The enemy of my enemy is my friend, she repeated to herself. And, considering the way the Xendzov brothers had tried to destroy each other for the past ten years, Kasimir Xendzov must be her new best friend. Right?

A lump rose in her throat.

I would marry the devil himself...

Slowly, Josie forced her feet off the sidewalk. Her legs wobbled as she crossed the street. She dodged a passing tour bus, flinching as it honked angrily.

There was no backing out now.

"Can I help you?" the doorman said inside the lobby, eyeing her messy ponytail, wrinkled T-shirt and cheap flip-flops.

Josie licked her dry lips. "I'm here to get married. To one of your residents."

He didn't bother to conceal his incredulity. "*You?* Are going to marry someone who lives *here?*"

She nodded. "Kasimir Xendzov."

His jaw dropped. "You mean His *Highness?* The *prince?*" he spluttered, gesticulating wildly. "Get out of here before I call the police!"

"Look, please just call him, all right? Tell him Josie Dalton is here and I've changed my mind. My answer is now yes."

"*Call* him? I'll do nothing of the sort." The doorman pinched his nose with his thumb and finger. "You must be delusional...if you think you can just walk in off the street..."

Josie rummaged through her backpack.

"His Highness's presence here is secret. He is here on *vacation...*"

"See?" she said desperately, holding out a business card. "He gave me this three days ago. When he proposed to me. At a salad bar near Waikiki."

"Salad bar," the doorman snorted. "As if the prince would ever..." He saw the embossed seal, and snatched the card from her hand. Turning over the card, he read the hard masculine scrawl on the back: *For when you change your mind.* "But you're not his type," he said faintly.

"I know," Josie sighed. Twenty pounds overweight, frumpy and unstylish, she was painfully aware that she was no man's type. Fortunately Kasimir Xendzov wished to marry her for reasons that had nothing to do with love—or even lust. "Just call him, will you?"

The man reached for the phone on his desk. He dialed. Turning away, he spoke in a low voice. A few moments later, he faced Josie with an utterly bewildered expression.

"His bodyguard says you're to go straight up," he said in shock. He pointed his finger towards an elevator. "Thirty-ninth floor. And, um, congratulations, miss."

"Thank you," Josie murmured, tugging her knapsack higher on her shoulder as she turned away. She felt the doorman watching her as she crossed the elegant lobby, her flip-flops echoing against the marble floor. She numbly got on the elevator. On the thirty-ninth floor, the door opened with a ding. Cautiously, she crept out into a hallway.

"Welcome, Miss Dalton." Two large, grim-looking bodyguards were waiting for her. In a quick, professional motion, one of them frisked her as the other one rifled through her bag.

"What are you checking for?" Josie said with an awkward laugh. "You think I would bring a hand grenade? To a wedding proposal?"

The bodyguards did not return her smile. "She's clear," one of them said, and handed her back the knapsack. "Please go in, Miss Dalton."

"Um. Thanks." Looking at the imposing door, she clutched her bag against her chest. "He's in there?"

He nodded sternly. "His Highness is expecting you."

Josie swallowed hard. "Right. I mean, great. I mean…" She turned back to them. "He's a good guy, right? A good employer? He can be trusted?"

The bodyguards stared back at her, their faces impassive.

"His Highness is expecting you," the first one repeated in an expressionless voice. "Please go in."

"Okay." *You robot,* she added silently, irritated.

Whatever. She didn't need reassurance. She'd just listen to her intuition. To her heart.

Which meant Josie was *really* in trouble. There was a reason her dying father had left her a large parcel of Alaskan land in an unbreakable trust, which she could not receive until she was either twenty-five—three years from now—or married. Even when she was a child, Black Jack Dalton had known his naive, trusting younger daughter needed all the help she could get. To say she could be naive about people was an understatement.

But it's a good quality, Bree had told her sadly two days ago. *I wish I had more of it.*

Bree. Josie could only imagine what her older sister was going through right now, as a prisoner of that other billionaire tycoon, Kasimir Xendzov's brother. Closing her eyes, she took a deep breath.

"For Bree," she whispered, and flung open the penthouse door.

The lavish foyer was empty. Stepping nervously across the marble floor, hearing the echo of her steps, she looked up at a soaring chandelier illuminating the sweeping staircase. This penthouse was like a mansion in the sky, she thought in awe.

Josie's lips parted when she saw the view through the floor-to-ceiling windows. Crossing the foyer to the great room, she looked out at the twinkling lights of the still-dark city, and beyond that, pink and orange sunrise sparkling across the Pacific Ocean.

"So...you changed your mind."

His low, masculine purr came from behind her. She stiffened then, bracing herself, slowly turned around.

Prince Kasimir Xendzov's incredible good looks still hit her like a fierce blow. He was even more impossibly handsome than she remembered. He was tall, around six foot three, with broad shoulders and a hard-muscled body. His blue eyes were electric against tanned skin and dark hair. The expensive cut of his dark suit and tie, and the gleaming leather of his black shoes spoke of money—while the ruthlessness in his eyes and chiseled jawline screamed *power*.

In spite of her efforts, Josie was briefly thunderstruck.

Normally, she had no problems talking to people. As far as she was concerned, there was no such thing as a stranger. But Kasimir left her tongue-tied. No man this handsome had ever paid her the slightest notice. In fact, she wasn't sure there *was* any other man on earth with Kasimir's breathtaking masculine beauty. Looking into his darkly handsome face, she almost forgot to breathe.

"The last time I saw you, you said you'd never marry me." Kasimir slowly looked her over, from her flip-flops to her jeans and T-shirt. "For *any* price."

Josie's cheeks turned pink. "Maybe I was a bit hasty," she stammered.

"You threw your drink in my face."

"It was an accident!" she protested.

He lifted an incredulous dark eyebrow. "You jumped up and ran out of the restaurant."

"You just surprised me!" Three nights ago, on Christmas Eve, Kasimir had called her at the Hale Ka'nani Hotel, where she was working as a housekeeper. "My sister told me to never talk to you," she'd blurted out when he introduced himself. "I'm hanging up."

"Then you'll miss the best offer of your life," he'd replied silkily. He'd asked her to meet him at a hole-in-the-wall restaurant near Waikiki Beach. In spite of knowing he was forbidden—or perhaps because of it—she was intrigued by his mysterious proposal. And then she'd been even more shocked to find out he'd meant a real proposal. *Marriage.*

"You ran away from me," Kasimir said quietly, taking a step towards her, "as if you were being chased by the devil himself."

She swallowed.

"Because I did think you were the devil," she whispered.

His blue eyes narrowed in disbelief. "This is your way of saying you'll marry me?"

She shook her head. "You don't understand," she choked out. "You…"

Her throat closed. How could she explain that even though he and his brother had ruined their lives ten years ago, she'd still been electrified by Kasimir's bright blue eyes when he'd asked her to marry him? How to explain that, even though she knew it was only to get his hands on her land, she'd been overwhelmed by too many years of yearning for some man, any man, to notice her—and that she'd been tempted to blurt out *Yes,* betraying all her ideals about love and marriage?

How could she possibly explain such pathetic, naive stupidity? She couldn't.

"Why did you change your mind?" he asked in a low voice. "Do you need the money?"

They did need to pay off the dangerous men who'd pursued them for ten years, demanding payment of their dead father's long-ago debts. But Josie shook her head.

"Then is it the title of princess that you want?"

Josie threw him a startled glance. "Really?"

"Many women dream of it."

"Not me." She shook her head with a snort. "Besides, my sister told me your title's worthless. You might be the grandson of a Russian prince, but it's not like you actually own any land—"

Whoops. She cut off in midsentence at his glare.

"We once owned hundreds of thousands of acres in Russia," he said coldly. "And we owned the homestead in Alaska for nearly a hundred years, since my great-grandmother fled Siberia. It is rightfully ours."

"Sorry, but your brother sold your homestead to my father fair and square!"

He took a step towards her.

"Against my will," he said softly. "Without my knowledge."

Josie took an unwilling step back from the icy glitter in his blue eyes. A self-made billionaire, Kasimir Xendzov was known to be a ruthless, heartless playboy whose main interest, even more than dating supermodels or adding to his pile of money, was destroying his older brother, who had cheated him out of their business partnership right before it would have made him hundreds of millions of dollars.

"Are you afraid of me?" he asked suddenly.

"No," she lied, "why would I be?"

"There are…rumors about me. That I am more than ruthless. That I am—" he tilted his head, his blue eyes bright "—half-insane, driven mad by my hunger for revenge."

Her mouth went dry. "It's not true." She gulped, then said weakly, "Um, is it?"

He gave a low, threatening laugh. "If it were, I would hardly admit it." He turned away, pacing a step before he looked back at her. "So you've changed your mind. But has it occurred to you," he said softly, "that I might have changed my mind about marrying *you?*"

Josie looked up with an intake of breath. "You—wouldn't!"

He shrugged. "Your rejection of me three days ago was definitive."

Fear, real fear, rushed through Josie's heart. She'd gambled her last money to come here. Without Kasimir's help, Bree would be lost. She'd be Vladimir Xendzov's possession. His *slave.* Forever. Her shoulders felt tight as hot tears rushed behind her eyes. Desperately, she grabbed his arm.

"No—please! You said you'd do anything to get the land back. You said you made a promise to your dying father. You—" She frowned, suddenly distracted by the hard muscle of his biceps. "Jeez, how much weight lifting do you do?"

He looked at her. Blushing, she dropped his arm. She took a deep breath.

"Just tell me. Do you still want to marry me?"

Kasimir's handsome face was impassive. "I need to understand your reason. If it's not to be a princess…"

She gave a choked laugh. "As if I'd marry someone for a worthless title!"

His dark eyebrow lifted. "For your information, my title isn't worthless. It's an asset. You'd be surprised how many people are impressed by it."

"You mean you use it as a shameless marketing tool for your business interests."

His lips curved with amusement. "So you do understand."

"I hope you're not expecting me to bow."

"I don't want you to bow." He looked up, his blue eyes intent. "I just want you to marry me. Right now. Today."

Staring at his gorgeous face, Josie's heart stopped. "So you do still want to marry me?"

He gave her a slow-rising smile that made his eyes crinkle. "Of course I want to marry you. It's all I've wanted."

He was looking down at her...as if he cared.

Of course he cares, she told herself savagely. *He cares about getting his family's land back. That's it.*

But when he looked at her like that, it was too easy to forget that. Her heart pounded. She felt...desired.

Josie tried to convince herself she didn't feel it. She didn't feel a strange tangle of tension and breathless need. She *didn't.*

Kasimir reached out a hand to touch her cheek. "But tell me what changed your mind."

The warm sensuality of his fingers against her skin made her tremble. No man had touched her so intimately. His fingertips were calloused—clearly he was accustomed to hard work—but they were tapered, sensitive fingers of a poet.

But Prince Kasimir Xendzov was no poet. Trembling, she looked down at his strong wrist, at his tanned, thick forearm laced with dark hair. He was a fighter. A warrior. He could crush her with one hand.

"Josie."

"My sister," she whispered, then stopped, her throat dry.

"Bree changed your mind?" Dropping his hand, he walked around her. "I find that hard to believe."

She took a deep breath.

"Your brother kidnapped her," she choked out. "I want you to save her."

She waited for him to express shock, elation, rage, *something*. But his expression didn't change.

"You…" He frowned, narrowing his eyes. "Wait. Vladimir *kidnapped* her?"

She bit her lip, then her shoulders slumped. "Well, I guess technically," she said in a small voice, "you could say she wagered herself to him in a card game. And lost."

His lip curled. "It was a lovers' game. No woman would wager herself otherwise." His eyes narrowed. "My brother always had a weakness for her. After ten years apart, they're no doubt deliriously happy they've made up their quarrel."

"Are you crazy?" she cried. "Bree hates him!"

"What!"

Josie shook her head. "He *forced* her to go with him."

His handsome face suddenly looked cheerful. "I see."

"And it's all my fault." A lump rose in her throat, and she covered her eyes. "The night after you proposed, my boss invited me to join a private poker game. I hoped I could win enough to pay off my father's old debts, and I snuck out while Bree was sleeping." She swallowed. "She never would have let me go. She forbade me ever to gamble, plus she didn't trust Mr. Hudson."

"Why?"

"I think it was mostly the way he hired us from Seattle, sight unseen, with one-way plane tickets to Hawaii. At the time, we were both too desperate to care, but…" She sighed. "She was right. There was something kind of…weird about it. But I didn't listen." She lifted her tearful gaze to his. "Bree lost everything on the turn of a single card. Because of me."

He looked down at her, his expression unreadable. "And you think *I* can save her."

"I know you can. You're the only one powerful enough to stand up to him. The only one on earth willing to battle with Vladimir Xendzov. Because you hate him the most." She took a deep breath. "Please," she whispered. "You can take my land. I don't care. But if you don't save Bree, I don't know how I'll live with myself."

Kasimir stared at her for a long moment.

"Here." He reached for the heavy backpack on her shoulder. "Let me take that."

"You don't need to—"

"You're swaying on your feet," he said softly. "You look as if you haven't slept in days. No wonder. Flying to Seattle and back…"

Without her bag weighing her down, she felt so light she almost felt dizzy. "I told you I went to Seattle?"

He froze, then relaxed as he looked back at her. "Of course you did," he said smoothly. "How else would I know?"

Yes, indeed, how would he? After almost no sleep for two days, she was starting to get confused. Rubbing her cheek with her shoulder, she confessed, "I am a little tired. And thirsty."

"Come with me. I'll get you a drink."

"Why are you being nice to me?" she blurted out, not moving.

He frowned. "Why wouldn't I be nice to you?"

"It always seems that the more handsome a man is, the more of a jerk he is. And you are very, very…"

Their eyes locked, and her throat cut off. Her cheeks burned as she muttered, "Never mind."

He gave her a crooked grin. "Whatever your sister might have told you about me, I'm not the devil. But I am being remiss in my manners. Let's get you that drink."

Carrying her backpack over his shoulder, he turned down the hallway. Josie watched him go, her eyes tracing the muscular shape of his back beneath his jacket and chiseled rear end.

Then she shook her head, irritated with herself. Why did she have to blurt out every single thought in her head? Why couldn't she just show discipline and quiet restraint, like Bree? Why did she have to be such a goofball all the time, the kind of girl who'd start conversations with random strangers on any topic from orchids to cookie recipes, then give them her bus money?

This time wasn't my fault, she thought mutinously, following him down the hall. He was far too handsome. No woman could possibly manage sensible thinking beneath the laser-like focus of those blue eyes!

Kasimir led her to a high-ceilinged room lined with leather-bound books on one side, and floor-to-ceiling windows with a view of the city on the other. Tossing her backpack on a long table of polished inlaid wood, he walked over to the wet bar on the other side of the library. "What will you have?"

"Tap water, please," she said faintly.

He frowned back at her. "I have sparkling mineral water. Or I could order coffee…"

"Just water. With ice, if you want to be fancy."

He returned with a glass.

"Thanks," she said. She glugged down the icy, delicious water.

He watched her. "You're an unusual girl, Josie Dalton."

Unusual didn't sound good. She wiped her mouth. "I am?" she echoed uncertainly, lowering the glass.

"It's refreshing to be with a woman who makes absolutely no effort to impress me."

She snorted. "Trying to impress you would be a waste of time. I know a man like you would never be interested in a girl like me—not *genuinely* interested," she mumbled.

He looked down at her, his blue eyes breathtaking.

"You're selling yourself short," he said softly, and Josie felt it again—that strange flash of heat.

She swallowed. "You're being nice, but I know there's no point in pretending to be something I'm not." She sighed. "Even if I sometimes wish I could."

"Unusual. And honest." Turning, he went to the wet bar and poured himself a short glass of amber-colored liquid. He returned, then took a slow, thoughtful sip.

"All right. I'll get your sister back for you," he said abruptly.

"You will!" If there was something strange about his tone, Josie was too weak with relief to notice. "When?"

"After we're wed. Our marriage will last until the land in Alaska is legally transferred to me." He looked straight into her eyes. "And I'll bring her to you, and set you both free. Is that what you want?"

Isn't that what she'd just said? "Yes," she cried.

Setting down his drink on the polished wooden table, he held out his hand. "Deal."

Slowly, she reached out her hand. She felt the hot, calloused hollow of his palm, felt his strong fingers interlace with hers. A tremble raced through her. Swallowing, she lifted her gaze to his handsome face, to those electric-blue eyes, and it was like staring straight at the sun.

"I hope it won't be too painful for you," she stammered, "being married to me."

His hand tightened over hers. "As you'll be my only wife, ever," he said softly, "I think I'll enjoy you a great deal."

"Your only wife *ever?*" Her brow furrowed. "That seems a little pessimistic of you. I mean—" she licked her lips awkwardly "—I'm sure you'll meet someone someday…"

Kasimir gave a low, humorless laugh.

"Josie, my sweet innocent one—" he looked at her with a smile that didn't reach his eyes "—you are the answer to my every prayer."

Prince Kasimir Xendzov hadn't started the feud ten years ago with his brother.

As a child, he'd idolized Vladimir. He'd been proud of his older brother, of his loving parents, of his family, of his home. Their great-grandfather had been one of the last great princes of Russia, before he'd died fighting for the White Army in Siberia, after sending his beloved wife and baby son to safety in Alaskan exile. Since then, for four generations, the Xendzovs had lived in self-sufficient poverty on an Alaskan homestead far from civilization. To Kasimir, it had been an enchanted winter kingdom.

But his older brother had hated the isolation and uncertainty—growing their own vegetables, canning them for winter, hunting rabbits for meat. He'd hated the lack of electricity and indoor plumbing. As Kasimir had played, battling with sticks as swords and jousting against the pine trees, Vladimir had buried his nose in business books and impatiently waited for their twice-a-year visits to Fairbanks. "Someday, I'll have a better life," he'd vowed, cursing as he scraped ice off the inside window of their shared room. "I'll buy clothes instead of making them. I'll drive a Ferrari. I'll fly around the world and eat at fine restaurants."

Kasimir, two years younger, had listened breathlessly. "Really, Volodya?" But though he'd idolized his older brother, he hadn't understood Vladimir's restlessness. Kasimir loved their home. He liked going hunting with their father and listening to him read books in Russian by the wood-burning stove at night. He liked chopping wood for their mother, feeling the roughness of an ax handle in his hand, and having the satisfaction of seeing the pile of wood climb steadily against the side of the log cabin. To him, the wild Alaskan forest wasn't isolating. It was freeing.

Home. Family. Loyalty. Those were the things Kasimir cared about.

Right after their father died unexpectedly, Vladimir got news he'd been accepted to the best mining college in St. Petersburg, Russia. Their widowed mother had wept with joy, for it had been their father's dream. But with no money for tuition, Vladimir had put off school and gone to work at a northern mine to save money.

Two years later, Kasimir had applied to the same college for one reason: he felt someone had to watch his brother's back. He didn't expect that he'd have the money to leave Alaska for many years, so he'd been surprised tuition money for them both was suddenly found.

It was only later he'd discovered Vladimir had convinced their mother to sell their family's last precious asset, a jeweled necklace hundreds of years old that had once belonged to their great-grandmother, to a collector.

He'd felt betrayed, but he'd tried to forgive. He'd told himself that Vladimir had done it for their good.

Right after college, Kasimir had wanted to return to Alaska to take care of their mother, who'd become ill. Vladimir convinced him that they should start their own business instead, a mining business. "It's the only way we'll be sure to always have money to take care of her." Instead, when the banks wouldn't loan them enough money, Vladimir had convinced their mother to sell the six hundred and thirty-eight acres that had been in the Xendzov family for four generations—ever since Princess Xenia Petrovna Xendzova had arrived on Alaskan shores as a heartbroken exile, with a baby in her arms.

Kasimir had been furious. For the first time, he'd yelled at his brother. How could Vladimir have done such a thing behind his back, when he knew Kasimir had made a fervent deathbed promise to their father never to sell their land for any reason?

"Don't be selfish," Vladimir said coldly. "You think Mom could do all the work of the homestead without us?" And the money had in part paid for their mother to spend her last days at a hospice in Fairbanks. Kasimir's heart still twisted when he thought of it. His eyes narrowed.

The real reason they'd lost their home had been Vladimir's need to secure the most promising mining rights. What mattered: a younger brother's honor, a mother's home, or his need to establish their business with good cash flow and the best equipment?

"Don't worry," his brother had told him carelessly. "Once we're rich, you can easily buy it back again."

Kasimir set his jaw. He should have cut off all ties with his brother then and there. Instead, after their

mother died, he'd felt more bound than ever to his
brother—his only family. They strove for a year to build
their business partnership, working eighteen-hour days
in harsh winter conditions. Kasimir had been certain
they'd soon earn their first big payout, and buy their
home back again.

He hadn't known that Black Jack Dalton, the land's
buyer, had put the land in an irrevocable trust for his
child. Or that, as recompense for Kasimir's loyalty,
hard work and honesty, at the end of that year Vladimir would cut him out of the partnership and cheat him
out of his share of half a billion dollars.

Now, even though Kasimir had long since built up
his own billion-dollar mining company, his body still
felt tight with rage whenever he remembered how the
brother he'd adored had stabbed him in the back. Even
once Kasimir regained the land, he knew it would never
feel like home. Because he'd never be that same loyal,
loving, idealistic, stupid boy again.

No. Kasimir hadn't started the feud with his brother.
But he would end it.

"I'm the answer to your prayer?" a sweet, feminine
voice said, sounding puzzled. "How?"

Kasimir's eyes focused on Josie Dalton, standing in
front of him in the library of his Honolulu penthouse.

Her brown eyes were large and luminous, fringed
with long black lashes—but he saw the weary gray shadows beneath. Her skin was smooth and creamy—but
pale, and smudged on one cheek with dust. Her mouth
was full and pink—but the lower lip was chapped, as
if she'd spent the last two days chewing on it in worry.
Her light brown hair, which he could imagine thick and
lustrous tumbling down her shoulders, was half pulled
up in a disheveled ponytail.

Josie Dalton was not beautiful—no. But she was attractive in her own way, all youth and dewy innocence and overblown curves. He cut off the thought. He did not intend to let himself explore further.

He cleared his throat. "I've wanted our land back for a long time." His voice was low and gravelly, even to his own ears. "I'll make the arrangements for our wedding at once."

"What kind of arrangements?" She bit her lip anxiously, her soft brown eyes wide. "You don't mean a—a honeymoon?"

He looked at her sharply. She blushed. Her pink cheeks looked very charming. Who blushed anymore? "No. I don't mean a honeymoon."

"Good." Her cheeks burned red as she licked her lips. "I'm glad. I mean, I know this is a marriage in name only," she said hastily, holding up her hand. "And that's the only reason I could agree to…"

Her voice trailed off. Looking down, he caught her staring at his lips.

She was so unguarded, so innocent, he thought in wonder. Soft, pretty. Virginal. It would be very easy to seduce her.

Fortunately, she wasn't his type. His typical mistress was sleek and sophisticated. She lavished hours at the salon and the gym as though it was her full-time job. Véronique, in Paris. Farah, in Cairo. Oksana, in Moscow. Exotic women who knew how to seduce a man, who kept their lips red and their eyes lined with kohl, who greeted him at the door in silk lingerie and always had his favorite vodka chilled in the freezer. They welcomed him quickly into bed and spoke little, and even then, they never quite said what they meant. They were easy to slide into bed with.

And more importantly: they were very easy to leave.

Josie Dalton, on the other hand, expressed every thought—and if she forgot to say anything with words, her face said it anyway. She wore no makeup and clearly saw her hair as a chore, rather than an asset. In that baggy T-shirt and jeans, she obviously had no interest in fashion, or even in showing her figure to its best effect.

But Kasimir was glad she wasn't trying to lure him. Because he had no intention of seducing her. It would only complicate things that didn't need to be complicated. And it would hurt a tenderhearted young woman whom he didn't want to hurt—at least not more than he had to.

No. He was going to treat Josie Dalton like gold.

"So what other…arrangements…are you talking about?" she said haltingly. She lifted her chin, her eyes suddenly sparkling. "Maybe a wedding cake?"

This time, he really did laugh. "You want a cake?"

"I do love a good wedding cake, with buttercream-frosting roses…" she said wistfully.

"Your wish is my command, my lady," he said gravely.

Her expression drooped, and she shook her head with a sigh. "But I'd better not."

He rolled his eyes. "Don't tell me you're on a diet."

"Do I look like I watch my weight?" she snapped, then flushed guiltily. "Sorry. I'm a little grumpy. My flight ran out of meals before they reached my aisle, and I haven't eaten for twelve hours. I would have bought something at the airport but I only have three dollars and thought maybe I should save it."

Her voice trailed off. Kasimir had already turned away, crossing to the desk. He pressed the intercom button.

"Sir?"

"Send up a breakfast plate."

"Two, Your Highness?"

"Just one. But make it full and make it quick." He glanced back at Josie. "Anything special you'd like to eat, Miss Dalton?"

She gaped back at him, her mouth open.

He turned back to the intercom and said smoothly, "Just send everything you've got."

"Of course, sir."

Taking her unresisting hand, Kasimir led her to the soft blue sofa and sat beside her. She stared at him, apparently mesmerized, as if he'd done something truly shocking by simply ordering her some breakfast when she said she was hungry.

"You were saying," he prompted.

"I was?"

"Wedding cake. Why you don't want it."

"Right." Ripping her hand away nervously, she squared her shoulders and said in a firm voice, "This is just a business arrangement, so there's no point to wedding cake. Or a wedding dress. I think it's best for both of us—" she looked at him sideways, not quite meeting his eyes "—to keep our marriage on a strictly professional basis."

"As you wish." He lifted an eyebrow. "You are the bride. You are the boss."

She swallowed, turning her head to look at him nervously. "I am?"

He smiled. "I know that much about how a wedding works."

"Oh." Josie's face was the color of roses and cream as she chewed on her full, pink bottom lip. "You're being very, um—" her voice faltered and seemed to stumble "—nice to me."

Kasimir's smile twisted. "Will you stop saying that."

"But it's true."

"I'm being strictly professional, just as you said. Courtesy is part of business."

"Oh." She considered this, then slowly nodded. "In that case…"

"I'm glad you agree." He wondered if she would still accuse him of kindness if she knew the truth about what he intended to do with her. Or exactly why she was the answer to his prayer.

An hour ago, he'd been on the phone in his home office, barely listening to his VP of acquisitions drone on about how they could sabotage Vladimir's imminent takeover of Arctic Oil. He'd been too busy thinking about how his own recent plan to embarrass his brother had blown up in his face.

Kasimir had long despised Bree Dalton, the con artist he blamed for the first rift between the brothers ten years ago. All this time, he'd kept track of her from a distance, waiting for her to go back to her old ways (she hadn't) or to agree to let Josie marry him to get the land (she wouldn't, and he could go to hell for asking).

Kasimir had finally decided to try another way: Josie herself.

Until they'd met at the Salad Shack a few days ago, all he'd known of Josie was in a file from a private investigator, with a grainy photograph. Six months ago in Seattle, the man had tested her by dropping a wallet full of cash in the aisle of a grocery store in front of her. Josie had run two blocks after the man's car, catching up with him at a stoplight, to breathlessly give the wallet back, untouched. "Girl's so honest, she's a nut," the investigator had grumbled.

So finally, Kasimir had come to a decision. Knowing his brother was recuperating from a recent car-racing injury in Oahu with a private weekly poker game at the Hale Ka'nani, he'd bribed the general manager of the resort, Greg Hudson, to hire the Dalton sisters as housekeepers. He'd hoped Vladimir would have a run-in with Bree Dalton, causing him a humiliating scene, but that was just an amusement. Kasimir's real goal in coming here had been to try to negotiate for the land, and the requisite marriage, directly with Josie Dalton.

He shouldn't have been surprised that she'd flung her soda at him and run out. Or that, according to the report he'd gotten from Greg Hudson, not only had there been no screaming match between Vladimir and Bree, they'd apparently fallen into each other's arms at the poker game. Bree had won back the entire amount of her sister's wager, then promptly accepted Vladimir's offer to a single-card draw between them—a million dollars versus possession of Bree.

Reintroducing the formerly engaged couple to happiness after ten years of estrangement, had never been Kasimir's plan. For the past day and a half, he'd been grinding his teeth in fury. He'd spent last night dancing at a club, women hitting on him right and left, until even that started to irritate him, and he'd gone home early—and alone.

Then, like a miracle, he'd been woken from sleep with the news that Josie Dalton was here and wished to marry him after all.

And now, here she was. He had her. She'd just changed his whole world—forever.

He could have kissed her.

"I will be happy to get you a cake," he said fervently. "And a designer wedding gown, and a ten-carat diamond ring." Reaching for her hand, he kissed it, then looked into her eyes. "Just tell me what you want, and it's yours."

Her cheeks turned a darker shade of pink. He felt her hand tremble in his own before she yanked it away. "Just bring my sister home. Safely away from your brother."

"You have my word. Soon." He rose to his feet. "I must call my lawyer. In the meantime, please take some time to rest." He gestured to the bookshelves of first-edition books. "Read, if you like. Your breakfast will be here at any moment." He gave a slight bow. "Please excuse me."

"Kasimir?"

He froze. Had Josie somehow guessed his plans? Was it possible her expressive brown eyes had seen right through his twisted, heartless soul? Hands clenched at his sides, body taut, Kasimir turned back to face her.

Josie's eyes were shining, her expression bright as a new penny, as she leaned back against the sofa pillows. His gaze traced unwillingly over the patterns on her skin, along the curve of her full breasts beneath her T-shirt, left by the soft morning light.

"Thank you for saving my sister," she whispered. She took a deep breath. "And me."

Uneasiness went through him, but he shook it away from his well-armored soul. He gave her a stiff nod. "We will both benefit from this arrangement. Both of us," he repeated stonily, squashing his conscience like a newly sprouted weed.

"But I'll never forget it," she said softly, looking at him with gratitude that approached hero-worship. Her brown eyes glowed, and she was far more beautiful than he'd first realized. "I don't care what people say. You're a good man."

His jaw tightened. Without a word, he turned away from her. Once he reached his home office, he phoned his chief lawyer to arrange the prenuptial agreement and discuss ways to break Josie's trust as quickly as possible. The discussion took longer than expected. When Kasimir returned to the library an hour later, he found Josie curled up fast asleep on the sofa, with a cold, untouched breakfast tray on the table beside her.

Kasimir looked down at her. She looked so young, sleeping. Had he ever been that young? She couldn't be more than twenty-two, eleven years younger than he was, and more stupidly innocent than he'd been at that age. In spite of himself, he felt an unwelcome desire to take care of her. To protect her.

His jaw set. And so he would. For as long as she was his prisoner—that was to say, his wife.

He reached a hand out to wake her, then stopped. He looked down at the gray shadows beneath her eyes. No. Let her sleep. Their wedding could wait a few hours. She deserved a place to rest, a safe harbor. And so he would be for her....

Carefully, he picked her up into his arms, cradling her against his chest. He carried her upstairs to the guest room. Without turning on the light, he set her gently on the mattress, beside the blue silk pillows. He stepped back, looking down at her in the shadowy room.

He heard her sweetly wistful voice. *I do love a good wedding cake with buttercream-frosting roses.*

Kasimir had told her the truth. She would be his only wife. He never intended to have a real marriage. Or trust any human soul enough to give them the ability to stab him in the back. This would be as close as he'd ever get to holy matrimony. For the few brief weeks of the marriage, Josie Dalton would be the closest he'd ever have to a wife. *To a family.*

He took a deep breath. She'd make an exceptional wife for any man. She was an old-fashioned kind of woman, the kind they didn't make anymore. From his investigator's reports, he knew Josie was ridiculously honest and scrupulously kind. Six months ago, a different private investigator had her under surveillance in Seattle. He'd dressed as a homeless street person, which should have rendered him invisible. Not to Josie, though. "She came right up to me to ask if I was all right," the man reported in amazement, "or if I needed anything. Then she insisted on giving me her brown-bag lunch." He'd smiled. "Peanut butter and jelly!"

What kind of girl did that? Who had a heart that unjaded and, well—soft?

Unlike Vladimir and Bree, unlike Kasimir himself, Josie deserved to be protected. She was an innocent. She'd done nothing to earn the well-deserved revenge he planned for the other two.

Even though it would still hurt her.

He felt another spasm beneath his solar plexus.

Guilt, he realized in shock. He hadn't felt that emotion for a long time. He wouldn't let it stop him. But he'd be as gentle as he could to her.

Turning away from Josie's sleeping form, he went back downstairs to his home office. He phoned his head secretary, and ten minutes later, he was contacted by Honolulu's top wedding planner. Afterward, he tossed his phone onto his desk.

Swiveling his chair, he looked out the window overlooking the penthouse's rooftop pool. Bright sunlight glimmered over the blue water, and beyond that, he could see the city and the distant ocean melting into the blue sky.

For ten years, he'd been wearing Vladimir down, fighting his company tooth and claw with his own, getting his attention the only way he knew how—by making him pay with tiny stings, death by a thousand cuts.

But getting Bree Dalton to betray Vladimir would be the deepest cut of all. The fatal one.

Rising to his feet, Kasimir stood in front of the window, hands tucked behind his back as he gazed out unseeingly towards the Pacific. He'd give his lawyer a few weeks to transfer possession of Josie's land back to his control. By then, once the two little lovebirds were enmeshed in each other, Kasimir would blackmail Bree into stealing his brother's company away.

He narrowed his eyes. Bree would crush Vladimir's heart beneath her boot, and his brother would finally know what it felt like to have someone else change his life, against his will, when Bree betrayed him.

She'd have no choice. Kasimir had all the ammunition he needed to make Bree Dalton do exactly as he wanted. A cold smile crossed his lips.

He had her sister.

CHAPTER TWO

JOSIE'S EYELIDS FLUTTERED, then flew open as she sat up with a sharp intake of breath.

She was still fully dressed. She'd been sleeping on an enormous bed, in a strange bedroom. The masculine, dark-floored bedroom was flooded with golden light from the windows.

How long had she been sleeping? She yawned, and her mouth felt dry, as if it was lined with cotton. Who had brought her here? Could it have been Kasimir himself?

The thought of being carried in those strong arms, against his powerful chest, as she slept on unaware, caused her to tremble. She looked down at the mussed white bedspread.

Could it possibly be his bed…?

With a gulp, Josie jumped up as if it had burned her. The clock on the fireplace mantel said three o'clock. Gracious! She'd slept for hours. She stretched her arms above her head with another yawn. It had been nice of Kasimir to let her sleep. She felt so much better.

Until she saw herself in the full-length mirror on the other side of the bedroom. Wait. Was that what she looked like? She took three steps towards it, then sucked in her breath in horror, covering her mouth with her hand.

Josie knew she wasn't the most fashionable dresser, and that she was a bit on the plump side, too. But she'd had no idea she looked *this* bad. She'd crossed the Pacific twice in the same rumpled T-shirt and wrinkled, oversize men's jeans that she'd bought secondhand last year. In her flight back from Seattle, she'd been crushed in the last row, in a sweaty middle seat between oversize businessmen who took her armrests and stretched their knees into her personal space. And she hadn't had a shower or even brushed her teeth for two days.

Josie gasped aloud, realizing she'd been grungy and gross like this when she'd been face-to-face with Kasimir. Picturing his sleek, expensive clothes, his perfect body, the way he looked so powerful and sexy as a Greek god with those amazing eyes and broad shoulders and chiseled cheekbones, her cheeks flamed.

She narrowed her eyes. She might be a frumpy nobody, but there was *no way* she was going to face him again, possibly on her fake wedding day, without a shower and some clean clothes. *No way!*

Looking around for her backpack, she saw it sitting by the door and snatched it up, then headed for the large en suite bathroom.

It was luxurious, all gleaming white marble and shining silver. Tossing her tattered backpack on the marble counter, where it looked extremely out of place, she started to dig through it for a toothbrush. Some great packing job, she thought in irritation. In the forty seconds she'd rushed around their tiny apartment in Honolulu, trying to flee before Vladimir Xendzov could collect Bree as his rightful property, Josie had grabbed almost nothing of use.

The top of a bikini—just the top, no bottom. Her mother's wool cardigan sweater, now frayed and darned. Some slippers. She hadn't even remembered to pack underwear. Gah!

Desperately, she dug further. A few cheap souvenirs from Waikiki. Her cell phone, now dead because she'd forgotten to pack the charger. A tattered Elizabeth Gaskell novel which had belonged to her mother when she was a high-school English teacher. A small vinyl photo album, that flopped open to a photo of her family taken a year before Josie was born.

Her heart twisted as she picked it up. In the picture, her mother was glowing with health, her father was beaming with pride and five-year-old Bree, with blond pigtails, had a huge toothless gap in her smile. Josie ran her hand over their faces. Beneath the clear plastic, the old photo was wrinkled at the edges from all the nights Josie had slept with it under her pillow as a child, while she was left alone with the babysitter for weeks at a time. Her parents and Bree looked so happy.

Before Josie was born.

It was an old grief, one she'd always lived with. If Josie had never been conceived, her mother wouldn't have put off chemotherapy treatments for the sake of her unborn child. Or died a month after Josie's birth, causing her father to go off the deep end, quitting his job as a math teacher and taking his seven-year-old poker-playing prodigy daughter Bree down the Alaskan coast to fleece tourists. Josie blinked back tears.

If she had never been born...

Her parents and Bree might still be happy and safe in a snug little suburban home.

Squaring her shoulders, she shook the thought away. Tucking the photo album back into her bag, she looked at her own bleak reflection, then grabbed her frayed toothbrush, drenched it in minty toothpaste and cleaned her teeth with a vengeance.

A moment later, she stepped into the steaming hot water of the huge marble shower. The rush of water felt good against her skin, like a massage against the tired muscles of her back and shoulders, washing all the dust and grime and grief away. Using some exotic orange-scented shampoo with Arabic writing—where on earth had Kasimir gotten that?—Josie washed her long brown hair thoroughly. Then she washed it again, just to be sure.

It was going to be all right, she repeated to herself. It would all be all right.

Soon, her sister would be safe.

Soon, her sister would be home.

And once Bree was free from Vladimir Xendzov's clutches, maybe Josie would finally have the guts to tell her what she felt in her heart, but had never been brave enough to say.

As much as she loved and appreciated all that Bree had sacrificed for her over the past ten years, Josie was no longer a child. She was twenty-two. She wanted to learn how to drive. To get a job on her own. To be allowed to go to bars, to date. She wanted the freedom to make mistakes, without Bree as an anxious mother hen, constantly standing over her shoulder.

She wanted to grow up.

Turning off the water, she got out of the shower. The large bathroom was steamy, the mirrors opaque with white fog. She wondered how long she'd been in the water. She didn't wear a watch because she hated to watch the passage of time, which seemed to go far too slowly when she was working, and rushed by at breakneck speed when she was not. Why, she'd often wondered, couldn't time rush by at work, and then slip into delicious slowness when she was at home, lasting and lasting, like sunlight on a summer's day?

Wrapping a plush white towel around her body, over skin that was scrubbed clean with orange soap and pink with heat, she looked at the sartorial choices offered by her backpack. Let's see. Which was better: a wool cardigan or a bikini top?

With a grumpy sigh, she looked back at the dirty, wrinkled T-shirt, jeans and white cotton panties and bra crumpled on the shining white tile of the bathroom floor. She'd worn those clothes for two days straight. The thought of putting them back over her clean skin was dreadful. But she had no other option.

Or did she...?

Her eyes fell upon something hanging on the back of the bathroom door that she hadn't noticed before. A white shift dress. Going towards it, she saw a note attached to the hanger.

Every bride needs a wedding dress. Join me at the rooftop pool when you're awake.

She smiled down at the hard black angles of his handwriting. She'd thought she hadn't wanted a dress, that she wanted to keep their wedding as dull and unromantic as possible. But now...how had he known the small gesture would mean so much?

Then she saw the dress's tag. Chanel. Holy cow. Maybe the gesture wasn't so small. For a moment, she was afraid to touch the fabric. Then she stroked the lace softly with her fingertips. It felt like a whisper. Like a dream.

Maybe everything really was going to be all right.

Josie exhaled, blinking back tears. She'd taken a huge gamble, using her last paycheck to come back to Honolulu, trusting Kasimir to help her. But it had paid off. For the first time in her life, she'd done something right.

It was a strangely intoxicating feeling.

Josie had always been the one who ruined things, not the one who saved them. She'd learned from a young age that the only way to make up for all the pain she'd caused everyone was just to take a book and go read quietly and invisibly in a corner, making as little trouble or fuss as possible.

But this time…

She tried to imagine her sister's face when Josie burst in with Prince Kasimir and saved her. Wouldn't Bree be surprised that her baby sister had done something important, something difficult, all by herself? *Josie,* her usually unflappable sister would blurt out, *how did you do this? You're such a genius!*

Josie smiled to herself, picturing the sweetness of that moment. Then she looked down at her naked body, pink with heat from the shower. Time to do her part, but maybe it wouldn't be so awful after all. How hard could it be, to get dressed in a fancy wedding gown, and marry a rich, handsome prince?

Pulling the white shift dress off the hanger, she stepped into it. Pulling it up her thighs, she gasped at the feel of the sensual fabric against her skin. It was a little short, though.

Josie frowned, looking down. It only reached to her mid-thigh. Maybe it would be all right, though. She reached back for the zipper. As long as it wasn't…

Tight. She stopped. The zipper wouldn't zip. Holding her breath, she sucked in her belly. Nervously, she moved the zipper up inch by inch, afraid she'd break it and ruin the expensive dress. Finally the zipper closed. She looked at herself in the mirror.

Her full breasts were pushed up by the tight dress, practically exploding out of the neckline. She looked way too grown-up and, well, *busty*. Bree would never have let her leave the house like this in a million years.

But it was either this or the dirty clothes. She decided she could live with tight. She'd just have to be careful not to bust a seam every time she moved.

Going to her backpack in mincing steps, she grabbed a brush and brushed her wet brown hair down her shoulders, leaving traces of dampness against the silk. She put on her pink flip-flops—it was either that or fuzzy slippers, and she was in Hawaii, after all—and some tinted lip balm. She left the bedroom with as much elegance as she could muster, her head held high.

Tottering down the stairs to the bottom floor of the penthouse, Josie went through the rooms until she finally found her way to the rooftop pool, with the help of the smiling housekeeper she'd found in the big kitchen. "That way, miss. Down the hall and through the salon."

The salon?

Josie went through a large room with a grand piano, then through the sliding door to the rooftop pool. She saw Kasimir at a large table, still dressed in his severely black suit, leaning back in his chair. He was talking on the phone, but when he saw her, his eyes widened.

Nervously, Josie walked along the edge of the pool towards him. She had to sway her hips unnaturally to move forward, and she felt a bead of sweat suddenly form between her breasts. The sun felt hot against her skin.

Or maybe it was just the way her bridegroom was looking at her.

"I'll talk to you later," he breathed to the person on the phone, never looking away from Josie, and he rose to his feet. His gaze seemed shocked as it traveled up and down her body. "What are you wearing?"

"The wedding dress. That you gave me. Should I have not?"

"That—" his voice sounded strangled "—is the dress I left you?"

"Yeah, um, it's a little tight," she said, her cheeks burning. She wasn't used to being the center of any man's attention, let alone a man like Prince Kasimir Xendzov. Then she bit her lip, afraid she'd sounded like she was complaining. "But it was really thoughtful of you to get me a wedding dress," she added quickly.

He slowly looked her up and down. "You look…"

She waited unhappily for his next word.

"…fine," he finished huskily, and he pulled out a chair for her. "Please sit."

Fine? She exhaled. Fine. She could live with *fine.* "Thanks."

But could she sit down? Clutching the edges of the short hem, she sat down carefully. The expensive craftsmanship paid off. The seams held. She exhaled.

Until, looking down, she saw she was flashing way too much skin. With the dress tugged so hard downward, her breasts were thrust up even higher, and the fabric now just barely covered her nipples for decency. Trying to simultaneously pull the dress higher over her breasts and lower over her thighs, she bit her lip, glancing up in chagrin.

Fortunately, to her relief, as he sat down across the table from her, Kasimir's gaze seemed careful not to drop below her eyes. He indicated the lunch spread across the table. "You've come at the perfect time."

She looked at the chicken salad, fresh fruit and big rolls of crusty bread. It all looked delicious. But even Chanel craftsmanship would only go so far. "I probably shouldn't," she said glumly.

"Don't be ridiculous. You must be starving. You fell asleep before breakfast. You've not had a decent meal for days." Taking a plate, he started to load it with a bit of everything. "We can't have you fainting during our wedding this afternoon."

She almost laughed aloud. Her? Faint from hunger?

Food had always been Josie's guilty pleasure. She felt self-conscious about the extra pounds she carried around, sure, but not enough to give up the pastries and candy she loved. Unlike Bree, who boringly ate the same healthy salad and nuts and fish every day, Josie loved trying exotic new cuisine. Maybe she didn't have the money or courage to travel around the world, but eating at a Thai or Mexican or Indian restaurant was almost as good, wasn't it? Especially when she found a half-price coupon. She looked at the delicious meal in front of her. And this was even better than half price!

She gave him a sudden grin. "Who says there's no such thing as a free lunch, huh?"

"Glad you understand." Placing the full plate in front of her, Kasimir gave her a wicked grin. "You are going to be my wife, Josie. That means, as long as you are mine, all you will know—is pleasure."

Their eyes locked, and she felt that strange flutter in her belly—a flutter that had nothing to do with cookies, couscous or even chocolate. "Okay," she whispered as heat pulsed through her body. She unconsciously licked her lips. "If you insist."

"I'll admit the dress is a bit tight. Women's fashions are often a mystery to me," he said huskily. "I very rarely pay attention to them—except when I'm taking them off."

"I bet," she said shyly, shaking a little. Could he see that she was a virgin with zero sexual experience? Could he tell? Suddenly unable to meet his eyes, she dropped her own back to her plate. Even across the table, he felt so close to her. And too good-looking. Why did he have to be so good-looking? Not to mention sophisticated and powerful. He looked like a million bucks in that dark vested suit.

Sitting back in his chair, he filled himself a plate, then pushed a pile of papers towards her. "You need to sign this."

"What is it?"

"Our prenuptial agreement."

"Fantastic," she said, looking up in relief.

His eyebrows raised. "Not the usual reaction I'd expect."

"Remember, I want to keep our arrangement nice and official." She started reading through the first pages, pausing to sign and initial in places. As she read, she took a bite of a crusty bread, then a nibble of the ginger chicken salad. It was surprisingly good, with carrots, lettuce and cilantro. She ate some more. "Have you found my sister yet?"

"I might have an idea where Vladimir could have taken her."

"Where?"

"I'll look into it further." He tilted his head. "*After* we are married."

"Oh. Right. The deal." She took a deep breath. "But she's safe?"

He snorted. "What do you think?"

She looked up. "You think she is?"

"She is crafty. And sly. I doubt even my brother will be able to control her," he said dryly. "It's more likely she'd be putting him through hell."

Feeling reassured, she leaned her elbows against the table. "You don't like my sister, do you?"

"She's a liar," he said evenly. "A con artist."

"Not anymore!" Josie cried, stung.

"Ten years ago, she told my brother your land was legally hers to sell. Then she tried to distract him from doing his due diligence with her big weepy eyes and a low-cut blouse."

Josie licked her lips. "We were desperate. My father had just died, and violent men were demanding repayment of his debts—"

"Of course." He shrugged contemptuously. "Every criminal always has some hard-luck story. But our company was still new. We wanted our family's land back, but we could little afford to lose the thousands of dollars in earnest money she planned to steal from us. She had Vladimir so wrapped around her finger, she would have succeeded..."

She shook her head vehemently. "She told me the whole story. By then she'd already fallen in love with your brother, and was planning to throw herself on his mercy."

"On his mercy? Right. I told him the truth about her, and he refused to believe me." He looked away. "I decided to fly back to our site in Russia, alone. At the airport, I drunkenly told a reporter the whole story. The next morning, when my brother found himself embarrassed in front of all the world, he pushed me out of our partnership. And out of a Siberian deal he signed two days later worth half a billion dollars."

"I'm sorry about the problems between you and your brother, but it wasn't Bree's fault!"

"No. It was Vladimir's. And mine." He narrowed his eyes. "But she still deserves to be punished."

"But she has been," Josie said, looking down unhappily at her empty plate. "She was going to tell your brother everything. To be honest, at any price. But he never gave her the chance. He deserted her without a word. And he left her to the wolves. Alone, and in charge of a twelve-year-old child." She lifted her gaze. "My sister has been punished. Believe me."

As he stared at her, his angry gaze slowly softened. "You alone are innocent in all this. I will bring her back to you. I swear it."

She gave an awkward laugh. "Stop it, will you? Stop being so—"

"You'd better not say *nice*," he threatened her.

She took a deep breath. "Just stop reminding me!"

"Of what?"

She spread her arms helplessly. "That you're a handsome, charming prince, and I—" She stopped.

"And you what?"

She blurted out, "I'm a total idiot who can't even remember to pack underwear!"

Oh, now she'd really done it. She wished she could clap a hand over her mouth, but it was too late. His eyes widened as he sucked in his breath.

"Are you telling me," he said in a low voice, "that right now, you're not wearing any underwear?"

Miserably, she shook her head, hating herself for blurting out every thought. Why, oh why, had she ever mentioned underwear? Why couldn't she keep her mouth shut?

His blue eyes moved slowly over her curves in the tight white dress. A muscle tightened in his jaw. "I see." He turned away, his jaw clenched. "We'll have to buy you some. After the wedding."

His voice was ice-cold. She'd offended him, she thought sadly. She buttered a delicious crusty roll, then slowly ate it as she tried to think of a way to change the subject. "Your Highness…"

He snorted. "I thought you said it was a worthless title."

"I changed my mind."

"Since when?"

She tried to grin. "Since I'm about to be a princess?"

"Just call me by my first name."

She hesitated… "Um, I'd rather not, actually. It just feels a little too personal right now. With you being so irritated…"

"I'm not irritated," he bit out.

"Your Highness…"

"Kasimir," he ordered.

She swallowed, looking away. But he waited. Taking a deep breath, she finally turned back to face him and whispered, "Kasimir."

Just his name on her lips felt very erotic, the *K* hard against her teeth, the *A* parting her lips, the *S* vibrating, sibilant against her skin as the *M-I-R* ended on her lips like a kiss.

He looked at her in the Hawaiian sunlight.

"Yes," he said softly. "Like that."

She swallowed, feeling out of her depth, drowning. "I like your name," she blurted out nervously. "It's an old Slavic name, isn't it? A warrior's name. 'Destroyer of the Peace.'" She was chattering, something she often did when she was nervous. "Very different from the meaning of your brother's…" *Uh-oh*. That topic wouldn't end well. She closed her mouth with a snap. "Sorry," she said weakly. "Never mind."

"Fascinating." His body was very still on the other side of the table, his voice cold again. "Go on. Tell me more."

She shrugged. "I've worked as a housekeeper for hotels for years, since I turned eighteen, and I listen to audio books from the library while I clean. It's amazing what you can learn," she mumbled. She gave him a bright smile. "Like about…um…botany, for instance. Did you know that there are only three types of orchid native to Hawaii? Everyone always thinks tons of orchids grow here in the rain forest, while the truth is that another place I once lived, Nevada, which is nothing but dry desert, has *twelve* different wild orchids in two distinct varieties. There was this, um, flower that…"

But Kasimir hadn't moved. He sat across from her beneath the hot Hawaiian sunshine, his arms folded as the water's reflection from the pool left patterns of light on his black suit. "You were telling me about the meaning of my brother's name."

She gulped. There was no help for it. "Vladimir. Well. Some people think it means 'He on the Side of Peace,' but most of the etymology seems to indicate the root *mir* is older still, from the Gothic, meaning 'Great in His Power.' And Vladimir is…" She hesitated.

Kasimir's eyes were hard now. She took a deep breath.

"'The Master of All,'" she whispered.

Hands clenched at his sides, Kasimir rose to his feet. Frightened by the fierce look in his eyes, she involuntarily shrank back in her chair. His hands abruptly relaxed.

"My brother is not all-powerful," he said simply. "And he will know it. Very soon."

"Wait." As he started to turn away, she jumped to her feet, grabbing his arm. "I'm sorry. I'm so stupid, always letting my mouth get ahead of my brain. My sister always says I need to be more careful."

"I'm not offended." Looking down at her, he gave her a smile that didn't quite meet his blue eyes. "You shouldn't listen to your sister. I respect a woman who speaks the truth without fear far more than one who uses silence to cover her lies."

"But I told you—she's not like that. Not anymore." With a weak laugh, she looked away. "If she were, we'd be rich right now, instead of poor. But she gave up gambling and con games to give me an honest, respectable life. And just look at the trouble I've caused her." She looked down at the floor. "I gambled at that poker game, and she had to sacrifice herself for me. Again."

He touched her cheek, forcing her to meet his gaze. "Josie." His eyes were deep and dark as a winter storm on a midnight sea. "The choice she made to sacrifice herself to my brother was not your fault. It was never your fault."

"Not my fault?" she repeated as, involuntarily, her eyes fell to his sensual lips. He seemed to lean towards her, and her own lips tingled, sizzling down her nerve endings with a strange, intense need. Somewhere in her rational mind, she heard a warning that she couldn't quite hear; her brain had lost all power over her body. Her traitorous heart went thump, thump in her chest. Still staring at his cruelly sensual mouth, she whispered, "How can you say it's not my fault?"

"Because I know your sister. And I know you." Cupping her face, he tilted her head back. "And other than my mother, who died long ago, I think perhaps you are the only truly decent woman I've known. And not just decent," he said softly. "But incredibly beautiful."

Josie's mouth fell open as she looked up. Her? Beautiful?

Was he—cripes—was it possible he was *flirting* with her?

Don't be ridiculous, she told herself savagely. *He's being courteous. Nothing more.* She had no experience with men, but she did know one thing: a devastatingly handsome billionaire prince would have no reason to flirt with a girl like her. But still, she felt giddy as she looked up at him, mesmerized by his blue eyes, which seemed so warm now, warm as a June afternoon, warm as one of the brief summers of her childhood in Alaska.

"Don't do that," he said.

"Don't what?"

"Look at me like that," he said softly.

She swallowed, lifting her gaze to his. "Then don't tell me I'm beautiful. It's…it's not something I've ever heard before."

"Then all the other men in the world are fools." His blue eyes burned through her. "Our marriage will be short, but for the brief time you are mine…" He put his hand over hers. "I am not going to stop telling you that you're beautiful. Because it's true." His lips curved up at the corners as he said softly, "And didn't I just say that one should always speak the truth?"

Stop, Josie ordered her trembling heart as she looked up at his handsome face. There would be no schoolgirl crushes on her soon-to-be husband! Absolutely none!

But it was too late. The deed was done.

"Are you ready?"

"Ready?" she breathed.

He smiled, as if he could see the sudden brutal conquest of her innocent heart. "To marry me."

"Oh. Right." She bit her lip. "Um, yeah. Sure."

Pulling her into the foyer, he took a bouquet of white flowers out of a waiting white box. He placed a bridal bouquet in her hand. "For you, my bride."

"Thank you," she whispered, fighting back tears as she pressed her face amid the sweetly scented flowers.

He scowled. "Don't you dare tell me no man has ever given you flowers before."

She hesitated. "Well…"

"You're killing me," he groaned. "The men you know must be idiots."

She gave him a wan smile. "Well, I don't really know any men. So it would be unreasonable to expect them to buy me flowers."

"You don't know any men?" He stared at her incredulously. "But you're so friendly. So chatty."

"I don't talk to cute ones. I'm too nervous. Besides—" she gave her best attempt at a casual shrug "—Bree won't let me date. She's afraid I'll get hurt."

His lips parted. "You've never been on a date?"

She shook her head. "I did have a sort of boyfriend once," she added hastily. "In high school. We met in chemistry class. He was…nice."

"Nice," he snorted. "With your rose-colored glasses, he probably had a mohawk, a spiked dog collar and a propensity for stealing," he muttered.

"That's not fair," she protested. "After all, I think you're nice. And you're not a thief."

Looking uncomfortable, Kasimir cleared his throat. "Go on."

"We went out a few times for ice cream. Studied together at the library. Then he asked me to prom. I was so excited. Bree helped me fix up a thrift-shop dress, and I felt like Cinderella." She stopped.

"What happened?" he asked, watching her.

She looked away. "He never showed up," she whispered. "He took another girl instead, a girl he'd just met." She lifted her gaze in a trembling smile. "But she put out. And I…didn't."

A low growl came from the back of Kasimir's throat.

Clutching the bouquet of white flowers, Josie stared down at the pattern of the polished marble floor. "I just think kissing someone should be special. That you should only share yourself with someone you love." She shuffled her pink flip-flops, echoing the sound across the high-ceilinged foyer. "I expect you think it's stupid and old-fashioned."

"No." Kasimir's voice was low. "I used to think the same."

Her jaw dropped as she looked up. "What?"

He gave a humorless smile. "Funny story for you. I was a virgin until I was twenty-two."

"You?" Josie breathed. The fact that he'd told her something so intimate caused a shock wave through her. "The international playboy?"

He snorted. "Everyone has a first experience. Mine was Nina. She worked at a PR firm in Moscow, and we hired her to help our new business. She was far older than me—thirty. We dated for a few months. After I lost my half of Xendzov Mining, I went back to Russia to see her. I was floundering. I had some half-baked idea that I'd ask her to marry me." He gave her a crooked smile. "Instead, I found her in bed with a fat, elderly banker."

Josie gasped aloud.

He looked away. "I thought I was in love with her." He gave her a crooked smile. "Virgins usually think that, their first time. But Nina just thought of me as a client. To her, sex was 'networking.' And when I no longer was a potentially lucrative PR account, she no longer had reason to see me."

"Oh," Josie whispered. Her brown eyes were luminous with unshed tears. "I'm so sorry."

He shrugged. "She did me a favor. Taught me an important lesson."

She swallowed, looking up at him. "But just because one woman hurt you, that's no reason to give up on love forever."

His lips twisted sardonically. "You wouldn't say that if you'd seen me standing outside her apartment in the snow and ice, with an idiotic expression on my face."

"But—"

"You'll be my only wife, Josie. Because you're temporary. And this sham marriage will be over in weeks." Giving her a smile that didn't meet his eyes, Kasimir held out his arm. "Come, my beautiful bride," he said softly. "Our wedding awaits."

An hour later, Kasimir and Josie exchanged wedding rings, speaking their vows in a simple ceremony in the office of a justice of the peace in downtown Honolulu. Kasimir couldn't look away from the radiant beauty of his bride.

Or believe that he'd told her so much about his past. He'd told her about his first experience with love. He'd told her he'd been a virgin at twenty-two. What the hell had possessed him?

He didn't care if she looked at him with her weepy

eyes and vulnerable smile. He'd never try to comfort
her again with a little piece of his soul.

From now on, he'd keep his damned mouth shut.

"And do you, Josephine Louise Dalton, take this man
to be your lawfully wedded husband, to have and to
hold, in sickness and in health, for richer or poorer, as
long as you both shall live?"

Josie turned to look at Kasimir, her soft brown eyes
glowing as she whispered, "I do."

Kasimir's gaze traced downward, from her beautiful face to her slender neck, to those amazingly sexy
curves in the tight, clinging white sheath.

And he'd keep his hands off her. His forehead burst
out in a hot sweat as he repeated the rule to himself
again.

He wasn't going to seduce Josie. He *wasn't*.

He had good reasons. All reasons he'd thought of
before he'd seen her in this dress.

Who'd known she was hiding all those curves beneath her baggy clothes?

He'd nearly gasped the first time he saw her, when
he'd been talking on the phone near his rooftop pool,
tying up loose ends with Greg Hudson. The man was
taking full credit for the way Bree Dalton and Vladimir
had left together after the poker game, and wanted a
bonus on top of the agreed-upon bribe. "I went to a lot
of work," Hudson whined. "I didn't just hire the Dalton girls, I got them to trust me. And I managed to get
your brother to leave with her. I think I deserve double."
Kasimir had been rolling his eyes when he'd looked up
and seen Josie in that tight white dress. "I'll talk to you
later," he'd said, hanging up on the man in midsentence.

But he knew the whole story now. Bree had taken
Josie's place at the poker table to try to win back her

little sister's debt. She'd succeeded, and had been walking away from the table free and clear, when Vladimir had taunted her into one last game.

It was Bree's fault she was in Vladimir's hands. Her own pride had been her downfall.

And it irritated Kasimir beyond measure that Josie blamed herself for her sister's predicament. No wonder her father had established the land trust for her. She'd give undeserving people the very shirt off her back. She needed to be protected—even from her own soft heart.

Although he wouldn't mind taking the shirt off her back. He looked at the way her full breasts plumped above her neckline, and the white lace clung tightly to her tiny waist and hips. He looked at the curvaceous turn of her bare legs all the way to her casual pink flip-flops, and realized she might need to be protected from him, as well.

Because he wanted her in his bed.

He hadn't planned to want her, but he did. And seeing the glow of hero-worship in her big brown eyes made it even worse. It made him want her even more. She was so different from his usual type of woman. She wasn't sarcastic or snarky or ironic. Josie actually cared.

I just think kissing someone should be special. That you should only share yourself with someone you love.

She clearly had no idea how powerful lust could be. Her first experience would hit her like a tidal wave. It would be so easy to seduce her, he thought. One kiss, one stroke. She would be totally unprepared for the fire. But she would be an apt student. He felt that in the tremble of her hand as he slid the ten-carat diamond ring on her finger. Saw it in the rosy blush on her cheeks as she placed the plain gold band on his. All he would have to do would be to kiss her, touch her, and she'd be lost in a maelstrom of pleasure she would not know how to defend herself against. She'd fall like a ripe peach into his hands.

Except he couldn't. *Wouldn't.*

Unlike anyone else he'd met for a long while, Josie was a good person with a trusting heart. It was bad enough that he'd be virtually holding her hostage over the next few weeks in order to blackmail her sister and get revenge on his brother.

Kasimir could be ruthless, yes, even cruel. But to people who deserved it. Not to a sweet, trusting, old-fashioned young woman like Josie. She deserved better.

So he wouldn't take his wife to bed. He would control himself. No matter how difficult it might prove to be.

"I now pronounce you man and wife." Adjusting the flower lei around his neck, the officiant looked between them. "You may now kiss the bride."

With an intake of breath, Josie looked up at Kasimir with a tremulous smile.

He hesitated. It would be appropriate to kiss her, wouldn't it? It would almost be weird *not* to kiss her.

But he feared taking even one taste of what was forbidden. Undecided, he leaned forward, torturing himself as he breathed in the scent of her hair, like summer peaches. He wanted to wrap his hands in her hair, lower his mouth to hers and plunder those pink lips, and see if they were as soft and sweet as they looked...

He couldn't seduce her. *Couldn't.*

Kasimir turned his head, giving her a brief, chaste peck on the cheek, before he drew away.

She blinked, then reached for her bouquet, giving Kasimir a small smile, as if she were tremendously relieved he hadn't given her a proper kiss. As if she hadn't been waiting breathlessly for one.

Neither of them were glad he hadn't properly kissed her. Even the officiant looked bewildered as he cleared his throat. "Sign here," he told Kasimir's attorney, who was their witness. They posed for photographs, to make their wedding look real, and they were done.

"Get busy," Kasimir told his attorney, handing him the marriage license and the camera. "I expect the land in Alaska to be in my name before the end of January."

Today was December twenty-seventh. The man looked flummoxed beneath his wire-rimmed glasses. "But sir...the legal formalities of getting the trust to transfer the land to Miss Dalton, and then having her sell it to you are complicated. It could easily take three or four months...."

"You have four weeks," he cut the man off. Plenty of time to blackmail Bree Dalton into handing over his brother's company. And too much time of having Josie—now his wife—enticing him with her body and the latent passion in her deep brown eyes. The first man to take her might be consumed by it.

But it wouldn't be him. Kasimir set his jaw. He wouldn't touch her.

At all.

Even if it killed him.

"Kasimir?" Josie's brow furrowed. "What's wrong?" She saw too much. "Nothing," he said shortly.

"Do you..." She paused, biting her lip. "You don't already regret marrying me...do you?"

"No," he said shortly. "I just don't want to make this marriage any harder for you than it has to be."

She glanced down at her Chanel gown, her beautiful bouquet, her enormous diamond ring. Her pink lips curved. "Well," she said teasingly, "this *has* been pretty tough to take."

"And I saved the best for last. Your cake."

"You didn't!" she cried happily. "What kind?"

"Three layers, with buttercream roses. You were sleeping, so I couldn't ask your favorite flavor. So each layer is different—white, yellow and devil's food."

Her eyes looked luminous. "You are so kind," she whispered.

He frowned at her.

"Don't you dare cry," he ordered.

"Don't be silly," she said, wiping her eyes. "Of course I'm not crying."

Kasimir cursed aloud. "How can the small kindness of cake make you weep?"

"You listened to me," she said, giving him a watery smile. "I'm not used to anyone actually listening to me. Even Bree just talks at me, telling me what I should want."

"No more. Remember, now you're a princess." He gave her a sudden cheeky grin. "Princess Josephine Xendzov." Reaching down, he stroked her cheek as he looked into her eyes. "Princess Josie, you're perfect."

"Princess." She gulped, then shook her head with a laugh. "If only the girls who teased me in high school could see me now!"

Setting his jaw, he looked down at her. "If any girls who teased you were here right now, I'd make them regret they were born."

Looking up at him, she gave a shocked laugh.

Then she blinked fast. She gave a sudden tearful sniff.

"Don't start that again," he said in exasperation. Grabbing her hand, he pulled her out of the justice of the peace's office and into the sunshine. The sky was a brilliant blue against the soaring skyscrapers of downtown Honolulu. Holding Josie's hand, Kasimir led her to the Rolls-Royce waiting for them at the curb.

"Kiss her!" Some rowdy tourists shouted from a nearby bus, spotting him in a black suit and Josie with her white dress and bouquet, standing beside a chauf-feured black Rolls-Royce.

Kasimir looked back at her. "They want me to kiss you."

Josie looked back at him breathlessly, her eyes huge with fear. "It's all right," she said awkwardly. "I know you don't want to. It's okay."

"Since this is my only wedding—" his hand tight-ened over hers as he pulled her closer "—this is my only chance to properly fulfill the traditions."

He felt her tremble in his arms, saw her lips part as she looked up at him, ripe for plunder. And he knew it would be easy, so easy, to possess her. Not just her lips, but her body. Her heart. Her soul.

"Josie," he said hoarsely, looking at her lips.

"Yes?"

He lifted his gaze. "You'll remember that our mar-riage is in name only. You know that. Don't you?"

Her cheeks went pale, and she dropped his hand with an awkward laugh. "Of course I know that. You think I don't know that? I know that."

"Good," he said, exhaling. Now he just had to keep on reminding himself. Turning away, he opened the door of the Rolls-Royce.

"I'm know I'm not your type," she chattered, climb-ing into the backseat of the car. "Of course I'm not your type."

"No," he growled. He climbed in beside her as his chauffeur closed the door. "You're absolutely not."

Her lips tugged downward, and she abruptly fell silent. But as the Rolls-Royce drew away from the curb, she turned to him suddenly in the backseat with pleading eyes. "So what *is* your type?"

His type. Kasimir's jaw clenched. It was time to draw a line in the sand. To end the strange emotional connection that had leapt up between them since he'd told her about Nina. He'd never told anyone about that. But Josie had looked so sad, so vulnerable, he'd wanted to comfort her.

He'd overshot the mark. Because for the last hour she'd been looking at him as if he were some kind of damned hero just for some flowers and cake and sharing a story from his past. Enough. The way his body was fighting him now, he needed Josie to be on her guard against him. To remind them both that he was exactly what the world thought he was—a heartless playboy— he opened his mouth to tell her frankly about Véronique, Oksana and all the rest.

Taking her hand, Kasimir looked straight into her eyes.

Then he heard himself say huskily, "My usual type isn't half as beautiful as you."

He sucked in his breath. Why had he said that? How had it slipped past his guard? Was he picking up the habit from Josie—randomly blurting things out? He risked a glance at her.

Josie's jaw had dropped. Her hand trembled in his own. Her eyes were shining.

He pulled his hand away. "But I'm heartless, Josie. You should know I'm not the good man you think."

"You're wrong," she whispered. "I can tell—"

He turned away, clawing back his hair as he stared out the window at the passing city. "I don't want to hurt you," he said in a low voice. "But I'm afraid I will."

The truth was, he was starting to like the glow of admiration in her eyes. Josie had a good heart. He saw that clearly. But oddly, she seemed to think he had a good heart, as well—which was an opinion that no one on earth shared, not even Kasimir himself. But some part of him didn't want to see that glow in her eyes fade.

Although it would. Once she found out the truth about him, no amount of cake or diamonds or flowers would ever convince Josie to forgive the man who'd blackmailed her sister.

It doesn't matter, he told himself harshly. He was glad she admired him. That delusion would keep her close. She would have no reason to try to leave. Not that she could. Turning to her, he asked abruptly, "Why did you use your passport as ID for the wedding license? Don't you drive?"

She shook her head with a sigh. "Bree is too afraid I'll get distracted by a sunset and crash, or forget where I parked, or maybe even give the car away to some beggar on the street. Not that we have a car," she said wistfully. "Our clunker that we drove south from Alaska died when we crossed the Nevada border."

"How can you not know how to drive?"

She bit her lip. "I would like to, but…"

"You are a grown woman. If you want to learn, learn. Nothing is stopping you."

"But Bree—"

"If she treats you like a child, it's because you still act like one. Mindlessly obeying her. I'm surprised she even let you get a passport," he said sardonically. "Isn't she afraid you might fly off to Asia and wreak havoc? Crash international stock markets in South America?"

She stared at him, wide-eyed. "How would I even do that?"

"Forget it," he bit out, looking out the window. "It just irritates me, how you've allowed her to control you. I can hardly believe you've bought into it for so long, looking up to her as if she's so much smarter than you, thinking that eventually, if you tried hard enough, you'd be able to earn her trust and respect—"

His voice cut off as he realized it wasn't Josie's sister he was talking about. Jaw tight, he glanced at her, hoping she hadn't noticed. His usual sort of mistress, who focused only on herself, wouldn't have registered a thing.

Josie was staring at him, her eyes wide.

"But Bree *is* smarter than me," she said in a small voice. "And it's okay. I don't mind. I love her just the same." She tilted her head. "Just as you love your brother. Don't you?"

Damn her intuitive nature. He turned away, his shoulders tight. "Loved. A long time ago. When I was too stupid to know better."

"You shouldn't give up on him. You should—"

"Leave it alone," he ground out.

"But you've spent the last ten years trying to destroy him—in this internecine battle—"

"Internecine?"

"Mutually destructive."

"Ah." His lips tugged up at the edges. "Well. Our rivalry has certainly been that. We've both lost millions of dollars bidding up the same targets for acquisition, sabotaging each other, planting rumors, political backstabbing. All of which Vladimir deserves. But I can hardly expect him just to take it without fighting back. No. In fact—" he tapped his knuckles aimlessly against the side of the car "—I'd have been very disappointed if he had."

"Oh," Josie breathed. "Now I get it."

Frowning, he looked at her. "Get what?"

"You're like little boys in some kind of quarrel, wrestling and punching each other till you're bloody. Till someone says 'uncle.' The reason you're fighting him so hard…is because you miss him."

Kasimir gave an intake of breath, staring at her. His shoulders suddenly felt uncomfortably tight. He was grateful when his phone rang. "Xendzov," he answered sharply.

"It's happened, Your Highness," his investigator said. "Even sooner than you expected. Your brother has started looking for Josie."

"Do you know why?" he bit out, extremely aware of Josie watching him anxiously in the back of the car.

"It could be at her sister's request. Or for some reason of his own. He tracked her commercial flight from Seattle to Honolulu. It's just a matter of time until he finds her on this island. With you."

Kasimir's hand tightened on his phone. "Understood."

"Who was that?" Josie asked after he hung up. "Was it about my sister?"

His lips tightened. "Change of plan." He turned to her. "We'll have to skip the cake."

"Did you find her?" she cried. "Where is she?"

"How would you like a surprise honeymoon?" he said evasively.

Josie scowled. "Why would I want that?"

Ouch. He tried to ignore the blow to his masculine pride. "You've never wanted to go to Paris?" he said lightly. "To stay at the finest hotels, to have a magnificent view of the Eiffel Tower, to shop in designer boutiques, to…"

His voice trailed off when he saw Josie shaking her head fiercely. "I just want my sister—home safe. As you promised!"

Kasimir sighed, telling himself they'd have been tracked to Paris, anyway, when he was surrounded by the inevitable paparazzi. He flashed her a careless smile. "Fine. No honeymoon."

"But do you know where Bree is?" she persisted.

"I might have a slight suspicion." It wasn't a lie. He knew exactly where Bree was, and he'd known since yesterday. She was at Vladimir's beachfront villa on the other side of Oahu. Too damned close for comfort. It was a miracle that for almost a week now, Kasimir had managed to keep it quiet that he was in Honolulu.

"Is she safe?" Josie grabbed his hand anxiously. "He hasn't—hurt her—in any way?"

Hurt her? Kasimir snorted. His investigator had seen Vladimir kissing her on a moonswept beach last night, while Bree, wearing a bikini, had been enthusiastically kissing him back. But at Josie's pained expression, he coughed. "She's fine."

"How can you know?"

"Because I know." Rubbing his throbbing temples, Kasimir leaned forward to tell his chauffeur, "The airport."

They'd already turned down the street of his penthouse as the driver nodded.

"Airport?" Josie breathed. "Where are we going?"

Kasimir smiled. "Let's just say I'm glad you have your passport…"

His voice trailed off as he saw Greg Hudson pacing on the sidewalk outside his building. He'd come to demand payment in person. A snarl rose to Kasimir's lips. *Damn his greedy hide.* If Josie saw her ex-boss, it would ruin everything. Intuitive as she was, she'd quickly figure out who'd bribed him to hire the two Dalton girls. And why. Then, married or not, she'd likely jump straight out of Kasimir's car, and that would be the end of his revenge.

Josie blinked. "Wait, are we back on your street?" She turned towards the chauffeur. "Could we please just stop for a moment at the penthouse, so I can pick up my bag before we go?" She glanced at Kasimir with a dimpled smile. "And I'll grab the cake."

The chauffeur looked at Kasimir in his rearview mirror, then said gravely, "Sorry, Princess."

"Tell him to stop," Josie said imploringly to Kasimir. She started to turn towards the window, her hand reaching instinctively for her door. In another two seconds, she'd see her ex-boss waiting outside the building, and Kasimir's plans would be destroyed.

He didn't think. He just acted. That was the reason, he told himself later, the only possible reason, for what he did next.

Throwing himself across the leather seat of the Rolls-Royce, he pulled her roughly into his arms. He heard her gasp, saw her eyes grow wide. He saw panic mingle with tremulous, innocent desire in her beautiful face. He saw the blush of roses in her pale cheeks, breathed in the sweet peaches of her hair. His hands cupped her face as he felt the softness of her skin.

And then, with a low growl from the back of his throat, Kasimir did what he'd ached to do for hours.

He kissed his wife.

CHAPTER THREE

JOSIE TRULY DIDN'T believe he was going to kiss her. Not until she felt his mouth against her own. As he lowered his head to hers, she just stared up at him in shock.

Then she felt his lips against hers, rough and hot, hard and sensual as silk. She gasped, closing her eyes as she felt the caress of his embrace like a thousand shards of light.

In the backseat of the Rolls-Royce, Kasimir pulled her more tightly against him, and she felt his power, his strength. He tilted her head back, deepening the kiss as his hands twined in her hair. Her eyes squeezed shut as she felt the hot, plundering sweep of his tongue, felt the velocity of the world spinning around her, as if they were at the center of a sandstorm. She was lost, completely lost, in sensations she'd never felt before, in his lips and tongue and body and hands. When he finally pulled away, she sagged against him, dazed beneath the force of her own surrender.

But Kasimir just sat back against the seat, glancing out the car window calmly. As if he hadn't just changed her whole world—forever.

"Why…" she whispered, touching her tingling, bruised lips. "Why did you kiss me?"

Kasimir glanced back at her. "Oh, that?" He shrugged,

then drawled, "The justice of the peace did tell me I was allowed to kiss you now."

Her heart was pounding. She tried to understand. "You did it to celebrate our wedding?" she said faintly. "Because you were overcome...by the moment?"

He gave a hard laugh. As the chauffeur drove the Rolls-Royce onto the highway, Kasimir looked away from her, as if he were far more interested in the shining glass buildings and palm trees and blue sky. "Exactly." His tone was sardonic. "I was overcome."

And she imagined she saw smug masculine satisfaction in his heavy-lidded expression.

Josie had never thought of herself as a violent person. If anything, she was the type to hide and quiver from conflict. But in this moment, she suddenly felt a spasm of anger. "Then tell me the real reason."

He looked at her. "You were handy."

She gasped. He hadn't kissed her to share the sacredness of the moment, or because he was overwhelmed by sudden particular desire for Josie. Oh, no. He'd kissed her just because she was *there*.

I'm heartless, Josie, he'd told her. *You should know I'm not the good man you think.*

Apparently he'd felt that words weren't enough of a warning. He'd decided to show her, and this was exhibit A.

And for that, he'd ruthlessly stolen her first kiss away.

"It meant nothing to you?" she choked out. "You were just using me?"

"Of course I was," he said coldly. "What else could a kiss be? You know the kind of man I am. I don't do commitment. I don't do hearts and flowers and sappy little poems so dear to the innocent souls of tender little virgins," he ground out. His eyes were fierce as he glared at her. "So get that straight—once and for all."

She stared at him, her mouth wide-open.

Then emotion tore through her, like fire through dry brush. It was an emotion she barely recognized. She'd never felt it before.

Rage.

Hot burning tears filled her eyes. Drawing back her hand, she slapped his face—hard.

The ringing sound of the blow echoed in the car. Even the chauffeur in the front seat flinched.

Blinking in shock, Kasimir instinctively put his hand to his rugged, reddened cheek as he stared down at her.

"I dreamed about my first kiss for my whole life," she cried. "And you stole it from me. For no reason. Just to prove your stupid point!"

He narrowed his eyes. "Josie—"

"I get it. You don't want me to fall in love with you. No worries about that!" A lump rose in her throat. "You turned a memory that should have been sacred into a mockery," she whispered. Tears spilled over her lashes as she looked away. "Don't ever touch me again."

Silence fell in the backseat of the limo. She waited for him to apologize, to say he was sorry.

Instead, he said in a low voice, "Fine."

She whirled to face him, eyes blazing. "I want your promise! Your word of honor!"

"You think I have a word of honor?" His handsome face was stark, his blue gaze oddly vulnerable as he looked down at her, his arms folded over his black vest and tie.

"Stop joking about this!" Her voice ended with a humiliating sob. "I mean it!"

Seeing her tears, he released his arms. He touched her gently on the shoulders.

"All right. I will never kiss you again," he said in a low voice. His blue gaze burned through her like white fire. "I give you my word of honor."

She swallowed, then wiped her eyes roughly with the back of her hand. "I don't like being used," she whispered. Squaring her shoulders, she looked up. "Just stick to our original deal. A professional arrangement. You get your land. I get my sister back safe."

"Yes." Matching her tone, he said, "We'll be at the airport in a few moments."

She suddenly remembered. "My backpack—"

"I'll have my housekeeper bring it to the airport." Pulling out his phone, he dialed and gave his orders. After he hung up, he asked Josie quietly, "What is so important in the backpack, anyway?"

"Nothing much," she said, looking down at her hands, now tightly folded over the white lace of her dress. "An old photo of my family. A sweater that used to belong to my mother. Before she—" Josie's lip trembled "—died. Right after I was born."

Silence fell.

"I'm sorry," he said gruffly. "I lost my own mother when I was twenty-two. I still miss her. She was the only truly good, decent woman I've ever known. At least until—"

His voice cut off.

"Until?"

"Never mind," he muttered.

Josie stared at him. Then her hand reached out for his.

Kasimir looked down at her hand. "You're trying to

make me feel better?" he said slowly. He looked up. "I thought you were ready to kill me."

"I was—I mean, I am." She swallowed, then whispered, "But I know how it feels to lose your parents. I know what it's like to feel orphaned and alone. And I wouldn't wish it on my worst enemy." She tried to smile. "Though I guess you've done all right, haven't you? Being a billionaire prince and all."

He stared at her for a long moment. "It's not always what it's cracked up to be." He looked away. "You asked me where we're going? I'm taking you home."

"To Alaska?"

He snorted, then shook his head. "Not even close." He looked down at her tight white dress. "We'll need to get you some new clothes."

She followed his gaze. Sitting down, her body was squeezed by the white sheath like a sausage, pressing her full breasts halfway to her chin. Her nipples were barely tucked in for decency. She gulped, fighting the urge to cover herself with her bouquet of flowers. She cleared her throat. "I was planning to wash all my dirty clothes today. Does this place we're going to happen to have a washer and dryer…?"

Her voice trailed off when she saw his gaze roaming from her breasts, to her hips, and back again. Her cheeks colored.

"I wish I'd never told you," she said grumpily, folding her arms and turning away.

"Told me what?"

"About the underwear."

Silence fell in the backseat of the car.

"Me, too," he muttered.

* * *

Josie craned her neck to look right, left, then up. And up some more.

"Unreal," she muttered.

Kasimir flashed her a grin. "I'm glad you like it."

"This is your *home?*"

"No." He smiled at her, looking sleek and shaved in a clean suit, having showered on their overnight flight. "My home is in the desert, a two-hour helicopter ride away. But this…" He shrugged. "It's just a place to do business. I come here as little as possible. It's a bit too…civilized."

Too civilized?

Josie shook her head as she looked back up at the beautiful Moorish palace, two stories tall, surrounded by gently swaying palm trees and the glimmer of a blue-water pool.

It was like a honeymoon all right, she thought. If you were really, really rich.

After sleeping all night on a full-size bed in the back cabin of Kasimir's private jet, she'd woken up refreshed. She'd looked out the jet's small windows to see a golden land rising beyond the sparkling blue ocean, and past that, sunlight breaking over black mountains.

"Where are we?" she'd breathed.

Kasimir had looked at her, his eyes shining. "Morocco." His smile was warm. "My home."

Now, they were standing in front of his palace in the desert outside Marrakech. She could see the dark crags of the Atlas Mountains in the distance, illuminated by the bright morning sun. Birds were singing as they soared across the wide desert sky. The pool glimmered darts of sunlight, like diamonds, against the deep green palm trees.

It was an oasis here. Of beauty, yes. She glanced behind her at the guardhouse beside the wrought-iron gate. But also of money and power.

"It's beautiful." She exhaled, then could no longer keep herself from blurting out, "So is she here?"

He looked at her blankly. "Who?"

"Bree." She furrowed her brow. "You said she was here!"

"I never said that. I said I had a slight suspicion of where she might be."

"Do you think she's in Morocco?"

His lips twisted. "Unlikely."

Josie glared at him. "Then why on earth did we come all the way here?"

"Hawaii was getting tiresome," he said coldly. "I wanted to leave. And I told you. This is where I do business..."

"Business!" she cried. "Your only business is finding Bree!"

"Yes." He tilted his head. "Once I have your land."

She gasped. "You said as soon as we were married, you'd save her!"

"No." He looked at her. "I said I'd save her *after* we got married. When I had possession of your land."

She shook her head helplessly. "You can't intend to wait for some stupid legal formalities..."

"Can't I?" Kasimir said sharply. "It would be easy for you to decide, after your sister is safely home, that you'd prefer not to transfer your land to me at all. Or to suddenly insist that I pay you, say, a hundred million dollars for it."

"A hundred million..." She couldn't even finish the number. "For six hundred acres?"

"You know what the land means to me," he said tightly. "You could use my feelings against me."

"I wouldn't!"

"I know you won't. Because you won't have the chance."

"Getting the land could take months!"

"I have the best lawyers in the country working on it. I expect to have it in my possession within a few weeks."

A few weeks? She forced herself to take a deep breath, to calm the frantic beating of her heart, so she could say reasonably, "I can't wait that long."

His lips pursed. "You have no choice."

"But my sister's in danger!" she exploded.

"Danger?" He looked at her incredulously. "If anyone's in danger, it's Vladimir."

Josie frowned. "What do you mean by that?"

He blinked. "She's always been his weakness, that's all," he muttered. He reached for her hand. "Come inside. I want to show you something."

He led her through the exotic green garden towards the palace, and as they walked past the soaring Moorish arches, she looked up in amazement. The foyer was painted with intertwined flowers and vines and geometric motifs in gold leaf and bright colors. Raised Arabic calligraphy was embedded into the plaster on the walls. She'd never seen anything quite so beautiful, or so foreign.

Josie's lips parted as, in the next room, she saw the ornamental stucco pattern of the soaring ceiling, which seemed to drip stalactites in perfect symmetry. "Are those *muqarnas?*" she breathed.

He looked at her with raised eyebrows.

"I love architecture coffee-table books," she said, rather defensively.

"Of course you do." He sounded amused.

Her eyes narrowed, and she tilted her head. "It's beautiful. Even though it's fake."

"Fake?" he said.

"The builder tried to make it look older, Moorish in design, but with those art-nouveau elements in the windows...I'm guessing it was built in the 1920s?"

He gave her a surprised look. "You got all that from a single coffee-table book?"

Her cheeks colored slightly. "I might have spent a few hours lingering over books at my favorite couscous restaurant."

He grinned at her. "Well, you're right. This was built as a hotel when Morocco was a French protectorate." He looked at her approvingly. "There's no way Bree is smarter than you."

Her heart fluttered. In spite of her best efforts, she was still beaming foolishly beneath his praise as he led her past a shadowy cloistered walkway to the open courtyard at the center of the palace. The white merciless sun beat down in the blue sky, but the center courtyard garden was cool, with lush flowers and an orange tree on each corner. Soft breezes sighed through palm trees, leaving dappled shadows over the burbling stone fountain.

"Josie?" Kasimir was staring at her.

She realized she'd stopped in the middle of the courtyard, her mouth open. "Sorry." Snapping her lips shut, she followed him across the courtyard to a hallway directly off the columned stone cloister.

He held a door open for her.

"This will be your room," he murmured. She walked

past him to find a large bedroom with high ceilings, sumptuously decorated, with two latticed windows, one facing the courtyard, the other the desert. "You will need something to wear while you're here."

"No, really," she protested. "All I need is a washer and a dryer—"

He opened a closet door. "Too late."

Peeking past him, she saw a huge closetful of women's clothes, all with tags from expensive designers. She said doubtfully, "Whose are these?"

"Yours."

"I mean, where did they come from? Were they... left here by your other, um, female guests?"

"Female guests." His lips quirked. "Is that what you call them?"

"You know what I mean!"

"I wouldn't come all the way to Marrakech for a one-night stand." His smile lifted to a grin. "Why would I bother going to the trouble?"

"Yeah, why," she muttered. Her husband could seduce any woman with a smile. He'd melted Josie into an infatuated, delusional puddle with a single careless, stolen kiss.

She scowled. "Look. I just want to know if I'm wearing clothes you bought for someone else."

He gave an exaggerated sigh. "They were purchased in Marrakech for you, Josie. Specifically for you. And if you don't believe me..." He gave her a wicked grin as he opened a drawer. "Check this out."

Her lips parted as she looked down at all the lacy unmentionable undergarments.

"You'll never have to go commando again," he said smugly. His eyes met hers. "Unless you want to."

She swallowed, then turned away as her cheeks burned. "Great… Thanks."

"And for your information," he said behind her, "I would never bring a female guest here."

She didn't meet his eyes. She was afraid he would notice how she was trembling. "I'm the first?"

"Ah," he said softly. "But you're more than a guest." Reaching over, he tucked a tendril of her hair off her face. "You are my wife."

As his fingertips stroked her skin, she felt his nearness, felt his powerful body towering over hers. Swallowing, she turned away, pretending to look through the expensive items in the closet to hide her confusion.

"Well?" he said huskily. "Do you see anything you like?"

Her heart gave an involuntary throb as she looked back at him.

"Yes," she said in a low voice. "But nothing that's right for me."

His blue eyes narrowed as he frowned. "But they're your size."

"That's not what I meant."

"Then what?"

She swallowed. "Look, I appreciate the gesture, but…" She stopped herself in her tracks, then blurted out, "They're all just too—fancy."

He drew back, blinking in surprise. "Too fancy?"

She nodded. "I like clothes I can be comfortable in. Clothes I can work in."

He looked at her. "But you wore that all night?"

She looked down at her tight wedding dress. "Well. I just put this back on. I slept naked."

Kasimir swallowed. "Naked?" he said hoarsely.

"Look, I really appreciate your sweet gesture, but

until I can wash my own clothes, couldn't I just borrow some of your old jeans?" she said hopefully. "Maybe an old T-shirt?"

The shock on his handsome face was almost comical. "You'd rather wear my old ratty work clothes than Louis Vuitton or Chanel?"

Not wanting to examine too carefully the reasons for that, she just nodded.

He snorted. "You're a very original woman, Josie Xendzov."

Josie Xendzov. Her heart did that strange thump-thump again. "So people have always told me."

"So what work are you planning to do around here, Princess? Dig trenches in the dirt? Change the oil in my Lamborghini?"

"You have a Lamborghini?" she said eagerly.

His lips curved. "You don't give a damn about designer clothes, but you're impressed by a car? You can't even drive!"

She shrugged. "My father had a Lamborghini when I was six years old. He had it shipped up to Alaska, delivered to our house in the middle of winter. The roads were covered with snow. Impossible to drive the Lamborghini with those wide performance tires."

Kasimir nodded. "You'd slide right into a snowbank."

"So Dad let me pretend to drive it in the driveway. For hours. I remember it was dark, except for flashes of the northern lights across the sky, and I drove the steering wheel so recklessly. Pretending to be a race-car driver. We both laughed so hard." She blinked fast. "It was the first time I ever really heard him laugh. Though I heard he used to laugh all the time before my mom died." She looked down at her feet. "I miss my family," she whispered. "I miss my home."

For a moment, he didn't move.

Then his warm, rough hands took her own. With an intake of breath, she looked up, waiting for him to tell her Black Jack Dalton had been a criminal who didn't deserve a Lamborghini. She waited for Kasimir to mock her grief, to tell her she should put the memory of childhood happiness away, like outgrown toys, discarded and forgotten.

Instead, Kasimir put his hand on the small of her back, pulling her close as he looked down at her.

"So you have a fondness for Lamborghinis, do you?" he said softly, searching her gaze. "They're not too fancy?"

Josie looked up at his ruggedly handsome face. Every inch of her body felt his touch on her back. She shook her head. "Nope," she whispered. "Not fancy."

"In that case..." With a wicked smile, he reached out to stroke her cheek as he said softly, "I know just what I'm going to do with you."

CHAPTER FOUR

Two HOURS LATER, Josie's body was shaking with fear.

Her hand trembled on the gearshift. "I can't believe you're making me do this."

"I'm not making you do anything."

She'd changed out of her tight dress, but in spite of wearing Kasimir's old rolled-up jeans and a clean, slightly tattered black Van Halen T-shirt, she didn't feel remotely comfortable. She'd showered, too, but that hadn't done her much good, either. Her forehead now felt clammy with sweat. The two of them were in the enormous paved exterior courtyard of the palace. In his Lamborghini.

And for the first time since she was a child, Josie was in the driver's seat.

"You wanted to learn how to drive," Kasimir pointed out.

"Not in your brand-new Lamborghini!"

"Snob, huh? So it's suddenly 'too fancy' for you after all?"

"You're laughing now. You'll be crying when I crash it straight into your pool."

He shrugged. "I'll buy a new one."

"Car or pool?"

"Either. Both."

She gaped at him. "Are you out of your mind? These things cost real money!"

"Not to me." Reaching over, he put his hand on her denim-clad leg. She nearly jumped out of her skin before she realized he was only pressing on her knee. "Push down harder on the clutch. Yes." He put his other hand over hers on the gearshift. "Move it like that. Yes," he said softly as he guided her. "Exactly like that."

Josie gulped, her heart pounding in her throat. She accelerated, then stalled. She stomped on the gas, then the brakes. She spun out, again and again, kicking up clouds of dust.

"You're doing great," Kasimir said for the umpteenth time, even as he was coughing from the dust. He gave her a watery smile, his face encouraging.

"How can you be so patient?" she cried, nearly beating her head against the steering wheel. "I'm terrible at this!"

"Don't be so hard on yourself," he said gruffly. "It's your first time."

Resting her head against the steering wheel, Josie looked at him sideways. Since she'd met Kasimir, it had been her first time for lots of things. The first time she'd ever been recklessly pursued by a man who wanted to marry her. The first time she'd felt her heart pound with strange new desire. The first time she'd ever been wildly, truly infatuated with anyone.

She looked down at the huge diamond ring on her finger, seeing the facets flash in the light. The first time she'd fully realized the depths of her bad luck, that she was married to a handsome prince, whose secretly kind heart would unfortunately never pound that way over her.

Never ever, her brain assured her.

Not in a million years, her heart agreed.

His phone rang, and he looked down at the number. "Excuse me."

"Sure," she said, relieved to take a break from driving, or whatever her tire-screeching, bloodcurdling version of driving might be. She stretched in her seat, yawning.

Then she noticed how Kasimir had turned his body away from her to speak quietly into the phone. He got out of the car altogether, closing the door behind him.

Who on earth was he speaking to? Josie's eyes narrowed. Clearly someone he didn't want her to know about. Was it information about Bree? Or—cripes, could he be talking to another woman, making plans for a romantic getaway as soon as he was safely rid of her?

She quietly got out of the driver's-side door.

Kasimir had turned away to speak into the phone. In a very low voice. *In Russian.* "My brother's private jet left for Russia? You're sure?" He paused. "And she's still with him? Very well. Get out of Oahu and head for St. Petersburg. As soon as you can."

Hanging up, Kasimir turned around. His eyes widened as he saw her standing beside him in the dust-choked driveway.

"What was that about?" she asked casually.

"Nothing that concerns you."

"You haven't found my sister?"

"Nope." He gave her a careless, charming smile. Lying to her. Lying to her face! "You've almost got the clutch down. Ready for more?"

She didn't move. "I studied Russian in school," she ground out. "For six years."

His expression changed.

"You found Bree," she whispered, hands clenching

at her sides. "She was on Oahu. And you didn't want me to know."

Kasimir stared at her, then resentfully gave a single nod.

Closing her eyes, Josie took a deep breath as grief filled her heart. "She was on Oahu. All the time we were there, we could have just driven across the island at any time and picked her up?"

"If we'd gone the moment you arrived at my penthouse—yes." Her eyes flew open. His cold blue gaze met hers. "We weren't married then. You could have walked away. I had no reason to tell you."

With a little cry, Josie leapt towards him. She pounded on his chest. "You bastard!"

He didn't move, or try to protect himself. "I don't blame you for being angry," he said softly.

"So that's why you brought me here?" Wide-eyed, she staggered back. "Damn you," she whispered. "How selfish can you be?"

He looked at her. "You already know the answer to that, or else you're a fool."

But she was. She was a fool, because she'd believed in his compliments and lies! Turning on her heel, she started to walk away.

He grabbed her wrist, turning her to face him. "Where do you think you're going?"

"To St. Petersburg," she flashed. "To save her, since you won't!"

"And just how do you intend to do that?" He sounded almost amused. "With no money and nothing to barter?"

She tossed her head. "Perhaps your brother is interested in trading for his old family homestead!"

She heard his ragged intake of breath. "You couldn't do that."

"Why not? It's mine now. Thanks for marrying me."

His hand tightened on her wrist. "That land belongs to me—"

"I signed a prenup, remember? It protected all your possessions and fortune you brought into our marriage. But it also protected mine!"

His blue eyes were like fire. "You—you, the last honest woman—would try to steal my land? And give it to my brother?"

"Why not? You stole my first kiss!" she cried, trembling all over. She looked away, blinking fast. "It should have been something special, something I shared with someone I loved, or might love someday. And you ruined it!" She turned on him fiercely. "You lied to my face from the moment I came back to Honolulu. You won't go save Bree until you legally get my land? You say you can't trust me? Fine!" She tossed her head. "Maybe I won't trust you, either!"

His expression was dark, even murderous. "Yes. I lied to you about your sister's whereabouts. And yes, kissing you was a mistake." His grip on her wrist tightened as he looked down at her. "But don't act like a traumatized victim," he ground out. "You enjoyed our kiss. Admit it."

"What?" She tried to pull away. "Are you crazy?"

He wrapped her in his arms, bringing her tight against his hard body. "Claim what you want. I know what I felt when you were in my arms," he growled. "I felt your body tremble. You looked at me with those big eyes, holding your breath. Parting your mouth, licking your lips. Did you not realize you were giving me an invitation?" Cupping her face, he glared at her. "It is the same thing you are doing now."

She swallowed, yanking her chin away as she closed her mouth with a snap. She blinked fast.

"Maybe I did want you to kiss me. *Then,*" she whispered. Wistfully, she looked towards the wrought-iron gate, towards the road to the Marrakech airport. "But I don't anymore. All I want now is for you to let me go."

For a moment, the only sound was the pant of her breath.

"Is being married to me really so awful?" he said roughly. "Was—kissing me—really so distasteful to you?"

She took a deep breath.

"No," she said honestly. She couldn't lie. She pushed away from him. "But I can't just wait around here for weeks, hoping she's all right. If you're in no hurry to save her...I'll make a deal with someone who is."

"You'll never even make it to Marrakech."

"I'll hitchhike into town," she tossed back. "And hock my wedding ring for a plane ticket to St. Petersburg."

"You'll never even be able to talk to him!"

She stopped. "My phone," she breathed aloud. "I'll call my sister's number. Either she will answer it, or Vladimir will. The battery is dead but I'll plug it in and..." Triumphantly, Josie glanced behind her. Then she saw his face.

With a gasp, she started to run towards the house.

She was only halfway across the inner courtyard, racing for her bedroom, when he came up behind her, scooping her up with a growl. "I won't let you call him."

She struggled in his arms. "Let me go!"

"Vladimir will never have that land." Beneath the

swaying palm trees of the sunny courtyard, next to the soft burbling water of the stone fountain, he slowly released her, and she felt the strength of his muscular form as she slid down his body. He gripped her wrists. "It's mine. And so are you."

She shook her head wildly. "You can't keep me prisoner here. I'll scream my head off! One of your servants will…"

"My servants will say nothing. They are loyal."

It was impossible to pull her wrists out of his implacable grip. Tears filled her eyes.

"Someone will talk," she whispered. "Someone will hear me. We're not that far from the city. I'll find a phone that works. Or email. There's no way you can keep me here against my will."

Kasimir looked down at her, then his eyes narrowed. He abruptly let her go.

"You're right."

She rubbed her wrists in relief. "You're letting me go?"

His sensual mouth curled in a devastating smile. He looked every inch a ruthless Russian prince, his blue eyes icy as a Siberian winter. "Wrong," he said softly.

Frightened of the coldness in his eyes, Josie slowly backed away. "Whatever you're planning, it won't work. I'll escape you…"

Their eyes locked, and shivers went through her.

"Will you?" he purred.

And coiling back like a tiger, he sprang.

Kasimir heard the loud whir of the helicopter flying away as he stood on thick carpets over the packed sand in his own grand tent, the largest and most luxurious in his camp, deep inside the Sahara Desert.

He looked down at his prisoner—that is to say, his dear wife—sitting on his bed. Tied up with a soft silken gag over her mouth, Josie was glaring at him with bright sparks of hatred in her eyes.

His eyes traced down her body. She still wearing his black T-shirt and oversized jeans from Marrakech, but from the flash of lacy bra strap, he knew she was wearing the sexy lingerie he'd given her underneath. His body tightened. He said softly, "What am I going to do with you?"

Josie answered him in a muffled, angry voice, and he had the feeling she was telling him what he should do with *himself,* and that her suggestion was not a courteous one.

Kasimir sighed. He should have guessed Josie might speak Russian—it was sometimes taught in Alaskan schools. He regretted that he'd let himself be caught in such a clumsy lie.

But at the moment, he regretted even more his promise never to kiss her again. A word of honor was a serious thing: unbreakable. He'd unknowingly broken a vow once, to his dying father, when Vladimir had sold their homestead behind his back. Kasimir wouldn't break another.

The truth was he'd been attracted to Josie Dalton from the moment they'd met on Christmas Eve, in the Salad Shack. Kissing her in the back of his Rolls-Royce yesterday, far from satiating his desire, had only made him want her more. Her shy, trembling, perfectly imperfect kiss had punched through him like a hurricane, knocking him over and sucking him down beneath the sensual undertow of her sweet, soft embrace.

Why did she have such power over him?

He felt a sudden hard thwack against his shin.

Exhaling, Kasimir looked down at her, sitting on his bed. "Stop trying to kick me, and I'll untie you."

"Mmph!" Josie responded angrily. If looks could kill, a lightning bolt would have sizzled him on the spot, leaving only the ash of his body to be carried away like smoke on the hot desert wind.

With a sigh, he reached down and untied the white sash from her mouth. "I warned you what would happen if you didn't stop screaming," he said regretfully. "You were driving the pilot crazy. Tark's been in some rough places, flown military missions all over the world. But even he had never heard the kind of curses that came shrieking out of your mouth."

Her mouth now free, Josie coughed. "You kidnapped me, you—" And here she let out a torrent of new invective against his manhood, his intelligence and his lineage in her sweet Sunday-school voice, that left him wide-eyed at her creative vulgarity.

"Ah, my dear." He gave a soft laugh. "I'm beginning to think you are not quite the innocent I thought you were."

"Go to hell!"

He tilted his head. "Who taught you to swear like that?"

"Your *mother*," she bit out insultingly. Then with an intake of breath, Josie looked up, as if she'd just remembered that his mother had died. She bit her lip, abashed. "I'm sorry," she said in a small voice. She held out her wrists. "Would you mind please untying me now?"

Kasimir stared at her. After the way he'd thrown her bodily into his helicopter, ignoring her protests, tying her up—she felt guilty for her single thoughtless insult? She was afraid of causing *him* pain?

Bending to untie her wrists, he muttered, "You are quite a woman, Josie Xendzov."

"So you keep telling me." She looked around his enormous, luxurious white canvas tent, from the four-poster bed to the luxurious Turkish carpets lining the hard-packed sand floor. A large screen of carved wood covered the wardrobe, illuminated by the soft golden light of a solar-powered lamp. "Where are we?"

"My home. In the Sahara."

"Where in the Sahara?"

"The middle," he said sardonically.

"Thanks." Narrowing her eyes she tossed her head. "I'm grateful you're not just going to leave me in chains. As your prisoner."

"It's tempting," he said softly. "Believe me."

As he loosened the knots around her wrists, he tried not to notice the alluring softness of her skin. Tried not to imagine how the white lacy bra and panties looked beneath her clothes. Tried not to think how easy it would be to push her back against his bed, to stretch back her arms, still bound at the wrists, against the headboard. To press apart her knees, still bound at the ankles. He tried not to think how it would feel to lick and caress up her legs, to the inside of her thighs, until he felt her tremble and shake.

No. He wouldn't think about it. At all.

A bead of sweat broke out on Kasimir's forehead. *His word of honor.* That meant his lips and tongue couldn't possibly yearn to suckle her full, ripe breasts. His hands could not ache to part her virgin thighs. He couldn't hunger to stroke and kiss her until he lost himself deep, deep, deep inside her hot wet core.

The bindings on her wrists abruptly burst loose and, as the rope dropped to the floor, Kasimir took a single staggering step back from her. He ran his hand over his forehead, feeling dizzy.

She rubbed her free wrists, looking up at him dubiously. "Are you all right?"

Blinking, he focused on her beautiful brown eyes, expressive and still slightly resentful, in the fading afternoon light. Her voice was like the cool water of an oasis to a man half-dead with thirst. Did she feel the same electricity? He'd been so sure of it in Honolulu. In Marrakech, he'd been absolutely confident of the answering desire in her eyes. But now, he wondered if that had just been a mirage in the desert, an illusion created by his own aching, inexplicable need.

Josie took a deep breath. "Please," she whispered.

"Yes," he said hoarsely. He wanted to please her. He wanted to push her back against the pillows and rip the clothes from her body. He wanted to thrust himself inside her until he felt her scream and explode with joy.

"Please—" she held out her ankles "—finish untying me."

Kasimir exhaled. "Right," he said unsteadily.

Holding himself in check, he knelt at her feet. From where she sat on the bed, her long legs were stretched towards him, her heels on the Turkish carpet. Even in the baggy jeans he'd loaned her, she had legs like a houri—the pinnacle of feminine beauty. As he undid the ropes, his fingertips unwillingly brushed against her calves, against the tender instep of her sole. He felt her shiver, and he stopped, his heart pounding. He looked up her legs, straight past her knees to her thighs, and the heaven that waited there, then to her breasts, then to her face. His body broke out into a hot sweat.

His word of honor.

With a twist and a rip, he yanked the rope off her

ankles. His own legs trembled as he rose to his feet. He clenched his hands at his sides, his body tight and aching for what he could not have.

"I shouldn't have tied you up," he said in a low voice. "I should have told Tark to go to hell and just let you scream curses at me for two hours."

"No kidding." She stared at him, waiting, then she gave a crooked smile. "So are you going to say you're sorry?"

"Mistakes were made," he said tightly, and that was the best he could do.

Her smile widened. "You're not used to saying you're sorry, are you?"

"I don't make it a habit."

"Too bad for you. It's a big habit with me. I say it all the time. You should try it."

"It's been a while." Kasimir's throat burned as he remembered the last time he'd apologized. Ten years ago, he'd arrived in St. Petersburg to discover his "interview" was all over the business news. He'd immediately phoned his brother, still in Alaska. Kasimir still writhed to remember the pitiful way he'd groveled. *I'm sorry. I didn't know he was a reporter. Forgive me, Volodya.*

But his brother had just used his confession against him, convincing Kasimir his mistake was a betrayal and they should end their partnership immediately. And all along Vladimir had secretly known a billion-dollar mining deal in Siberia was about to come through.

"How long has it been since you apologized?" Josie asked softly.

Kasimir shrugged. Saying sorry was tantamount to admitting fault, and he'd learned that humbly asking for forgiveness was a useless, self-destructive exercise, like flinging your body in front of a speeding train. It could only end in being flattened. "Ten years."

Her jaw dropped. "Seriously?"

"I have to go." His shoulders felt tight in his suit jacket. "Just stay here, all right? I'll be back in a few minutes."

"Where are you going?"

"To change out of these clothes. And take a quick shower." From the corner of his eye, he saw her immediately glance at her old backpack on the floor. He could almost see the wheels turning in her mind. Fine, let her dig for her phone. Let her try to use it out here—with no way to recharge the dead battery and no connection even if she'd had power. He looked back at her. "Make yourself comfortable. But don't try to leave the encampment," he warned. "You're in the middle of the desert. There is no way for you to escape, so please don't try."

"Right." Josie nodded, her expression blank and bland. "No escape."

"I mean it," he said sharply. "You could die a horrible death, lost in the sand."

"Die a horrible death. Got it."

With a sigh, he tossed back the heavy canvas door, and went to a nearby smaller bathing tent. He knew Josie was up to something, but she'd soon see there was nowhere to go. He twisted his neck to the left, cracking his vertebrae. She'd hopefully spend the next ten minutes trying to get her phone to work. He gave a low laugh.

Taking off his suit, he used silver buckets filled with cool, clean water to wash the grime of civilization off his skin. He exhaled, feeling his shoulders relax, as they always did here. He changed into the traditional male caftan over loose-fitting pants. His body felt more at ease in a lightweight djellaba than he'd ever felt in a suit. He loved the natural wildness of the desert, so much more rational and merciful than the savage corporate world.

As he left the bathing tent, Kasimir looked up at the endless blue sky, at the white-sand horizon stretching to eternity. There were eight large white tents, most of them used by his Berber servants who maintained this remote desert camp, surrounding the deep well of an oasis. On the edge of the camp was a pen for the horses, and farther away still, a helicopter pad. He'd given up trying to drive here. He'd destroyed three top-of-the-line Range Rovers trying to drive over the sand dunes before he'd finally given up on driving altogether and turned to horses and helicopters.

Now, he looked across the undulating sand dunes stretching out to the farthest reaches of the horizon. Sand muffled all sound at this lonely spot on the edge of the Sahara. The sun was falling in the cloudless blue sky.

His oasis in the desert was as far from Alaska as he could possibly get. He had no memories here of the bleak, cold snow. Or of the only promise he'd ever broken.

Yet.

Kasimir sighed. He was starting to think it was a mistake to wait until he had the land before he searched for Bree. Not just because it was making Josie so unhappy, but also because it was growing agonizing for him to be near his wife and unable to touch her.

"Sir." One of his most trusted servants, a man in a blue turban, spoke to him anxiously in Berber. He pointed. "Your woman..."

Kasimir's lips parted as he saw Josie struggling up a

nearby dune, kicking off her flimsy flip-flops, her bare feet sinking in the sand to her knees.

A sigh escaped him. He should have known that mere warnings of death wouldn't be enough to stop Josie from trying single-handedly to rush off to save that sister of hers. Irritated, he went after her.

Catching up with her easily, he grabbed her hand and pulled her all the way to the top of the dune. Then he abruptly released her.

"Look where you are, Josie," he raged at her. "Look!"

With an intake of breath, Josie turned in a circle, looking in every direction from the top of the dune. It was like standing in the middle of an ocean, surrounded by endless waves of sand.

"There's a reason why I brought you here," he said quietly. "There is nowhere for you to go."

She went in circles for five minutes before the truth of his words sank in on her, and she collapsed in a heap on the sand. "I can't stay here."

Kasimir knelt on the sand beside her. Reaching out, he tucked some hair away from her face. "I'm still going to save your sister. So stop trying to run away," he said gruffly. "Okay?"

Wiping her eyes, she sat on the sand, looking at him. "You can't just expect me to just sit here and do nothing, and leave her fate in Vladimir's hands. Or yours!"

"I thought you said I was a good man with a good heart."

She hiccupped a laugh, then sniffled. "I changed my mind."

His jaw tightened. "Your sister is in no danger. Vladimir has done nothing worse to her than making her scrub the floor of his villa."

"How do you know?"

"His housekeeper in Hawaii was not pleased to see him treating a female guest so rudely. But Bree has always been my brother's weakness. That is why I—" *Why I arranged for them to cross paths in Hawaii,* he almost said, but cut himself off. He could hardly admit that now, could he? Josie's trust in him was on very tenuous ground already. He set his jaw. "I've just found out he has her at his palace in St. Petersburg, where his company is busy with a merger."

"And he's not—bothering her?"

His lips curved. "From what I've heard, her greatest suffering has involved too much shopping at luxury boutiques with his credit card."

Josie frowned. "But Bree hates shopping," she said uncertainly.

"Maybe you don't know her as well as you think." He stood up, then held out his hand. "Just as she does not truly know you."

She put her hand into his. "What do you mean?" she said softly.

"She's spent the last decade treating you like something fragile and helpless. You are neither." He pulled her up against him, looking down at her. "You are reckless, Josie. Powerful. Fearless."

"I am?" she breathed, looking up into his eyes.

"Didn't you know?" He searched her gaze. "You risk yourself to take care of others. Constantly. In a way I cannot imagine."

She bit her lip, looking down.

His hand tightened on hers. "No more escape attempts. I mean it. I swear to you that she is safe. Just be patient. Stay here with me. From this moment, you will be treated not as a prisoner, but as an honored guest."

"*Honored guest?* You said I was more."

"I cannot treat you as my wife," he said huskily. "Not anymore."

"What do you mean? Of course you…"

"I cannot make love to you." His eyes met hers. "And since we kissed in Honolulu, it's all I can think about."

He heard her intake of breath.

"But I gave you my word of honor. I will not touch you. Kiss you. Make love to you for hours on end." Kasimir's larger hand tightened over hers. He looked down at her beautiful face, devoid of makeup. Her luminous brown eyes were the sort a man could drown in. And her lips… He shuddered. "You are safe, Josie," he whispered. "Until the end."

She slowly nodded. Holding her hand, he turned to lead her down the dune. They walked sure-footedly down the spine of sand, pausing to collect her discarded shoes, until they reached the encampment below. He thought about the cake he'd ordered for her, left behind in Honolulu. He'd order a wedding feast for her tonight. He would do everything he could to treat her as a princess—as a queen. That much he could do.

At the door of his tent, he glanced back to tell her how he planned to make her evening a happy one. Then he saw how her shoulders were slumped in his old black T-shirt, how the jeans he'd loaned her had unrolled at the hem, to drag against the ground. Her face was sad.

Something twisted in Kasimir's chest.

He suddenly wanted to tell her he was sorry. Sorry he'd brought her here. Sorry he'd dragged her into his plans for revenge. And sorry above all that when she discovered the blackmail against her sister, it would be a crime that even Josie's heart would be unable to forgive. She would despise him—forever. And he was starting to realize hers was the one good opinion he'd regret.

But when he opened his mouth to say the words, they caught in his throat.

Clenching his jaw, he turned away, pointing at the wardrobe. "You have fresh clothes here." He gestured towards the large four-poster bed, the sumptuous wall-to-wall Turkish carpets. "I will ask the women to bring you refreshment and a bath. When you are done, we will have dinner." He gave her a smile. "A wedding feast of sorts."

But she didn't smile back. She didn't seem interested, not even in the bath—a rare luxury in the desert. Sitting down heavily on the edge of the bed, she lifted her gaze numbly.

"I don't want to stay here with you," she whispered.

She was so beautiful, he thought. His gaze traced from her full, generous mouth down the curve of her long, graceful neck. Like a swan. So unself-conscious, as if she had no idea about her beauty, about the way her pale skin gleamed like cream in the shadows of the tent, or the warmth and kindness that caused her to glow from within, as if there were a fire inside her.

And that fire could be so much more. Standing beside the bed, he felt how alone they were in his private tent. He could push her back against the soft mattress and see the light brown waves of her hair fall like a cascade against the pillows. He could touch her skin, stroke its luminescence with his fingertips and see if it was as soft as it looked.

He had to stop thinking about this. Now.

Kasimir turned away, stalking across the tent. He flung open the heavy canvas flap of the door, then stopped. Standing in the late-afternoon sun, he heard the sigh of the wind and the distant call of desert birds.

Shoulders tight, without turning around, he said in a low voice, "I never should have kissed you."

He heard her give a little squeak. He slowly turned back to face her.

"I was wrong." He took a deep breath. And then, looking into her shocked brown eyes, he spoke the words he hadn't been able to say for ten years. "Josie," he whispered, "I'm sorry."

CHAPTER FIVE

An hour later, Josie was in the tent, bathed, comfortable and wearing clean clothes. And more determined than ever to escape.

Okay, so her phone didn't work and her impulsive escape attempt had been laughable. But she couldn't stay here. Whatever Kasimir thought, she couldn't just be patient. She had no intention of abandoning Bree for weeks in her ex-boyfriend's clutches and trusting all would be well.

Why had Kasimir even insisted on keeping her here? There was no reason he couldn't have her sign some kind of letter of intent or something, promising to give him the property. Something just didn't add up. She felt as if she'd become almost as much a prisoner as Bree was. Two prisoners for two brothers, she thought grimly.

And yet…

Josie brushed her long brown hair until it tumbled softly over her shoulders. Somehow, he'd also made her feel free. As if she, of all people, could be daring enough to travel around the world, learn to drive on a Lamborghini and boldly catch a powerful man in a lie.

You are reckless, Josie. Powerful. Fearless.

Could he be right? Could that be the voice inside her,

the one she'd ignored for so long, the one she'd been scared to hear?

Dropping the silver-edged brush, she pulled her hair back into a ponytail. Well, she was listening to it now. And that meant one thing: maybe she would have accepted being in a cage once…

But she'd be no man's prisoner now.

Josie stood up in her pale linen trousers and a fine cotton shirt she'd found in the wardrobe, in her exact size. She'd just come back from the bathing tent, where she'd been delightfully submerged in hot water and rose petals. As she'd watched the Berber servants pour steaming water into the cast-iron bathtub, she'd felt as though she was in another century. In *Africa*. In Morocco.

"He's called the Tsar of the Desert," one of the women had whispered. "He came here with a broken heart."

Another woman tossed rose petals into the fragrant water. "But the desert healed him."

A broken heart? *Kasimir?* If she hadn't already heard his story about his lost love, Josie would have found that hard to believe. With a shiver, she pictured him, all brooding lips and cold eyes…and hard, broad-shouldered, muscular body, towering over her. A man like that didn't seem to have feelings. She would have assumed he didn't have a heart to break.

But now she knew too much. An orphan who'd been stabbed in the back by his beloved older brother. A romantic who'd waited to lose his virginity, then fallen for his first woman, even planning to propose to her. If she'd known Kasimir when he was twenty-two…

Josie shivered. She would have fallen for him like a stone. A man with that kind of strength, loyalty, integrity and kindness was rare. Even she knew that.

She knew too much.

Now, as she left his tent, she looked out at the twilight. *Stop having a crush on him,* she ordered herself. She couldn't let herself get swept up in tenderness for the young man he'd once been—or in desire for the hard-eyed man he'd become. She couldn't get caught up in the romance of the desert, and start imagining herself some intrepid lady adventurer from a 1920s movie matinee. Kasimir was *not* some Rudolph Valentino-style sheikh waiting to ravish her, or love her.

No matter how he'd looked at her an hour ago.

I never should have kissed you. I was wrong. Josie, I'm sorry.

She pushed away the memory of his haunted voice, and hardened her heart. She couldn't completely trust him—no matter how handsome he was, or how he made her feel. There was something he wasn't telling her. And she wasn't going to stick around to find out what it was.

The air was growing cool in the high desert. She saw the darkening shadows of dusk lit up by torches on both sides of the oasis. It looked like magic.

She'd find a chance to escape. And this time, she wouldn't just run off. She'd figure out a plan. She'd seen horses on the edge of the encampment. Perhaps she could borrow one. She'd never been much of a planner. Bree had the organized mind for that. Josie was more of a seat-of-your-pants type of girl.

She'd figure it out. She'd seize her chance. Sometime when Kasimir wasn't looking.

Josie looked for him now, turning her head right and left. She pictured his handsome face, so intense, so ruthless. No wonder, under the magnetic force of his complete attention, she'd once felt infatuated—at least before she'd realized he was a liar and kidnapper. Her brief crush wasn't anything to be embarrassed about. With Kasimir's chiseled good looks, electric-blue eyes and low, husky voice—and the sensual stroke of his practiced fingertips, rough against her skin—any woman would have felt wildly attracted. But her crush was over now. Her hands tightened. She wasn't going to let him stop her from doing what she needed to do.

But it couldn't hurt to be fortified with dinner before her escape. Her stomach growled. Calories would give her energy, which would give her ideas. Josie looked around for the dining tent. The sun was setting at a rapid pace.

A man in an indigo turban bowed in front of her. "Princess," he said in accented English.

Princess…? She blushed. "Oh. Yes. Hello. Could you please tell me where Kasimir—Prince Kasimir—might be?"

The man smiled then gestured across the encampment. "You go, yes? He waits."

"Yes, of course," she stammered. "I'll hurry."

Josie went in the direction he'd pointed. She wasn't sure she was going the right way, until she suddenly saw a path in the sand, illuminated by a line of torches in the dusk.

She followed the path, all the way up the spine of the tallest sand dune. At the top, she discovered a small table and two chairs on a Turkish carpet, surrounded by glimmering copper lanterns.

Kasimir rose from one of the chairs. "Good evening." Coming forward, he bent to kiss her hand. She felt the heat of his lips against her skin before he straightened to look at her with dark, sizzling blue eyes as he said huskily, "You look beautiful."

She gulped, pulling back her hand. "Thank you for

the clothes, and the bath," she said weakly. "I hope you haven't been waiting long."

He gave her a warm smile that took her breath away. "You are worth waiting for."

Silhouetted in front of the red-and-orange twilight, Kasimir looked devastatingly handsome in the long Moroccan djellaba with its intricate embroidery on the edges and loose pants beneath. His head was bare, and the soft wind ruffled his black hair as he pulled back her chair. "Will you join me?"

Holding out her chair was such an old-fashioned, courtly gesture. And in this setting, with this particular man, it was extremely romantic. In spite of her best efforts, a tremble rose inside her. *I do not have a crush on him anymore,* she told herself firmly, but apparently her legs hadn't gotten the message, because they turned to jelly.

She fell into her chair. He pushed it back beneath the table, and as she felt his fingertips accidentally brush her shoulders, she couldn't breathe. She didn't exhale until he took his own seat across the small table.

"How lovely," she said, looking around them. "I never would have thought a table could be brought up here. It's enchanting...."

"Yes," he said in a low voice, looking at her. "Enchanting."

Their eyes locked in the deepening twilight, and spirals of electricity traveled down Josie's body to her toes, centering on her breasts and a place low and deep in her belly. Looking at the hard angles of his chiseled face, she felt uneasy. She suddenly wanted to lean across the table, to touch and stroke the rough dark stubble of his jawline, to run both her hands through his wind-tousled black hair....

What was she thinking? Nervously, she looked down at the flickering lanterns that surrounded the carpet. She was relieved to see four servants with platters of food coming up the path illuminated by torches in the dusk.

"I've ordered a special dinner tonight that I hope you'll enjoy," her captor said softly. "Would you care for some white wine?"

She gulped. "Sure," she said, trying to seem blasé, as if drinking wine in the Sahara with billionaire princes was something she did every day. Oh, good heavens. With her billionaire prince *husband*.

Pouring wine from a pitcher into a crystal-and-gold goblet, he handed it to her. Smoothly, she lifted it to her lips. She didn't much like the smell, but she took a big drink anyway.

Then she sputtered, and nearly choked. Making a face, she pulled the glass away from her lips.

"Don't you like it?" Kasimir asked in surprise.

"Like it?" She blurted out. "It tastes like juice that's gone bad!"

He laughed, shaking his head. "But Josie, that's exactly what wine is." He tilted his head, giving her a boyish grin. "Though I don't think the St. Raphaël winery will be using those exact words in their ads anytime soon. No wine, huh?"

"I didn't like it."

"I never would have guessed. You hide your emotions so well."

For an instant, they smiled at each other, and Josie's heart suddenly twisted in her chest. Then, turning away, he lifted his hand in signal. "I'll get you something you'll like better."

He spoke in another language—Berber?—to one of the servants, and the man left. After serving their dinner, the other three, too, departed, leaving Kasimir and Josie to enjoy a private dinner in the Sahara, beneath the shadows of red twilight.

"Ooh." Looking down at the table, Josie saw a traditional Moroccan dinner, full of things she loved: *tajine,* a zesty saffron-and-cumin-flavored chicken stew—pickled lemons and olives, carrot salad sprinkled with orange-flower water and cinnamon and couscous with vegetables. She sighed with pleasure. "You have no idea how often I ate at the Moroccan restaurant, trying to imagine what it would be like to travel here."

"How often?"

"Every time I got my hands on a half-off lunch coupon."

He grinned at her, then the smile slid from his face. His expression grew serious.

"So," he said in a low voice, "does that mean you forgive me? For bringing you here?"

She looked in shock at the vulnerability in his eyes. Something had changed in him somehow, she thought. The warm, generous man sitting across from her in exotic Moroccan garb seemed very different from the cold tycoon in a black suit she'd met in Hawaii. Had the desert really made him so different? Or was it just that she knew too much about the man behind the suit?

"I don't like that you lied to me about Bree," she said slowly. "Or that you brought me out here against my will. But," she sighed, taking a bite of the *tajine* as she looked at the sunset, "at the moment it's a little hard for me to be angry."

He swallowed. Reaching across the table, he briefly took her hand. "Thank you."

She shivered as their eyes met. Then he released her as the servant returned with a samovar of filigreed metal. He left it on the table in front of Kasimir, then disappeared.

"What's that?" Josie said, eyeing it nervously.

He smiled. "You'll enjoy it more than wine. Trust me."

She wrinkled her nose. "I'd enjoy anything more than that," she confessed.

"It's mint tea."

"Oh," she sighed in pleasure. She watched him pour a cup of fragrant, steaming hot tea. "This is kind of like a honeymoon, you know."

He froze. "What do you mean?"

"The bath with rose petals. This wonderful dinner. The two of us, in Morocco. It's like something out of a romantic movie. If I didn't know better, I would have thought…"

Whoa. She cut herself off, biting down hard on her lower lip.

He looked up from the samovar. "You'd have thought what?"

"You were trying to seduce me," she whispered.

His shoulders tightened, then he shrugged, giving her a careless smile belied by the visible tension in his body. "I could only dream of being so lucky, right?" He swept his arm over the horizon, over the tea and the lanterns, with a sudden playful grin. "You can see the tricks I'd use to lure you."

"And I'm sure they'd work," she said hoarsely, then added, "Um, on someone else, I mean." Looking away quickly, she changed the subject. "How did you find this place?"

He set down the elegant china cup on the table in front of her. Sitting back in his chair, he took a sip of his own wine. "After Nina dumped me, I had the bright idea that I should go see every single place where I held mining options. After our partnership dissolved, I still held the mining rights in South America, Asia and Africa." He gave her a crooked smile. "Vladimir was happy to let those lands go. He didn't believe I'd ever find anything worth digging."

"But you proved him wrong."

"Southern Cross is now a billion-dollar company, almost as wealthy as his." His lips curved. "I left St. Petersburg with total freedom—no family, no obligations, almost no money, nothing to hold me back. Every young man's dream."

"It sounds lonely."

He took a drink from his crystal goblet. "I bought a used motorcycle and got out of Russia, crossing through Poland, Germany, France, Spain—all the way to the tip of Gibraltar. I caught a ferry south to Africa, then in Marrakech, I took roads that were barely roads—"

"You wanted to disappear?" she whispered.

He gave a hard laugh. "I did disappear. My tires blew up, my engine got chewed up by sand. I was dying of thirst when they—" he nodded towards the encampment "—found me. Luckiest day of my life." He took another gulp of wine. "They call this place the end of the world, but for me, it was a beginning. I found something in the desert I hadn't been able to find anywhere."

"What?"

He put his wineglass down on the table and looked at her. "Peace," he whispered.

For a moment, they both looked at each other, sitting alone on an island amid an ocean of sand in the darkening night.

"What would it take to make you give up the war with your brother?" Josie asked softly.

"What would it take?" His eyes glittered in the deepening shadows. "Everything that he cares about."

"It's just so...sad."

He looked at her incredulously. "You're sad? For him? For the man who took your sister?"

She shook her head. "Not for him. For you. You've wasted ten years of your life on this. How much more time do you intend to squander?"

He finished off his wine in a gulp. "Not much longer now."

The brief, cold smile on his face made her shiver. "There," she breathed. "That smile. There's something you're not telling me. What is it?"

Kasimir stared at her for a long time, then turned away. "It's not your concern."

She watched the flickering shadows from the lanterns move like red fire against his taut jaw. He clearly wanted to end the subject. *Fine,* she told herself. What did she care if Kasimir wasted his life on stupid revenge plots? She didn't care. She *didn't*.

She bit her lip, then said hesitantly, "Is hurting your brother really more important to you than having a happy life yourself?"

"Leave it alone, Josie," he said harshly.

Josie knew she should just be quiet and drink her mint tea but she couldn't stop herself from replying in a heated tone, "Maybe if you just talked to him, explained how he'd hurt you—"

"He'd what, apologize?" Kasimir ground out. "Give me back my half of Xendzov Mining, wrapped in a nice gold bow?" His lips twisted. "There must be limits even to your optimism."

She looked up quickly, her cheeks hot. "You keep

telling me to be honest, to be brave and bold, but what have you done lately that was any of those things?"

He looked at her.

"If I weren't bound by my vow," he said, "I'd do the bravest, boldest, most honest thing I can think of. And that's kiss you."

She sucked in her breath.

Exhaling, Kasimir looked up, tilting his head back against his chair. "Look at the stars. They go on forever."

Josie stared at him, her lips tingling, her heart twisting in her chest. Then she slowly followed his gaze. He was right about the stars. They had never looked so bright to her before, like twinkling diamonds above a violet sea. Looking at them, she felt so small, and yet bigger, too, as if she were part of something infinite and vast.

"You really want to kiss me so badly?" she heard herself say in a small voice.

"Yes."

"And it's not just because I'm—handy?"

He groaned. "I never should have said that. I knew I was wrong to kiss you. I was trying to act like it was no big deal." His lips quirked upward. "Hoping maybe you wouldn't notice that it was."

Her own lips trembled. "Oh, I noticed."

Their eyes locked across the table. As they faced each other, alone in the desert, the full moon had just lifted above the horizon. The world seemed suspended in time.

"But why me?" she choked out. "You could kiss any woman you wanted. And we both agreed I'm not your type…."

Tilting his head, Kasimir looked at her. "You keep talking about my type. What is my type?"

She looked down at her plate, which had been filled with enough *tajine* and bread for your average Moroccan lumberjack. It was now empty—and just a moment ago, she'd been considering going back for seconds. She bit her lip. "She's thin and fit. She spends hours at the gym and rarely eats anything at all."

He gave a slow nod. "Go on."

Josie looked down at her linen trousers and plain cotton blouse that had felt so good, but now seemed dowdy and dumpy. "She's very glamorous. She wears tight red dresses and six-inch stiletto heels." She ran a hand over her ponytail. "She has her hair styled every single day in a top salon." She pressed her bare lips together. "And she wears makeup. Black eyeliner and red lipstick."

He gave her a crooked smile. "Yes. Even when I wake up beside her in bed, her lipstick is perfectly applied."

"What, you mean when you wake up in the morning?" Josie blinked, pulled out of her reverie. "How is that even possible? Do magic makeup fairies put lipstick on her in the middle of the night or something?"

He lifted a dark eyebrow. "Obviously, she gets up early, to freshen up her makeup and hair before I wake up."

Josie dropped her fork with a clang against her plate. "Sheesh! What a waste of time!" She thought of how much she loved sleeping in on mornings she didn't have to work. And if she happened to be sharing a bed with a man—a man like Kasimir—there surely would be better ways to wake up. Not that she would know. Her cheeks flared with heat as she pushed away the thought. She scowled, folding her arms. "You would never know the flaws of a woman like that. So long as she's wearing lots of lipstick and a tight red dress, you don't really know her at all."

Kasimir stared at her in the moonlight.

"You're right," he said softly. "And that's why I want you."

Josie dropped her folded arms. "What?"

"More than I've ever wanted any woman." He sat forward in his chair, his eyes intense. "I know your flaws. They're part of what makes you so beautiful."

She swallowed, looking down as she mumbled, "I'm dowdy and frumpy."

"You don't need sexy clothes for your natural, effortless beauty."

"I'm a klutz." She looked down at her empty plate, feeling depressed. "And I eat too much."

"You eat the exact right amount for your perfect body."

"My what?" She gasped out a laugh, even as her throat ached with pain. "You don't have to sugarcoat it. I'm chubby."

"Chubby?" He shook his head. "You drove me insane in your wedding dress. You taunted me in that sliver of white lace, teasing me with little flashes of your breasts and thighs until I thought I'd go mad." Standing up, he walked around the table. "You have the type of figure that men dream about," he said quietly. "And if you haven't noticed, I'm a man."

Kasimir stood over her now, so close their bodies almost touched. Her body sizzled as her lips parted.

"But I'm plain," she whispered. "I'm naive and silly. I blurt out things no one cares about."

He knelt beside her chair. "Your beauty doesn't come from a jar." He took her hand gently in his own. "It comes from your heart."

His palm and fingertips were warm and rough against hers. And Josie suddenly realized that he wasn't just being courteous. He wasn't trying to give compliments to an honored guest. He wasn't even flirting, not really.

He actually believed what he was saying to her.

A lump rose in her throat. How she'd longed to hear those words from someone, anyone, let alone a devastatingly handsome man like Kasimir....

But she couldn't let herself fall for it. *Couldn't.* She swallowed. Her voice was hoarse as she said, "I'm nothing special."

"Are you joking?" His hand tightened over hers. "How many women would have spent their last money to cross an ocean—and agree to marry a man like me—just to save an older sister who's perfectly capable of taking care of herself?"

Josie's whole body was shaking. With an intake of breath, she pulled away. "Anyone would have—"

"You're wrong." He cut her off. "And that is what's different about you. You're not just brave. Not just strong. You don't even know your own power. You are—" he kissed the back of her hand, causing a flash of heat across her body as he whispered "—an elemental force."

Her body felt as if it was on fire. A breeze blew through the desert night, cooling her skin. Her heart pounded in her chest. She looked up at him.

The wind caught at his black hair, blowing it against his tanned skin, against his high cheekbones that looked chiseled out of marble in the silver moonlight and flickering glow of the lanterns.

"Now do you understand? Now do you believe?" he said softly. "I want you, Josie. Only you."

He reached out to stroke her cheek, and the sensuality of that simple touch caused her whole body to shake. Against her will, her gaze dropped to his mouth. Could she...? Did she dare to...?

Kasimir's hand dropped.

"But I will be true to my word. And I am almost glad you bound me by it." He gave her a small, wistful smile. "Because we both know that you are far too good for a heartless man like me."

Searching his gaze, she swallowed. "Kasimir—"

His expression shuttered. "You are tired." Rising to his feet, he held out his hand. "I will take you back to the tent."

But Josie didn't feel tired. Every sense and nerve in her body was aware of the stars, the night, the desert. From a distance, she could hear the call of night birds. She breathed in the exotic scent of spice on the soft warm wind. She'd never felt so alive before. So awake.

Because of him.

Kasimir's handsome face was frosted by moonlight, giving his black hair and high cheekbones a hard edge of silver. He looked like a prince—or a pirate—from a far-off time. Euphoria sang through her body, through her blood. *Like an elemental force.*

As if in a trance, Josie reached for his hand. Without a word, he led her down the sand dune towards the encampment. She was distracted by the feel of his hand against hers, by the closeness of his powerful body. Her feet were somehow as sure-footed as his as they walked lightly over the sand, down past the flickering torches blazing through the night, illuminating their path.

Kasimir led her into his private tent. They faced each other, and as they stood beside the enormous four-poster bed, which suddenly seemed to dominate the luxurious tent, Josie's knees felt weak. Her lips felt dry, her heart was pounding.

He looked down at her with smoldering eyes, as if only a hair's breadth kept him from pushing her back against the bed and covering her body with his own. As if some part of him were waiting—praying for her to say the magic words: *Kasimir, I release you from your promise.*

Josie clenched her hands into fists at her sides. And, in a supreme act of will, stepped back from him.

"Well," she choked out. "Good night."

He tilted his head, frowning. "Good night?"

"Yes," she stammered. "I mean, thank you for our wedding night. I mean, our wedding feast. It was delicious. I'll never forget how you tasted—I mean, how the *tajine* tasted." *Oh, for heaven's sake.* Squaring her shoulders, she cried out, "But good night!"

"Ah." His sensual mouth curved at the edges. He took a step towards her. Josie almost lifted her arms to push him away. That was surely the reason she yearned to put her hands against his chest, to touch the powerful plane of his muscles through his djellaba and see if they could possibly be as hard as they looked. "Josie," he murmured, "I don't think you understand." He leaned his head down towards her with a gleam in his eye. "This is my private tent."

She licked her lips. "And you're giving it to me as your guest? No." She shook her head. "I couldn't possibly accept. I'm not kicking you out of your bed."

"Thank you." His eyebrow lifted as he said evenly, "And I'm not going to allow you to run away."

"What?" She jumped, flushed with guilt. "What makes you think I'm planning to run away?"

He put his hand over his heart in an old-fashioned

gesture, even as his eyes burned through her. "If you run out into the desert alone, you will die in the sand."

She swallowed nervously. "I would never..."

"Then give me your word." In the dim light of the tent, lit by only a single lantern, his gaze seemed to see straight through her soul. He put his hand on her cheek.

"My word?" she echoed softly.

"As I gave you mine. Not just a promise. But your sacred word of honor—" his eyes met hers "—that you won't try to leave."

She sucked in her breath, knowing what a word of honor meant—to both of them. Her cheeks were burning as she licked her lips. "What would be the point? Do you really think I'm that much of an idiot to—"

"I think you are an incurable optimist. And when it comes to people you love, you make reckless decisions with your heart. I cannot allow you to put yourself at risk. So I intend to sleep here. With you. All night."

"Here?" she squeaked. She frantically tried to regroup, to think of a way she could still try to escape. Maybe if she waited until he was deeply asleep in the middle of the night... She licked her lips. "So you're going to sleep where—on those pillows? Or on the carpet, across the doorway of the tent?"

"Sorry. I'm not sleeping on the floor." Coming closer to her, he smoothed a tendril of hair off her face, looking down at her with something like amusement. "Not when I have a nice big bed."

She furrowed her brow, then with an irritated sigh, she rolled her eyes. "You mean after all that song and dance about me being your honored guest, you want the bed, while I get the floor?" She folded her arms, scowling.

Then she saw a spot on the floor not too far from the

door. He was actually doing her a favor. She brightened. This would be almost too easy! Looking up, she saw his suspicious, searching glance, and tried to rearrange her own face back into a glower. She tossed her head, pretending she was still really, really mad. "Fine. I'll sleep on the floor like a prisoner. Whatever."

"I'm afraid that solution is also unacceptable," Kasimir said gravely, looking down at her with his midnight-blue eyes. "There is only one way I can make sure you do not try to sneak out in the night the moment I am asleep."

She stared at him in dawning horror.

"We are going to share this bed," he said huskily.

CHAPTER SIX

"No way!" Josie exploded. "I'm not sharing a bed with you!"

She folded her arms and stuck out her chin, glaring at Kasimir in a way that told him everything he needed to know.

He'd been right. She'd been planning to escape.

Narrowing his eyes, Kasimir folded his arms in turn and glared right back at her. "If I cannot trust you, I will keep you next to me all night long."

She now looked near tears. "You're being ridiculous!" She unfolded her arms. "Can't you just trust me not to escape?"

His eyebrow lifted. "Sure. I told you. All you need to do is give me your word of honor."

Her eyes widened, and then her shoulders sagged as she looked away.

"I can't," she whispered.

Kasimir brushed back some long tendrils of light brown hair that had escaped her ponytail. "I know."

Her brown eyes were bright with misery as she looked back at him. "How did you guess?"

"Ah, *kroshka*." He looked down at her trembling pink lips, at her cheeks that were rosy with emotion. "I can see your feelings on your face." His jaw tightened. "But you saw how deep we are in the desert. Even with your reckless optimism, you cannot think that running away on foot in the middle of the night is a good idea."

"That wasn't my plan," she mumbled.

"If you try to flee, you'll die. You'll be swallowed up by the desert and never be found again."

Her shoulders slumped further, and she wouldn't meet his eyes. "I wouldn't…" She took a deep breath, then lifted her eyes, shining with unshed tears that hit him like a knife beneath his ribs. "I just can't share a bed with you," she whispered.

His hands clenched.

"Damn you, can't you understand?" He had to restrain himself from shaking her. "It's either share a bed with me, or I'll tie you up as you were before, and leave you to sleep on the floor!"

She didn't answer.

"Well?" he said sharply.

"I'm thinking!"

He exhaled, setting his jaw. "I'm not going to seduce you. Surely you know that by now. What more can I do to prove it to you?"

"You don't have to do anything," she said in a small voice. "I believe you."

"Then what are you so afraid of?"

She looked at him in the dim light of the flickering lantern as they stood alone together in his tent.

"But what if I touch you?" she whispered.

Kasimir's whole body went hard so fast he nearly staggered back from the intensity of his desire. He held his breath, staring down at her as he choked out, "You—"

"Just accidentally, I mean," she said, her cheeks red. "I might roll over in bed in the middle of the night and put my arms around you while I'm sleeping. Or something. You might wake up and, well, get the wrong idea…"

The wrong idea? Kasimir's mind was filled with dozens of ideas, and all of them seemed exactly *right*. He looked at the way she was chewing her full, pink lower lip. A habit of hers. He wanted to lean forward and taste its sweetness for himself. To part her mouth with his own and stroke deep inside with his tongue. To push her back against the blue cushions of the bed, to feel her naked skin against his, and bury himself deep inside her.

"Well, would you?" she said awkwardly. "Or would you know it was all…an innocent mistake?"

Kasimir cleared his throat, forcing the seductive images of her from his mind. "You don't need to worry," he said, hoping she didn't notice the hoarseness of his voice. "I do not make a habit of pouncing on virgins in the middle of the night."

She stared at him, then gave him a sudden, irrepressible smile that caused a dimple in her cheek. "Why? Is there some other time you prefer to do it?"

She was teasing him! His lips parted in surprise, then he gave a low laugh, shaking his head. "For your information, I've never been anyone's first lover."

Josie blinked. "Ever?"

"No," he said softly. "You were my first 'first' kiss."

"I was?"

"And I've changed my mind," Kasimir said in a low voice. "I'm not sorry about kissing you. Because I'll never forget how it felt."

For an instant, they looked at each other in the flickering light.

"Nor will I," she whispered.

The night wind shook noisily against the canvas of the tent, and he forced himself to turn away. "Change for bed."

"Change clothes in the same tent? Forget it!"

"You can change behind the screen. I won't look."

"Can't you please wait outside?"

"And give you the chance to run off in the dark? No."

"But I don't have a nightgown." She choked out a nervous laugh. "Am I supposed to sleep naked?"

Naked. He squeezed his eyes shut, imagining the full, bare curves of her naked body, hot and smooth beneath his hands. He shuddered, his body aching. He realized he had clenched his hands again. His fists were as hard as the rest of him.

Stop it, he ordered his body, which ignored him. He exhaled.

"Look in that trunk." He waved his hand behind him without looking towards her. "Over there. They should fit."

"Really? Thanks." He heard her go to the trunk and dig through it before she went towards the wooden screen painted with designs of flowers. "I guess I owe you."

"You can pay me back by not getting yourself killed," he growled, still not turning around. "What was your plan of escape, anyway?"

"My plan?" When he heard her voice muffled behind the screen, he knew it was safe to turn around. He saw her arms lifting over the top of the painted wooden panels as she pulled off her shirt. She tossed it over the screen, followed by the white lacy bra he'd given her. He swallowed, feeling hot. She gave a low laugh. "You're right, it was completely stupid. I hadn't figured out the exact details, but I was going to steal a horse from your pen, fling myself on it and ride bare-back into the sunset."

"Do you have experience with horses?"

"Absolutely none." She tossed her pants over the top of the screen with a merry laugh. "Now that I'm considering my plan in a more rational light, I'm kind of relieved you figured it out."

Josie was naked behind the screen—or nearly so, just wearing the lacy white panties he'd had purchased for her in Marrakech. He tried not to think about it. Because in a moment, they'd be lying beside each other in his big bed.

He had the sudden feeling that it was going to be a long night.

"Pretty nightgown," she mused behind the screen. "And modest, too."

He was grateful for that, although in his current state of mind he knew he'd be aroused by her even if she was covered from head to toe. Turning away, he pulled off his djellaba, leaving his chest bare, wearing only his lightweight, loose-fitting pants. "Just so you know," he said, "I generally sleep in the nude."

He heard her gulp.

"But not tonight," he said quickly.

"Good." She breathed an audible sigh of relief. "I've never seen a naked man before, and tonight doesn't seem like the time to start."

He couldn't even disguise the hoarseness of his voice this time. "Never?"

Lifting on her tiptoes, she peeked over the screen, looking at him over the painted wooden panels. Her eyes lingered over his bare chest as she purred, "Never."

Kasimir didn't breathe till she ducked back behind the screen. Her arms lifted as she pulled the nightgown over her head. The loose fit of his pants had never felt so uncomfortably tight before.

"Is it safe to come out?" she called.

"Safe as it will ever be," he muttered.

Josie came around the screen in a silver silk nightgown, bias-cut in a retro style, which went to her ankles, but left her arms bare. "Thanks for this. It's very retro. Nineteen forties."

"I told my staff to ransack the vintage shops, and avoid designer boutiques. Warned them not to get all 'fancy.'"

"I love this." She stroked the silk over her belly. "It's...soft."

His fingers itched to discover that for himself. He didn't let himself move. "Glad you approve."

Their eyes met. His forehead broke out into a sweat. At the same moment, they both abruptly turned towards the water basin, causing their hands to brush.

Josie ripped back her hand as if he'd burned her. "You go ahead."

"No, be my guest."

"All right." Keeping a safe distance, she quickly washed her face and brushed her teeth, then walked a semi-circle around him towards the bed. She was afraid to touch him, which meant she felt the same electricity, after all. Knowing she wanted him made this all the harder.

Or maybe it was just him.

As he brushed his teeth, out of the corner of his eye he watched her climb into bed, watched the silk of her nightgown move as sensuously as water over her curves. Putting down his toothbrush, he splashed cold water on his face, wishing he could drench his whole body with it.

Josie hesitated, biting her lip prettily as she glanced at him. "Do you care which side—"

"No," he ground out.

She frowned. "You don't have to be so rude…"

He looked at her, and something in his face made her close her mouth with a snap. Without another word, she jumped into bed and pulled the covers all the way up to her chin.

"Ready." Her voice was muffled.

He put out the flickering lantern light. Stretching his tight shoulders, he climbed in beside her. They each took opposite sides of the bed in the darkness, neither of them moving as the wind howled against the canvas roof.

"Kasimir?" her soft voice came from the darkness a moment later. "What will you do…when all this is over?"

"You mean our marriage?"

"Yes."

He leaned his head back against the pillow, folding his arms beneath his head. "I'll have everything I ever wanted."

"You mean the land?"

He exhaled with a flare of nostril. "Among other things."

"But you're not planning to live in Alaska, are you?"

Live at the old homestead? He inhaled, remembering nights sharing the cold attic room with his brother. Remembering the constant love of his hardworking parents, and how he'd bounded up eagerly each morning to start his chores.

As a boy, Kasimir had felt so certain of what mattered in the world. Home. Family. Loyalty.

"No, I won't go back," he said quietly.

"Then why do you want it so badly? Just because of your promise to your father?"

"It was a deathbed vow…" He stopped. He'd told himself that same lie for years, but here in the darkness, lying in bed beside her, he couldn't tell it again. "Because I don't want Vladimir to have it. He doesn't deserve a home. Or a brother."

"What about you?" Josie said softly. "What do you deserve?"

Kasimir looked away from her, towards his briefcase, which looked distinctly out of place in the corner of the tent. "Exactly what I will get," he said. Retribution against his brother and the Mata Hari who'd caused their rift. Total ownership of both Xendzov Mining and Southern Cross. That would make him happy. Give him peace.

It would. It had to. Looking at her shadowy form in the darkness, he turned the question back on her. "What will you do? With your life?"

"I don't know." She swallowed. "Bree always talked about sending me to college, but even if we had the money, I'm not sure that's what I want."

"Why not? You'd be good at it."

She gave a regretful laugh. "Bree should have been the one to go. She's a planner. A striver. Though she dropped out of high school to help support me." He could hear the self-blame in her voice. Then she laughed again. "But maybe she was glad. She was impatient with school. She's always had an eye to the bottom line. If not for those old debts threatening us, she'd be running her own business by now."

"I didn't ask about Bree's dreams," he said roughly. "I asked about you. What do *you* want?"

She paused. "You're going to think it's stupid."

"Nothing you want is stupid," he said, then snorted. "Except maybe stealing my horse and riding off alone into the desert."

"Not one of my best ideas," she admitted. For a long moment, they lay silently beside each other in the darkness. Kasimir started to wonder if she'd fallen asleep, then she turned in the darkness. Her voice was muffled as she said, "I never really knew my mother. She died a month after I was born. She was supposed to start chemo, then found out she was pregnant. She didn't want to put me at risk."

"She loved you."

Her voice trembled. "She died because of me," she said softly. "When I was growing up, my father and Bree were always away on their moneymaking schemes. I was mostly alone in a big house, left with a babysitter who got paid by the hour."

Kasimir's heart ached as he pictured Josie as a child—even more tenderhearted and vulnerable than she was now—feeling alone, unwanted, unloved.

"And from that moment, even as a kid, I knew what I wanted someday. And it wasn't college. It wasn't even a career."

"What is it?" he said in a low voice.

He heard her shuddering intake of breath.

"I want a home," she whispered. "A family of my own. I want to bake pies and do piles of laundry and weed our garden behind the white picket fence. I want an honest, strong husband who will never lie to me, ever, and who will play with our kids and mow our lawn on Saturdays. I want a man I can trust with my heart. A man I can love for the rest of my life." She stopped.

Kasimir's heart lurched violently in his chest. For a moment, he couldn't speak.

"See?" she said in a voice edged with tears. "I told you it was stupid."

He exhaled.

"It's not stupid," he said tightly. For a moment, he closed his eyes. Then he slowly turned to face her in the darkness. His vision adjusted enough to see her eyes glimmer with tears in the shadows of the bed.

I want an honest, strong husband who will never lie to me. A man I can trust with my heart.

Kasimir suddenly envied him, Josie's future husband, whoever he might be. He would deserve her, give her children, provide for her. And she would love him for the rest of her life. Because she had that kind of loyalty. The kind of heart that could love forever.

The irony almost made him laugh. Kasimir envied her next husband. Because even though he was married to her now, Kasimir couldn't be that man. He wasn't her partner, or even her lover. Not even, really, her friend.

But he could be.

"After I pay you for the land," he said, "you and your sister will be free of those old debts. You'll be able to pursue your dreams." He ignored the lump in his throat. "Whatever they might be."

"You're going to pay me?" she gasped. "I thought our deal was just a direct trade—the land for my sister."

"And I always intended to pay you full market value," he lied.

He heard her intake of breath. "Really?" she said wistfully.

No. He'd pay her double the market value. "Yes."

"You don't know what this means to me," she choked out. "We won't have to hide from those men anymore. We'll be free. And if there's any money left after the debts, Bree could use it to start her bed and breakfast."

"Is that what will make you happy?" he said. "Using the money so your sister can fulfill her dreams?"

"Yes!" she cried. "Oh, Kasimir…" He felt her hand against his rough, unshaven cheek, turning him towards her. He saw the tearful glitter of her eyes. "Thank you. You are—you are…"

With a joyful sob, she threw her arms around him.

Kasimir's arms slowly wrapped around her as her silken negligee slid against the bare skin of his chest. Their bodies pressed together in the bed, and as he felt her soft body against his own, he became all jumbled inside, twisted up and down and turned around.

He put his hand against her cheek. "Josie…" he said hoarsely.

In the shadowy tent, beneath the covers of the bed, he could see her beautiful eyes. He could barely hear her ragged breathing over the pounding of his own heart.

Her skin felt so soft beneath his fingertips. Her arms were bare and wrapped around his naked back. Their faces were inches apart. He wanted to kiss her, hot and hard and deep. He wanted to take her and let his promises fade like mist into the night.

Using every bit of willpower he possessed, he dropped his hand. He pulled away, rolling to the farthest edge of his bed.

"Good night," he choked out.

Silence fell. Then she said softly behind him, "Good night."

Kasimir heard her move to the other side of the bed. He exhaled, closing his eyes. He could still see her beautiful, innocent face, her curvaceous body sheathed in diaphanous silk, shimmering like waves in the flickering light.

He listened to the wind blowing against the tent, the

distant whinny of horses, the call of servants' voices across the encampment. And he still heard Josie's voice, sweet and innocent, filled with the trembling edge between desire and fear.

But what if I touch you? she'd asked.

Kasimir didn't have to touch her to feel her. Lying next to her in the soft bed, with blankets warming them in the cool, arid night, there was a desert of empty space between them, but her slightest tremble was an earthquake.

In just a few weeks, once her land was his, Kasimir would trade her for what he wanted most. He would seize control of Xendzov Mining. He'd get justice against those who'd wronged him. He'd finally win.

He should be glad. Excited. His teeth should have been sharpening with anticipation.

But as he listened to Josie's soft, even breathing, all he could think about was what he would soon lose.

He glanced over at her in the darkness. She didn't care about vengeance or money. She wanted to give away her fortune to make her sister happy. She gave everything she had, without worrying if she'd get anything back in return. She didn't even try to protect her heart.

Thank you, Kasimir. He remembered the joy in her voice when she'd thrown her arms around him. *You are...you are...*

He was a selfish bastard with a jet-black heart. He'd kissed her, kidnapped her, kept her prisoner, but she kept forgiving him, again and again.

Rolling onto his back, Kasimir stared up bleakly at the swoop of the tent's canvas, gray with shadow.

Was there some way to keep her in his life? Some way to bind her to him so thoroughly that she'd have no choice but to forgive him the unforgivable?

* * *

Two days later, Josie stared up at him with consternation. "You have to be joking."

"Come on," Kasimir wheedled, holding out his hand beneath the hot afternoon sunshine. "You said you wanted to do it."

Glancing back at the tallest sand dune, she licked her lips. "I said it looked fun in theory."

"You know you want to." Wind ruffled his tousled black hair as he smiled down at her. He was casually dressed, in a well-worn black T-shirt that hugged his muscular chest and large, taut biceps and low-slung jeans on his hips. He looked relaxed and younger than she'd ever seen him. He lifted a dark eyebrow wickedly. "You're not scared, are you?"

Josie licked her lips. When he looked at her with that mischievous smile, he made her want to agree to absolutely anything.

But—this?

Furrowing her brow, she looked behind her. Three young Berber boys, around twelve or thirteen years old, were using brightly colored snowboards to career down the sand, whooping and hollering in Berber, the primary language of the tribe, but the boys' joyous laughter needed no translation.

Josie and Kasimir had been sitting outside the dining tent, lazily eating an early dinner of grapes, flatbread and lamb kabobs, when the boys had started their raucous race. As Josie sipped mint tea, with Kasimir drinking a glass of Moroccan rosé wine beside her, she'd said dreamily, "I wish I could do what they're doing. Be fearless and free."

To her dismay, Kasimir had immediately stood up, brushing sand off his jeans. "So let's go."

Now, he was looking at her with challenge in his eyes. "I have an extra sandboard. I'll show you how."

She scowled. "You know, saying something looks fun and being brave enough to actually do it, are two totally different things!"

"They shouldn't be."

"It looks dangerous. Bree would never let me do it."

"Another good reason."

Josie stiffened. "I wish you would quit slandering Bree—"

"I don't care about her," he interrupted. "I care about *you*. And what you want. Your sister isn't here to stop you. I'm not going to stop you. You say you want to do it. The only one stopping you is you."

She looked up at the dune. It was very tall and the sand looked very hard. She licked her lips. "What if I fall?"

He lifted an eyebrow. "So what if you do?"

"The kids might laugh, or—" she hesitated "—you might."

"Me?" He stared at her incredulously. "Is that a joke? You'd let fear of my reaction keep you from something you want?" His sensual lips lifted as he shook his head. "That doesn't sound like the Josie I know."

She felt a strange flutter in her heart. Kasimir thought she was brave. He thought she was bold.

And she was, when she was with him. She barely recognized herself anymore as the downtrodden housekeeper she'd been in Hawaii. Tomorrow was New Year's Eve, but for Josie, the New Year—her new life—had already begun.

She'd be able to pay off their debts. She hugged the thought to her heart like a precious gift. They'd be free of the dark cloud of fear that had hung over them for ten years, forcing them to stay under the radar with low-paying, nondescript jobs. Bree would be able to start her business. Josie would never feel like a burden again to anyone.

But it would come at a cost. Josie looked up at Kasimir. He could be a rough man, selfish and unfeeling, and yet beneath it all…he truly was a good man. His generosity would change her life.

But she would never see him again. And that thought was starting to hurt. Because she couldn't kid herself.

She'd stopped thinking of their marriage as a business arrangement long ago.

Yesterday, Kasimir had taught her how to ride a horse. Very patiently, until she lost her fear of the big animals' teeth and sharp hooves, until she started to gain confidence. She was still a little sore from their ride that morning, traveling across the dunes to the nearest village, to bring medicine from Marrakech. As she and Kasimir galloped back together across the desert, his eyes had been as blue and bright as the wide Moroccan sky. She lost a new fragment of her heart every time he looked at her with that brilliant, boyish smile.

Just as he was looking at her now.

"Well?" His hand was still outstretched with utter confidence, as if he knew she would not be able to resist.

"Is it soft? Like powder?"

He laughed. "No. It'll leave bruises."

"Sounds fun," she muttered.

"Do you want to try it or not?"

She swallowed, then looked at the boys zooming down the sand dune at incredible speed, on boards lightly strapped to their feet. Heard their roars of laughter and delight. Maybe it wasn't hard. Maybe it was actually quite easy. All she had to do was make the choice.

Josie's eyes narrowed. She was done being afraid—of anything. Done living a life smaller than her dreams.

Holding her breath, she put her hand in his own.

He pulled her close. "Good," he said in a low voice. "Let's do it. Right now."

His face was inches from her own, and a tremble went through her that had nothing to do with fear. Every time Kasimir looked at her, every time he spoke to her, she felt her heart expand until she felt as if she was flying.

Let's do it. Right now.

His grip on her hand tightened. Then he abruptly turned away, disappearing into a nearby tent. And she exhaled.

It had been torture sleeping next to him the last two nights. She'd been so aware of him beside her, it was a miracle she'd gotten any rest at all. Especially the first night, when they'd been talking so late into the darkness, and he'd told her he meant to pay for her land. She'd been so ecstatic that she'd thrown her arms around him. He'd held her so tightly, his eyes dark on hers, and for one moment, she'd thought, really thought, he might break his promise. And here was the really shocking thing...

She'd *wanted* him to.

Her lips had tingled as she'd waited breathlessly for him to lower his mouth savagely to hers and pull her hard against his body. She'd ached to stroke her hands down his hard, tanned chest, laced with dark hair. She'd yearned to feel his pure heat and fire. Her body still shook with the memory of how she'd wanted it. And looking at him, she'd known he felt the same.

But he'd hadn't touched her.

When he'd abruptly turned away, she'd felt bereft—disappointed. Almost heartbroken.

Which made no sense at all. She admired commitment to promises, didn't she? And while they'd been thrown together in a very intimate way, it wasn't as if they had—or ever would have—a real marriage.

She needed to keep reminding herself of that.

Kasimir returned to the table outside the dining tent. He had two snowboards hefted over his shoulders as if they weighed nothing. "Let's go."

Smiling, and far lighter on her feet, she led the way to the top of the dune.

"Like being faster than me, huh?" he said, quirking his eyebrow.

She grinned. "Absolutely."

"We'll see." He answered her with a wicked smile. "Sit down right here."

Obediently, Josie plunked back on the warm sand in her cotton button-down shirt and soft linen pants. As he knelt on the sand in front of her, in his form-fitting T-shirt and loose cargo shorts, she wondered how brave she could really be. He'd promised not to kiss her.

But there was no rule about her kissing him.

"You're going to love this," he said, pulling off her sandals.

She shivered. His hands brushed against the hollows of her bare feet, and her mouth went dry. "I'm sure," she murmured.

He was inches away from her. She could just lean forward and kiss him. Press her lips against his. Could she do it? Was she brave enough?

Kasimir's blue eyes met hers, and he smiled. She wondered how she'd ever thought him cold in Honolulu.

Here, he was warm and bright as the blazing desert sun. "Are you nervous?"

"Yes," she whispered, praying he couldn't guess why.

"Don't be."

She gave a soft laugh. "That's easy for you to say."

He placed her bare feet into the straps attached to the board. Standing up, he grabbed her hands and pulled her upright. Josie swayed a little, getting used to the balance. She hadn't been on a board in a long time. She tested the sand with a slight lean and twist. Without snow boots, the ankle support was nonexistent. Turning corners would be nearly impossible.

Kasimir stepped into his own modified snowboard, and his arm shot out to grab her when she started to tilt. "Ready?"

She felt a flash of dizzying heat with his hand on her arm. "Yes," she breathed. "I just need a second to build my courage."

"So." He gave her a slow-rising grin. "Are you interested in racing me?"

"Racing?" Josie looked dubiously over the edge of the dune. It wasn't as steep as some of the mountains she'd snowboarded in Alaska, but that was ten years ago. To say her skills were rusty was an understatement. And boarding down sand was going to be like sailing down a sheet of ice. "I'm not sure that's a good idea."

"I thought you said you liked being faster than me."

"I do."

"Then racing me should be right up your alley." His masculine grin turned downright cocky. "I'll even give you a head start."

Laughter bubbled up to her lips, barely contained. He clearly believed he would be faster. "Um. Thank you?"

"And if you win, you'll get a prize."

"What do you have in mind?"

"Your own private tent," he said recklessly. "For the rest of the time we're in the Sahara."

Her lips parted. Somehow that prize didn't excite her as much as it once would have. "And what about if you win?"

Kasimir looked down at her, and something in his glance made her hold her breath.

"You'll share my bed," he said softly, "and let me make love to you."

CHAPTER SEVEN

SHARE HIS BED?

Josie's lips parted, her heart beating frantically as she looked up at him.

Let him make love to her?

She'd been trying to build up enough courage to kiss him. What would it be like to have him make love to her?

With a shuddering breath, she looked up at him. "I thought you said our marriage was in n-name only."

"I changed my mind," Kasimir said huskily. "You know I want you. And I've come to enjoy your company. There's no reason we shouldn't be…friends."

"Friends who will divorce in a few weeks."

"We could still see each other." He looked at her. "If you want."

Her lips parted. "If *I* want?"

"I would very much like to still see you, after we are divorced." His blue eyes seared through her soul. "For as long as you are still interested in seeing me."

Josie sucked in her breath. For as long as *she* wished to see him? That would be forever!

She looked back over the edge of the dune. It didn't look so frightening anymore. Not with this new challenge. Not with her very virginity on the line.

But…

What about saving herself for love, for commitment, for a lifetime?

She looked back at him. Was Kasimir the man? Was this the time? Was this how she wanted to remember her first night, for the rest of her life?

Her heart pounded in her throat.

Should she let her husband take her virginity?

"Just so you know," she said hesitantly, "my babysitter taught me to snowboard."

"Even better." He gave her a cheeky grin. "So with your head start, you have pretty good odds."

She couldn't help but smile at his smug masculine confidence. "Bree's the gambler, not me."

He gave her a long look beneath the blazing white sun.

"Are you sure about that?" he said softly.

On the other end of the dune, with a loud shout, the boys pushed off again, going straight down, good-naturedly roughhousing and cutting in front of each other as they skidded down the sand.

Josie closed her eyes, took a deep breath, and made her choice.

"I'll do it."

"Excellent."

His blue eyes were beaming. He clearly expected that this would be no contest and that he would easily overtake her. He didn't know that the entirety of the choice was still hers. Would she let him beat her? Or not?

Before her courage could fail her, she breathed, "Just tell me when to go."

"One…two…three…*go!*"

Hastily, Josie tilted her snowboard and went off the edge, plummeting down the dune. Her body remembered the sport, even though her brain had forgotten, and her board picked up speed. For a glorious instant, she flew, and wild joy filled her heart—joy she hadn't felt for ten years.

Then she remembered: if she won, she would sleep alone.

And if she lost, *he would seduce her.*

Slow down, she ordered her feet, and though they protested, she made them turn, her body leaning to drag the board against sand as hard and glassy as ice. It was hard to slow down, when her body yearned to barrel down the dune, like the reckless child she'd once been.

"You'll never win that way," Kasimir called from the top, sounding amused. "Turn your feet to aim straight down."

Josie choked back a wry laugh. He had no idea how hard she was trying *not* to do that. A bead of sweat formed on her forehead from the effort of fighting her body's desire to aim the snowboard straight down and plummet at the speed of flight. Couldn't he tell? Couldn't he see she was actually forcing herself *not* to win?

"Ready or not..."

Behind her, he pushed off the top of the dune. Smiling, she looked up at him as he glided past her on his snowboard. She saw the joy in his face—the same as when they'd galloped together across the desert that morning.

"You are mine now, *kroshka!*" he shouted, and flew past her.

Let me fly fast, half her heart begged.

Let him seduce you, the other half cried.

Then Josie turned her head when she heard a scream at the bottom of the hill. One of the roughhousing boys had lost control and crashed into the other, sending the smaller one skidding down the hard sand in panicked yells. The smaller boy, perhaps twelve years old, had a streak of blood across his tanned face and a trail of red followed him across the pale sand.

Josie didn't think, she just acted. Her knees turned, she leaned forward and she flew down the hill. She had a single glimpse of Kasimir's shocked face as she flew right past him. But she didn't think about that, or anything but the boy's face—the boy who moments before had seemed like a reckless, rambunctious teenager, but who now she saw was barely more than a child.

She reached the bottom of the dune in seconds. Ten feet away from the boy, she twisted hard on her snowboard, digging in for a sharp stop, causing sand to scatter in a wide fan around the boy's friends, who were struggling up towards him. Josie kicked off her snowboard in a single fluid movement and leapt barefoot across the hot sand.

"Are you all right?" she said to the boy in English. His black eyes were anguished, and he answered in sobbing words she didn't understand.

Then she saw his leg.

Beneath the boy's white pants, now covered with blood, she saw the freakish-looking angle of his shin.

She blinked, feeling as though she was going to faint. Careful not to look back at his leg, she reached her arm around the boy's shoulders. "It'll be all right," she whispered, forcing her voice to offer comfort and reassurance. "It'll be all right."

"It's a compound fracture," Kasimir said behind her. She turned and got one vision of his strangely calm face, before he twisted around and spoke sharply in Berber to the other two boys. They scattered, shouting as they ran for the encampment.

Kasimir knelt in the sand beside her. He looked down at the injury. As Josie cuddled the crying boy, Kasimir spoke to him with incredible gentleness in his voice. The boy answered him with a sob.

Carefully, Kasimir ripped the fabric up to the knee to get a closer look at the break. Tearing off a corner of his own shirt, he pushed it into Josie's hand. "Press this just below the knee to slow down the blood."

His voice was calm. Clearly he was good in a crisis. She was not. She swallowed, feeling wobbly. "I can't—"

"You can."

He had such faith in her. She couldn't let him down. Still feeling a bit green, she took a deep breath and pressed the cloth to a point above the wound as firmly as she could.

Rising to his feet, Kasimir crossed back across the sand and returned a moment later with his snowboard. Turning it over to the flat side, he dug sand out from beneath the boy and gently nudged the board beneath the injured leg. He ripped more long bits of fabric from his shirt, giving Josie a flash of his hard, taut abs before he bent to use the board as a splint.

The boy's parents arrived at a run, his mother crying, his father looking blank with fear as he reached out to hold his son's hand. Behind them another man, dark-skinned, with an indigo-colored turban, gave quick brusque orders that all of them obeyed, including Kasimir. Five minutes later, they were lifting the boy onto a makeshift stretcher.

Josie's knees shook beneath her as she started to follow. Kasimir stopped her.

"Go back to the tent," he said. "There's nothing more

you can do." His lips twitched. "Can't have you fainting on us."

She swallowed, remembering how she'd nearly
fainted at the sight of the boy's injury. "But I want to
help—"

"You have," he said softly. He glanced behind him.
"Ahmed's uncle is a doctor. He will take good care of
him until the helicopter arrives." He pushed her gently
in the other direction. "He'll be all right. Go back to
the tent. And pack."

Josie watched anxiously as the boy was carried to
the other side of the encampment. He disappeared into
a tent, with Kasimir and the others beside him, and she
finally turned away. Dazed, she looked down at her
clenched hands and saw they were covered in blood.

Slowly, she walked back to the tent she shared with
Kasimir. She went to the basin of water and used rose-
scented soap to wash the blood off her hands. Drying
her hands on a towel, she sank to the bed.

Go back to the tent. And pack.

She gasped as the meaning of those words sank in.
She covered her mouth with her hand.

She'd won. By pure mischance, she'd won their race.

There would be no seduction. Instead, from this
night forward, she'd be sleeping alone in a separate tent.

Once, Josie would have been relieved.

But now...

Numbly, she rose from their bed. Grabbing her
backpack, she started to gather her clothes. Then she
stopped, looking around the tent. Kasimir always
dumped everything on the floor, in that careless masculine way, knowing it was someone else's job to follow after him and tidy up. Looking across the luxurious
carpets piled thickly across the sand, Josie's eyes could

see the entirety of her husband's day: the empty water bucket of solid silver. The hand-crafted sandalwood soap. His crumpled pajama pants. And in a corner, his black leather briefcase, so stuffed with papers that it could no longer be closed, none of which he'd glanced at even once since the day they'd arrived here.

In the distance, she heard a sound like rolling thunder.

Tears rose to her eyes, and she wiped them away fiercely. She didn't want to leave him. This was the place where they whispered secrets to each other in the middle of the night. The bed where, if she woke up in the middle of the night, she'd hear the soft sound of his breathing and go back to sleep, comforted that he was beside her.

No more.

When she was finished packing, she grabbed her mother's tattered copy of *North and South*. For the next hour as she waited, sitting on the bed, Josie tried to concentrate on the love story, though she found herself reading the same paragraph over and over.

Kasimir's footstep was heavy as he pushed aside the heavy cotton flap of the door. She looked up from her book, her heart fluttering, as it always did at the breathtaking masculine beauty of his face, the hard edge of his jawline, dark with five o'clock shadow, and the curved edge of his cheekbones. His blue eyes looked tired.

Setting down the book on the bed, Josie asked anxiously, "Is he going to be all right?"

"Yes." He went to the basin and poured clear, fresh water over his dirty hands. "His uncle put a proper splint on his leg. The helicopter just left to take them all to the hospital in Marrakech."

"Thank heaven," Josie whispered.

Kasimir didn't answer. But as he dried his hands, she saw the shadows beneath his eyes, the tightness of his shoulders.

Without a word, she came up behind him. Closing her eyes, she wrapped her arms around his body, pressing her cheek against his back until she felt his tension slowly relax into her embrace.

A moment later, with a shudder, he finally turned around in her arms to face her.

"You were the first to reach him," he said in a low voice. "Thank you."

Her eyes glistened with tears. "It was nothing."

Kasimir gave her a ghost of a smile. "You were much faster than I thought."

"I told you my father and Bree were gone a lot," she said in a small voice. "My babysitter was a former championship snowboarder from the Lower Forty-Eight."

"You grew up in Anchorage, didn't you?" He gave a low, humorless laugh. "Had a season pass at Alyeska?"

"Since I was four years old." She gave him a trembling smile. "If it's any consolation, I'm faster than Bree, too. She's horrible on the mountain. Strap skis or a snowboard on her feet and she'll plow nose-first into the snow."

"I'll keep that in mind."

"But you and I," she said quickly, "it was a close race…"

"Not even." He bared his teeth in a smile. "You won by a mile."

With an intake of breath, Josie searched his gaze. "Kasimir, you have to know that I never meant to—"

"And I see you've packed. Good." He glanced down at her backpack. "I'll show you to your new tent."

"Fantastic," she said, crestfallen. Against her will, she hungrily searched his handsome face, his deep blue eyes, his sensual lips. She didn't want to be away from him. *She didn't.* "If not for the accident," she said, glancing at him sideways, "the race could have ended very differently…"

"Josie, please," Kasimir growled. "Do not attempt to assuage my masculine pride. That would just add insult to injury." Picking up her backpack, he tossed it over his shoulder. "I'll send over your trunk of new clothes later. You'll likely only be here at the camp for another week or two."

"Just me? Not you?"

He set his jaw. "I'm going to go look for your sister."

"I thought you said it was too soon," Josie said faintly.

He gave her a smile that didn't quite reach his eyes. "I'll leave you and go get her. Both the things you wanted. It's your lucky day."

It was ending. He was leaving her. She thought of the time she'd wasted, longing for him to kiss her and doing nothing. Waiting—always waiting—with a timid heart!

"But you said you couldn't trust me. That if you brought back my sister early, I might demand a hundred million dollars for my land…"

He gave a hard laugh. "You're more trustworthy than anyone in this crazy, savage world. Including me." Grabbing her upper arms, he looked down at her. "Serves me right," he muttered. "I never should have tried to get around my promise."

"Take me with you."

His eyes widened, then he slowly shook his head. "It'll be better…for your sake…for both of us…it's best that we separate."

"Separate," she echoed, feeling hollow.

"Until the land comes through."

She swallowed. "Until we divorce."

His lips curved into a humorless smile. "You know what, I'm almost glad I lost." He tucked a loose tendril of her brown hair behind her ear, then looked straight into her eyes. "Save yourself, Josie. For your next husband. For a man who can deserve you. Who can love you," he added softly.

Turning away, Kasimir started to walk towards the door.

"I intended to lose the race," she blurted out.

She heard his intake of breath. He slowly turned to face her.

"Why?" he asked in a low voice.

She gulped. She had to be brave. To tell the truth. And do it now. Now, without thinking about the risk or cost. Now.

Josie crossed the tent to him. Standing up on her tiptoes, she put her hands on his shoulders and looked straight into his startled blue eyes. "Because I wanted you to seduce me," she whispered.

And leaning forward, she kissed his lips.

So much for his brilliant intelligence. Kasimir had thought he was so smart, finding a loophole around his promise. Passing her in their race down the dune, he'd felt triumphant, his body tight, knowing he all but had her in his arms.

Then there was a scream, and she'd flown past him. She was such an accomplished snowboarder that she'd had no problem handling the textural differences between snow and sand. And she'd seen the source of the scream, the injured boy, half a second faster than he had. It was enough to make any man feel slow. Stupid and slow.

Which was exactly how Kasimir had felt pacing the tent of the boy's family as his uncle, a doctor trained in Marrakech, worked on the boy's ugly compound fracture with his limited instruments at hand. Kasimir had looked down at the sobbing boy, wishing he could do more than order a helicopter on his satellite phone, wishing they didn't have to wait so long, and most of all, dreading the long, jarring journey the boy would face traveling to the hospital in Marrakech.

After Ahmed was loaded on the helicopter with a stretcher, Kasimir had evaded the tearful thanks of Ahmed's family. Shoulders tight, he returned to the tent where Josie waited—not for his seduction, but for her freedom.

The whole afternoon, from start to finish, had left the acrid sourness of failure in his mouth.

And then—Kasimir had tasted the sweetness of Josie's lips against his.

She'd reached her hands around his shoulders, lifting up on her tiptoes, and he'd just stared down at her in shock, telling himself he was completely misreading the situation. Josie, the inexperienced virgin, wouldn't make the first move.

Why would she kiss him? He was a man who stood for nothing and no one. She was an angel who knew how to fly.

I intended to lose the race. Because I wanted you to seduce me.

He heard a soft sigh from the back of her throat. Saw her close her eyes. And she pressed her soft, trembling lips to his.

He didn't immediately respond. He was too amazed.

But when she grew shy, and started to draw away, a growl came from the back of his throat. Closing his eyes, he roughly pulled her back against his body and returned her kiss with force, with all the passion and longing he'd tried so hard not to feel. He let himself feel it—all of it—and desire overwhelmed him as it never had before.

Her lips parted as he deepened the kiss. She returned his embrace awkwardly, hungrily. And it was the best kiss of his life.

Outside the tent, he heard the rising wind flapping and rattling against the heavy waxed canvas. But he was lost in her. Her lips were so soft, her body so womanly, her soul so pure. As he ran his hands down her back, over her loose cotton shirt, he felt the press of her breasts against his muscled chest. Her brown hair now tumbled down her back in waves, tangling in his fingers.

It could have been hours or even days that he kissed her, standing with her in his arms, holding her body tightly against his own. He flicked her mouth lightly with his tongue, guiding her lips, teaching her to kiss. His tongue brushed against hers, luring her to explore further. With a sigh of pleasure, she leaned towards him, her arms tightening around his shoulders.

Josie. So reckless. So beautiful. She had such strange power. She made him want things he shouldn't want…. Made him feel things he didn't know he could still feel….

Lifting her into his arms, never ending their kiss, he carried her to the four-poster bed he'd shared with her in painful chastity for two nights. As he laid her back against the mattress, he looked down at her beautiful face.

"Tell me you don't want me," he said hoarsely. "Tell me to leave you be."

He held his breath, as if waiting for a verdict of his life or death. She shook her head slightly. His heart twisted.

Then her full, pink lips lifted into a tender smile. Her brown eyes shimmered, glowing with desire, and she reached up for him, pulling him down against her in clear answer.

He felt her body beneath him, and knew he'd never again suffer the agony of sleeping beside her without being able to touch her. Because nothing on earth would stop him from taking her now.

Cupping her face, he kissed her passionately, stretching her back against the bed. His hands moved up and down her body until he finally reached beneath her cotton shirt. He felt her trembling hands stroke his bare chest beneath his own ripped shirt, torn into bandages on the dune. Her satin-soft fingertips ran along his flat belly and bare chest, and he gasped at the amazing sensation. He kissed down her throat, and his fingers were suddenly clumsy as he tried to unbutton her shirt, finally popping off the buttons in his desperation to feel the warmth of her skin against his own.

Yanking her shirt off her body, he threw it to the carpet and was mesmerized by full breasts barely contained within a lacy black bra. He sucked in his breath. Distracted, he didn't notice her tugging on his T-shirt until suddenly it was pulled off over his head. He felt the exploratory touch of her fingertips over his flat nipples and down the light dusting of black hair that pointed like an arrow down his muscled body.

Josie. Was this really going to happen? His heart was in his throat as he looked down at her. Here, now?

Outside, the hot wind howled against the tent as he kissed her deeply, pushing her down beneath him, against the soft pillows. He cupped his hands over her bra, feeling the weight of her breasts beneath his hands. He pushed her legs apart with his knee, grinding himself slowly against her, with only fabric separating them. She trembled as he liberated one large breast completely from the bra, watching the rosy nipple pucker and harden beneath the warmth of his breath before he suckled her.

In a single movement, he unclasped the bra and tossed it aside. Leaning back over her, he felt her shiver as he slowly kissed down her neck. Pressing her full breasts together, he kissed the crevice between them, licking her skin.

He felt her fingers tangle in his dark hair as she gasped, clutching him to her. He kissed down to the soft curve of her belly, feeling her tremble, feeling the damp heat of her skin. He slowly pulled off her linen pants, lingering against her thighs and the secret hollow beneath her knees. He removed his cargo shorts. Wearing only his silk boxers, which at the moment were uncomfortably tight, he slid his hips between her legs. Instinctively, she swayed as he rocked himself against her, back and forth over her lacy black panties. He heard her intake of breath as her hands clutched his shoulders, holding him against her.

His lips lowered to suckle a full, pink nipple. He lightly squeezed her breast, pushing her nipple more deeply into his mouth. He heard her soft muffled gasp as he ran his tongue in a swirling motion, nibbling and sucking, as his hand toyed with the other nipple. And all the while, he was slowly grinding himself against her, with only the thin separation of silk between them.

Her hands suddenly gripped his hair. "Stop."

Kasimir sucked in his breath as he pulled back. His body ached as he held himself in check, looking down at her. It would kill him, but if she wanted him to stop....

Josie reached up, running her hands down his bare chest, to the edge of his silk boxers. She looked up, her cheeks red, her eyes bright. "I want to see you. To touch you."

He exhaled.

"Yes."

With tantalizing slowness, she ran her hands along the edge of the waistband, and then—*and then*—he held his breath as she reached beneath the silk. She stroked the hardness of his shaft, running her fingers along the ridges and tip.

He heard a low hoarse gasp, and realized it was his own. Her eyes were huge as they met his. And then...

She suddenly smiled.

It was a smug, feminine smile, full of infinite mystery and pride—as if she'd realized the depths of power she held over him, as she held him completely in her hands.

She pulled down the silk, revealing his body completely to her gaze. She ran her hand over him, exploring. His breathing became ragged. He closed his eyes. Her slightest touch made him wild. He felt as though he could explode at any moment...

No. His eyes flew open, narrowed. With a growl, he pushed her back against the bed. Pulling at her panties, he tugged them slowly down her legs and tossed them to the carpeted sand. He stroked her calves, her knees, then moved back upward, to her thighs. Gently, he pushed her legs apart.

He felt her tremble at being so exposed. She tried to close her knees.

"What are you doing?" she breathed.

"Surrender to me," he whispered. And he lowered his head.

First, he kissed her inner thighs. Then he moved higher. Holding her against the mattress, he stretched her legs wide. For a moment, he just allowed her to feel the warmth and sensation of his breath. Then, very slowly, he moved his kisses to the core of her pleasure. She abruptly stopped struggling.

He took a long, delicious taste. "Like honey," he murmured.

She gave a soft gasp beneath him. He licked her again, swirling his tongue lightly against her, then widening his tongue fully. He pushed a single thick fingertip an inch into her tight, wet core.

She cried out, writhing beneath him as she gripped the sheets. Licking her, sucking her hard nub, he thrust a second finger inside her gently, and she moved her hips unthinkingly, twisting in an agony of need. He lapped her with his tongue, swirling against her taut center, as he felt her tense up. Her back arched off the bed, higher, higher still, until she exploded with a scream of joy.

And just in time. His whole body was sweaty and aching from holding himself back. As she exploded in her pleasure, he could no longer wait. In a swift mindless movement, he drew back and positioned himself between her legs. Lowering his head, he kissed her mouth, and then thrust himself roughly inside her, sheathing himself deep, deep, deep.

CHAPTER EIGHT

JOSIE GASPED AGAINST his lips as he thrust inside her, and she felt an unexpected fleeting pain.

Still deep inside her, he did not move, allowing her to gently stretch to accommodate him. His mouth was motionless against hers in a suspended kiss as she grew accustomed to the now dulling pain. She barely heard the wind outside, or felt the soft mattress beneath her and the weight of him over her. She was overwhelmed by the huge feel of him inside her.

Then, keeping his body still, he flicked his tongue against hers, tantalizing her with a hot, seductive kiss as she grew accustomed to the thick feel of him, like silk and steel inside her. The pain receded, like a wave drawing back beneath her feet. He pressed his naked body over hers, cupping her face with one hand to kiss her more deeply, and her hand trailed down his shoulder to his back as pleasure began to build anew inside her.

She'd never known the pain would be so great—and yet so suddenly gone. She'd never known pleasure could be so intense, so explosive—and could just as suddenly begin again. Sex was a more intense experience than she'd ever imagined. It left her breathless and weak.

So did he.

Josie's heart raced, pounding frantically in her throat,

as she looked up at his handsome, sensual face. She'd been bold and daring enough to tell him the truth, and this was her reward. *This*.

Their hot, naked bodies twisted and moved together, sweaty, hard, sliding. She ran her hands down his chest, feeling his hard muscles and taut hollows. His body felt as amazing as it looked. Pulling him down against her, she kissed his shoulder, tasting and nibbling the salt of his skin.

With a shudder, Kasimir pushed her back against the bed, kissing down her throat. She gasped, tilting her head.

He finally began to move inside her, riding her. He filled her in a way she'd never imagined, deeper with each thrust. Her hands scratched slowly down his back, finally clutching his hard backside. She felt new tension inside her, coiled to spring. She felt the tautness of his muscles, heard the hoarse pant of his breath, and knew he was fighting to keep his body under control.

And *she* was causing that. She was the one driving him wild with desire. Her. Plain, frumpy Josie.

But she wasn't that Josie anymore. He'd changed her. Or she'd changed herself. But either way, she'd become the woman she'd always known she was born to be. Brave. Reckless. Even a little wicked…

His eyes closed. His sensual lips parted in a silent gasp as he pushed inside her, filling her to the hilt, stretching her to the breaking point. He was trying not to hurt her, she realized. He was still holding himself back.

Reaching her arms around his shoulders, she dug her fingernails into his flesh and whispered, "Don't be afraid."

His eyes flew open. He looked down at her with a choked intake of breath.

Giving him a little smile, she ran her hand softly down his hard, muscular body. "Stop holding back."

A growl came from the back of his throat, ending in a hiss. Pushing her back hard against the bed, he pushed more roughly inside her, riding her faster and deeper.

Now it was deepening pleasure. Their intertwined bodies tangled in desperate passion, clutching each other tightly as her hips lifted to meet each explosive thrust. Josie heard the hot wind howling outside and didn't care if a sandstorm flung the tent up into the sky. She was already flying....

The new pleasure continued to soar, rising and surpassing the first. It was deeper and different and sharper than before. Clutching his shoulders, she hung on for dear life as the pleasure grew so big it was almost too much to bear. Finally, it exploded inside her. Sucking in her breath, she tossed back her head and screamed with joy, heedless of who might hear, as she fell, fell, fell, plummeting off the edge of reason.

In that same instant, she heard his low answering roar. He slammed inside her with one final deep thrust, gripping her tightly with a low hoarse shout.

His muscular, sweaty body was heavy as he collapsed on top of her. Rolling next to her on the bed, he clutched her to his heart. A smile traced Josie's lips as she closed her eyes, pressing her cheek against his chest. She felt changed, reborn in his arms. She'd been born to be his wife....

It could have been minutes later, or hours, when Josie's eyes flew open in the darkness. She realized she hadn't just given her virginity to Kasimir tonight.

She'd given him her heart.

So this was how it was to fall in love. In all the books she'd read, all the movies she'd seen, she'd dreamed and wondered how it would be. What it would feel like, when she gave herself to a man completely.

It was like this. Overwhelming. Powerful. Sweet and full of longing. But also...

Terrifying.

Because loving him was an astoundingly simple thing to do. She'd been dazzled by him from the moment they'd met. Infatuated before they were wed. But now...she was in love. Truly and deeply in love for the first time.

Josie swallowed, slowly turning to look at the handsome face of the man sleeping beside her. One side of his face was turned toward the silver moonlight glowing softly through the white canvas. The other side of his face was in shadow, dark and harsh.

And that was Kasimir's soul. This was the man she'd given herself to—body and heart. The man she loved had one side filled with light. This side encouraged, protected, demanded, respected. He was strong and calm in a crisis; he'd rushed to the side of the injured boy.

But Kasimir's other half...was filled with darkness.

There are rumors about me, he'd said. *That I am more than ruthless. That I am half-insane, driven mad by my hunger for revenge.*

But loving him changed everything. She no longer wished to escape him. Or even to be his make-believe wife for a few weeks in a marriage of convenience.

Josie wanted to be his real wife. Always and forever. Complete with children and the white picket fence.

But Prince Kasimir Xendzov was not a white-picket-fence kind of man.

She turned her head, blinking back tears. Such a risk.

Such a stupid risk. She loved the good in him—the man he'd once been, the man he could be again.

But the pain of past betrayals had warped his soul, turning him dark and ruthless. Giving him reason to keep the world at a distance. Her heart twisted in her chest.

Could she make him see that forgiving his brother wouldn't be weakness, but strength—freeing him for a new life? Could she show him that the world could be so much more? She yearned to show him his life, his future, had just begun.

Just as hers had…

With a low sigh, she nestled closer to him in bed. His eyes remained closed, but his strong arms instinctively pulled her closer against the warmth of his body.

It felt so protective, so good. Closing her eyes, she pressed her cheek against his chest.

She would find a way. She yawned, safe and sleepy in his arms. Kasimir had changed her life.

For so long, Josie had been afraid. Since she was twelve, Bree had protected her like a mother hen, not letting her take risks, warning her about the evils of the world. Josie had listened. After all, Bree, older by six years, was the smart one. The strong one. Josie was the burden. The helpless, hapless one. The one who, just by being born, had caused her mother to die. What right did Josie have to ask for anything at all? What right to speak her mind, to make a fuss, to live her dreams?

But Kasimir had changed her, completely and irrevocably. He'd forced her to be who she really was inside. And shown her that living boldly was the only way to honor the sacrifice her mother had made, and the life she'd been given.

He'd done that for her. She yearned to do something

for him. She wanted to teach him that being vulnerable, that trusting others, could be his greatest strength. Josie snuggled deeper into his arms. She would help him break free from the chains of anger and revenge....

Morning sunlight was bright against the white canvas of the tent when Josie opened her eyes. She sat up abruptly. She was alone amid the tangled sheets of the bed. Much of the tent, too, was empty. She saw his packed suitcase beside her own backpack at the door. Weird. Were they going somewhere?

But where was Kasimir?

Kasimir. Just his name was like a song in her heart. Rising from the bed, she splashed fresh cool water on her face from the basin, then pulled on a clean T-shirt, a cotton skirt and sandals from the wardrobe and went outside.

Her heart pounded as she looked for him. She was going to tell him she loved him. Now. Today. The instant she saw him.

But where was he? All of the servants in the encampment seemed to be rushing around strangely, boxing up, packing. She wondered if they were tidying up from the wind storm the night before. Maybe it had been a big one. Not that Josie had noticed. She'd been too distracted by the sensual storm in their bed. A sweet smile lifted her lips. She started towards one of the women, to ask if she'd seen Kasimir. Then Josie stopped.

He was standing alone on the highest dune. His powerful dark silhouette dazzled her. He was like the sun—her northern star.

With an intake of breath, she climbed the sand dune towards him, as fast as she could go. Looking around, she realized she'd come to love the vastness and beauty of the desert. It didn't feel so lonely anymore, or make her feel small.

As long as she was with Kasimir, the world was a wondrous place.

She stopped. Was she making a mistake to tell him she loved him? Would it ruin everything?

She looked at him again, and her shoulders relaxed. Her momentary fear floated away, evaporating like dark smoke into the blue sky, like a shadow beneath the bright Moroccan sun. She didn't have to be afraid. Not anymore. Kasimir had believed in her.

And now, she believed in herself.

"I'm not afraid," she said aloud. Her legs regained their strength. She started to walk towards his broad-shouldered shadow on the top of the dune, silhouetted against the bright sun.

A warm desert wind blew against her skin, tossing tendrils of her hair in her face as she reached him. She was so happy to see his handsome face that tears filled her eyes. "Kasimir. There's something I need to…"

"I have good news," he interrupted coldly.

She looked at him more closely. His desert garb was gone. No more tight black T-shirts. No more cargo shorts or jeans, either. Instead, he was back in his dark suit with a tie and vest. He looked exactly like the same dangerous tycoon she'd first met in Honolulu.

In the distance, she heard a loud buzzing noise. Suddenly feeling uncertain, she echoed, "Good news?"

He gave a single sharp nod. "I'm taking you with me. To Russia. So I can get your sister."

"Oh," Josie said faintly. "That is good news."

It was. But why was his handsome face so expressionless, as if they were total strangers? Why did he seem so suddenly distant, as if they hadn't spent last night ripping off each other's clothes? Why did he look at her as if he barely knew her when just hours before he had been gasping with sweaty pleasure, deep inside her?

"Time to go," he said flatly.

Looking at him in his suit, Josie suddenly felt cold in the warm morning air. The joyful, emotional barbarian with the unguarded heart, the one who'd taught her to ride horses, to snowboard sand, to make love—was gone. She bit her lip. "When?"

He glanced behind him, and she saw an approaching helicopter in the wide blue sky. "Right now."

Shivering, she wrapped her arms around her body, feeling chilly in her cotton shirt. They stood only a few feet apart on the sand, but there was suddenly a deep, wide ocean between them that she didn't understand.

His cruel, sensual lips curved. "We're leaving to find your sister. Aren't you happy?"

"I am," she said miserably. Then, reminding herself she was brave and bold, she lifted her gaze. "But why are you acting like this?"

He blinked. "Like what?"

"Like…" She looked straight into his eyes. "Like last night meant nothing."

"It meant something." He took a step towards her, his face hard as a marble statue. "It meant…a few hours of fun."

It was like a stab in the heart. "Fun?"

Kasimir gave her a coldly charming smile, looking every inch the heartless playboy the world believed him to be. "Oh, yes." He tilted his head, looking at her sideways. "Definitely fun."

For an instant, Josie could hardly breathe through the pain. Then she saw a flash of something in his expression, something quickly veiled and hidden. Her eyes widened as she searched his gaze.

"You're deliberately pushing me away," she breathed.

His expression hardened as he set his jaw. "Don't."

"Last night meant something to you. I know it did!"

"It was an amusement, just to pass the time. But that time is over. Let's get this done. Get our divorce. Then we'll never have to see each other again."

She licked her lips as the approaching helicopter grew louder. "But you said…we could still be friends…."

"Friends?" He gave a harsh, ugly laugh. "You really think that would work? You expect me to give up my life and join you in your fairy-tale world, where families love and forgive?" He slowly walked around her, his eyes glittering in the white sun. "Tell me. Are you already picturing me mowing the lawn outside your storybook cottage with the white picket fence?"

"You're using my dreams against me?" she whispered. His sneer ripped through her heart. She blinked back tears. "Why are you being so cruel?"

Kasimir stopped. The helicopter landed on the pad some distance behind him, causing sand to fly in waves. His black hair whipped wildly around his face as he looked down at her. When he finally spoke, his voice had changed.

"Whatever happened between us last night," he said quietly, "cannot last. Someday soon you will learn the truth about me. And you will hate me."

She shook her head fiercely. "I will never—"

"I'm not giving up my revenge." His blue eyes suddenly blazed. Reaching out, he grabbed her shoulders. "Don't you understand? You can't make me give it up, no matter how good or kind you are, or how you look at me. I'm never going to change, so don't even try."

"But you can," she choked out. A single tear spilled over her lashes. "You could be so much more…."

A flash of raw vulnerability filled his stark blue eyes as he stared down at her. "A woman like you would be a fool to care about a man like me," he said in a low voice. "Don't do it, Josie. Don't."

She stared at him with an intake of breath.

"It is growing late." The cold mask reasserted itself on his handsome face. Abruptly releasing her, he turned towards the waiting helicopter. "Time to go."

An ache filled her throat.

"It's too late already," she whispered, but he'd already turned away.

CHAPTER NINE

HAPPINESS COULD BE corrosive as acid, when you knew it wasn't going to last.

Kasimir gripped the phone to his ear as he stared at the snowy Russian forest outside the window of the dark-walled study. Greg Hudson's voice was grating on the other end of the line.

"So—the New Year's Eve ball tonight? I am tired of waiting," the man complained.

"Yes. And once you are paid," Kasimir replied tightly, "you will never contact me again, or speak of our deal to anyone."

"Of course, of course. I just want the money you owe me. Especially since my boss at the Hale Ka'nani found out about your bribe and fired me."

"You are sure Vladimir and Bree are attending the ball?"

"Yes. I've been watching them, as you said. You owe me extra, for freezing my butt off in Russia. I could be sipping piña coladas on a beach right now."

"Eleven o'clock." Kasimir tossed his phone across the desk. With a deep breath, he looked back out the window. It was the first time he'd seen snow in ten years.

And a million miles from where he'd woken up that

morning. In the heat of the Sahara, waking in Josie's arms to the soft pink dawn, Kasimir had known perfect happiness for the first time in his adult life. He'd held her, listening to the soft sound of her breath as she slept. For thirty seconds, he'd known peace. He'd known joy. And the feelings were alien and terrifying....

Then he'd known that it would all soon end.

So let it end, he thought grimly. After returning to Marrakech, and a stop for the necessary travel documents, he'd taken Josie to Russia in his private jet, to this small remote dacha—a luxurious cabin in the forest outside St. Petersburg.

He'd been cold to her. He'd done what needed to be done. He was hanging on to his control by a thread. He knew what she wanted. He couldn't give in.

He could *not* let himself care for Josie. He couldn't listen to her alluring whispers about a different future. She made him feel things he did not want to feel. Uncertain. Raw. With a heart full of longing for a world that did not, could not exist.

It was time to face reality.

Tonight. New Year's Eve. He would wait until he could speak to Bree Dalton alone, at the exclusive luxury ball at the Tsarina's palace. He would give her his blackmail ultimatum. Now. Before Josie convinced his heart to turn completely soft.

He exhaled.

And once he'd done it...he would tell Josie the truth about who he was. The kind of man who felt nothing, who got what he wanted at any cost. For once and for all, he would wipe that look of adoration off her face. Because he would not, could not give up his plans for revenge. Or keep Josie from finding out about it. For their time together in the Sahara, he'd been happy, truly happy. But it was all about to end.

So let it end. Now. Before the corrosive happiness of caring for Josie, and knowing she'd soon leave, burned his soul straight to ash.

"Kasimir?" Her sweet voice spoke behind him. "Who were you talking to on the phone?"

He whirled around to face her in the dacha's dark study. The decor was very masculine. But then, he'd borrowed this country house from an old acquaintance, Prince Maksim Rostov, who was spending the week of New Year's in California with his wife, Grace, and their two young children.

Kasimir cleared his throat. He kept his voice as cold as he could. "No one that concerns you."

Josie's beautiful eyes filled with hurt. "I thought, now we were in Russia, maybe we could talk...."

"There's nothing to talk about." He told himself he was doing her a favor. This small hurt would be nothing compared to how she'd feel when she discovered he'd kept her prisoner all this time to blackmail her sister.

Let her learn the truth of his dark heart by degrees.

He had to let her go.

He had to push her away.

Now. Before she made him surrender his very soul.

Kasimir straightened the black tie of his tuxedo. "I have to go."

Her brown eyes were deep with unspoken longing. "Go where?"

"Out," he said shortly.

She bit her lip. "In a tuxedo...?"

"Bree and Vladimir will be at the most exclusive New Year's Eve ball in the city. I'm going to go have a little chat." He stopped, then kissed her briefly, not on her lips, but on her forehead. He gave her a smile that didn't meet his eyes. "Your sister will be surprised to hear we're married."

"Take me with you," she said.

He shook his head. "Sorry."

"I need to explain to her why I married you." She swallowed. "She'll be so disappointed in me, that I did it to break my father's trust...."

"Bree? Disappointed in you?" he said harshly. His eyes blazed. "You gave up everything to save her." Forcing his shoulders to relax, he pulled a colorful, brightly decorated phone out of his pocket. "And you can explain that."

She blinked. "What are you doing with my dead phone?"

"All charged up now. I'll give it to her so she can call you here. Tonight."

Kasimir could see the emotions fighting for domination in her expression. But what she finally said was, "Thanks. That is very—kind..."

Kind. Again. Scowling, he turned away. "I have to go."

"Wait," she choked out.

He stopped at the door. He looked back at her.

Josie's beautiful eyes were huge, her soft cheeks pale. "Just tell me one thing," she whispered. "Do you—do you regret taking me to bed last night?"

His eyes met hers.

"Yes," Kasimir said simply, and as he saw her face crumple, he knew it was true. He regretted that for the rest of his life, he'd be haunted by the memory of a perfect woman he could never deserve. A woman he could never have again. A woman who would despise him forever the instant she heard he'd blackmailed her sister.

"Oh." It was the kind of gasp a person makes when they'd just been punched in the gut. She blinked fast, fighting back tears. He wanted to comfort her. Instead, he said, "I'll be back after midnight. Don't wait up."

"Happy New Year," she whispered behind him, but he kept walking, straight out of the house.

As his chauffeur drove him away from the dacha, heading down the lonely road through the snowy forest, Kasimir looked up at the icy moon in the dark sky. His hands tightened in his lap. He missed her. After ten years alone, without ever letting down his guard to another human soul, he missed Josie. He missed his wife.

But his days with her were numbered. They were ticking by with every minute on the clock. And so this had to be done. Although suddenly, even in his mind, he didn't like to specify what *it* was.

It was betraying her.

The New Year's Eve ball was in full swing when he arrived at the elegant palace outside St. Petersburg. Beautiful, glamorously dressed women stared at him hard as he stepped out of the expensive car, and he felt their eyes travel down the length of his tuxedo as they licked their red lips.

In another world, he would have been only too glad to take advantage of the pleasurable services clearly on offer. But not now. Kasimir looked down at the plain gold wedding band on his finger. There was only one woman his body hungered after now. The one woman who would soon leave him, no matter how much he cared. Turning away, he backed into the shadows, avoiding notice as much as he could. Watching. Looking.

"There you are," Greg Hudson said from behind a potted plant. He nodded towards the dance floor. "Your brother and *Bree,*" he panted her name, "are over there."

Kasimir's lip curled as he looked from the man's greasy hair to his totally inappropriate sport jacket, which barely covered his pot belly. With distaste, he withdrew an envelope from his pocket.

Hudson's eyes lit up, but as he reached for the envelope, Kasimir grabbed his wrist. "If you even hint to Vladimir I'm here, I will take back every penny, and the rest out of your hide."

"I wouldn't—couldn't—" With a gulp, the man backed away. "So goodbye, then. Um. *Da svedanya.*"

Turning away with narrowed eyes, Kasimir looked out at the dance floor. He moved slowly through the people, on the edge of the party. Then he saw his brother.

Seeing Vladimir's face was almost startling. For a split instant, Kasimir saw him walking ahead in the snow on the way to school, always ahead of him, whether chopping firewood, chasing newborn calves through the Alaskan forest, or fishing frozen lakes for hours through a cut-out hole in the ice. *Wait for me, Volodya,* Kasimir had always cried. *Wait for me.* But his brother had never waited.

Now, Kasimir's jaw set.

In the last ten years, Vladimir had grown more powerful, more distinguished in his appearance and certainly richer. He also now had faint lines at his eyes as he smiled down at the woman in his arms.

Bree Dalton. The older sister that Josie had sacrificed so much, risked so much, to save. And there was Bree, laughing and flirting and apparently having the time of her life in his great-grandmother's peridot necklace and a fancy ball gown.

Watching them with dark thoughts, Kasimir waited in the shadows until Vladimir left Bree alone on the dance floor. And then Kasimir approached her. He talked to her in low, terse tones. And five minutes later, he left Bree on the dance floor, her face shocked and trembling with fear.

Serves her right, Kasimir thought with cold fury as he left the Tsarina's palace. Josie had been so desperate to save her, and Bree had been enjoying herself all this time as Vladimir's mistress. A tight ache filled his throat.

So much for Josie's *sacrifice.*

And still, after everything she'd done for Bree, when Josie had briefly spoken to her sister, she'd still tried to apologize.

Kasimir exhaled as his chauffeur turned the black Rolls-Royce farther from the palace and through the snowy, frozen sprawl of St. Petersburg. Letting the two sisters briefly speak on the phone had been a calculated gamble.

Where are you? Bree had gasped. There was a pause, in which Kasimir overheard Josie's blurted-out apology, begging her sister's forgiveness for her marriage of convenience. Panicked, Bree had cried, *But where are you?*

He'd taken the phone away before Josie could blurt out that she was right here, in St. Petersburg, not in Morocco at all. Now, Kasimir silently looked out at the moonlit night, at passing fields of snow, laced with black trees.

It was just past midnight. A brand-new year. As he traveled out into the countryside, towards the dacha, he should have been feeling triumphant. His brother had no idea he was about to lose his company, his lover, everything.

Bring the signed document to my house in Marrakech within three days, Kasimir had told Bree coldly.

She'd answered, *And if I fail?*

He'd given her a cold smile. *Then you'll never see your sister again. She'll disappear into the Sahara. And be mine. Forever.*

Now, Kasimir clawed back his hair as he stared out the window at the moonlit night, with only the occasional lights of a town to illuminate the Russian land in the darkness.

In seventy-two hours, Bree would meet him in Marrakech and provide him with a contract, unknowingly signed by Vladimir, that would give him complete ownership of Xendzov Mining OAO. He should have been ecstatic.

Instead, he couldn't stop thinking about how Josie had felt, soft and breathless, in his arms all night, as the hot desert wind howled against their tent, and they slept, naked in each other's arms, face-to-face, heart-to-heart. Her reckless, fearless emotion had saturated his body and soul. He couldn't forget the adoration in her eyes last night—and the shocked hurt in them today.

His hands shook at the thought of the conversation he'd soon have with his wife. Looking down, he realized he was twisting the gold ring on his left hand so hard his fingertip had started to turn white. He released the ring, then exhaled, leaning back in the leather seat. The last lights disappeared as they went deeper into the countryside. Dawn was still hours away on the first of January, the darkest of deep Russian winter.

The car finally turned down a quiet country road surrounded by the black, bare trees of a snowy forest. Past the empty guardhouse, the car continued down a road that was bumpy and long. The trees parted and he saw a large Russian country house in pale gray wood, overlooking a dark lake frosted with moonlight.

The limo pulled in front of the house and abruptly stopped. For a moment, he held his breath. The chauffeur opened his door, and Kasimir felt a chilling rush of cold air. Pulling a black overcoat over his tuxedo, he stepped out into the snowy January night.

As he walked towards the front door, the gravel crunched beneath his feet, echoing against the trees. In the pale gleaming lights from the windows, he could see the icicles of his breath.

As the chauffeur drove the car away towards the distant barn that was used as a garage, Kasimir went to the front door and found it was unlocked.

Surprised, he pushed open the door. He walked into the dark, silent foyer. The house was silent. As the grave.

Where were the bodyguards?

"Hello?" he called harshly. No answer. With a sickening feeling, he suddenly remembered the guardhouse had been empty, as well. With no one minding the door, anyone could have walked right in and found Josie sleeping, helpless and alone.

He sucked in his breath. This was a safe area, but he had plenty of enemies. Starting with his own brother. If somehow—somehow—Vladimir had found out he was here...

"Josie!" he cried. He ran up the stairs three steps at a time. He rushed down the hall to their bedroom. If anything had happened, he would never forgive himself for leaving her.

He knocked the door back with a bang against the wall. In the flickers of dying firelight from the old stone fireplace, he saw a shadow move in the bed.

"Kasimir?" Josie's voice was sleepy. She sat up in bed, yawning. "Was that you yelling?"

Relief and joy rushed through him, so great it nearly brought him to his knees. Without a word, he sat down on the bed and pulled her into his arms. In the moonlight from the window, he saw her beautiful, precious face, her cheeks lined with creases from the pillow, her messy hair tumbling over her shoulders, auburn in the red glow from the fire's dying embers.

"What is it? What's wrong?"

Kasimir didn't answer. For long moments, he just sat on the bed, holding her. Closing his eyes, he inhaled the scent of vanilla and peaches in hair, felt the sweet softness of her body pressed against his own.

"Kasimir?" Her voice was muffled against his chest. He finally pulled back, gripping her shoulders as he looked down at her.

"Where are the bodyguards?" he said hoarsely. "Why are you alone?"

"Oh… That." To his surprise, she shrugged, then gave him a crooked grin. "They got in this big fight, arguing over which of them got to watch some huge sports event on the big screen in the basement and which poor slob would be stuck watching me. So I told them in Russian that I didn't need anyone watching me. I mean—" she gave a little laugh "—I've been sleeping on my own for a long time. My whole life. I mean—" she suddenly blushed, looking at him "—until quite lately." Drawing back, she looked at him. "You aren't mad, are you?" she said anxiously. "I promised them you wouldn't be mad."

"I will fire them all," Kasimir said fervently. Pulling her hard against his body, he pressed his lips to hers in a kiss that was pure and true and that he wished could last forever—but he feared would be their last.

This time, she was the one to pull away. "You don't

really mean that," she said chidingly. "You can't fire them. They had to obey me. I'm your wife."

"Of course they had to obey you," he growled.

"Good," she sighed. She pressed her cheek against his chest, then sat up in sudden alarm. "The phone line got cut off when I tried to talk to Bree. Was she mad? Did you cut the deal with Vladimir? When will I see her?"

Kasimir looked down into her beautiful, trusting face, feeling heartsick. "She's safe and happy and you'll see her in three days." His jaw clenched, and he forced himself to say, "But there's something I need to tell you."

Josie shook her head, narrowing her eyes with a determined set of her chin. "I have something to tell you first."

"No—"

She covered his mouth with her small hand. She looked straight into his eyes. And she said the five words that for ten years, he'd never wanted to hear from any woman.

"I'm in love with you," Josie whispered.

With an intake of breath, he pulled back, his eyes wide. He looked at her face, pink in the warm firelight. "What did you say?" he choked out.

Josie's eyes were luminous as she looked up at him with a trembling smile. Then she said the words again, and it was like the home he'd dreamed of his whole life. "I love you, Kasimir."

"But—you can't." He realized his body was shaking all over. "You don't."

"I do." Her eyes glowed like sunlight and Christmas and everything good he'd ever dreamed of. "I knew it last night, when you held me in your arms. And I had to tell you before I lost my courage. Because even if you're mean to me, even if you push me away, even if you divorce me and I never see you again…" She lifted her gaze to his. "I love you."

Standing up, Kasimir stumbled back from her. Pacing three steps, he stopped, clawing his hair back wildly as he faced her in the moonlight. "You're wrong. Sex can feel like love, especially the first time. When you don't have enough experience to know the difference…"

Pushing aside the quilts, she slowly stood up in her plaid flannel nightgown. "I know the difference." Her eyes pierced his. "Do you?"

His heart started to pound.

He didn't want to think about how being with Josie was so different from anything he'd ever experienced before. Couldn't. "Don't you understand what kind of man I am?" he said hoarsely. "I'm selfish. Ruthless. I've spent ten years trying to destroy my own brother! How can you love me?"

Coming towards him, she put her hand over his. "Because I do."

A tremble went through him then that he couldn't control. Outside, through the windows, the sky was turning lighter as dawn rose pink and soft. It was New Year's Day.

"You should hate me," he whispered. "I want you to hate me."

Reaching up, Josie cupped his cheek, her palm soft against the rough bristles of his jawline. "You don't have to be afraid."

He stiffened. "Afraid?"

"Of loving me back," she said quietly. She took a deep breath. "You want to love me. I think you already do. But you're afraid I'll hurt you or leave you. What will it take for you to see you have nothing to fear? I've never loved anyone before, but I know one thing. I will love you," she whispered, "for always."

Their eyes locked in the gray shadows of the bedroom. The icy wind rattled the window, and the fire crackled noisily.

"There. I'm done." Tears shone in her eyes as she gave him a trembling smile. "Now what did you want to tell me?"

And just like that, Kasimir suddenly knew.

He couldn't tell Josie the truth. Because he wanted her in his life. No, it was more than just wanting her.

He couldn't bear to let her go.

Kasimir's throat ached. But even if he lied to her now, he wouldn't be able to keep the truth from her for long. In three days, when he took her to Morocco for the exchange, she'd discover what he'd done. That he'd been keeping her prisoner all this time. Even she could not forgive that.

Unless…

Was there any way he could keep her as his wife? Any way he could keep her in his bed, with that innocent, passionate love still shining so brightly in her eyes?

Slowly, Kasimir lifted his hand to stroke the softness of her hair. "What I wanted to tell you is…" He took a deep breath. "I missed you."

Josie sighed in pleasure, closing her eyes, pressing her cheek against his chest in an expression that was protective, almost reverent.

In the warmth and comfort of her arms, Kasimir closed his stinging eyes against his own weakness for the lie. Then, in the wintry Russian dawn, against the cold blank slate of a brand-new year, he lowered his mouth to hers for a forbidden kiss. And then another. Until they were tangled together, and he was lost.

Josie had been feeling hurt, with an aching heart, when he'd left her in his tuxedo, to go to the New Year's Eve ball without her. Then she'd been struck by a thought so sudden and overwhelming that it had made her stand still.

Her husband, for all his wealth and power, was completely alone.

Josie couldn't imagine having no family, except a brother who was an enemy. She knew that Bree, for all her overbearing ways, still loved her fiercely. The two sisters had each other's backs—always. But who had Kasimir's back?

No one.

Who loved him on this wide, lonely earth?

Nobody.

Realizing this, Josie's wounded heart had abruptly stopped aching. The tears had disappeared. He had no one who believed in him—no one he could trust. No wonder he'd devoted his life to the success of a business that had never been his childhood dream, to earning money he didn't really need, and most of all—to destroying his only family. His brother.

No wonder his moral compass was so askew. No wonder, when they'd spent the night together in bed and she'd given him her heart, as well as her body, he hadn't known how to react.

But he'd never been loved as she could love him.

Kasimir expected her to stop caring about him the instant he did something cold or rude. Well, he didn't know the type of woman he was dealing with. Josie had been ignored and dismissed her whole life. She'd never once let that stop her from believing the best of people and giving them everything she could.

She knew Kasimir had darkness inside him. She accepted that it was part of him. But as long as he was honest with her, honorable and true, she didn't care. Everyone had flaws. She did. It wouldn't stop her from loving him, the only way she knew how to love someone.

All the way.

Josie loved him. Come what may.

At that simple decision, peace had come over her. The bodyguards, who'd been arguing over who would be stuck watching the crying woman instead of the two-hundred-inch projector screen in the basement, had been astonished when she'd suddenly stopped pacing and told them in clumsy Russian to go watch the game. She'd gone alone to the kitchen. She'd made herself some Russian tea. After speaking briefly to her sister, who sounded very shocked indeed that Josie had married Kasimir, she'd brushed her teeth, put on her nightgown and gone to bed. Rehearsing what she would tell him, she'd waited for her husband to come home.

She'd fallen asleep, but it didn't matter. She hadn't used a word of her little rehearsed speech anyway. She'd just taken one look at the gray bleak shadows on Kasimir's face, at the tight set of his shoulders, and spoken the truth from her heart.

Now, pulling back from his sudden hungry kiss, Josie looked at him. His eyes seemed haunted, tortured, dark as a midnight sea. But he cared for her. She could see it. Feel it. Reaching up, she cupped his cheek. He put his rough hand over hers, then pressed his lips to her palm in a lingering kiss so passionate that her soul thrilled inside her body.

And looking at him, she felt no more trembling

fear. She felt only the absolute knowledge, down to her bones, that her love for him was meant to be.

This time, Kasimir was the one who was shaking, as if he felt her words of love like a physical blow. She tried to imagine what his life had been like for the last ten years, unloved and alone—never knowing what it was to be protected and sheltered by another human soul.

Starting today, and for the rest of his life, he would know. She would shelter him. Protect him.

Beside the bed, she pulled the black overcoat off his unresisting body. She removed his tuxedo jacket and dropped it to the floor. Pushing him to sit on the bed, she knelt and unlaced his black Italian leather shoes, then she reached up for his black tie.

He grabbed her wrist. "What are you doing?"

She exhaled, then leaned up, smiling through her tears.

"Let me show you," she whispered.

His eyes widened. His hand numbly released her.

Pulling off his tie, Josie undid the top button of his white tuxedo shirt, then the waistband of his black trousers. She removed all his clothes, one by one, then pushed him back against the bed. Looking down at him, she yanked her long nightgown up over her head. She kicked off her panties. For a split second, she shivered in the cool winter air as they stared at each other, both naked in the flickering firelight, against the misty gray dawn. Then she pulled the goose-down comforter over them.

Beneath the blanket was their own world. She wrapped her arms around his hard, shivering body, trying to warm them both. She kissed his forehead. Then his cheek. Then...

Suddenly, staying warm was not a problem. She felt

hot, burning hot, with his naked skin against her own. She kissed him, clutching him to her, and a growl came from the back of his throat.

Putting his hands on both sides of her face, Kasimir kissed her back fiercely, possessively, almost violently. Rolling her body beneath him, he kissed slowly down her neck, running his hands over her naked skin as if it were silk. As if he wanted to explore every inch of her.

Insane, intoxicating need overwhelmed her. If he couldn't say the three words that she yearned to hear, she needed to feel his love for her.

"Take me," she whispered. "Now."

He sucked in his breath, searching her eyes. Then, gripping her hips, he pulled back, then thrust inside her, filling her so deeply, all the way to the heart.

She gasped, gripping his shoulders. He wrapped his arms around her, pressing his hard body against her own, and she felt the heat of his breath against her skin as he rode her slow and hard and deep. She cried out, clutching him to her. Drawing back, he looked straight into her eyes, holding her gaze as he plunged one last time, deep, so deep, that she shuddered all around him, as he shuddered inside her.

Afterward, tears ran down Josie's cheeks as she felt his strong arms around her, keeping cold winter away. *She loved him so.* And when Kasimir reached for her again a brief time later, to show her his love again and again, she knew that fairy tales were true. They had to be. Because even if he couldn't speak the words, he loved her. His body proved it.

They were in love. Weren't they? That meant everything would be all right. Didn't it? So they'd be together forever.

Wouldn't they?

* * *

Two and a half days later, in the rustic, dark-walled study of the country house, Kasimir dialed Bree Dalton's number with shaking hands. When she did not answer, he gritted his teeth and called a number he hadn't called for ten years. A number he knew by heart.

Kasimir had waited till the last possible moment to call. For three days now, he'd racked his brain to think of a way to keep both Josie and his revenge. But Bree expected her sister in exchange for the signed contract. There was no solution. Only a choice.

But such a choice. Kasimir had already sent his bodyguards with the luggage to the nearby private airport, where his jet was ready to take them to Marrakech. But then, five minutes ago, outside in the snow with Josie, watching her sparkling eyes as she made a snowman, he suddenly knew the answer.

He wanted Josie more than anything else. So the solution was screamingly obvious.

He would give up his revenge.

He would take Josie to some place where her sister and Vladimir would never find her.

He took a deep breath as Vladimir answered his phone.

"It's me," he ground out.

"Kasimir," his brother replied in a low voice. "About time."

Vladimir didn't sound surprised to hear from him. Strange. And stranger still that after ten years of silence, it seemed as if no time had passed between them. He sounded exactly the same.

"You might as well know, I tried to blackmail Bree," he said abruptly, "into signing your company over to me."

"She already told me," Vladimir replied. "Your plan to turn us against each other didn't work."

Kasimir stopped. "You already know? So what do you intend to do?"

"I am willing to make the trade."

He sucked in his breath. "You're willing to give up your billion-dollar company? For the sake of a woman who once lied to you?" His jaw hardened. Vladimir must really love Bree. "Too bad. I've changed my mind. I no longer have any intention of divorcing Josie, for any price. You can keep your stupid company. In fact... there's no reason for us ever to talk. Ever again."

"Kasimir, don't be a fool," his brother said tersely. "You can still—"

Kasimir turned his head as he heard Josie coming in from the snowy garden. He hung up, dropping his phone into his pocket.

"Why did you run off like that?" She was laughing, wearing a white hooded coat, halfcovered with snow. "We're not even done. The poor snowman only has one eye." Puppy-like, she tried to shake the snowflakes off her coat. Her eyes sparkled like a million bright winter days, and the sound of her laughter was like music. "Ah," she sighed. "I've missed winter!"

He'd never seen anything, or anyone, so beautiful. As he looked at her, his heart twisted with infinite longing.

And he realized: *he loved her.*

His eyes narrowed, and he knew he wouldn't let anyone take Josie away from him. He'd keep her. At any cost.

"I have something to tell you," he said softly. He pulled off her white hooded coat, covered with snow, off her shoulders and dropped it to the floor. "It's important."

Josie gave him a teasing, slow-rising smile. "Hmm. Knowing you…" She tilted her head, pretending to consider, then lifted an eyebrow. "Does that something involve a bed?"

"Ah. You know me well," he answered with a wicked grin. "But no." Growing more serious, he gently used the pads of his thumbs to wipe away the snowflakes from her creamy skin, and those tangled in her eyelashes. Looking down into her eyes, he saw eternity in those caramel-and-honey-colored depths. And he whispered the words in his heart. "I love you, Josie."

Her lips parted in shock. Tears filled her eyes as a sob escaped her. "You love me?"

He cupped her cheek. "Will you stay with me and be my wife?" He gave her a crooked, cocky smile, even as his hands trembled. "Not just now, but forever?"

"Forever," she breathed. A single tear streamed down her cheek. "Yes," she choked out. She threw her arms around him. "Oh, yes!"

He pulled back from her embrace to look down at her. "But there's just one thing." He looked down at her. "If you stay with me as my wife—you must never see Bree again."

"What?" She wiped her eyes with an awkward laugh. "What are you talking about?"

"I saw your sister with my brother at the ball. Laughing. Kissing. They are together now." He set his jaw. "So you must choose. Them…" He tucked back a long tendril of her hair and said in a low voice, "Or me."

Josie blinked fast. "Maybe if we all just talked together, we could…"

"No," he cut her off.

Josie stared at him, her brown eyes glittering. She swallowed, then whispered, "You can't ask this of me."

"I must." He pulled her into his arms. His hands moved to her back, getting tangled in her lustrous, damp brown hair. He kissed her temple, her cheek, her lips. "Choose me, Josie," he whispered against her skin. "Stay with me."

She trembled in his arms, uncertain. Knowing he'd asked her the deepest sacrifice of her life, he persuaded her in the only way he could. He lowered his mouth to hers, kissing her with his soul on his lips, holding nothing back. He kissed her with every bit of love and longing and passion in his heart, until even Kasimir was dizzy as the world seemed to spin around their embrace.

"Let me show you the world," he whispered. "Every day can be more exciting than the last. Choose me."

Her arms twisted around his shoulders as she sighed against his lips. "I can't…"

He kissed her again. In the distance, he dimly heard noises outside the dacha—the call of the birds, the crack of wood in the bare forest.

With a sob, Josie pulled away. A single tear fell unheeded down her cheek. "I love you both." She drew a deep breath like a shudder, then lifted her gaze and whispered, "But if I must choose, I choose you."

Kasimir's heart almost stopped in his chest.

Josie chose him.

It was a selfish thing he'd asked of her, he knew. Selfish? Unforgivable. And yet this amazing woman had chosen him. Over everything and everyone she'd ever loved. He got a lump in his throat. "Thank you, Josie," he said in a low voice. "I'll honor your sacrifice. For the rest of our lives…."

The outside door banged against the wall. Whirling around, Josie gasped, "Bree!"

As if in slow motion, Kasimir turned his head.

Vladimir and Bree stood in the open doorway.

"Josie." The slender blond woman ran quickly towards her younger sister. "Are you all right?"

"Of course I'm all right," Josie tried to reassure her. "You're the one who's been in trouble." She patted her sister's shoulders as if to be sure she was really there. "But are you okay?" she said anxiously. She scowled at Vladimir. "He didn't—hurt you?"

"Vladimir?" Bree looked astonished. "No. Never."

"What are you doing here?"

"We came to save you."

"Save me?" Looking bewildered, Josie looked at Kasimir with a smile then tilted her head. "Oh. You mean from my marriage." She sighed. "I knew you'd be upset I married Kasimir, but you don't need to worry. It started out as a business arrangement, yes, but now we're in love and…"

Her voice trailed off as she looked at the faces of the others. Vladimir folded his arms, glowering at Kasimir. He stared back at his brother warily.

What's going on?" Josie breathed, looking bewildered.

Kasimir set his jaw. He'd been so close—so close to getting her away forever. But now he had no choice but to tell her *everything*—before the others did. He turned to her, his arms folded.

"There's something I need to tell you," he said tightly. "Something I need to explain."

"Go on," she said uncertainly.

He desperately tried to think of a way to make her understand, to forgive. "It was… I thought it was fate." He tightened his hands into fists at his sides. "When you fell into my lap."

He parted his lips to say more, then stopped.

"Kasimir threatened me on New Year's Eve," Bree stated. "He said if I didn't trick Vladimir into signing over his company, he would make sure I never saw you again!"

Josie gasped.

Her sister scowled. "I had to get the contract signed by midnight tonight, or Kasimir was going to make you disappear into the desert forever. Into his harem, he said!"

Josie's face went pale. "No," she breathed. She turned to him. "It's not true," she whispered. "Tell me it's not true. It's some kind of—misunderstanding between you and my sister. Tell me."

Kasimir's shoulders and jaw were so tense they hurt as he looked down at her. "I was going to explain, the night I came back on New Year's Eve. Having you with me, when Bree was with Vladimir, it just seemed—well, I told myself I'd be a fool not to take advantage of the situation." He paused, then forced himself to continue. "I...I was the one who arranged for you and your sister to get jobs in Hawaii."

"You did!"

He gave a single terse nod. "I hoped to convince you to marry me. And I hoped Vladimir would see Bree."

"You mean you hoped I'd cause a scene," Bree retorted.

"Which you did," Vladimir murmured, giving her a wicked grin. She blushed.

"That's neither here nor there," she said primly.

But Josie's soft brown eyes didn't look away from Kasimir's face. "That's why you took me from Honolulu to Morocco?" The color had drained out of her rosy cheeks, leaving her skin white as Russian snow. "You weren't keeping me safe—you were keeping me hostage? To blackmail my sister?"

Kasimir's heart twisted in his chest. "Josie." He swallowed. "If you'll just let me explain…."

And again, she waited, still with a terrible, desperate hope in her eyes. As if there could be any way Kasimir could explain his actions that didn't make him a selfish monster. He took a deep breath. "I did do a terrible thing. But an hour ago, I called and told them the deal was off. I told Vladimir he could keep his company. All I wanted was you." Urgently, he grabbed her hands in his own and looked down at her. "Doesn't that mean something?" he said softly. "I called off the blackmail. For you."

For a moment, Josie's eyes glowed. For that split second, he thought it was all going to be all right.

Then her expression crumpled. "But you were going to separate me from my sister forever, rather than confess how you tried to blackmail her. You were going to force me to give her up, her friendship, her love, for the rest of my life, rather than tell me how you threatened her—with my *safety!*"

"I was afraid." Words caught in his throat. He felt her hands starting to slip away and he tried to grab them, hold on to them. "I was afraid you wouldn't understand. I couldn't take the risk you wouldn't forgive me…."

She pulled her hands away. "If even an hour ago, you'd confessed everything, I think even then I could have forgiven you," she whispered. "But not for th-this." Her teeth chattered. "You d-demanded that I make that horrible choice. When it was never necessary. Even knowing what it would cost me!"

"I'm sorry," he said in a low voice.

Her eyes widened, then narrowed. "You never loved me," she choked out. "Not if you could do that."

Desperately, he took a step towards her. "It was the only way I could keep you!"

She flinched. Closing her eyes, she exhaled. "I always wondered why a man like you would be interested in a woman like me. Now I know." She opened her eyes, and tears spilled over her lashes. "I was just a possession to you. Someone to be married for the sake of land in Alaska, then traded for your brother's company. Then kept at your whim, as what? Your mistress, your sex slave?"

"My wife!"

"You never thought of...of *me*. How I would feel. You either didn't think about it, or you didn't care."

"It's not true!" With a deep breath, he said, "Yes, I tried to use you to get revenge on my brother. But everything changed, Josie, when I...I fell in love with you."

She stared at him. Turning away with a sob, she pressed her face against her sister's shoulder.

"Please," Kasimir whispered, taking a step towards her. "Doesn't it mean anything that I gave up what I wanted most—the company that should have been mine?"

"You don't have to give it up." Vladimir stepped between them, his face grave. Reaching into his coat, he pulled out a white page. "Here it is."

For an instant, Kasimir stared blankly at the page. He took it from his brother's hand. Looking down, he sucked in his breath. "It's the contract I gave Bree." He looked up in shock. "It transfers your shares in Xendzov Mining to me. You signed it."

"Let this be the end," Vladimir said. "I was wrong to force you out of our company ten years ago. I was angry, and humiliated, and my pride wanted vengeance. But I was the only one to blame. So take back what I owe you, with interest. Take it all. And let this be the end of our war."

Kasimir's mouth was dry. "You're just giving it to me?" His voice was hoarse. "Just like that?"

"Just like that."

"A lifetime's work. You're throwing it away?"

Vladimir's forehead creased. "I'm trading it. For the happiness of the woman I love. The woman who will soon be my wife." His blue eyes, the same shade as Kasimir's own, were filled with regret as he said softly, "And to make amends to the little brother I always loved, but have sometimes treated very badly."

A lump rose in Kasimir's throat.

"I should have waited for you," Vladimir said in a low voice, "all those days we walked to school in the snow." Glancing behind him, he gave a sudden snort. "And I should have listened when you said Bree Dalton was a wicked creature, not to be trusted..."

"Hey," she protested behind him.

Lifting a dark eyebrow, Vladimir gave her a sensual smile. "You know you're wicked. Don't try to deny it." Then he looked back to Kasimir, his expression serious. "I was wrong to cut you out of my life," he said humbly. "Forgive me, brother."

Kasimir's world was spinning. He gripped the contract like a life raft. "You can't mean it," he said. "You've put your whole life into Xendzov Mining. How can you just surrender? How can you let me win?"

"For the same reason that, an hour ago, you were willing to let it go." Vladimir gave a crooked smile. "I've won a treasure far greater than any company. The life I always wanted. With the woman I always loved.

You reunited us in Hawaii. And I have you to thank for that."

"I was trying to hurt you," he said hoarsely.

His older brother's smile lifted to a grin. "You did me the biggest favor of my life. Now you're taking the mining company off my hands, I'm off to Honolulu. I've just bought the Hale Ka'nani resort for Bree."

"You did what?"

"Oh, Bree," Josie breathed, clutching her sister's arm. "Just like you always dreamed!"

"I dreamed of running a little bed-and-breakfast by the sea." Bree's lips quirked as she looked at Vladimir. "Trust you to buy me a hundred-million-dollar hotel for my birthday!"

"It was way easier than trying to buy you jewelry," he said, and she laughed.

Kasimir's throat hurt as he looked down at the signed contract in his hand. He had the company he'd always wanted. He'd soon have Josie's land in Alaska. He even had his brother's apology.

He'd won.

And yet, he suddenly didn't feel that way. He looked past Vladimir and Bree to the only thing that mattered.

"Can you forgive me, Josie?" he whispered. "Can you?"

She looked up from Bree's shoulder. Her cheeks were streaked with tears, her face pale.

His heart fell to his feet. He tried to smile. "It's in the marriage vows, isn't it? You have to forgive me. For better, for worse. Can't we just agree that you're the better, and I'm the worse—"

Josie held up her hand, cutting him off. He stared at her, feeling sick as he waited for the verdict. She'd never looked so beautiful to him as she did at that moment, when he knew all he deserved was for her to walk out the door.

"I was willing to give up everything." She sounded almost bewildered. She put her hand to her forehead. "*Everything*. How could I have been so stupid?" She looked up, her eyes wide. "I was willing to give up everything for you. My family, my home, my life—everything that makes me *me*. For a romantic dream! For *nothing!*"

Kasimir's heart stopped in his chest. "It's not a dream. Josie—"

"Stop it!" Her sweet, lovely face hardened as her eyes narrowed. "It *was* a dream. I knew you were ruthless. I knew you were selfish. But I didn't know you were a liar and more heartless than I ever imagined!"

"I'm sorry," he whispered. He swallowed. "If you'll just—"

"No!" She cut him off every bit as ruthlessly as he'd once done to her, again and again. He flinched, remembering. She took a deep breath, and her voice turned cold. "As soon as my land in Alaska is transferred to your name, there's only one thing I want from you."

"Anything," he said desperately.

Josie lifted her chin, and for the first time, her brown eyes held a sliver of ice. He saw her soul there, what he'd done to her, in a kaleidoscope of blue and green and shadows, glittering like a frost-covered forest, frozen as midnight. "I want a divorce."

CHAPTER TEN

ALMOST FOUR WEEKS later, Josie watched her sister and Vladimir get married in a twilight beachside ceremony in Hawaii.

Seeing their happiness as they spoke their wedding vows, a lump rose in Josie's throat. The sun was setting over the ocean as they stood barefoot in the sand, the surf rushing over their feet. Bree wore a long white dress, Vladimir a white button-down shirt and khakis, and they both were decked in colorful fresh-flower leis. As the newly married couple kissed to the scattered applause of friends and family surrounding them on the beach, Josie felt a hard twist in her chest. She told herself she was crying because she was so happy Bree had found love at last.

Josie had filed for divorce the day before.

When her lawyer had called yesterday morning to tell her that the land in Alaska now officially belonged to Kasimir, Josie had thanked him, and told him to file papers for their divorce.

She'd had no choice. She'd given Kasimir all her trust and faith, and he'd still selfishly asked her to make a sacrifice that would have destroyed her—a sacrifice that didn't even have to be made, if he'd just been honest enough to confess!

But her heart was breaking. She'd loved him so. She loved him still.

She'd never forget when Kasimir had told her he loved her on that cold winter day in Russia. She'd thought she would die of happiness. Now, Josie looked down, her tears dripping like rain into the bouquet of flowers she held as matron of honor.

Love. Kasimir hadn't known the meaning of the word. He'd never loved her. All the time she'd spent worshipping him, all the sunny optimistic hopes she'd had that she could change him—what a joke. She felt like a fool. Because she was one.

Blinking fast, Josie watched Bree's fluffy white puppy happily entwining herself around the happy couple, before running up and down the beach in pure doggy joy. She'd been like Snowy, she thought. Like Kasimir's slavishly adoring pet, waiting by the door with his slippers in her mouth. Pathetic.

And now he'd gotten what he wanted all along. His brother's company and his apology. Seducing Josie had just been a way for the notoriously ruthless womanizer to pass the time.

Everything changed, Josie. She had the sudden memory of his haunted eyes. *When I...I fell in love with you.*

She squeezed her eyes shut. No. She didn't believe it. Kasimir was just a man who didn't know how to lose, that was all. He'd wanted to keep her, but not enough to pursue her back to Hawaii. He'd let her go, and had never bothered to contact her since. If he'd loved her, he would have tried to fight for her. He hadn't.

Should she still tell him?

Josie shivered. Still standing in the surf on the beach, surrounded by applauding friends and her new husband, Bree looked at her sister with worried eyes.

Straightening her shoulders, Josie forced her lips into a quick, encouraging smile. She couldn't let Bree know. Not yet.

She exhaled as the group started walking back up the beach towards the Hale Ka'nani for the reception.

Bree was working sixteen-hour days as the new owner of the five-star resort and loving every minute of it. Her first act had been to double the salaries of the hotel's housekeepers. The second was to fire the vendors who'd been double-charging their accounts. Employee morale had skyrocketed since the tyrannical reign of their hated ex-boss, Greg Hudson, had ended.

And both sisters' futures were brighter than Josie had ever imagined. Thanks to Vladimir, there were no longer angry men demanding that Josie and her sister repay their dead father's debts. Without a company to run, he had pronounced himself—at thirty-five—to be retired. But Bree confided she thought he missed working. "Not for the money. But for the fun."

Fun? Josie had shaken her head. But who was she to judge what made people happy? Life was wherever your heart was.

Her own life had become unrecognizable. She'd left Honolulu a poor housekeeper, desperate, broke and completely insecure. Now, she'd started spring classes at the University of Hawaii, and instead of living in a dorm, she had her own luxurious beach villa, right next to her sister's at the Hale Ka'nani. She'd finally gotten her driver's license—and she'd bought herself a brand-new, snazzy red two-seater convertible. For which she'd paid cash.

But she was going to have to return the convertible to the dealer. And see if she could exchange it for something that had room for another passenger in the back.

Josie put her hand over her belly in wonder. As the small, intimate wedding reception began in the open-air hotel bar, and Bree and Vladimir cut their wedding cake together beneath the twinkling fairy lights in the night, she still couldn't quite believe it. How could she be pregnant? She blushed. Well, she knew, but she'd never thought it could happen.

Pregnant. With Kasimir's baby.

A soft smile traced her lips. She was starting to get used to the idea. Maybe Kasimir didn't love her. Maybe Josie's heart would never recover. But he'd still given her the most precious gift of all.

A child.

No one knew yet. She was afraid of what Bree would say. At twenty-two, Josie was young to be a mother. Other women her age were worried about the next frat party or calculus test.

But thanks to Kasimir, there was at least one thing Josie would never need to worry about: money. The day after she left Russia, before he'd even gotten the land in Alaska, he'd placed an amount in her bank account that she still couldn't even quite comprehend, because it had so many zeroes at the end.

"Josie? Is everything okay?"

Looking up, she saw Bree in front of her. Her long blond hair tumbled over her flower lei and white cotton dress as she looked at her sister with concern.

"You look beautiful," Josie whispered. "I'm so happy for you."

"Cut the crap. What's wrong?"

Trust her sister to see right through her. Forcing her lips into a smile, she said, "It's your wedding. We can talk later."

"We'll talk now. Is it Kasimir?" Bree's gaze sharpened. "Has he tried to contact you?"

"Contact me?" Josie gave a low, harsh laugh. "No."

Bree scowled. Then grabbing Josie's hand, she pulled her out of the outdoor bar and into a quiet, dark gazebo in the shadowy garden overlooking the cliff. "Look, you're better off without him," she said urgently. "Plenty of other fish in the sea. You'll find someone really great, who appreciates you—"

Josie flinched. "I know," she quickly said to end the horror of the conversation.

"Then what?"

She paused. "Let's talk about it a different day. After your honeymoon."

"Honeymoon?" Bree grinned. "I'm living in Hawaii, in my dream job, with the man I love! I'll be on honeymoon for the rest of my life!"

"I'm so happy for you," Josie repeated, ignoring the ache in her throat. Resisting the urge to wipe her eyes, she looked down at the wet, soft grass beneath her feet. "After years of taking care of me, you deserve a lifetime of love and joy."

"Hey." Bree lifted her chin gently. "So do you. And I can't be happy until I know what's going on."

Josie blinked back tears, trying to smile. "You've always been a mother hen."

"Always." Her older sister looked into her eyes. "So you might as well tell me what's going on, or I'll be pecking at you all night."

Josie took a deep breath.

"I'm...I'm pregnant," she whispered.

Her sister gasped. "Pregnant? Are you sure?"

She nodded.

Bree took a deep breath, then visibly gained control of herself. "It's Kasimir's." It was a statement, not a question.

"He doesn't know." Josie looked away, blinking back tears. "And I don't know if I should tell him."

"Are you going to keep the baby?"

Josie whirled to face her. "Of course I am!"

"You could consider adoption…"

"I'm not giving up my baby!"

"You're just so young." Bree's hazel eyes were full of emotion. "You have no idea how hard it is. What you're in for."

"I know." Josie swallowed. "You were only six when Mom died, and eighteen when we lost Dad. All these hard years, you've taken care of me…"

"I loved every minute."

Josie looked at her skeptically.

"All right," Bree allowed with a grin, "maybe not every *single* minute." She paused. "I was so scared at times for you."

"Because I was always screwing up," Josie said sadly.

"You?" Her sister's lips parted, then she shook her head fiercely beneath the colored lights of the wooden gazebo. "I was scared I would fail you. Scared I'd never be the respectable, honest, careful mother you deserved, no matter how hard I tried."

Something cracked in Josie's heart.

"That's why you hovered over me?" she whispered. "I thought I was a burden to you, forcing you to give up ten years to look after me."

"I felt like the luckiest big sister in the world to have a sweet kid like you to look after." Bree took a deep breath. "But you don't know what it's like to raise a child. To fear for them every moment." She looked down at the wet hem of her white dress. "To pray that your own stupid mistakes won't hurt the sweet, innocent one you love so, so much."

"You worried you might make a mistake?" Josie said in amazement. Shaking her head, she patted her sister's shoulder. "You gave me a wonderful childhood that I'll never forget." Josie bit her lip, and forced herself to say what she'd been too afraid to say before. "But I'm all grown up now. You don't need to be my mother any more. Just be my sister. My friend." She looked at her. "Just be my baby's aunt."

Bree stared at her. Then, bursting into tears, she pulled Josie into her arms, hugging her tightly.

"You'll be a wonderful mother," she choked out, wiping her eyes. "You're the strongest person I know. You've always been so fearless. You've never been afraid of anything."

"Me?" Josie cried.

Bree gave a laugh, shaking her head as she smiled through her tears. "The stunts you used to pull. Snowboarding in Alaska. While I was hesitating over the safest way, or worrying about the risks, you'd just fly straight past me, head-first. And that's how you love." She looked at Josie. "You're still in love with him, aren't you?"

Josie's lips parted. Then, wordlessly, she nodded.

"Are you going to tell him? About the baby?"

"Should I?"

With a rueful little smile, Bree shook her head. "That's a choice that only you can make." She paused. "Because you're right, Josie. You're all grown up."

Josie hugged her sister tight, then pulled away, wiping her eyes. "I do love him. But he doesn't love me. I know now that he's never going to come for me. I'll never see him again."

"I don't know about that." There was a strange expression on Bree's face as she looked at a point above her ear.

Frowning, Josie turned around.

And saw Kasimir standing behind her, just outside the dark gazebo, in the warm Hawaiian night.

Kasimir's heart was thudding in his throat.

Josie's big brown eyes looked up at him in shock, as if she thought she was dreaming. She was chewing her pink bottom lip in an adorable way, wearing a simple pink cotton bridesmaid's dress, with her soft brown hair hanging in waves over her bare, tanned shoulders.

So beautiful. So incredibly beautiful. Seeing her face, breathing the same air, almost close enough to touch—Kasimir felt alive again for the first time since she'd left him. Especially when he saw she was still wearing her wedding ring.

Kasimir ran his thumb over his own gold wedding band. He'd never taken it off. It had become a part of him.

And so had she.

When he'd burst into the wedding reception, he'd immediately looked for Josie. Instead, he'd seen his brother standing near the bar. It had taken all of Kasimir's courage to tap him on the shoulder.

Still laughing at a friend's joke, Vladimir had turned around. The smile dropped from his face. "Kasimir," he whispered. "I didn't expect you."

"Then you shouldn't have sent me an invitation."

"No—that's not what I meant. I—"

"It's all right. I know what you meant. And until a few hours ago, I didn't know I was coming either." Reaching into the pocket of his jacket, Kasimir pulled out the contract. He pushed it into his brother's hand. "I can't take this. I don't want it."

His brother stared down at the signed contract now in his hand. "Why not?" he said faintly.

Kasimir blinked fast. "The truth is, I never really cared about taking over your company."

His brother snorted. "You gave a damned good impression."

Kasimir tilted his head and gave a low chuckle. "All right. Maybe I did want it. But what I wanted even more," he said in a low voice, swallowing against the ache in his throat, "was to have my brother back." He lifted his eyes. "I've missed you. I don't want to run your company. But..." He paused. "A merger... We could run Xendzov Mining and Southern Cross together. As partners."

Vladimir stared at him. "Partners?"

"We'd have the second-largest mining company in the world. With your assets in the northern hemisphere, and mine in the southern.... We could dominate. Win. Together."

Vladimir blinked, his eyes dazed. "You'd give me a second chance? You'd trust me with your company? After the way I betrayed you?"

Kasimir gave him a crooked smile. "Yeah."

"Why?"

"Because we're brothers. But no more big-brother-little-brother stuff. From now on, we're equals." He tilted his head, quirking a dark eyebrow. "What do you say?" Nervously, Kasimir held out his hand. "Will you be my business partner? Will you be my brother again?"

Vladimir stared at him for a long moment. Then he pushed his hand aside roughly.

Kasimir sucked in his breath.

His brother suddenly pulled him against his chest in a bear hug. His voice was muffled. "I've missed you. What do I say? Hell, yes. To all of it."

When the hug ended, both brothers turned away.

"Sand in my eyes," Kasimir muttered, wiping them with his hand.

"Stupid wind. Lifting sand from the beach." Wiping his own eyes, Vladimir cleared his throat in the windless night, then looked back at him and smiled, with his eyes still red. "From now on, we're equals. Through and through."

Kasimir snorted. "About time you figured that out."

"And by the way, your timing couldn't be better. Thanks for coming to save me. Turns out I'm no good at running a hotel." He gave a sudden grin. "This will save my wife the trouble of firing me."

Kasimir laughed. "Although she might miss you when you start commuting to Russia on a daily basis."

"Hmm." He grew thoughtful. "About that…"

The brothers spoke for a few minutes, and then Kasimir sighed. "I am sorry I missed your wedding."

"So am I." Vladimir punched him on the shoulder. "But having you back is the best wedding present any man could ask for." He lifted an eyebrow with a grin. "Though something tells me you didn't just come here for wedding cake. Or even a business deal."

"You're right." Kasimir took a deep breath. "Where is she, Volodya?"

At the use of his old nickname, Vladimir's eyes glistened. "Sorry," he said gruffly. "Sand again." He gestured towards a nearby cliff. "There. Talking to my wife."

Kasimir had looked past the outdoor bar to a gazebo, strung with colorful lights, on the edge of a cliff. He saw a moving shadow. *Josie*. At last! He'd turned to go, then stopped, facing his brother. He'd said in a low voice, "I'm glad we're friends again."

"Friends?" Vladimir's smile had lifted to a grin. "We're not friends, man. We're *brothers*."

Kasimir was glad and grateful beyond words that after ten years of estrangement, he and Vladimir were truly brothers again. But even that, as important as it was, wasn't the reason he'd flown for almost twenty-four hours straight from St. Petersburg across the North Atlantic to Alaska, and then across the endless Pacific to Hawaii.

Now, Kasimir took a deep breath as he looked down at Josie, facing him beneath the gazebo in the moon-swept night. At the bottom of the cliff, he could hear the ocean waves crashing against the shore, but it was nothing compared to the roar of his own heart.

"What—what are you doing here?" Josie stammered. The music of her sweet, warm voice traveled through his body like electricity.

"My brother invited me to the wedding."

"You missed it," she said tartly.

"I know." He'd known he was too late when from the window of his plane, he'd seen the red sunset over Oahu. But the lights of Honolulu had still sparkled like diamonds in the center of the sunset's red fire, against the black water. Like magic. Because he knew Josie was there. "But the real question is," he whispered, "am I too late with you?"

Josie's lips parted.

Looking between her sister and Kasimir, Bree cleared her throat. "Um. I think I hear my husband calling me."

She hurried away from the gazebo, her wedding

gown flying behind her. And for that alone, Kasimir could have forgiven her anything.

Turning, Josie started to follow. Kasimir grabbed her arm. "Please don't go."

"Why?" She looked at him. "What could we possibly have to talk about?"

"Vladimir and I worked through things," he said haltingly. He gave an awkward smile. "In fact, we've decided to combine our companies. Be partners."

Her jaw dropped. "You did?"

"I was in Alaska this morning, at the homestead. I had everything I ever wanted. And I suddenly realized something."

"What?" she whispered.

He looked at her. "I realized there's no point in having everything," he said softly, "if you can't share it with people you love."

Josie looked at him, her eyes wide. Swallowing, she looked away. "I'm happy you and your brother are friends again."

"Not friends." Kasimir grinned, remembering. *"Brothers."*

Josie looked at him, her eyes luminous and deep. "I'm glad," she said softly. Then she looked down. "But that doesn't have anything to do with me. Not anymore."

Kasimir knew his whole life depended on his next words. "He's not the reason I came back to Honolulu, Josie."

She looked up. "He's not?"

He shook his head, then looked down wryly at his dark wrinkled suit, white shirt and blue tie. "Do you know I haven't changed clothes for twenty-four hours?" He loosened his tie, then pulled it off. "When my lawyer said the land in Alaska was finally mine, I left

St. Petersburg straight from the office. All I could think was I wanted to go home." His lips twisted. "But all I saw in Alaska was a rickety old cabin, piles of snow and a silent forest. It wasn't home." Looking straight into her eyes, he whispered, "Because it wasn't you."

Josie looked up at him, not even trying to hide the tears spilling over her lashes.

With a trembling hand, he reached out and brushed a tear from her cheek. "You're the home I've been trying to find for my whole life, Josie. You're my home."

"Then why did you let me go so easily?" she whispered.

Kasimir took a deep breath, closing his eyes, allowing the warm air to expand his lungs. "After you left," he said in a low voice, "I tried to convince myself I'd won. Then I tried to convince myself that you deserved a better man than me. Which you do. But this morning, in Alaska, I realized something that changed everything."

"What?" she faltered.

He looked straight into her eyes. "I can be that man." He took her hand in his own, and when she didn't pull it away he tightened his grasp, overwhelmed with need. "I can be the man who will mow the lawn by your white picket fence," he vowed. "The man who will be by your side forever. Worshipping you. For the rest of your life."

"But how can I believe you?" Josie wiped her eyes. "Our whole marriage was based on a lie. How can I ever give you my whole heart again?"

Kasimir stared at her, his heart pounding. He finally shook his head. "I don't know." He gave a low laugh, running his hand through his dark, tousled hair. "I wouldn't blame you for telling me to go to hell. In fact, I sort of figured you would."

"Then why come all this way?"

"Because you had to know what was in my heart," he whispered. "I had to tell you how you changed me. Forever. You made me want to be the idealistic, loyal person I once was. The man I was born to be."

Covering her face with her hands, she wept.

Falling on his knees before her, Kasimir wrapped his arms around her. "I'm so sorry I tried to separate you and your sister, Josie. I was selfish and I was a coward. Losing you was the one thing I thought I couldn't face."

He felt her stiffen, then slowly, her hand rose to stroke his hair. It was the single sweetest touch of his life.

Kasimir looked up, his eyes hot with unshed tears. "But I should have thought of you first. Put *you* first. Now, all I want is for you to be happy. Whether you choose to be with me. Or—" he swallowed "—without—"

"Shut up." She put her finger to his lips, and his voice choked off. She said slowly, "I've learned I can live without you."

Kasimir's heart cracked inside his chest. He'd lost her. She was going to send him away, back into the bleak winter.

"But I've also learned," Josie whispered, "that I don't want to." Her brown eyes were suddenly warm, like the sky after a sudden spring storm. "I tried to stop loving you. But once I love someone, I love for life." Her lips lifted in a trembling smile. "I'm stubborn that way."

"Josie," he breathed, rising to his feet. He cupped her face, searching her gaze. "Does this mean you'll be my wife? This time for real?"

Reaching up, she said through her tears, "Yes. Oh, yes."

"You better make her happy!" Bree yelled. They turned in surprise to see Vladimir and his bride standing amid the flowers beyond the gazebo. Bree's eyes were shining with tears as she sniffed. "You'd better..."

"I will," Kasimir said simply. He turned back to Josie and vowed with all his heart, "I will make you happy. It's all I will do. For the rest of my life."

And he lowered his head to kiss her, not caring that Bree and Vladimir stood three yards away from them, with all the partygoers of the wedding reception behind.

Let them look, he thought. *Let all the world see.*

Taking Josie tenderly in his arms, Kasimir kissed her with all the passion and promise of a lifetime. When he finally pulled away, she pressed her cheek against him with a contented sigh, and they stood together, holding each other in the moonswept night.

He could get used to Hawaii, he thought. In the distance, he heard the loud roar of the surf against the shore. He heard the wind through the palm trees, heard the cry of night birds soaring across the violet sky. And above it all, he heard the pounding of his own beating, living heart—his heart which, now and forever, was hers.

"I wish we could stay here," Josie said softly, for his ears only. She looked back at the other couple. "That we could live nearby, and all our children could someday play together on the beach..."

"About that..." Thinking of the decision he and his brother had just made, to build the world headquarters of their merged companies right here in Honolulu, Kasimir looked down at her with a mischievous grin. "I have a surprise for you."

"A surprise, huh?" Tears glistened in Josie's eyes as

she shook her head. A smile like heaven illuminated her beautiful face. "Just wait until you hear the one I have for you."

EPILOGUE

THE DAY JOSIE placed their newborn daughter in her husband's arms was the happiest day of her life, after eight
months of joyful days.

All right, so her pregnancy hadn't been exactly easy.
She'd been sick her first trimester, and for the last trimester, she'd been placed on hospital bed rest. But even
that hadn't been so bad, really. She'd made friends with
everyone on her hospital floor, from Kahealani and
Grace, the overnight nurses who were always willing
to share candy, to Karl, the head janitor who told rivet-
ing stories about his time as a navy midshipman with
a girl in every port.

The world was full of friends Josie just hadn't met
yet, and in those rare times when there was no one
around, she always had plenty of books to read. Fun
books, now. No more textbooks. She'd made it through
spring semester, but now college was indefinitely on
hold.

The truth was, Josie didn't really mind. Her real
life—her real happiness—was right here. Now. Living
with Kasimir in their beach villa, newly redecorated
complete with a white picket fence.

Now, Josie smiled up from her hospital bed at Kasi-

mir's awed, terrified, loving face as he held his tiny
sleeping daughter for the first time.

"Need any help?"

"No." He gulped. "I think."

Looking at her husband holding their baby, tears
welled up in Josie's eyes. They were a family. Kasimir loved working with his brother as partners in their
combined company, Xendzov Brothers Corp. But for
both princes, the way they did business had irrevocably changed. They still wanted to be successful, but the
meaning of success had changed. "I want to make a difference in the world," Kasimir had said to her wistfully,
lying beside her in the hospital bed last week. "I want
to make the world a better place."

Josie hit him playfully with a pillow. "You do. Every
time you bring me a slice of cake."

"No, I mean it." He'd looked at her out of the corner
of his eye. "I was thinking…we could put half our prof-
its into some kind of medical foundation for children.
Maybe sell the palace in Marrakech for a new hospital in the Sahara." He stopped, looking at her. He said
awkwardly, "What do you think?"

"So what's stopping you?" With a mock glare, she
tossed his own words back at him. "The only one stopping you is *you*."

"Really? You wouldn't miss it?"

She snorted. "We don't need more money, or another
palace." She thought of little Ahmed breaking his leg
on the sand dune, far from medical care. "I love your
hospital idea. And the foundation, too."

He looked down at her fiercely. "And I love you."
Cupping her face, he whispered, "You're the best,
sweetest, most beautiful woman in the world."

Nine months pregnant and feeling ungainly as a whale, having gained fifty extra pounds on banana bread, watermelon and ice cream, Josie had snorted a laugh, even as she looked at him tenderly. "You're so full of it."

"It's true," Kasimir had insisted, and then he kissed her until he made her believe he was an honest man.

Josie smiled. Kasimir always knew what to say. The only time she'd ever seen him completely without words was when she'd told him she was pregnant that night of Vladimir and Bree's wedding. At first, he'd just stared at her until she asked him if he needed to sit down—then, with a loud whoop and a holler, he'd pulled her into his arms.

With the divorce cancelled, he'd still insisted on re-marrying her and doing it right, with their family in attendance. He'd actually suggested that they wed immediately, poaching Bree and Vladimir's half-eaten wedding cake, and grabbing the minister yawning at the bar. But rather than steal her sister's thunder, Josie had gotten him to agree to a compromise.

Tearing up the pre-nup, they'd married three days later, at dawn, on the beach. The ceremony had been simple, and as they'd spoken vows to love, cherish and honor each other for the rest of their lives, the brilliant Hawaiian sun had burst through the clouds like a benediction.

Then, of course, this being Hawaii, the clouds had immediately poured rain, forcing the five of them—Josie, Kasimir, Bree, Vladimir and the minister—to take off at a run for the shelter of the resort, with their leis trailing flower petals behind them. And once at the hotel, Josie had discovered the ten-tiered wedding cake

her husband had ordered her—enough for a thousand
or two people, covered with white buttercream flowers
and their intertwined initials.

Her husband's sweet surprise was the most delicious
cake of her life. Good thing too. Remembering, she gave
a sudden grin. They were still eating wedding cake out
of their freezer.

Josie glanced through the window in the door of her
private room in the Honolulu hospital. In the hallway,
she could see Bree pacing back and forth, a phone to her
ear, telling Vladimir the happy news of the birth. Vladimir was still in St. Petersburg, finalizing the company's move to Honolulu. They were a very high-powered
couple. Bree was having the time of her life running
the Hale Ka'nani resort, which was already up in prof-
its, having become newly popular with tourists from
Japan and Australia. Vladimir and Bree did hope to
start a family someday, but for now, they were having
too much fun working.

Not Josie, though. All she wanted was right here.
She looked at Kasimir and their daughter. Right now.
A home. A husband. A family.

"Am I doing this right?" Kasimir said anxiously,
his shoulders hunched and stiff as he cradled his baby
daughter.

She snorted, leaning forward to stroke the baby's
cheek with one hand. "You're asking me? It's not like
I have more experience."

"I'm a little nervous," he confessed.

"You?" she teased. "Scared of an eight-pound baby?"

"Terrified." He took a deep breath. "I've never been
a father before. What if I do something wrong?"

She put her hand on his forearm. "It won't matter."

Tears spilled over her lashes as she smiled, loving him so much her heart ached with it. "You're the perfect father for her, because you love her." She looked down at the sleeping newborn in his arms. "And Lois Marie loves you already."

Kasimir's eyes crinkled. "Lulu is the best baby in the world," he agreed, using their baby's nickname. They'd named her after the mother Josie had never known. The mother who, along with her father, she would always remember. Josie would honor them both by being true to her heart. By singing the song inside her.

Holding hands, Kasimir and Josie smiled at their perfect little daughter, marveling at her soft dark hair, at her tiny hands and plump cheeks.

Then a new thought occurred to Josie, and she suddenly looked up in alarm. "What if I'm the one who doesn't know how to be a mother?" she asked.

"You?" Her husband gave a laugh that could properly be described as a guffaw. "Are you out of your mind? You'll be the best mother who ever lived." Cradling their tiny baby, securely nestled in the crook of his arm, he reached out a hand to cup Josie's cheek. "And I promise you," he whispered, "for the rest of my life, even if I make a mistake here or there, I'll love you both with everything I've got. And if I screw up, or if we fight, I'll always be the first to say I'm sorry." He looked at her. "I give you my word."

Reaching up, Josie wrapped her hand around his head, tangling her fingers in his dark hair. "Your word of honor?"

His eyes were dark. "Yes."

She took a deep breath.

"Show me," she whispered.

And as Kasimir lowered his head to hers, proving

his words with a long, fervent kiss, Josie felt his vow in her heart like bright sun in winter. And she knew their bold, fearless life as a family, complicated and crazy and oh, so happy, had just begun.

* * * * *

THE GREEK BILLIONAIRE'S
BABY REVENGE

To Pete, the sexiest, smartest and best.
Every day, I love you more.

CHAPTER ONE

SNOW WAS FALLING so hard and fast that she could barely see through the windshield.

Anna Rostoff parked her old car in the front court-yard of the palace, near the crumbling stone fountain, and pulled on the brake. Her hands shook as she peeled them from the steering wheel. She'd nearly driven off the road twice in the storm, but she had the groceries and, more importantly, the medicine for her baby's fever.

Taking a deep breath, she hefted the bag with one arm and climbed out into the night.

Cold air stung her cheeks as she padded through soft snow and ascended sweeping steps to the gilded double doors of the two-hundred-year-old palace. They were conserving electricity in favor of paying for food and diapers, so the windows were dark. Only a bare thread of moonlight illuminated the dark Russian forest.

We're going to make it, Anna thought. It was April, and spring still seemed like a forlorn dream, but they had candles and a shed full of wood. Once she found work as a translator she'd be able to make a new life with her four-month-old baby and her young sister. After months of hell, things were finally looking up.

She lifted her keys to the door.

Her eyes went wide as a chill descended her spine. The front door was open.

Barely able to breathe, she pushed into the grand foyer. In the shadows above, an ancient, unseen chandelier chimed discordantly as whirling flurries of snow came in from behind, whipped by a cold north wind.

"Natalie?" Anna's voice echoed down the hall.

In response, she heard a muffled scream.

She dropped the groceries. Potatoes tumbled out across the floor as she ran down the hall. Gasping, she shoved open the door into the back apartment.

A figure stood near the ceramic tile fireplace, his broad-shouldered form silhouetted darkly in the candlelight.

Nikos!

For one split second Anna's heart soared in spite of everything. Then she saw the empty crib.

"They took the baby, Anna," Natalie cried, her eyes owlish with fear behind her glasses. Two grim bodyguards, ruddy and devilish in the crackling firelight, flanked her sister on either side. She tried to leap from the high-backed chair, but one of Nikos's men restrained her. "They came in while I was dozing and snatched him from his crib. I heard him cry out and tried to stop them—"

Misha. Oh, God, her son. Where was he? Held by some vicious henchman in the dark forest? Already spirited out of Russia to God knew where? Anna trembled all over. Her baby. Her sweet baby. Sick with desperation and fear, she turned to face the monster she'd once loved.

Nikos's expression was stark, almost savage. The man who'd laughed with her in New York and Las Vegas, drinking ouzo and singing in Greek, had disappeared. In his place was a man without mercy. Even in the dim light she could see that. Olive-skinned and black-haired, he was as handsome as ever, but something had changed.

The crooked nose he'd broken in a childhood fight had once been the only imperfection in classic good looks. Now his face had an edge of fury—of cruelty. He'd always been strong, but there were hard planes to his body that hadn't been there before. His shoulders were somehow broader, his arms wider, as if he'd spent the last four months beating his opponents to a pulp in the boxing ring. His cheekbones were razor-sharp, his arms thick with muscle, his blue eyes limitless and cold. Looking into his eyes was like staring into a half-frozen sea.

Once she'd loved him desperately; now she hated him, this man who had betrayed her. This man who, with kisses and sweet words whispered against her skin at night, had convinced her to betray herself.

"Hello, Anna." Nikos's voice was deep, dangerous, tightly controlled.

She rushed at him, grabbing the lapels of his black cashmere coat. "What have you done with my baby?" She tried to shake him, pounded on his chest. *"Where is he?"*

He grabbed her wrists. "He is no longer your concern."

"Give me my child!"

"No." His grip was grim, implacable.

She struggled in his arms. Once his touch had set her body aflame. No longer. Not now that she knew what kind of man he really was.

"Misha!" she shrieked helplessly.

Nikos's grasp tightened as he pulled her closer, preventing her from thrashing her arms or clawing his face. "*My son* belongs with me."

It was exactly what she'd known he'd say, but Anna still staggered as if he had hit her. This time Nikos let her go. She grabbed the rough edge of the long wooden table to keep herself from sliding to the floor. She had to be strong—strong for her baby. She had to think of a way to save her son.

In spite of her best efforts, a tear left a cold trail down her cheek. Wiping it away furiously, she raised her chin and glared at Nikos with every ounce of hate she possessed. "You can't do this!"

"I can and I will. You lost the right to be his mother when you stole him away like a thief in the night."

Anna brought her hands to her mouth, knowing Nikos could use his money and power and man-eating lawyers to keep her from her son forever. She'd been stupid to run away, and now her worst nightmare had come true. Her baby would grow up without her, living in Las Vegas with a heartless, womanizing billionaire and his new mistress...

"I'm so sorry, Anna," Natalie sobbed behind her. "I tried to stop them. I tried."

"It's all right, Natalie," Anna whispered. But it wasn't all right. It would never be all right again.

A door slammed back against the wall, causing Anna to jump as a third bodyguard entered from the kitchen and placed a tray on the table. Steam rose from the samovar as Nikos went to the table and poured undiluted tea, followed by hot water, into a blue china cup.

She stared at her great-grandmother's china teacup. It looked so fragile and small in his fingers, she thought. It could be crushed in a moment by those tanned, muscular hands.

Nikos could destroy anything he wanted. And he had.

"I've been here two weeks," Anna said bitterly as she watched him take a drink. "What took you so long?"

He lowered the cup, and his unsmiling gaze never once looked from hers.

"I ordered my men to wait until you and the child were separated. Easier that way. Less risk of you doing something foolish."

Stupid. Stupid. She never should have left her baby—not even to go to an all-night market in St. Petersburg. After all, Misha wasn't really sick, just teething and cranky, with a tiny fever that barely registered on her thermometer.

"I was stupid to leave," she whispered.

"It took you four months to figure that out?"

Anna barely heard him. No, the really stupid move had been coming here in the first place. After four months on the move, always just one step ahead of Nikos's men, and with money running out, Anna had convinced herself that Nikos wouldn't be staking out her great-grandmother's old palace. Now mortgaged to the hilt, the crumbling palace was their family's last asset. Natalie was trying to repair the murals in hopes that they'd be able to find a buyer and pay off their paralyzing debt. A fruitless hope, in Anna's opinion.

As fruitless as trying to escape Nikos Stavrakis. He was bigger than her by six inches, and eighty pounds of hard muscle. He had three bodyguards, with more waiting in cars hidden behind the palace.

The police, she thought, but that hope faded as soon as it came. By the time she managed to summon a policeman Nikos would be long gone. Or he'd pay off anyone who took her side. Nikos Stavrakis's wealth and power made him above the law.

She had only one option left. Begging.

"Please," she whispered. She took a deep breath and forced herself to say in a louder voice, "Nikos, please don't take my child. It would kill me."

He barked a harsh laugh. "That's what I'd call a bonus."

She should have known better than to ask him for anything. "You...you heartless bastard!"

"Heartless?" He threw the cup at the fireplace. It smashed and fell in a thousand chiming pieces. "Heartless!" he roared.

Suddenly afraid, Anna drew back. "Nikos—"

"You let me believe that my son was dead! I thought you both were dead. I returned from New York and you were gone. Do you know how many days I waited for the ransom note, Anna? Do you have any idea how long I waited for your bodies to be discovered? Seven days. You made me wait seven damn days before you bothered to let me know you were both alive!"

Anna's breaths came in tiny rattling gasps. "You betrayed me. You caused my father's death! Did you think I'd never find out?"

His dark eyes widened, then narrowed. "Your father made his own choices, as you have made yours. I'm taking my son back where he belongs."

"No. Please." Tears welled up in her eyes and she grabbed at his coat sleeve. "You can't take him. I'm—I'm still breastfeeding. Think what it would do to Misha to lose his mother, the only parent he's ever known..."

His eyes went dark, and Anna wanted to bite off her tongue. How could she have drawn attention to the fact that she'd not only denied Nikos the chance to experience the first four months of their child's life, but she'd broken her promise about their son's name?

Then he bared his teeth in the wolflike semblance of

a smile. "You are mistaken, *zoe mou*. I have no intention of taking him away from you."

She was so overwhelmed that she nearly embraced him. "Thank you—oh, God, thank you. I really thought..."

He took a step closer, towering over her. "Because I'm taking you as well."

He should have savored this moment.

Instead, Nikos was furious. For four months he'd fantasized about taking vengeance on Anna. *No, not vengeance*, he corrected himself. *Justice*.

Some justice. His lip curled into a half-snarl. Bringing Anna back to Las Vegas, where he'd see her face across his table every day? That was the last thing he wanted.

He'd intended to take his son and leave, as she deserved. But from the moment he'd first seen his baby son a surge of love had risen in him that he'd never felt before. At that moment he'd known he could never allow his son to be hurt. He'd kill anyone who tried.

For four months he'd hated Anna. But now...

Hurting her would hurt his son. His child needed his mother. The two were bonded.

The payback was off.

He cursed under his breath, narrowing his eyes.

Anna had lost all her pregnancy weight, and then some. Under her coat's frayed edges he could see the swell of her breasts beneath her tight sweater, see the curve of her slender hips in the worn, slim-fitting jeans. There were hungry smudges beneath her cheekbones that hadn't been there before, and tiny worry lines around her blue-green eyes. The tightly controlled secretary was gone. Her long dark hair, which she'd always pulled back in a tight bun, now fell wild around her shoulders. It was…sexy.

Anna slowly exhaled and stared up at him, her eyes pleading for mercy. Even now, she was the most beautiful woman he'd ever seen. Her aristocratic heritage showed in the perfect bone structure of her heart-shaped face, and in every move she made.

Once he'd been grateful for her skills. He'd admired her dignity, her grace. He'd known Anna's value. As his executive secretary, she'd run interference with government officials, employees, vendors and investors, making decisions in his name. She'd reflected well both upon him and the brand of luxury hotels he'd created around the world. Even now he still missed her presence in his office—the cool, precise secretary who'd made his business run so smoothly. She'd made it look easy.

It made him regret that he'd ever slept with her.

It made him furious that he was still so attracted to her.

Misha, indeed. A Russian nickname for Michael? Anna had promised to name their son after Nikos's maternal grandfather, but it didn't surprise him that she'd gone back on her word. She was a liar, just like her father.

"I had Cooper pack your things," he bit out. "We're leaving."

"But the storm—"

"We have snow chains and local drivers. The storm won't slow us down."

Anna glanced from Nikos to the empty crib, and the fight went out of her. Her shoulders sagged.

"You win. I'll go back with you," she said quietly.

Of course he'd won. He always won. Although this victory had come harder than he'd ever imagined, at a price he hadn't wanted. Already sick of the sight of her, he growled, "Let's go."

But as he turned away Anna's throaty voice said, "What about Natalie? I can't leave her here. She has to come with us."

"What?" her sister gasped.

Nikos whirled back with a snarl on his lips, incredulous that Anna was actually trying to dictate the terms of her surrender. Another Rostoff woman in his house? "No."

"No way, Anna!" Her sister echoed, pushing up her glasses. "I'm not going anywhere with him. Not after what he did to our father. Forget it!"

Anna ignored her. "Look around, Nikos. There's no money. I was planning to get a job as a translator to support us. I can't just leave her."

"I'm twenty-two! I can take care of myself!"

Anna whirled around to face her young sister. "You barely speak Russian, and all you know about is art. Mother doesn't have any more money to send you, and neither do I. What do you expect to eat? Paintbrushes?"

The girl's eyes filled with tears. "Maybe if we went to Vitya he would…"

"No!" Anna shouted.

Who was Vitya? Nikos wondered. Another impoverished aristocrat like Anna's father had been? For most of Anna's young life he'd forced his family to live off the charity of wealthy friends. She'd once dryly commented that that was how she'd learned to speak fluent French, Russian, Spanish and Italian—begging the Marquis de Savoie and Contessa di Ferazza for book money.

Although of course that had been before Alexander Rostoff had realized it would be simpler to just embezzle the money.

Aristocrats, he thought scornfully. Rather than live in the comforts of Nikos's house near Las Vegas, his brownstone in New York, or his villa in Santorini, Anna had kidnapped his baby son and moved from one cheap apartment to another.

His lip curled as he looked around the room. The back of the palace had been turned into a cheerless Soviet-era apartment. It was a little disorienting to be smack in the real thing, especially since Anna seemed to be using nineteenth-century standards to light and heat the room.

"How could you force my son to live like this?" he abruptly demanded. "What kind of mother are you?"

Anna's turquoise eyes widened as she gripped the gilded edge of a high-backed chair. "I kept him warm and safe—"

"Warm?" Incredulously, he looked at the single inadequate fireplace, the flickering candles on the wooden table, the frost lining the inside of the window. "Safe?"

Anna flinched. "I did the best I could."

Nikos shook his head with a derisive snort as Cooper, his right-hand man and director of security, entered the room. He gave Nikos a nod.

Nikos made a show of glancing at his sleek platinum watch. "Your things are packed in the truck. Are you coming, or should we toss your suitcases in the snow?"

"We just need a minute for Natalie to pack her things—"

"Perhaps I have not made myself clear? There is no way in hell that I'm taking your sister with us. You're lucky I'm bringing you."

Anna folded her arms, thrusting up her chin. He knew that expression all too well. She was ready to be stubborn, to fight, to prolong this argument until he had to drag her out of this place by her fingernails.

"Stay, then." He turned to leave, motioning for Cooper and his bodyguards to follow. "Feel free to visit our son next Christmas."

Precisely as he'd expected, Anna grabbed his arm.

"Wait. I'm coming with you. You know I am. But I can't just abandon Natalie."

He tried to shake off her grip, but she wouldn't let go. He looked into those beautiful blue-green eyes, wet with unshed tears. What was it about women and tears? How were they able to instantly manufacture them to get what they wanted? Well, it wouldn't work on him. He wouldn't be manipulated in this way. He wouldn't let her...

"You might have to go with him, Anna," Natalie said defiantly. "But I don't. I'm staying."

Nikos glanced at Anna's sister. The girl had fought like a crazed harpy to protect her nephew. Now, she just looked heartbreakingly young.

Something like guilt went through him. Angrily, he pushed it aside. If the Rostoffs were penniless, it wasn't his fault. As his secretary, Anna had been paid a six-figure salary for the last five years—enough to support her whole family in decent comfort.

So where had that money gone? He'd never seen Anna splurge on clothes or jewelry or cars. She bought things that were simple and well made but, unlike his current secretary, she avoided flashy luxury.

Anna's sister didn't look terribly royal either. In her bulky sweatsuit, covered by an artist's smock, she stood by the frost-lined window with a bowed head. She was staring wistfully at the broken pieces of the blue china teacup he'd smashed against the fireplace.

His jaw tightened.

He gestured to Cooper, who instantly came forward. "Yes?"

"See that the girl has all the money and assistance she requires to live here or return to New York, as she wishes." In a lower voice, he added, "And find a replacement for that damn cup. At any price."

Cooper gave a single efficient nod. Nikos turned to Anna. "Satisfied?"

Anna raised her chin. Even now, when he'd given her far more than she deserved, she was defiant. "But how do I know you'll keep your word?"

That one small question made fury rise tight against his throat. He always kept his word. Always. And yet she dared insinuate that he was the one who was untrustworthy. After her father had stolen his money. After she herself had stolen his child.

He hated her so much at that moment he almost *did* leave her behind. He wanted to do it. But not at the cost of hurting his son. Damn her.

Gritting his teeth, he said, "Call your sister when we reach Las Vegas. You'll see I've kept my word."

"Very well." Anna's face was pale as she knelt beside her sister. "You'll accept his help, won't you, Natalie? Please."

The girl hesitated, and for a moment Nikos thought she would refuse. Then her expression hardened. "All right. Since he's only paying back what he took from Father."

What the hell had Anna told her? Surrounded by bodyguards, he didn't have the time or inclination to find out. He'd tried to spare Anna the truth about her father, but he was done coddling her. It was time she knew the kind of man he really was. He would enjoy telling her.

And more than that, Nikos promised himself as they left the palace. Once they'd returned to his own private fiefdom in Las Vegas he would make her pay for her crimes. In private. In ways she couldn't even imagine.

Oh, yes, he promised himself grimly. She'd pay.

CHAPTER TWO

RIDING IN THE limo from the Las Vegas airport to Nikos's desert estate twenty miles outside the city gave Anna an odd sense of unreality.

In one long night she'd left darkness and winter behind. But it wasn't just the bright morning light that threw her. It wasn't just the harsh blue sky, or the dried sagebrush tumbling across the long private road, or the feel of the hot Nevada sun on her face.

It was the fact that nothing had changed. And yet everything had changed.

"Hello, miss," the housekeeper said as they entered the grand foyer.

"Welcome back, miss," a maid said, smiling shyly at the baby in Anna's arms.

The moment their limo had arrived inside the guarded gate the house steward and a small army of assistants had descended upon Nikos. He walked ahead with them now, signing papers and giving orders as he led them through the luxurious fortress he called a home. Members of his house staff had already spirited away her luggage.

Where had they taken it? Anna wondered. A guestroom? A dungeon?

Nikos's bedroom?

She shivered at the thought. No, surely not his bedroom. But for most of her pregnancy his room had been her home. She'd slept naked in his arms on hot summer nights. She'd caressed his body and kissed him with her heart on her lips. She'd dreamed of wearing his engagement ring and prayed to God that it would last. She'd been so sure that if he left her she would die.

But in the end she'd been the one who left.

Because the moment he'd found out she was pregnant he'd fired her. She'd gone from being his powerful, trusted assistant to a prisoner in this gilded cage. He'd ordered her to take her leisure, practically forcing her into bedrest, although she'd had a normal, healthy pregnancy.

Nikos had taken the job she loved and given it to a young, gorgeous blonde with no secretarial skills. He'd ordered the household staff to block the calls of her mother and sister. Then, during her final trimester, he'd suddenly refused to touch her. He'd abandoned her to go and stay, with his secretary Lindsey on hand, at the newly finished penthouse at L'Hermitage Casino Resort.

That should have been enough to make Anna leave him. That should have been more than enough. But it hadn't been until she'd found those papers showing that Nikos had deliberately destroyed her father's textiles company that she'd finally been fed up. Anna's hands tightened. Running away had been an act of self-defense for her and her child.

But now they were back. As Anna entered a wide gallery lined with old portraits, she could smell the flowers of the high desert. Spring was swift in southern Nevada, sometimes lasting only weeks. Wind and light cascaded through high open windows, oscillating the curtains. Her footsteps echoed in the wide hall as she followed Nikos and his men.

But a woman was with them, too: the perfect blonde who'd replaced Anna in Nikos's office, and in his bed. Anna watched Lindsey lean forward eagerly, touching his arm. She blinked, surprised at how much it hurt to see them together.

Nikos was impeccably gorgeous, as always. He'd showered and changed on the plane, and now wore dark designer slacks and a crisp white shirt that showed off his tanned olive skin. It wasn't just his height that made him stand out from the rest of his men, but his aura of power, worn as casually as his shirt.

Nikos had always stood out for her. Even now, looking at him, Anna felt her heart ache. It was too easy to remember the years they'd spent working together. In spite of his arrogance, she'd admired him. He'd seemed so straightforward and honest, so different from her former employer, Victor. Plus, Nikos had never tried to make a pass at her. For five years he'd taken time not just to teach her about the business, but also to rely upon her advice. At least until that night thirteen months ago when he'd shown up wild-eyed on her doorstep, and everything had changed between them forever.

But her job had meant everything to her. For the first time in her life she'd felt strong. Capable. Valued. Was it any wonder that, even knowing her boss was a playboy, she'd fallen so totally under his spell?

As if he felt her gaze, Nikos glanced back to where she trailed behind with the baby. His eyes were dark, and a shiver went through her.

"He hates you, you know."

Anna glanced up at Lindsey, who was standing next to her. She had a scowl on her pouting pink lips, though she looked chic in a dark pinstriped suit with a tucked-in waist and miniskirt. Her tanned legs stretched forever into impossibly high heels.

Anna felt dowdy in comparison, wearing the same T-shirt and jeans from last night, with a sweater tied around her waist. Her hair, which hadn't been washed or combed since yesterday, was pulled back in a ponytail. She'd been afraid to leave her baby alone on the plane, even for the few minutes it would have taken to shower.

Next to Lindsey, Anna felt a million years old, worn out from running away, working odd jobs, trying to get by, raising her child. Lindsey was fresh and young, glossy and free. No wonder Nikos preferred her. The thought stung, even though she told herself that it didn't hurt.

"I don't care if he hates me." Anna nervously twisted her great-grandmother's wedding ring around her finger, fiddling with its bent-back tines and empty setting. She couldn't let Lindsey know how vulnerable she felt on the inside, how scared she was that the younger woman would soon take everything Anna cared about. She already had Nikos and her job. Would Misha be next?

Lindsey lifted a perfectly groomed eyebrow in disbelief. "You really think you've gotten away with it, don't you? You actually think Nikos will take you back."

Anna smoothed back a tuft of Misha's dark hair. "I don't want to be taken back. I'm here for my son. Nikos can rot in hell for all I care."

The girl gave Misha a crocodile smile that made Anna's skin crawl. "Yeah, right. As if anyone would believe that." Her perfectly made-up eyes narrowed. "But Nikos doesn't want you. He's got me now, and

I keep him very satisfied, trust me. We'll be getting married soon."

Anna couldn't keep herself from glancing at Lindsey's left hand. It was bare. Remembering Nikos's wandering eye when she'd been just his secretary, Anna almost felt sorry for the girl. "Has he proposed?"

"No, but he—"

"Then you're kidding yourself," she said. "He'll never propose to you or anyone else. He's not the marrying kind."

Grinding her white teeth, Lindsey stopped in the hallway, and grabbed Anna's wrist. Her long acrylic nails bit into Anna's skin.

"Listen to me, you little bitch," Lindsey said softly. "Nikos is mine. Don't think for a second you can come back with your little brat and—"

Nikos spoke from behind her. "This is cozy. Catching up on office gossip?"

Lindsey whirled around, spots of hot color on her cheeks. "We…uh, that is…"

Anna hid a smile. But her pleasure at the blonde's discomfiture was short-lived as Nikos turned to her, reaching for the diaper bag on her shoulder.

"I need this."

"What? Why?" Anna stammered. The diaper bag held her whole life. Bought at a secondhand shop, it was overflowing with documents, diapers, wipes and snacks. It was the one item that Anna had taken with her everywhere since Misha's birth.

"For my son." As he took the bag, he brushed her shoulder carelessly with his hand. An electric shock reverberated across her body. For a single second it stopped her heart.

Then she realized that Nikos was taking Misha away from her.

And handing both bag and baby to her replacement.

"No!" Anna cried out, shaking herself out of her stupor. "Not to *her*!"

Nikos stared straight back at her, as if he were marking her over the barrel of a gun. "Good. Fight me. Give me a reason to throw you out of my house. I'm begging you."

Anna opened her mouth. And closed it.

"I thought so." He turned back to Lindsey. "Take my son to the nursery. I'll follow in a moment."

She tossed Anna a look of venomous triumph. "With pleasure."

As they passed him, Nikos kissed the baby on the forehead. "Welcome home, my son," he said tenderly.

Anna watched as Lindsey disappeared down the hall toward the nursery. She could see her baby's sweet little head bobble dangerously with every swaying step and clackety-clack of the girl's four-inch heels against the marble floor. She wondered if Nikos had destroyed all of Natalie's hand-painted murals and her own carefully chosen antique baby furniture. *He probably ordered Lindsey to redecorate the nursery from a catalog*, she thought, and her heart broke a little more.

As much as she'd hated being on the run, this was worse. Here, every hallway, every corner, held a memory of the past. Even looking at Nikos was a cruel reminder of the man she'd once thought him to be, the man she'd respected, the man she'd loved. That was the cruelest trick of all.

"You don't like Lindsey, do you?" Nikos said, watching her.

"No."

"Why?"

Did he want her to spell it out? To admit that she still had feelings for him in spite of everything he'd done? Not in this lifetime.

"I told you. After you fired me, I got calls at the house from vendors and managers at the worksite, complaining about her cutting off half your calls and screwing up your messages. Her mistakes probably cost the company thousands of dollars. It nearly caused a delay in the liquor license."

Nikos pressed his lips together, looking tense. "But you said those complaints stopped."

"Yes," she retorted. "When you had the house staff block all my calls. Even from my mother and sister!"

"That was for your own good. The calls were causing you stress. It was bad for the baby."

"My mother and sister needed me. My father had just died!"

"Your mother and sister need to stand on their own feet and learn to solve their own problems, rather than always running to you first. You had a new family to care for."

She squared her shoulders. She wasn't going to get into that old argument with him again. "And now you have a new secretary to care for you. How's she doing at solving all your problems? Has she even learned how to type?"

His jaw clenched, but he said only, "You seem very worried about her capabilities."

Oh, yeah, she could just imagine what Lindsey's *capabilities* were. Still shivering from Nikos's brief touch, bereft of her baby, Anna could feel her self-control slipping away. She was tired, so tired. She hadn't slept on the plane. She hadn't slept in months.

The truth was, she hadn't really slept since the day Nikos had rejected her in the last trimester of her pregnancy, leaving her to sleep alone every night since.

She rubbed her eyes.

"All right. I think she's vicious and shallow. She's the last person I'd entrust with Misha. Just because she's in your bed it doesn't make her a good caretaker for our son."

He raised a dark eyebrow. "Doesn't it? And yet that's the whole reason that *you* are the caretaker of my son now…because you were once in my bed."

Their eyes met, held. And that was all it took. Memories suddenly pounded through her blood and caused her body to heat five degrees. A hot flush spread across her skin as a single drop of sweat trickled between her breasts. It was as if he'd leaned across the four feet between them and touched her. As if he'd taken possession of her mouth, stroked her bare skin, and pressed his body hot and tight on hers against the wall.

One look from him and she could barely breathe.

He looked away, and she found herself able to breathe again. "And, as usual, you are jumping to the wrong conclusions," he said. "Lindsey is my secretary, nothing more."

Anna had been his secretary once, too. "Yeah, right."

"And whatever her failings," he said, looking at her with hard eyes, "at least she's loyal. Unlike you."

"I never—"

"Never what? Never tricked a bodyguard into taking you to the doctor's office so you could sneak out the back? Never promised to name my son Andreas, then called him something else out of spite? I did everything I could to keep you safe, Anna. You never had to work or worry ever again. All I asked was your loyalty. To me. To our coming child. Was that too much to ask?"

His dark eyes burned through her like acid. She could feel the power of him, see it in the tension of hard muscles beneath his finely cut white shirt.

A flush burned her cheeks. The day of her delivery, surrounded by strangers in a gray Minneapolis hospital, she'd thought of her own great-grandfather, Mikhail Ivanovich Rostov, who'd been born a prince but had fled Russia as a child, starting a difficult new life in a new land. It had seemed appropriate.

But, whatever her motives, Nikos was right. She'd broken her promise. She pressed her lips together. "I'm…sorry."

She could feel his restraint, the way he held himself in check. "You're sorry?"

"A-about the name."

He was moving toward her now, like a lion stalking a doomed gazelle. "Just the name?"

She backed away, stammering, "But some might say y-you lost all rights to name him when you—" Her heels hit a wall. Nowhere to run. "When you—"

"When I what?" he demanded, his body an inch from hers.

When he'd ruined her father.

When he'd taken a mistress.

When he'd broken her heart…

"Did you ever love me?" she whispered. "Did you love me at all?"

He grabbed her wrists, causing her to gasp. But it was the intensity in his obsidian gaze that pinned her to the wall.

"You ask me that now?" he ground out. But there was a noise down the hall, and he turned his head.

Three maids stood with their arms full of linens, gawking at the sight of their employer pressing Anna against the wall. It probably looked as if they were having hot sex. Heaven knew, they'd done it before, though they'd never been caught.

He lifted a dark eyebrow, and the maids scattered.

With a growl, he grasped Anna's wrist and pulled her into the privacy of the nearby library. He shut the heavy oak door behind him. The sound echoed against the high walls of leatherbound books, bouncing up to the frescoed ceiling, reverberating her doom.

His dark eyes were alight with a strange fire. "You really want to know if I loved you?"

She shook her head, frightened at what she'd unleashed, wishing with all her heart that she could take back the question. "It doesn't matter."

"But it does. To you."

"Forget I asked." She tried desperately to think of a change of subject—anything that would distract him, anything to show that she didn't care. But he was relentless.

"No, I never loved you, Anna. Never. How could I? I told you from the start I'm not a one-woman kind of man. Even if you'd been worthy of that commitment— which obviously you're not."

Pain went through her, but she raised her chin and fired back, "I was loyal to you when no other woman would have been. You kept me prisoner. You fired me from the job I loved. When you took Lindsey in my place I should have left you. But it wasn't until I saw what you did to my father…"

"Ah, yes, your sainted father." He gave a harsh laugh. "Those papers you found, Anna, what did they prove?

That I withdrew all financial support from your father's company?"

"Yes. Just when he needed you most. He'd been doing so well, finally getting the company back on its feet, but just when he needed extra cash to open a new factory in China, to compete in the global market—"

"I withdrew my support because I found out that your father embezzled my investment—millions of dollars. There was no new factory, Anna. He'd laid off most of his workers in New York, leaving Rostoff Textiles nothing more than a shell. He used my investment to buy cars and houses and to pay off his gambling debts to Victor Sinistyn."

"No." A knife-stab went through her heart. "It can't be true." But even as she spoke the words she remembered her father's frenetic spending in those days. He'd stopped pressuring her to marry Victor, and instead had suddenly been prosperous, buying a Ferrari for himself, diamonds for Mother and that crumbling old palace in Russia. He wanted to remind the world of their royalty, he'd said, that the Rostoffs were still better than anyone.

"I didn't tell you," Nikos continued, "or press charges, because I was trying to protect you. I cut off his lines of credit and informed the banks that I was no longer responsible. If he'd just asked me for the money I would have given it to him, for your sake. But he stole from me. I couldn't allow that to continue."

She turned to stare blindly at a nearby gold and lacquer globe. Turning the smooth surface of the world, her fingers rested near St. Petersburg. She wished with all her heart that she was still there, in the dark, cold, crumbling palace without a ruble to her name. She wished Nikos had never found her and dragged her back to luxury. Russia was numb peace compared to this hell.

"And so he went bankrupt. Then died from the shame of it." She closed her eyes, fighting back tears.

"He was weak. And a coward to leave his family behind." She felt his hand on her shoulder as he brushed back her hair with his thick fingers. "I'm done protecting you from the truth. You stole from me. Just like him."

Barely controlling her body's involuntary tremble at his touch, she blinked fast, struggling to contain tears that threatened to spill over her lashes. She pressed her nails hard against her palms. *If he sees me cry, I'll kill myself.*

"I hate you," she whispered.

His grip on her shoulder tightened. "Good. We're even."

"Let me go."

Pressing her back against the wall of leather-bound books, he ran his hand along the bare flesh of her arm. "You chose to come back with me. Did you think it would cost you nothing?"

Heaven help her, but even now, hating him, she wanted to run her hands along his back, to touch the strength of his muscles and the warmth of his skin. She wanted to lace her fingers through the curls of his short dark hair and pull him down to her, to taste the sweet hardness of his mouth.

Oh, God, what had come over her? Trembling from the effort, she forced her body to stay still and betray nothing. "You're not some medieval warlord. You can't toss me in a dungeon and torture me into surrender."

He gently traced the back of his hand down her cheek. "We have no dungeons here. But I could keep you in my bedroom. Every night. And you wouldn't escape." He whispered in her ear. "You wouldn't want to."

She sucked in her breath as a hard shiver rocked her body. She couldn't stop it even though she knew, pressed against her as he was, he'd be able to feel the movement.

He rewarded her with a smug, masculine smile. "Would you like that, Anna?" he murmured against the soft flesh of her ear, his breath hot on the tender skin of her neck. "Would you like to sleep against me again? Or would I have to tie you to the bed and force you to remember how good it once was between us?"

She felt his closeness and power over her and she hated it, even as part of her longed for him with all the strength of her body's memory.

"I don't want you," she gasped, but even as she spoke the words she felt her traitorous body slide against him, melding every soft curve against his well-muscled form.

"We'll see."

He leaned forward, lowering his head. Involuntarily she closed her eyes, licking her lips as her body moved against him.

She felt the warmth of his breath. She could smell his skin, a scent of soap and hot desert sun and something more—something she couldn't describe but that made her yearn for him with all the ferocity of her heart, as she'd once hungered for Christmas as a child.

But Nikos was in no hurry. The seconds it took before his lips finally touched hers were exquisite torture. And when he finally kissed her the world seemed to whirl around them, making her dizzy, making her knees weak.

She'd expected him to savage her lips, to try and break her in his embrace. But his kiss was gentle. Pure. Just like the very first time he'd kissed her, long ago, that night he'd shown up at her door half-mad with confusion and grief…

He deepened the kiss, brushing his hand through her hair as his tongue caressed her own. She clung to him, returning his caress with a rising passion.

He lingered possessively in her arms, kissing her neck and murmuring endearments in Greek. A sigh of pleasure came from deep within her as she ran her hands through his dark, wavy hair.

Then, without warning, he released her.

She blinked up at him, dazed. Caressing the inside of her wrist with a languorous finger, he looked down at her with cold, dark eyes.

"You hate me enough to kidnap my son," he observed coolly. "But then you kiss me like that."

He dropped her wrist and stepped away from her. As if she disgusted him. Rejecting her. Again.

Her whole body went white-hot with humiliation as she realized that his gentle kiss had been more savage than any forceful assault. Nikos was too strong for brute force. All he had to do was give her the chance to betray herself. One loving, lying kiss from him, and all her feeble defenses had burned to the ground.

She took a deep breath, trying to regain her balance. "You surprised me, that's all. It was just a kiss. It meant nothing."

"It meant nothing to me. But to you…" He looked down at her with a sardonic light in his dark eyes. "I own you, Anna. You're mine in every way. It's time you understood that."

She tightened her hands into fists, fighting for calmness, for some vestige of dignity. "You don't own me. You can't *own* someone."

He stepped back from her. His face was a dark silhouette against the sunlight flooding the high library windows. She could see the cruel twist to his sensual lips as he stared her down.

"You're mine. And I will make you suffer for betraying me."

He meant it, too. She could see that. And she knew how he'd make her suffer. Not by hurting her body—no. But by breaking her will. By breaking her heart. By making her desire him, by giving her pleasure in bed such as she'd never imagined until it ultimately destroyed her soul.

He would poison her with love.

A sob rose to her lips that she couldn't control.

"Enjoy your time with our son," he said. He stepped back through the tall library doors, closing them behind him as he departed with a low, grim parting shot. "Because for the rest of your days and nights you are mine."

Revenge.

As Nikos strode down the hall toward the east wing of the house he smiled grimly, remembering the way Anna had melted into his arms. The bewildered look in her eyes after he pulled away. She was putty in his hands. Like the old song promised, that single kiss had told him everything he needed to know.

She still wanted him.

She still cared for him.

That was her weakness.

Now that he knew, making her suffer would be easier than he'd ever imagined. He'd already begun, by telling her the truth about her worthless excuse for a father. She didn't want his protection? Fine. He was done protecting her.

He would see her twist and pant helplessly, like a

butterfly pinned to a display. He would see the pain in her eyes every day while he mercilessly pounded her heart into dust. Maybe then, someday, she would understand what she'd done to him by stealing his child.

His son was all that mattered now. He was the one who needed Nikos's protection...and love.

"I waited for you in the nursery," he heard Lindsey say from down the hall. "When you didn't come, I gave him to the nanny."

He turned to see Lindsey leaning against the wall in a sultry pose. "I was delayed," he replied in a clipped voice.

"That's okay." She skimmed a hand over a tanned thigh barely covered by her short skirt, curving her red lips into a smile. "Finding you alone is even better."

God, no. Another of Lindsey's clumsy attempts at seduction? He was in no mood.

"I gave you the rest of the morning off," he said shortly. "The negotiations for the Singapore bid can wait."

"That's not why I came looking for you."

No, of course it wasn't. Unlike Anna, who'd taken her job so personally, Lindsey would never stick around on a holiday. Her work was barely up to par on regular days.

He hated that he still had Lindsey as his secretary. She wasn't a fraction of the employee Anna had been. He should have fired her long ago. But firing her would have been like admitting that he'd made a mistake.

"What do you want, Lindsey?" he asked wearily.

She toyed with the slit of her short skirt with her long French-manicured nails, making sure he could see the top edge of her thigh-high stockings. "The question is, what do *you* want, Nikos?"

It was the most blatant invitation she'd ever tried.

Once, he might have taken her up on her offer, buried his pain in the sweet oblivion of pleasure. No longer. His experience with Anna had taught him that sex could give a worse hangover than tequila and Scotch.

"Just go to the casino office and wait for my call," he said, walking past her.

Nikos found his son in the nursery, held in the plump arms of his new nanny. The white-haired Scotswoman had recently finished raising an earl's son from babyhood to university, and Nikos had hired her at an exorbitant rate. His son must have the best of everything. "Good morning, Mrs. Burbridge."

"Good morning, sir." She smiled at him, holding up the baby. "Here to hold your son?"

"Of course." But, looking at the baby, he suddenly felt as if he were facing a firing squad. What did he know about babies? He'd never held one before. Nikos had been an only child, or close enough, and he'd never exactly been the sort of man to ooh and ah over the children of friends.

Feeling nervous, Nikos gathered his child from the nanny's protective embrace and held him awkwardly underneath the arms.

"No, er…Mr. Stavrakis, tuck him closer to you. Under his bum."

Nikos tried, but he couldn't seem to get it right. The baby apparently agreed. He looked up at Nikos, and his lower lip started to tremble. He screwed up his face and started to wail.

"I…I seem to be doing this wrong," Nikos said, breaking into a cold sweat.

"Don't take it personally, sir," Mrs. Burbridge said in her friendly Scottish burr. "The bairn is just tired and hungry. He'll soon be right again with a bit to eat. Is his mum about? Or should I make a bottle?"

But Nikos could hardly hear her words over his son's panicked cries. He felt helpless. Useless. *A bad father*.

"He... I... I'll come back when he's not so tired." He thrust the baby back into Mrs. Burbridge's arms and fled.

Or at least he started to. Until he saw Anna standing in the doorway of the nursery, staring around the room with an expression of wonder.

"You didn't change the room," she breathed in amazement. With apparent ease, she took the baby from Mrs. Burbridge and cuddled him close. His cries subsided to small whimpers as Anna looked from the painting of animals and trees on the wall to the soft blue cushions of the window seat. "I was sure you'd have Lindsey redecorate."

Lindsey? Redecorate his house? She could barely manage to type his letters.

"Why would I do that?" Nikos said uncomfortably. "Damn waste of time."

But the truth was he'd loved this nursery. Once. Mostly he'd loved the way Anna's face had lit up when she designed it.

This was the first time he'd been in here since that awful day Cooper had called him to say that Anna was missing. Nikos had been sure she'd been kidnapped. Or worse.

It had been one of the police detectives who'd first dared to ask, "Is it possible the woman's just left you, sir?" Nikos had nearly punched the man for even suggesting it. Because, in spite of his arguments with Anna over her job and her family, Nikos had known he could trust her. He'd never trusted anyone more in his life.

And she'd made him look like a fool.

"Ah, so you're Mum, then? I'm Mrs. Burbridge, the new nanny. A pleasure to meet you, Mrs. Stavrakis."

"I'm not Mrs. Stav— A nanny?" Anna glanced at Nikos in surprise. "Is that really necessary? I can take care of Misha, as I always have."

Nikos stared at the baby. That name still grated on him. He could probably still change it to Andreas. *No*, he thought. Even he thought of his son as Michael now—Misha. Too late to change his name. Too late for a lot of things.

His own son didn't know him. He clenched his hands.

"I'm terribly sorry, Mrs. Burbridge, but we don't need you—"

"Mrs. Burbridge stays," he interrupted, glaring at Anna. "Since I don't know how long you'll be here."

"What do you mean, how long I'll be here?" she demanded. "I'm here until Misha is grown and gone. Unless," she added, "you want to give me joint custody?"

The idea was enough to make him shudder with the injustice of it, but he showed his teeth in a smile. "Your presence here is based upon my will and my son's needs. The day he doesn't need you anymore you'll be escorted to the gate. When he's weaned, perhaps? A few months from now?"

He had the satisfaction of seeing Anna's face go white.

She wasn't the only one. Mrs. Burbridge was edging uncomfortably toward the door. "I…er…now that you're both here with your son, I can see you have much to discuss. I'll go and take my tea, if you'll pardon me…"

Nikos barely noticed the woman leave.

"You can't throw me out," Anna said. "I'm his mother. I have rights."

"You're lucky you're not in jail. You have no idea how much I'd love to hand you to my lawyers. Letting them stomp you like grapes in a vat would give me a great deal of joy."

She looked scared, even as she raised her chin defiantly. "So why don't you do it, then?"

"Because my son needs you. For now." He came closer to her. "But that won't last forever. In the meantime, just give me an excuse, the slightest provocation, and you're out the door."

"You can't force me away from my son!"

"I can't?" He gave her a hard look, then shook his head with a disbelieving snort. "You and your whole aristocratic family really think the world revolves around you and your wants, don't you? To hell with everybody else."

"That's not true!"

"You're too much of a bad influence to raise my child. You're a thief, and the daughter of a thief. Your family mooched off others their whole pathetic lives. Your father was a selfish, immature bastard who never cared about anyone but himself, no matter what it cost the people who loved him—"

He stopped himself, realizing it was no longer Anna's father he was talking about.

She gave him a knowing glance, causing his teeth to set on edge. She knew too damn much. Ever since the night they'd conceived Michael, when he'd been stupid enough to spill his guts, she'd known the chinks in his armor. He hated her for that.

It had been the confusion and pain of finding out about his father that had sent Nikos to her house last year, expecting his perfect secretary to fix the ache as she fixed everything else in his life. But he hadn't expected to end up in Anna's bed. No matter how gorgeous she was, he never would have slept with her if he'd been in his right mind. Anna had been too important to his work—too important in his life—for him to screw it up that way. But, seeking comfort, he'd fallen into her bed and they'd conceived Michael. He'd never had a moment's peace since.

His son started to whimper again.

Anna snuggled the baby close. "You're hungry, aren't you?" With some hesitation, she looked up, biting her lip. "Nikos, I need to feed the baby. Do you mind?"

Itching for a fight, Nikos sat down on the blue overstuffed sofa, pretending to make himself comfortable. "No, I don't mind at all." He indicated the nearby rocking chair.

She stared at him in amazement. "You think I'll do it in front of you?"

"Why not?"

"You're out of your mind."

"What? Are you scared?" He raised his eyebrows. "You have no reason to be. I've seen everything you have to offer."

Although that was true, it wasn't true at all. With her loose ponytail, that left dark tendrils cascading against her white skin, she looked very different from the tightly controlled, buttoned-up woman he remembered. And even in the baggy T-shirt she was wearing he could see that her breasts were larger. They'd been perfect before. He remembered them well, remembered cupping them in his hands, licking slowly across the full nipples, until she'd moaned and writhed beneath him, making love to them after he'd brought her to climax—twice—with his mouth. What were her breasts like now beneath that shirt?

He suddenly realized he was rock-hard.

He was supposed to torture *her*, not the other way around. He willed the desire away. He didn't want her. He didn't want her.

"Fine. Stay. I don't care," she said, although he could tell by the defiant expression on her beautiful pale face that she cared very much. Grabbing the diaper bag with her free hand, she set it down with a plop on the floor by the cushioned rocking chair. Rummaging through the bag, she pulled out several items before she found a blanket. A small vial fell out and rolled across the floor. He picked it up. The label was in Russian.

"What's this?"

"Baby painkiller," she said. "He's teething."

"At his age?"

"It's a little early, but not uncommon." Her fingers seemed clumsy as she used the blue blanket, decorated with safari animals, to cover both baby and breast before she pulled up her T-shirt. The baby's wails immediately faded to a blissful silence, punctuated with contented gulps.

It shouldn't have been erotic, but it was. Every movement she made, every breath she took, seemed electric in Nikos's overcharged state.

He pressed his lips together, remembering how her whole body had trembled when he'd kissed her in the library. The way she'd melted into his arms when he'd brushed his lips against hers.

And before. After they'd found out she was pregnant he'd barely left her side for six months. Every inch of his skin, every cell of his body tingled with the memory. Remembering lovemaking so hot that it had nearly set his bed on fire. Not just his bed. When they hadn't been fighting about the way he'd forced her to relax and take care of herself, they'd made love everywhere—in the kitchen, the conference room, the home theater. Against the wall in the courtyard one rainy day. And in the back of his helicopter the time he'd wanted to fly her over the Grand Canyon. They'd never made it off the ground.

She glanced up at him now, her turquoise eyes so cool and distant. *I'm too good for you,* her eyes seemed to say. She had a royal bloodline of a thousand years. The great-granddaughter of a Russian princess, she was a fantasy of ice and fire. He'd never experienced any woman like her.

Watching her now, nursing his son, he came to a sudden decision.

She deserved to suffer.

But there was no reason to make himself suffer as well.

Tonight. He would have her in his bed tonight.

CHAPTER THREE

A SLOW BURN spread across Anna's cheeks as Nikos watched her nurse their child. She pulled the blanket a little higher, making sure her breast was covered, but she could still feel his eyes on her. It made her feel naked.

Funny to think she'd once dreamed of this moment, of nursing their baby in the gorgeous, spare-no-expense baby suite she'd decorated, with Nikos sitting beside her. A happy family. She'd dreamed that Nikos would love her, be faithful to her, and someday propose to her.

Now the dream tasted like ashes in her mouth.

Perhaps he hadn't purposefully set out to ruin her father, but he'd kept his involvement in his business a secret. If Anna had known, she could have found a way to save her father from himself, to prevent the depression after his bankruptcy that had caused him to drink himself to death. Nikos should have told her. Instead, he'd tried to shield her from everything, as if she were a helpless doll. It was as if the moment she'd become pregnant he'd suddenly lost all trust in her and in the world around them.

Thank God she'd given up on waiting for him to love her. Too bad it had taken her so long to wise up. After five years as his secretary, watching his revolving door policy with women, she'd been stupid to ever think he would ever change.

But for her to run away had been trading one stupidity for another. She'd dragged her newborn baby from Las Vegas to Spain to Paris, always on the run, living in cheap, tiny apartments with paper-thin walls and mattresses that sagged in the middle. Even in her great-grandmother's old palace there'd been no heat or electricity.

That was no life for a baby. In trying to do better for her child, she'd done worse. Nikos had been right to criticize her. Misha deserved a life of comfort and security.

And he deserved to spend time with the father who loved him.

But how could Anna remain here with him and survive? Nikos had made his intentions clear. He would shred her apart without remorse. Glancing at him now, she shivered at the darkness in his eyes. No, she couldn't stay here. That path led to endless days of seduction…a lifetime of heartbreak.

She silently cursed herself. Last year, when Nikos had unexpectedly shown up on her doorstep, she'd opened her arms…her bed…her soul. She should have slammed the door in his face, thrown all her bags into her car and headed east on Interstate 15. If she had, she might have still been in New York. Working. Single. Free.

But then Misha would never have been born.

That focused her. The past didn't matter. Her mistakes were old news. Her son was all that mattered now. And she wasn't going to let him grow up in this cold house with that cold brute.

But how could someone as small and powerless as Anna fight a billionaire ensconced in his own private fortress? He had money, power, and the added immunity of having no heart. What weapons did she have against him? Her family had no money. Her heart was an easy target.

What power did an impoverished single mother have in the world?

Then she had an idea.

An awful, terrible, dangerous idea.

Nikos touched her knee. She jumped in her seat, causing the baby to give a whimper of protest.

"We need to talk. Alone. We'll have Mrs. Burbridge watch Michael tonight." He gave her a lazy smile that belied the predatory look in his eyes. His strong, wide fingers lightly traced the edge of her knee through her jeans. "We'll have dinner. Discuss our future."

Anna could imagine the type of reacquaintance he had in mind. She felt relatively sure that it wouldn't involve a night of bowling or picquet. She trembled with anticipation and fear. He meant nothing less than full-scale seduction—which she wouldn't be able to resist. Even knowing that he caressed her with a cold heart and punishment on his lips.

She cleared her throat. "I would love to have dinner with you tonight, but, um, I'm afraid I have other plans."

He quirked an eyebrow. "Plans?"

"Yes, plans. Big plans." She swayed furiously back and forth in the plush rocking chair.

"Fascinating. With whom?"

She glanced down at the baby. "With a man."

He followed her gaze with amusement. "Anyone I know?"

She scowled, knowing it was hopeless to continue when they both knew that she was a terrible liar. "All right, I'm going to spend the evening with my son."

"Michael won't mind if his parents spend time alone together tonight. Mrs. Burbridge is trustworthy, Anna. She comes highly recommended and I had her thoroughly vetted, believe me. Michael will be happy with her."

"You called him Michael," she said suddenly.

"So? It's his name."

"You accept that?"

She saw a flash of anger in his face which was quickly veiled. "It is done and over with."

"You know I'm sorry about—"

"Forget about it. I have. Let's talk about tonight. Shall we have Cavaleri serve us dinner under the stars? By the pool?"

Yeah, the pool. Which was conveniently adjacent to the poolhouse, the Moroccan stone fountain, and the manmade waterfall—all places where they'd made love during their brief months of happiness.

Not happiness, she reminded herself fiercely. *Illusion.*

"No, thanks," she said. "I heard it might rain tonight."

"Would you prefer we have dinner at L'Hermitage?"

Her breath caught at his suggestion. L'Hermitage Casino Resort. All the years she'd spent organizing the details of its creation, and she hadn't even seen the inside since it opened. She ached to see it. In so many ways L'Hermitage was a part of her. She and Nikos had worked on it together. She'd never formally studied architecture, or interior design, but he'd still taken her suggestions to heart. She missed that.

"We'll have dinner at Matryoshka," Nikos continued.

Yes, her heart yearned. But she forced herself to take the safe course. She turned away.

"You can do whatever you want," she said crisply.

"But after Misha's asleep I will stay in my room alone. I plan to get a sandwich and take a long, hot bath."

He gave her another lazy half-smile, toying with her. "That sounds pleasant. I'll join you."

"You'll find a locked door."

"This is my house, Anna. Do you really think you can keep me out?"

She took a deep breath. He was right, of course. He had the key to every lock. And even if he didn't, he could break down the door with one slam of his powerful arms. He'd find a way into her room, and that would be that.

Of course he wouldn't need violence. One kiss and she'd fall at his feet like a harem girl, without a mind or will of her own.

Victor. The name of the Very Bad Idea pounded in her brain. He was her only hope to escape. Her only hope to survive.

It's too dangerous, she tried to argue with herself. But her former employer had ties both in Las Vegas and in Russia, and the wealth to employ lawyers who could face the best Nikos had to offer. The two men already hated each other—ever since the day Nikos had stolen Anna away to be his executive secretary. If Victor was still in love with her, he'd be willing to help... For a price. Whose price was worse?

Talk about a rock and a hard place. Would there be any way for her to pit the two men against each other and emerge unscathed, without giving body and soul to either one?

She glanced at Nikos from beneath her lashes. His power seemed like a tangible thing. It scared her. No, she couldn't risk getting Victor involved. It was too dangerous. Someone would end up getting hurt.

With as much grace as she could muster, she gently lifted Misha out from beneath the blanket, pulling down her shirt.

"He's asleep," she said softly. She carefully laid him down on the soft mattress of the crib. Nikos came to stand beside her, and for a moment they watched their child sleep. The baby's arms were tossed carelessly above his head, and his long dark eyelashes fluttered against his plump, rosy cheeks as his breath rose and fell. She whispered, "Isn't he beautiful?"

"Yes."

She bit her lip at his abrupt tone, feeling guilty again about what she'd done. No matter how she hated him, how could she have separated a child from his father?

She took a deep breath. "I...I owe you an apology, Nikos. I should never have taken Misha away from you."

"No." His voice was low.

She licked her lips. Might as well get it all over with. "And I'm sorry for blaming you for my father's death," she said in a rush. "You invested in his company and he took advantage of you. He's the one who chose to drink himself to death. I just wish you'd told me, so I could have tried to do something to save him before it was too late." She paused, then sighed. "I guess we've both made a mess of things in our own way, haven't we?"

He drew back, his eyes cold. "My only mistake was trying to take care of you."

She was trying to be penitent, but his words caused resentment to surge through her anew. She backed away from the crib, keeping her voice soft so as not to wake their sleeping child. "Oh, I see," she said furiously. "So was it for my *welfare* that you cheated on me during my pregnancy?"

He followed her across the room, clenching his jaw in

exasperation. He shook his head. "What are you talking about? I never cheated on you. Although at this point I wish I had. Are you trying to make up lies to use against me in court? That's a new low, even for you."

She could hardly believe he'd try to deny it. "What about Lindsey?"

"What about her?"

"You might as well admit she was your mistress. She told me everything." Anna stared blindly at the five-foot-high stuffed giraffe sitting on the powder-blue sofa in the corner. "Lindsey often came here during the last months of my pregnancy, supposedly to ask questions about her job. But I think the real reason was to torment me with details of your affair."

For a moment there was silence in the shaded cool of the nursery.

"Lindsey told you that we were lovers?" His voice was matter-of-fact, emotionless.

"She told me everything." Her throat started to hurt as the pain went through her heart again, ripping the wound anew. "How often you made love. How she believed you'd ask her to marry you."

"It's a lie."

"Of course *that* part was a lie. She was obviously delusional. You'll never propose to anyone." She gave a bitter laugh. "I almost feel sorry for her. You use women when it suits you. But you'll abandon her like you abandoned me."

He became dangerously still. "You think I—abandoned you?"

"I wasn't so sexy anymore, was I? The last three months of my pregnancy you wouldn't touch me, you pushed me away, and finally you just left altogether. You replaced me with a younger, slimmer model."

He looked down at her with narrowed eyes as his nostrils flared. "And that's really what you really think of me? After all our years working together you think I would reject and abandon the woman carrying my child."

She pushed away all the wonderful memories of them working, laughing, dancing together. Of nights under the stars. Days spent together in bed.

Wordlessly, she nodded.

"Damn you, it's well known that having sex during the final trimester can induce early labor—"

"I had a healthy pregnancy!" Anna cried. "But you kept me prisoner for nine months. I let you do it because I thought you were just worried about our child. But you kept me away from my family and my work, keeping me helpless and alone. Then you left to live with your gorgeous young mistress. Make up some cockamamie story about early labor if you want, but the truth is you just didn't want me anymore!"

"Anna, you know that's not—"

"I gave you everything, and you broke my heart." She turned away, barely holding back tears as she looked down at her sleeping son. "Go, Nikos. Just leave. That's what you do best, isn't it?"

He grabbed her shoulders, whirling her around. "I can't believe this. *That's* why you kidnapped my son and caused me four months of hell? Because of some damned lies Lindsey told you?"

His hands tightened painfully, and she was suddenly aware of his body close to hers. His breath brushed her cheek, sending waves of heat up and down her body. Her gaze fell to his mouth.

She licked her own lips unconsciously. "Lindsey is your lover. Why won't you just admit it? You didn't hesitate to tell me the brutal truth this morning about my father. I thought you said you were done protecting me!"

He pulled her close, wrapping his muscled arms tightly around her as he whispered in her ear, "Damn you, Anna."

He abruptly released her, striding for the door.

"I'll be back for dinner," he tossed at her without a backward glance. "I expect you to be waiting for me when I return."

She stared after him, still shivering. She had no doubt as to what he expected of her. To be waiting for him in lingerie, holding two flutes of champagne, hot and ready for his seduction. He thought she was weak. He thought that, even though she hated him, she would be powerless to resist.

No, she thought. No way.

Resting one hand protectively on her son's crib, Anna narrowed her eyes.

Whether he was more dangerous or not, Anna had to get Victor's help so she could get out of this house. She had no choice. Because when Nikos had told her that Lindsey's words were lies, she'd found herself wanting to believe him. Aching to believe him.

Being this close to Nikos was killing her.

She'd go to Victor's club tonight. She'd beg for his help. In exchange, she would promise to work for him again—something she'd sworn she'd never do. She'd do anything short of becoming his lover. And once she had Victor's help Nikos would see who was powerless and weak.

She clenched her hands into fists, remembering the arrogant way he'd demanded that she wait for him tonight. She'd be waiting, all right.

Waiting to give him the shock of his life.

* * *

Nikos poured himself a small bourbon from the crystal decanter in his office on the fourth floor of L'Hermitage.

He swished the glass and leaned back against the desk, staring out through the wide windows overlooking the Las Vegas strip. The brilliant blue sky and desert sun were beating down on the palm trees and garish architecture. The blacktop of Las Vegas Boulevard reflected waves of heat on the camera-wielding tourists, the gamblers and the drunken, ecstatic newlyweds.

He took a sip of bourbon. The normally smooth flavor was tasteless. Staring at the amber-colored liquid, he set down the glass and rested his head against his hands.

At last he understood.

He'd thought Anna had left because he'd tried to protect her during her pregnancy. He'd fired her because he'd sworn he'd be damned if his child's mother would ever have to work—not after he'd watched his own mother work herself to death. He'd blocked Anna's phone calls because he'd too often found her pacing while she solved problems at the casino building site, or tried to solve the endless foolish problems of her mother and sister. In both cases she'd been taking on problems that other people should have handled for themselves. Her first priority should have been her child, to the exclusion of all else. Why had she not seen that? Why had she been unable to let the weight of responsibility rest on him? Why had she fought his efforts to keep his fragile new family safe and protected?

Perhaps he should have told her about her father's initial request for an investment, but Alexander Rostoff had asked Nikos to keep it quiet. Later, when Nikos had discovered the embezzlement, Anna was already pregnant, and upsetting her had been the last thing he'd wanted to do. Anna already took too much on where her family was concerned.

But he couldn't believe that his real mistake, what had truly driven Anna away, had been leaving her bed.

She'd been so beautiful in her final trimester, lush with curves and ripe with his child, that Nikos had known there was no way he could keep his hands off her. He'd read in a pregnancy book that late-term sex could be a factor in early labor, so he'd forced himself to leave her, moving to his newly finished penthouse at L'Hermitage. To an empty bed and a lonely apartment. For her sake. For their child's sake.

And she'd taken that as rejection?

In leaving Anna's bed he'd given up the greatest pleasure he'd ever known. He'd even told her why he was leaving, but apparently she hadn't believed him. Instead of being grateful, she'd been angry at his sacrifice.

He clenched his jaw. Hell, how could she have felt otherwise after what Lindsey had told her?

Furious, he rose from his desk and paced his office, crossing to the opposite wall of one-sided windows that overlooked the main casino floor. Leaning against the glass, he stared down at the wide expanse of elegant nineteenth-century Russian architecture, the soaring ceilings with high crystal chandeliers and gilded columns, packed in with slot machines, card tables and well-heeled gamblers.

He spotted Lindsey weaving through the crowds, rushing toward the employee elevator. She was carrying a bag from a high-end lingerie store in the Moskva Shopping Complex within the casino. Even after he'd ordered her to wait for him here at the office she'd taken time to go shopping. Unbelievable.

He missed Anna.

Anna, the perfect secretary. Anna, who'd read his mind. Anna, who'd solved problems before he'd even known they existed.

He'd first met her in New York, when Victor Sinistyn had pitched that ridiculous idea for an Elvis-themed hotel-casino called Girls Girls Girls. The meeting had been an utter waste of his time. With twenty boutique hotels around the world, Stavrakis Resorts were known for their elegance, not for their go-go dancers.

Nikos had noticed Sinistyn's executive assistant, with her cool efficiency and aristocratic demeanor. He'd needed someone who could handle the complex details of running a billion-dollar business while still maintaining the image of his company. He'd needed someone with understanding and discretion, who wouldn't let herself be bullied—not even by him.

Anna Rostoff had been everything he'd wanted and more. Hiring her away from Victor Sinistyn had caused him no end of grief, for the man had been a furious thorn in his side ever since. But Sinistyn's enmity had been a small price to pay. For five years he and Anna had worked together, traveling around the world in his private jet, often working around the clock. She'd never complained. She'd never failed him. She'd never made a mistake. And he'd compensated her accordingly. When he'd found out she was sending most of her salary to support her mother and younger sister in New York, he'd given her a raise that had sent her salary skyrocketing deep into six figures.

He'd known by then that she was indispensable to his empire. Indispensable to *him*.

"I'm here." Lindsey's voice was panting as she leaned against the doorway. She'd stashed the lingerie bag somewhere *en route*, and now brought a hand to her heaving chest. "I was…um…"

"Stuck in traffic?" he said laconically.

"Right. Stuck in traffic." She looked relieved. "You know Las Vegas Boulevard is a nightmare this time of day."

"Don't worry." Standing over his desk, he leaned forward and gave her a lazy smile. "You're just in time."

"In time?" Her eyes lit up, and her hips swayed as she came toward him. Harsh afternoon sunlight hit her tanned face as she stretched a manicured hand to caress his cheek. "Past time, I'd say."

He removed Lindsey's hand.

"Stop it, Lindsey. It's not going to happen."

The desire for release was strong in him. The desire to forget, to bury himself in flesh and curves and the hot scent of woman. To pull her long hair back, exposing her throat for plunder, to possess her mouth and see the answering spark of desire in her eyes…

He wanted a woman. God, yes. Just not this one.

He wanted the woman who was at home right now, hating him.

Undeterred, Lindsey stroked his thigh. "Why do you think I took this stupid job? I know we'd be perfect together. I'll make you wild. I'll make you so hot and worked up that you'll forget that tramp—"

He cut her off, his tone ruthlessly cold. "You told Anna that we were lovers. When she was pregnant and vulnerable you lied to her. I want to hear it from your mouth."

"All right." Lindsey dropped the seductive pose, and her young, pretty face took on the hard, calculating look of a hustler. "But, the way I see it, I was doing you a favor."

He turned to his desk and pressed a button. Two guards appeared at his door.

"Please escort Miss Miller out of the casino," he said coldly. "Her employment here is done."

The color drained from her face, leaving her pale beneath her tan. "What?"

"A severance check will be waiting for you at the casino office downstairs. You'll find I've been more generous than you deserve."

"You can't be serious!"

"For every minute you argue with me I'll instruct Margaret to subtract a thousand dollars from your check."

She sucked in her breath. "Fine!" She turned on her designer heel and stalked out, grabbing her shopping bag just outside the door. She stopped and glared at him.

"It's not my fault she left, you know. She was having your kid and you still wouldn't marry her. Pathetic." She shook the lingerie bag at him. "And now you'll never see me in *this*!"

He should have gotten rid of her a long time ago, he mused, his ears still ringing with the noise of the slammed door. It took him a moment to realize he was hearing the phone. Shaking his head, he picked up the receiver.

"Yeah?"

"You're not going to like this, boss," Cooper said.

"What's wrong?" Nikos's heart gave a weird thump. "Michael?"

"The baby's fine. With his nanny. But Anna took off. I didn't stop her, since she didn't take the boy. I had her followed, like you said. She took the Maserati."

Nikos nearly choked on his bourbon. Anna had snuck out? Leaving their son behind? When it was almost dusk? Driving his favorite car?

That was her idea of going under the radar?

"Where did she go?"

"That's the part you're not going to like." Coop paused. "She walked into Victor Sinistyn's club ten minutes ago."

"And you waited ten minutes to tell me?" he said tersely.

"Wait, boss. You don't want to go there alone—I'm getting some of the guys—"

"I can do this alone!"

Nikos slammed down the phone and headed for the door. He went straight to his private garage and jumped on his Ducati motorcycle. Swerving through the traffic on Las Vegas Boulevard, he headed downtown.

Fremont Street was gritty, for all of its brilliant lights. This was where the hardcore gamblers came to play, far from the lavish themed hotels and the families with cameras and strollers. This was the original Las Vegas, and its hard-edged glamor showed its tarnish like an aging showgirl.

Victor Sinistyn had turned his failed casino concept into a dance club. Outside of Girls Girls Girls there was a long line of lithe, scantily-clad twenty-somethings, waiting to drink and dance.

Nikos leapt off his motorcycle, tossing his keys to a valet. The bouncer recognized Nikos as he strode arrogantly forward, bypassing the line.

"No bodyguards tonight, Mr. Stavrakis?"

"Where's your boss?" Not waiting for an answer, Nikos pushed past him.

Inside the club, colored lights were pulsing through the darkness to the beat of the music. The place was a cavern, a rebuilt warehouse with an enormous high ceiling, and it shook with the rhythm of the dancing crowd. The air was steamy, hot, redolent of sex and skin.

And then he saw her, wearing a tiny halter top and low-slung jeans that made her look virtually naked.

Dancing with Victor Sinistyn.

The man smiled down at Anna as they danced, running his hands possessively down her bare skin. She gave him a strained smile as she stepped back from him, swaying her body, moving down to her knees before she rose again. She leaned back, arms over her head, and her full breasts strained the fabric, nearly popped out of her flesh-colored top. But apparently Sinistyn wasn't satisfied with just looking.

Grabbing her shoulders, he pulled her bare belly against him and ground his body against hers, nuzzling her neck. Anna didn't struggle, but Nikos had a glimpse of her pale face. She looked as if she were gasping for air. Why was Anna allowing him to manhandle her?

He saw the Russian's hands move toward her breasts. With a savage growl, Nikos started to push roughly through the crowd. All he could think was that if Sinistyn kept touching her he'd kill the man in his own club.

CHAPTER FOUR

"THERE, WE'VE HAD our dance." Anna panted, drawing away. "Please can we talk now?"

"The music's not over yet," Victor said, pulling her back close.

That was what she was afraid of—that this music would never end. Her skin crawled where he'd touched her. "But I need to ask you something important, Victor. A life-and-death favor."

"Then you should be trying to please me now," Victor replied, flashing his teeth in a grin as he moved his body against hers. He was handsome, Anna thought, amid the heat and the lights and the pounding rhythm of the dance music. She could see why her sister had had a crush on him since girlhood. Too bad he had such an ugly soul.

Aware that she was playing with fire, Anna wanted to run from him, far away from this dance floor.

But where would she go?

Besides, though he might have hurt business rivals in the past, he would never hurt her, she tried to reassure herself. She'd known Victor since she was eighteen years old, when he'd gone into business with her father and had personally asked Anna to become his secretary. True, she'd spent five years fending him off, but now she had no other choice but to ask for his help. If she didn't want to be completely at Nikos's mercy she needed a favor from the only man who could fight him and win.

"Victor—"

"Call me Vitya, like you used to."

That was Natalie's nickname for him, not hers. "Victor, please, if we could only—"

A hand suddenly gripped her wrist, pulling her away. "Get away from her, Sinistyn," Nikos said.

"Stavrakis." Narrowing his eyes, Victor wrapped his arm around Anna's waist, pulling her back so hard he almost yanked her off her feet. "You've got some nerve to come into my club and start throwing orders. Get out before I throw you out."

"You? You'll throw me out? Or do you mean one of your goons will do it for you?" Nikos drawled lazily, in a tone that belied the threat in his posture. "We both know you wouldn't have the guts to do it yourself."

Victor smiled at him, showing sharp teeth. He looked over the dance floor. Anna noticed his bodyguards hovering close by. Apparently, this gave Victor courage. "I don't see Cooper with you tonight. It was a mistake to leave your guard dogs at home, you Greek—"

Anna physically came between them, pushing them apart. She felt sick. She'd thought Nikos would wait for his bodyguards, giving her at least thirty minutes to privately conclude her business with Victor. Having him come so quickly, and alone, had shot her plan apart.

"Please, let me go," she said to Victor. "I need to talk to Nikos anyway. I—I'll talk to you more later."

For a moment Victor looked as if he were going to pummel the smirk off Nikos's face anyway. Then he shrugged and said shortly, "As you wish, *loobemaya*. Go. Until later."

He walked off the dance floor. Nikos looked as if he meant to deliver some rejoinder, but Anna grabbed his hands, forced his attention back to her. "What are you doing here?"

Nikos's anger came back to focus on her. "The question, madam, is what are *you* doing here? Dancing with him? Dressed like that?"

"I can dress as I please—"

He interrupted her. "You will never see Victor Sinistyn again, do you understand?"

"No, I don't. You're not my husband. You're nothing—"

With a growl, he dragged her off the floor, through the crowds and out of the club. She struggled, unable to escape his iron grip.

Outside, the cooling desert air felt fresh against her overheated skin. She took several deep breaths, trying to calm her fears as he retrieved his motorcycle from the valet.

This was going to work. It *had* to work. She'd use the threat of Victor to force Nikos to give her joint custody of her son. And set her free.

Tossing a tip to the valet, Nikos threw a muscular leg over the motorcycle's seat. For a moment Anna's gaze lingered on his body, on the way his snug black T-shirt accentuated the muscles of his chest and his flat belly, on the tight curve of his backside in the dark designer jeans.

"Get on," he ordered, his eyes like ice.

Carefully, Anna climbed up behind him on the motorcycle. She gave a little squeak as he revved the engine and roared down the street without a word of warning.

She held him close, her body pressed against his back. Her tight suede halter top thrust her breasts upward, and they felt exquisitely sensitive, the nipples hardening as they brushed against the muscles of his back. She tightened her grip on his waist, her dark hair flying in the wind.

"You'll never go to that club again," he said in a low voice, barely audible over the roar of the engine.

"I'll do as I please."

"Promise me right now, or I swear to God I'll turn around and burn the place to the ground."

She felt his body tense beneath her grip as he waited. His deliciously hard body felt so good beneath her hands. It was enough to make her lose all rational thought.

Perhaps she could give in to this one request, she thought. She didn't want to go back to the stupid club again, anyway. She had no intention of letting Victor paw at her more on the dance floor.

Next time she'd meet him somewhere else. Like a library.

"All right," she said. "I promise."

She felt his body relax slightly. "Good."

A few moments later he pulled the motorcycle beneath the brilliant marquee of L'Hermitage Casino Resort.

Like the Parisian and Venetian hotels down the street, L'Hermitage's architecture was an imposing fantasy. Much of the design had been based upon the stately nineteenth-century palaces of St. Petersburg, but the centerpiece of the building was a reproduction of St. Basil's Cathedral in Red Square, with its distinctive onion-shaped domes.

Tossing his keys to the valet, he took her by the

hand—more gently this time—and led her through the front door for her first inside look at the finished project that had consumed them both for nearly four years.

She gazed upward at the high ceiling as he led her through the main floor of the casino. The architecture had triangular shaped Russian arches over doors, watched over by painted angels. Soaring above the slot machines and roulette tables, a simulated horizon held the breathless hush of a starlit sky on a cold winter night.

"It's beautiful," she whispered.

He smiled at her then, an open, boyish smile, and it nearly took her breath away. "Wait until you see the rest."

On the other side of the main casino floor they entered the Moskva Shopping Complex, which was built like several outdoor streets within the casino. The storefronts and streetlights, the ambient light and even the sounds of birds far overhead, made Anna feel as if she was walking through a fairytale Russian city.

"It's just like I dreamed." She looked at the expensive shops, Gucci and Prada and Tiffany, and her fingers tightened around his. "You made our dream a reality."

He stared at her, then slowly shook his head. "We did it together, Anna. I couldn't have created L'Hermitage without you."

She blinked as tears filled her eyes. He appreciated all the work she'd done, the heart she'd poured into her work.

He looked her full in the face. "I've missed you."

Anna felt her heart stop right in the middle of the ebb and flow of the busy street. The chic people hurrying into the stores seemed to blur around her. Could it be true? Just by seeing her with Victor, could Nikos have realized he missed her? Needed her?

Loved her?

Her heart gave a strange thump. Words trembled on her lips. Horrible words she couldn't possibly say, because they couldn't possibly be true. Could they?

"You...you've missed me?"

"Of course," he replied. "No other secretary has ever been your equal."

"Oh." The thump moved from her heart to her throat. She turned to face the large building behind her.

"Matryoshka," she murmured, over the miserable lump in her throat. She stared up at the restaurant's imposing domes of unpainted wood, like a miniature cathedral tucked inside the fairytale street. She had to change the subject before he realized what she'd been thinking. Before she despised herself more for being foolish enough to think he actually cared for her.

"Wait until you see the inside," he said, taking her hand. "You'll think you're inside the Terem Palace."

A slender, well-dressed *maître d'* stood at a podium just inside the restaurant.

"We'd like the table by the window," Nikos said.

The *maître d'* didn't bother looking up from his reservation page. "That particular table is booked for four months," he said, sounding bored. "And we have nothing available for tonight—not a thing—not even if you were the King of—"

Mid-sneer, the man glanced up. He saw Nikos, and his jaw went slack. He suddenly began to cough.

"One moment, sir," he said breathlessly. "We'll get your table ready, for you and for your lovely lady, straight away."

Two minutes later the *maître d'*, now fawning and

polite, had left them at the best table in the restaurant. A little awed in spite of herself, Anna looked around.

The interior of Matryoshka had been designed in seventeenth-century Muscovite style, with intimate low ceilings made of stucco and covered with frescoes of interweaving flowers and the nesting dolls that inspired the restaurant's name. Elaborate tiled ovens and *koko-shnik*-shaped arches were lit by flickering candles on the tables and torches on the walls.

As a waiter came to tell them about the specials, Nikos cut him off. "We'll both have the salmon with caviar and champagne sauce," he said, closing his menu. "And Scotch—neat."

"Wait." Anna stopped the waiter with a hand on his arm. "I would like Chicken Kiev, please. And *kulich* for dessert," she added, referring to the Easter fruitcake. "And sparkling water to drink." She closed her menu, matching Nikos glare for glare. "Not Scotch."

Caught in the crossfire, the waiter glanced nervously at Nikos, who nodded.

After the young man was gone, Nikos bit out, "I didn't mean the Scotch for you. I know you're nursing."

"Even if I weren't nursing I wouldn't want it. Or caviar, either. Ugh."

He gave her a humorless smile. "A Russian who dislikes caviar? Next you'll be telling me you have no taste for vodka."

"I don't appreciate you trying to order for me. I'm not a child."

"I was treating you like a lady," he said coolly, leaning back in his chair.

"Oh? And is that how you justify telling me who my friends can be?"

"Sinistyn's not your friend," Nikos bit out. "He'll use you and toss you aside."

She gave him an angry glare. "And you want to be the only one who does that to me?"

As the waiter placed their drinks on the table, Nikos looked affronted, furious. "You cannot even compare—"

"Save it. I've known Victor since I was eighteen. Our fathers were friends—although they chose to make their living in very different ways. I was Victor's secretary for five years. I know him better than you do."

Unfortunately she understood him well enough to know that everything Nikos said about him was true. But she wasn't going to say that.

Nikos's hands clenched on the table. "Just how *well* do you know him?"

Anna tilted her head and watched him narrowly. "He's asked me to marry him several times."

He glanced at the stained-glass window. The expression on his face was half hidden, but his jaw was hard. "What?"

"I've always said no, but that might change. I won't be your pawn, Nikos. I won't take your punishment forever. I won't allow you to threaten me with losing my child. And if what it takes to match you is to marry Victor…"

She let her voice trail off.

Nikos blinked, very slowly. When he opened his eyes, for the first time since he'd dragged her back to Las Vegas, they were wary. He was looking at her not as a victim to punish but as a challenging adversary. "What do you want?"

"You know what I want. My freedom."

"I won't let you take Michael from me. Ever. Get that."

"Then you can expect a very prolonged custody battle. If Victor and I take you to court, it'll be splashed in the papers. A full media circus."

"Is that really what you want?" he said in disbelief. "The two of us pulling at our child like a rope in a tug-of-war?"

"Of course not!" She had no intention of starting a romance with Victor, let alone making him Misha's stepfather, but she was praying Nikos wouldn't call her bluff. "I don't want to ask Victor for help, but what choice have you given me?"

The torches around them flickered in silence for several seconds before Nikos tossed his napkin down on the table. "Fine. You win."

Nikos abruptly rose from the chair. Anna watched in amazement as he strode across the restaurant and out the door.

She'd won?

He was going to give her joint custody? He was going to let her leave Las Vegas? Let her have her own life back?

She could hardly believe it. In a few days she'd be back in New York, looking for a new job. She knew she wouldn't find anything as invigorating as working at Stavrakis, but at least she'd be able to take pride in supporting herself and her son. Nikos would insist on child support, of course, but she'd put that money into a trust fund for Misha later. That way it would be clear to everyone, including herself, that Nikos had no hold on her. She'd never give him power over her again.

And to make sure of that she wanted some space between them. The whole country would be a nice start.

Their dinners were served, and she took a bite of her Chicken Kiev. Delicious. She stared into the flickering flame of the torch on the wall. It had almost been too easy. She was actually disappointed Nikos had capitulated so quickly. After the way he'd treated her, her blood had been up for a fight.

"Enjoying your meal?" the waiter asked, refilling her water glass with a smile. "You look happy."

"I am."

"Because you're in love? I am too," the young man added, and before she could dispute his assumption he leaned forward to joyfully whisper, "I'm proposing to my girlfriend tonight."

"That's wonderful!"

"But what's this?" He peered at Nikos's untouched plate. "Mr. Stavrakis didn't like his salmon?"

"He, um, got called away." Anna handed the waiter her own empty plate, which she'd all but licked clean. If it weren't for the caviar spread over the salmon, she'd have eaten Nikos's dinner, too.

"In that case, I'll bring your dessert. An extra big slice," he promised, then winked at her. "Everyone should celebrate tonight."

She definitely felt like celebrating. But as she dug into the fruitcake a few moments later she noticed her breasts were starting to hurt. Back at the estate, Misha would be getting hungry. She needed to return to the dance club, retrieve the Maserati and get back.

"Is there anything else I can do for you, miss?" the waiter asked.

"Um…the bill?"

"Mr. Stavrakis always takes care of his guests. I'd lose my job if I brought you a bill. Sorry. Standing orders."

She breathed a sigh of relief. Matryoshka was very expensive. As it had been Nikos's choice to bring her here, and he'd ditched her in the middle of the meal, her conscience would allow him to pay. Heck, his accountants would probably get a tax advantage out of it.

But just as she was about to leave Nikos sat down heavily in the chair across from her.

"What are you doing here?" she blurted out, chagrined. Could he have already gotten a lawyer to draw up the custody papers?

He frowned at the empty table. "Where is my dinner?"

"Long gone. My Chicken Kiev was delicious, though." She shook her head wryly. "Thanks for ditching me. I had a nice conversation with the waiter. He's in love. He's going to propose," she said airily.

"To you?" Nikos said sharply.

Anna snorted a derisive laugh. "Yes. To me. I have that kind of power over men."

He took a small sip of Scotch. Casually, almost dismissively, he tossed a small box on the table, pale blue as a robin's egg. "Here."

Frowning, she opened it.

Inside the box, nestled on black velvet, she saw a huge diamond ring set in platinum. The facets of the enormous stone, which had to be at least ten carats, sparkled up at her in the candlelight. It took her breath away.

She twisted her great-grandmother's stoneless ring around her finger nervously. Nikos's diamond was so big it wouldn't have even fit inside the Princess's empty setting. The diamond was bigger than a marble. Excessive to the point of tackiness. And yet…

She swallowed, looking up at him. "What is this? Some kind of trick?"

"No trick," he said. "We will be married tonight."

The rush that went through her then was like nothing she'd ever felt. *Nikos wanted to marry her.* Just as she'd dreamed for so long. Even when she'd known it was impossible—even when, as his secretary, she'd watched him go from one sexual conquest to another, she'd had secret dreams that she might someday be the woman to tame him.

"Put it on," Nikos said.

But it wasn't the earnest pleading of a lover—it was an order. Utterly cold and without emotion.

And just like that the pleasure in her heart evaporated.

Nikos didn't want to marry her.

He wanted to *own* her.

This was his way of dealing with the threat of Victor. Rather than calling for his lawyer, rather than negotiating for joint custody of Misha, he figured it was easier to just buy her off with a ring. He thought Anna could be purchased for the price of a two-hundred-thousand dollar trinket and some meaningless words.

"What do you take me for?" she said in a low voice.

"As my wife. To have—" his eyes raked over her "—and to hold."

She swallowed. His dark eyes were undressing her, right there in the restaurant. As if he were considering the very real possibility of pulling her to him, ripping off her clothes, and making love to her on there on the table, with the entire restaurant watching.

He still intended to coldly seduce her. He still meant to take his pound of flesh for what she'd done. And if he were her husband, his power over her would increase tenfold.

Just give in, her thought whispered. Give in to her desire. Give in to his power. Then he couldn't send her away from Misha ever again. She would be his wife. She would be above Lindsey and the other women like her—she would be Mrs. Stavrakis. And though Nikos hated her now, perhaps someday…

No. She had to get a hold of herself. Even if someday Nikos forgave her, she would never, ever forgive him. He didn't love her. And it was worse than that. He didn't even trust her enough to work or to make any decisions about her own life.

He said he wanted to protect her, but he really wanted to lock her away, like a parakeet in a tiny gold cage.

Could she put aside every ounce of pride and self-preservation and marry a man who hated her? Allow herself to be bound to him forever?

"No," she whispered.

His dark eyebrows pushed together like a stormcloud. "What did you say?"

She trembled at his anger even as she braced herself for more. She wouldn't bend. She wouldn't submit. She wouldn't sell herself for the hopeless, destructive illusion that he might someday trust her, respect her, love her.

"I said no." Snapping the box shut, she held it out to him. "Sorry, Nikos. I'm not for sale."

CHAPTER FIVE

NIKOS STARED AT HER, hardly able to believe his ears.

"Don't you understand?" he said. "I'm giving you what you wanted. I'm making you my wife."

"How very generous. But I only wanted that when I was in love with you. Not anymore." When he didn't take the box, she tossed it on the table between them. Such a small thing, but it separated them like a stone wall two feet thick. "Now I just want to be free."

She shifted in her chair, brushing her dark hair off her bare shoulders. He looked around the restaurant that they'd conceived together. To his fevered imagination it seemed that every man in the room was watching Anna. Her lovely pale skin, the dark hair cascading in riotous waves down her back, those almond-shaped turquoise eyes challenging him. The beige halter top barely covered her full breasts, and her dark low-rise jeans revealed her flat belly.

God, she was gorgeous. He'd never wanted her more.

"You will marry me, Anna," he said. "We both know it will happen."

"Death and taxes are inevitable. But marriage?" She gave him a humorless smile. "No."

"I don't particularly want to marry you, either. But my son's happiness means more to me than my own."

He saw her lips tighten at that. Good, so she understood how much he cared for Michael.

But there was more to it than that.

From the moment Nikos had seen Anna dancing with Victor Sinistyn in the club, something had changed in him that he couldn't explain. He only knew that Anna belonged to him and no other man. He had to stamp his possession on her for all the world to see.

The idea had haunted him. In the club, on his motorcycle, as he'd walked with Anna through the casino. He'd kept thinking it would be simple enough to marry her. Hell, they were already in Las Vegas. And once she wore his ring he knew she would be utterly loyal to those vows. There would be no more arguments or fear of betrayal. No custody battle splashed in the papers. It was the perfect solution.

He'd just never thought she would refuse him.

"You will marry me for the sake of our son."

"Never."

Nikos raked a hand through his dark hair in frustration. This wasn't how it was supposed to go. He was accustomed to his employees rushing to fulfill his orders, and his mistresses had always done the same.

"You will be rich—richer than your wildest dreams," he pointed out. "I will deny you nothing."

She snorted incredulously. "You think I care about that? If I'd wanted to marry for money, I could have done it long ago."

"Meaning you'd have married Victor Sinistyn?"

"Yes. I could have." She paused. "I could still."

Nikos tightened his hands into fists, cracking his knuckles. A flood of unwelcome emotion swept through him.

He remembered watching Anna in the dance club,

the way she'd swayed against Sinistyn, gyrating beneath the flashing lights. He remembered the way the skin on her taut belly had glistened, how her low-slung jeans had barely covered her hips as she swayed.

No other man but Nikos should touch her. Ever.

Especially not Victor Sinistyn. How could Nikos allow Anna to throw herself away on a man like that? How could he allow his son to have this man for a step-father?

There was only one way to make sure that never happened. She would agree to his proposal.

He had to convince her.

"Why don't you give the ring to Lindsey?" Anna said sweetly as she rose from the table. "I'm sure she'd be more than willing to marry you. Now, if you'll excuse me, I need to go home and feed my son."

Home.

He had a sudden image of her in bed, and he relaxed. Bed was a place where they'd always understood one another very well. A slow smile spread across his lips. Once they were home he would take her in his arms and she would not be able to deny him anything…

"I will take you home," he said.

"But I left your car at the club—"

"That will be arranged. The fastest way to get to my estate is on the bike." He raised an eyebrow. "Unless you're afraid to be that close to me again?"

She tossed back her hair with a deliberate casualness that didn't fool him for a second. "Don't be ridiculous."

"Good." He rose from his chair, reaching out for her hand. "Let's go."

She stared at him for a moment, her eyes wide as the sea, then with obvious reluctance gave him her hand.

It felt small and cool in his own. "Fine," she said with a sigh. "Take me."

Oh, he intended to.

But she hung back, glancing back at the table. "What about the ring? Are you just going to leave it?"

Nikos shrugged. Since the jewelry hadn't worked, it was of no further use to him. All he could think about now was that her skin felt warmer by the second. He yearned to touch her all over, to feel her hands on his body.

"Is everything all right, Mr. Stavrakis?" the waiter asked nervously behind him. "I hope there was no problem with your dinner?"

His eyes focused on the young waiter who'd served Anna earlier. He looked scared, holding a platter of dirty dishes on his shoulder.

"Your tip's on the table," Nikos replied abruptly. Then he turned back to push Anna out of the restaurant.

He heard a loud gasp, and the clatter of dishes falling to the floor as the waiter saw the ring, but he didn't wait for thanks. All he could think was that he had to get Anna home and in his bed. Within minutes they were roaring down the highway on his motorcycle.

The moon was full, casting shadows over the sagebrush and distant mountains. Anna clung to Nikos on the back of the motorcycle, her dark hair whipping wildly around her face as they sped across the wide moonlit desert.

She tightened her grip on his narrow waist, pressing her body against his. He was driving like a bullet, and the wind was cold against her bare arms and back. But that wasn't the reason she was shivering.

She was burning like a furnace, lit up from within. She knew why Nikos was driving down the highway as if all the demons of hell were in hot pursuit. She'd seen it in his dark eyes. She'd felt it in the way he'd touched her. In the way he'd taken possession of her hand and pulled her from the casino.

He was going to make love to her. Until she couldn't see straight. Until she couldn't think.

Until she agreed to marry him.

She felt beads of sweat break out on her forehead, instantly wiped away by the cool desert wind.

It terrified her how badly she wanted him in return. She was barely keeping herself in check. She was afraid she'd give in.

To sleeping with him.

To everything.

Had anyone ever defied Nikos for long? Was it even possible?

She shivered again.

"Cold, my sweet?" Nikos asked in a husky voice as they pulled into the ten-car garage. Turning off the engine, he set the kickstand and gently took her hand, pulling her off the bike. He ran his fingers down the inside of her wrist as he pulled her close. "You won't be cold for long."

She backed away. "I—need to go feed Misha," she gasped out, and hurried down the hall. She was surprised and relieved beyond measure when he didn't follow her.

Afterward, as she closed the nursery door, leaving a well-fed, slumbering baby behind her, she was just congratulating herself on escaping her fate when she heard his voice.

"I shouldn't have called you a bad mother. It's not true."

She whirled around to see Nikos step forward in the moonlit hallway, his face half hidden by shadows.

Gulping a breath, she looked down at the floor. "Nikos!"

He came closer and lightly brushed her wind-tangled hair off her shoulders. "I'm sorry I said it. You are good with him."

She knew that his brief kindness was part of his plan to wear her down, but unfortunately it was working. Those were words she'd been so desperate to hear, especially from him.

Damn! Biting her lip, she threw a look of longing at the guest bedroom the housekeeper had assigned her. It was only ten feet down the hall, but it might as well have been a million miles away as he took her in his arms.

He stared at the way her teeth rubbed against her lower lip. "You're so beautiful," he whispered, lightly tracing his finger against her cheek. "And so wild. So much passion behind that prim, dignified secretary. For all those years I never knew."

She started to tremble. She had to get out of here. She had to escape. She was already perilously close to giving in.

Swallowing, she tried to pick a fight. "Where's Lindsey tonight?"

"I have no idea. I fired her."

"You did—what?"

"She was never my lover, Anna. She fed you lies out of some deluded hope that she might be someday. But she was never my type."

"What's your type?" she retorted feebly, trying to hide her shock about Lindsey.

He blinked, then shook his head, giving her a predatory smile. "Arrogant Russian-born women with black hair, cat-shaped eyes and a tart mouth." He leaned forward to breathe in her hair, whispering in her ear. "I remember the sweet taste of you. Tart and sweet all over, Anna…"

She struggled not to remember, not to feel anything as his voice washed over her senses. "Lindsey really wasn't your lover?"

"Since that first night we were together you've been the only one." He ran his finger gently along her lips. "You're the mother of my child. I need you, Anna. In my home. In my bed."

Oh, my God. She was dizzy with longing, unable to speak.

"You are meant to be my wife." He kissed her softly on the forehead, her cheeks. "It is fate."

"But I—I don't want you," she managed, her heart threatening to jump out of her rib cage.

"Prove it," he whispered. Encircling her body with his strong arms, he slowly traced his hand down her bare back. She could feel the warmth of his skin, the strength of his hand.

"I don't," she insisted, but her voice was so weak that even she didn't believe it.

He backed her up against the wall between a large plant and a Greek statue in the wide, dark hallway. "Are you sure?"

The only thing of which she was sure was that the strain of not reaching for him was causing her physical pain. She flattened her trembling palms against the wall as he gently ran his hand through her tangled dark hair. His fingers brushed against the sensitive flesh of her earlobe. He traced lightly down her neck.

"I always get what I want, and I've never wanted any woman like I want you…"

Lowering his mouth to hers, he kissed her. His lips were gentle and oh, so seductive. Pressing her hands against his chest, she willed herself to resist. To remember the cruel way he'd humiliated her before.

I won't give in this time. I won't...

But even as she made token resistance she felt her body surrender. Her head leaned back as his tongue teased her, as his lips seared her own. She felt her mind, soul, everything float away until only longing was left.

"No!" With her last bit of willpower she pushed him away. She tried to push past him toward her room, but he blocked her. She stumbled over her high-heeled sandals, kicking them off as she turned and ran down the hall. He pursued her, as single-minded as a wolf stalking a deer. She raced outside, banging the door behind her.

In the courtyard, dark clouds had spread across the sky, and she could smell coming rain. Silver threads of moonlight laced the sky, barely holding back the storm.

Barefoot, Anna tripped across the mosaic tiles of the courtyard, skirting the edge of the pool's shimmering water. Her pale skin glowed in the moonlight as she ran beneath the dark shadows of palm trees.

Nikos caught her in front of the enormous Moroccan fountain, his arms wrapping around her from behind.

"I need you, Anna," he said huskily in her ear, holding her body against his own. "And you need me. Don't deny it."

Kissing her neck from behind, he ran his hands over her, cupping her breasts in the suede.

Sucking in her breath, she whirled to face him. Angry words fell unspoken as she saw his face. His handsome, strong face, made somehow even more masculine with the dark bristles of a five o'clock shadow on his chin. In the snug black T-shirt and dark jeans he didn't look like a billionaire tycoon. He looked like a biker, dangerous and dark, and a devil in bed.

He was right. She wanted him.

Needed him.

Could so easily love him…

"I can't," she gasped aloud.

"Can't?" He held her even tighter.

In spite of her resolve, honesty poured out of her. "I can't fight you anymore…"

His sensual lips curved into a smile as he reached his hand behind her head and pulled her into a hot, hard kiss. She returned the kiss hungrily, tasting blood in the intensity of their mutual need. His blood? Hers? She didn't care. All she knew was that she'd been denied his touch for too long. If he stopped kissing her now she would die.

She wanted to possess him as thoroughly and savagely as he'd possessed her soul…

She pressed her hands against his back, desperate to pull him closer, but it wasn't enough. She brought her hands between them, beneath his shirt, running her hands up his taut belly. She heard him gasp as she explored the trail of hair up his chest, feeling the hard planes of his torso. He'd always been strong, but his muscles were bigger now, harder than they'd ever been. And more…

"What's this?" she murmured aloud, but didn't wait for an answer. She yanked on the black T-shirt, and he let her pull it off his body. She lightly traced a hard ridge across his naked collarbone, then found another one over his ribs.

"You have new scars," she whispered.

He shrugged, a deceptively careless gesture. "I

worked some aggression out in the boxing ring while you were gone."

"I'm sorry—"

"I'm not. I'm stronger now. No one will ever have to do my fighting for me again."

Unlike most rich men, she thought in a daze. Unlike Victor.

Nikos ran his hands up and down her halter top, caressing the soft suede, pressing her breasts upwards until they threatened to spill over. He reached beneath the top, cupping and weighing their fullness, then bent to nuzzle between them. The dark stubble of his chin was rough against her tender skin, sending prickles all over her body as he licked his way slowly to her neck. He sucked at the crook of her shoulder, causing pain and pleasure and a mark of possession.

She moaned softly, arching into him. He pushed her back roughly against the tiled wall of the courtyard. Her eyelids fluttered, and as if in a dream she saw the splash of colorful tile in the moonlight, heard the burble of the stone fountain.

She couldn't let this happen...

She couldn't stop herself from letting it happen...

Dazed and unsteady, she threw her arms back against the wall for support. He pressed his hands on the small of her back, pulling her closer, tighter. His naked chest pressed against her, the hard muscles of his arms wrapped around her bare arms. Their legs were tangled as she felt the naked skin of his taut belly against her own. He kissed her hard, running his hands through her hair.

He ran his hands along the sides of her jeans. Jeans! She cursed the choice. Why hadn't she worn a skirt? He grabbed her backside, lifting her up so she could wrap her legs around him. She could feel how hard he was, how ready for her. She wanted him to take her here, now, against the wall, before she had time to think.

"God, I want you," he whispered. "For the last year you're the only woman I've been able to think about. Just you. Only you."

She took a deep breath. "Then take me."

There. She'd said it. Right or wrong, she'd dared to admit what they both already knew: she wanted him. Her cheeks felt hot; she felt like a hoyden. She took a deep breath. "But please be gentle. My—my doctor said the first time I had sex after the baby might feel like… like I was a virgin. It might hurt."

He pulled back abruptly, giving her a searing look. "I would never hurt you, *agape mou*."

At that moment she believed him. "I know."

But he still hesitated, looking troubled. She realized that he was holding himself back because he didn't want to cause her pain. He still cared about her. For the first time she felt the magnitude of her own power over him, and it thrilled her.

She smiled up at him, tracing the beauty of his slightly crooked nose with her fingertip, touching his bare scars. He was a warrior, fierce and powerful, and frightening in his beauty.

But, powerful as he was, she realized she could match his fire.

Bracing her hands on his shoulders, she unwrapped her legs from his body. Backing away, she reached behind her and untied her halter top. It fell into her hands, leaving her upper body naked. Moonlight briefly drenched her skin in an opalescent glow the color of pearls, then disappeared behind the dark clouds that were rapidly covering the sky.

She stood in front of him in the semidarkness, straight and tall. She'd never been this brave before. Even during the months of their affair she'd always let him take the lead. Nervous at her own daring, she looked into his face.

His expression was strained. With a low growl he lifted her back into his arms, pressing her against the wall. The feeling of his skin against her own, without the halter top to separate them, was exquisite. But it wasn't enough—still not nearly enough.

Clasping her wrists tightly in one massive hand, he pulled her arms over her head, kissing down her body as he moved his other hand between her legs. Her earlier fear of pain was already forgotten as she moved against him, wanting to feel more. To feel *him*. Above her, she could hear the howl of rising wind, and she felt small drops of rain against her overheated skin. Her hair whipped wildly as she leaned her head back, hardly able to breathe, out of her mind with longing.

"I take it all back," she gasped. "Don't be gentle. Don't make me wait. Take me now."

He gave her a lazy smile as his fingers caressed her through her jeans. "You want me to take you here? Against the wall?"

"Yes. And I don't give a damn who might see." She only knew that if he kept stroking her through her jeans she was going to come any second.

But he didn't make a move to pull off her jeans. Instead he kept stroking her, moving his chest against hers, plundering her mouth with his own.

"Stop," she panted. Pushing his hand away, she strained toward him, her hands fumbling at his zipper. "I want to feel you inside me—"

"No." He grabbed her hands. "Wait."

A roll of thunder shattered the clouds and cold rain began to fall, splattering across the courtyard and pool. Wind howled across the desert, rattling the palm trees high above them as they stared at each other.

"I want you. But—" He blinked, as if trying to clear his mind of a fog, shaking his head like a wolf scattering water from his fur. "This is a mistake. When I make love to you again it will be in a bed…"

She saw a glimmer of hope. "My bedroom is—"

"As my wife," he finished.

They stared at each other in the moonlight, whipped by wind and hard rain. Anna was suddenly aware that she was standing half naked, with cold, hard rain sleeting down her bare breasts.

She'd just thrown herself at him.

And he'd refused her. Her cheeks flushed with shame.

"If you wait for me to marry you, you'll wait forever," she retorted, blinking back angry tears. He'd only been trying to prove his power over her, and she'd fallen for it yet again. She reached down to the tiled floor and snatched up her halter top, now ruined in the rain. Her hands shook as she tied the strings in back. Her teeth chattered as she said, "Just being your mistress nearly killed me. I will never be your wife, Nikos. Never."

Beneath the darkness of the desert storm she could barely see his face for shadows. But his voice was low and dangerous, resonant with the certainty that only came from power. "We'll see."

The next morning, Nikos growled at the housekeeper's cheery greeting as she brought his breakfast to the table. She set down a cup of strong Greek coffee and a plate of eggs, bacon and toast, then left. He stared blankly at the morning editions of the *Wall Street Journal* and the local *Review-Journal* and cursed himself for a fool.

He hadn't slept all night, and it was his own damned fault.

It was not in his nature to be patient, but he'd left Anna in the courtyard and gone to his bedroom alone. Where he'd tossed and turned until dawn.

He swore softly to himself. If he'd just made love to Anna last night, perhaps he'd already be free of this spell.

He took a gulp of the hot coffee. He'd need all the help he could get to make it through the day. He had to secure a new secretary to replace Lindsey, the negotiations for the land lease bid for his new casino resort project in Singapore were at a critical juncture, and all he could think about was getting Anna in bed. He was so wound up he couldn't see straight.

He was off his game. Just when his business urgently needed his attention. It was intolerable.

And the worst thing was he had no idea how to convince Anna to be his wife. It was the best thing for everyone. Damn it, why couldn't she see that?

He'd already reasoned with her. Fired Lindsey. Bought her a two-hundred-thousand-dollar ring. He'd offered Anna wealth and the protection of his name, and she'd thrown them back in his face.

Even seducing her hadn't made her agree to his proposal. For a man accustomed to negotiation, he was in a tough spot. What was left to offer?

"More toast, Mr. Stavrakis?"

He growled in reply. Accustomed to his moods, the housekeeper gave him a cheerful nod. "By the way, thank you for hiring Mrs. Burbridge. She's already popular among the staff. And such a sweet baby you have too, sir, if you don't mind me saying so."

"Thank you," he bit out, then picked up the nearest paper to signal the end of the conversation. After the housekeeper had left he took several bites of food, then threw his paper down and went to look for Anna.

He found her at the pool, and watched her for several seconds from the doorway before she saw him.

She was in the water, holding Michael. The baby was laughing and splashing as she skimmed him through the water in the warm morning sun. Anna held him close, pointing out things in the courtyard. "And those are palm trees, and a fountain. That's the blue sky, and the water is blue too. It's going to be hot today," she said to the baby, smiling. "So different from your great-grand-mama's old palace, isn't it, Misha?"

Nikos envied her playful ease with the baby. He felt like an outsider looking at a loving family. It wasn't supposed to be this way. Having a child was his chance for a fresh start. To have a family of his own. To be the father he himself had never had. Damn it, how had everything gone so wrong?

It should have made him resent her, reminded him to hate her, but instead he felt only envy and a whisper of loneliness. Anna was simply in the pool doing nothing, splashing and wading, but he could tell she was having the time of her life because she loved just spending time with their child.

He'd been wrong to think about taking Michael away from her. Even if he'd been cruel enough to do it, Anna never would have accepted it. She would have fought him all the way. She had absolute loyalty and a single-minded devotion to those she loved.

His eyes went wide.

That was how he could get Anna to marry him.

Not jewelry. Not money. Not even sex.

Love. Love was the glue that would bind her.

He had to make Anna fall in love with him—fall so hard and fast that she'd not only marry him but would spend the rest of her life trying to get his love in return.

Which, of course, he wouldn't give her. He wasn't a fool. Loving her would make him weak when he most needed to be strong. How could he guard his family, protect them as they deserved, if his judgment was impaired? He'd never allowed himself to love anyone, and he never intended to.

But her loving him—that was something else. She had a character that was born for devotion. If she loved him it would ensure her loyalty for a lifetime. It would keep his son safe with a loving mother, and he'd be protected from stepfathers like Sinistyn.

It couldn't be that hard to make Anna love him, he reasoned. She'd said she loved him before, though he hadn't realized it at the time. All he needed to do was repeat those same conditions and she would do so again.

But she must never suspect what he was doing. She had to think she was falling for him of her own free will.

He narrowed his eyes, watching as Anna laughed with their baby, splashing in the pool, tilting her lovely pale face back to drink in the warm Nevada sun.

What carrot could he dangle in front of her to convince her to be with him and spend unguarded time together?

What if he allowed her to work as his secretary again? Just for a few days? Of course, it would be temporary. And, hell, he'd actually be grateful for Anna's help in selecting a new secretary. Maybe she could even help polish the negotiations for the Singapore deal.

But it wouldn't take long. A week, maybe just a few days of working together. He'd put on the charm. He'd spout nonsense about his *feelings*, if that was what it took. He'd wine her and dine her until she surrendered her body and soul.

And what a body. Her skin was pale as a Russian winter, but she looked sexy as hell, barely decent beneath a tiny string bikini that matched the alluring turquoise of the water. She'd certainly never worn anything like *that* when she was his mistress. She'd never flaunted her curves, never tried once to tease him. She hadn't had to; she'd driven him wild even as a buttoned-up secretary who wore her hair in a bun and covered up her body with elegant loose-fitting suits.

But who was this siren in her place? String bikini today. Tight jeans and clinging halter top yesterday. Had Anna really changed so much?

He saw her give a worried glance at the sun and, cuddling the baby to her chest, she climbed up the wide pool steps. She pulled sunscreen out of the old, frayed diaper bag sitting on the stone table near the fountain. Sitting back on a nearby lounge chair, she sat the chubby baby down on her flat belly and playfully tickled him while slathering him with sunscreen.

She reached for a wide-brimmed hat on the edge of the stone table. Her nearly nude body stretched beneath the bikini, revealing the side swell of her breasts.

Mrs. Burbridge nearly ran into him as she hurried around the courtyard doorway.

"Oh! Excuse me, sir."

He'd been so intent on watching Anna that he hadn't heard the plump woman come up behind him. He straightened. "My fault, Mrs. Burbridge."

"I was just going to ask Mrs. Stav—er, Miss Rostoff—" she flushed with embarrassment as she tripped over the name "—if she wanted me to take the baby inside. She didn't sleep well last night, so I thought perhaps she'd like a bit of a rest."

"She didn't sleep well?"

"She has the room next to mine. I heard her pacing. Jet lag, I suppose, poor dear."

So Anna had slept as badly as he had. Nikos would be willing to bet money it hadn't been jet lag that had troubled her all night.

His lips curved up in a smile. *Perfect.* It was all coming together. By the end of the week—by the end of the day, if he was lucky—Mrs. Burbridge would never have to trip over Anna's name again. She would be Mrs. Stavrakis.

Anna was barely back in the pool with Misha when she saw Mrs. Burbridge standing by the water's edge. But it wasn't the appearance of the Scotswoman that set her hackles on edge. It was the man behind her, who was staring at her like an ant under a microscope, as if he'd never seen a woman in a swimsuit before.

"Would you like me to take the bairn, Miss Rostoff?" Mrs. Burbridge asked. "I thought you might like a wee rest."

Since it was only ten o'clock in the morning, she was sure the "wee rest" was Nikos's idea. He wanted to get her alone, so he could finish his seduction and convince her to be his bride.

Not in this lifetime.

Anna turned to wade in the other direction, holding the baby close as if she feared the older woman might fling herself in the pool, orthopedic shoes and all, and wrestle Misha away. "No, thank you, Mrs. Burbridge. We're happy as we are."

She waited for Nikos to demand that she give up the baby, but to her surprise he didn't. "Obviously she's not tired," she heard him tell the nanny. "I think we'll just spend some time together as a family."

Anna heard Mrs. Burbridge leave and looked back, hoping that Nikos had left too. No such luck. He was standing by the pool, watching her with an inscrutable expression. His presence was like a dark cloud over the sun. It made her tense, remembering how easily she'd almost given herself to him last night, how much she still wanted to feel him inside her. The argument between longing and fury had kept her up all night. Twice she'd nearly weakened and gone to his room. It was only by the sheerest self-preservation that she hadn't woken up this morning in his bed, with a big engagement ring on her finger.

At least then she'd also have woken up with a big smile on her face. She shook the thought away.

"Well?" she said, giving him her haughtiest stare— the one her mother had used to give to other people's servants when they sneered at their family as "charity cases" and purposefully ruined their meals or their laundry behind their employers' backs. Until Anna was eighteen, when her father had returned the family to New York and gone into business with Victor, their life had been full of insult and insecurity.

And after that Victor had had power over them. That was why she would never allow herself to be dependent upon someone else for her livelihood again. Better to starve in a garret and have her pride.

At least that was what she'd thought before she became a mother. Now she wasn't so sure. What was her own pride compared to the safety and well-being of her child?

"What do you want?" she demanded irritably.

Instead of answering, Nikos sat down on the tiled edge of the pool. He folded his legs beneath him, looking strangely at ease, almost boyish. Her eyebrows rose at the sight of Nikos, in his elegant Italian wool trousers and crisp white shirt, sitting on the dusty tile floor of the courtyard. "I want you to teach me how to be a parent."

Her jaw dropped ever so slightly. "What do you mean?"

He glanced at Misha. "You know I never had a father. Not a real one, at any rate. I have no idea how to be one. I'm afraid to hold my own son."

Anna waited for him to point out that it was all her fault for stealing Misha for the first four months of his life, but again Nikos surprised her. He said instead, in a tone that was almost humble, "I need you to teach me how to be a father."

It's a trick, she warned herself, but for the life of her she couldn't see how. She licked her lips nervously. She glanced at the precious babe in her arms. He needed a good father, and, although she was far from a parenting expert, she was at least an expert on her own baby. How could she refuse?

"I suppose I could try," she said reluctantly.

"So you agree?"

"When do you want to start?"

"Now."

"Get a swimsuit, then."

"That would take too long." In a fluid motion, he pulled his shirt over his head and tossed it aside. Kicking off his shoes, he looked at her, and she suddenly realized what he was going to do.

"You can't be serious!"

"Anna, you know I'm *always* serious," he said, and jumped into the pool, trousers and all.

She turned away, protecting the baby from the enormous splash as he landed in the deep end of the pool. When he rose from the water his hair was plastered to his head. He spouted water like a fish, and his expensive Italian trousers were almost certainly ruined, but he was *laughing*.

Oh, my God. The sound of his laugh. She hadn't heard that for a long, long time. Nikos's laugh, so hearty and bold and rare, like a fine Greek wine, had first made her love him.

He swam over towards the shallow end, until his feet touched the bottom, and then he walked towards her, parting the water like a Greek god. He was six feet two inches, and the water only lapped his waistband when he reached her. His muscular torso glistened in the hot sun, and rivulets of water ran down his body. She nervously licked her lips as he put one hand on her bare shoulder and with the other gently caressed their baby's head.

"Will you show me how to hold him?"

She carefully set Misha in his arms, showing him how to hold the baby close to his chest.

"Hi," he said, looking down at the baby in his arms. "I know you've never had a father. This is my first time being one. We'll learn how to do this together."

Carefully, he moved deeper into the pool, until the baby laughed at the pleasurable feeling of the water against his skin. Nikos joined in his laughter as Misha joyfully splashed the water with his pudgy hands.

He kissed the baby's downy head and whispered, so

low that Anna almost didn't hear, "I will always be here to help you swim, Michael."

Anna watched with her heart in her throat. She'd thought she was in danger before. But now, watching him with their son, holding him tenderly, she saw in Nikos everything she'd ever wanted. A strong man who wasn't afraid to be playful.

This was the father she wanted for her child.

The husband she'd always dreamed of for herself.

She tried to push those troublesome thoughts away. It wasn't the real Nikos, she told herself. He was trying to trick her, to lure her in for the sake of his revenge. He wouldn't stop until he'd crushed her, heart and soul.

For the rest of the morning she waited for Nikos to revert to his usual arrogant, cold personality, but he never did.

They were like a happy family. It left her amazed. And shaken.

When she left the pool to go feed and change Misha for his nap, Nikos climbed out behind her. The ruined Italian trousers dripped and sloshed water behind him. She glanced at them with a rueful smile. "Sorry about your pants."

"I'm not." He gave her a grin. He looked relaxed and something else…contented? Had she ever seen him look that way before? "Besides, I can get more. I haven't had that much fun in ages. I felt like a kid again."

She snorted. "If it was that great, maybe next time in the pool I'll wear a snowsuit."

"Please don't," he said lazily. "I like the bikini."

The look he cast over her made her suddenly feel warm all over, in a way that had nothing to do with the hot desert sun.

"You didn't like my outfit last night."

"That was different," he said. "That was for another man."

She waited for him to lash into her accusingly, demanding that she never see Sinistyn again, but he just turned away to head back into the house. "I'm going to slip into something a little less wet," he said with a wink. "After Michael's asleep come see me in the office, will you? I have a proposal."

A proposal? Thank heavens, she thought as she hurried back to the nursery with her cranky, yawning baby. Nikos's behavior had been starting to confuse her. But she knew that as soon as she met him in the office he would start tossing out demands. He'd try to kiss her senseless until she agreed to his marriage proposal.

That she could deal with. It was his new playfulness, his kindness and love for his son, that she didn't know how to handle.

She showed up at the office with a T-shirt and shorts over her bikini, ready for battle. She was so ready, in fact, that she could hardly wait for him to take her in his arms. All the kisses in the world wouldn't convince her to marry him, but since she'd managed to get through last night unscathed, she was willing—no, eager—to let him try...

But he didn't touch her. The enormous mahogany desk that filled his home office had a light lunch spread at one end, while he sat working at the other, surrounded by piles of disorganized papers that were also stacked on the floor. He somehow managed to ignore the mess, focusing on his laptop.

He was dressed now, in a T-shirt and casual button-down shirt. He greeted her with a smile and nodded toward the food. "I had the housekeeper bring lunch. I figured you'd be hungry."

JENNIE LUCAS   303

"You figured right," she said, and went straight for the gourmet sandwiches and the fruit and cheese tray. Nursing left her hungrier than she'd ever been before, and thirstier too. She gulped down some sparkling water. She waited, but he still seemed intent on his laptop. She cleared her throat.

He looked up, as if he'd forgotten she was there.

"Um…why did you want me to join you here?" she asked, confused at his behavior. "You said you wanted to ask me something?"

"Oh. Right. I need your help. I'm closing my bid on the land lease for a new casino in Singapore, and since I fired Lindsey I have no executive assistant."

A thrill went through Anna. He wanted her back! She'd always taken such pride in her work, and she and Nikos had connected creating L'Hermitage. She tried to temper her growing hope. "But what about Margaret? Or Clementine in your New York office? They could quickly come up to speed."

"I need them where they are. The New York office are up to their necks getting zoning approval for the Battery co-op. And Margaret has her hands full with L'Hermitage. I need to hire someone new as my personal assistant, and I'll be leaving for Singapore in ten days. I need your help."

Her heart started to beat, thump, thump. Returning to work for Stavrakis Resorts would be a dream come true. She wondered if the baby would like traveling around the world.

"All right," she said, trying to hide her elation. "Since you need me."

"I was hoping you'd say that." He pushed a piece of paper down the desk.

To her confusion, Anna saw that it was a résumé. "What's this?"

"The first candidate." He looked at her with his velvety brown eyes, and a warm smile traced his lips. "To replace you."

CHAPTER SIX

ANNA FELT AS IF she'd just been suckerpunched.

"Replace me?" She thrust the résumé back at him, as if it burned her fingers. "Why would I help you replace me? This job was my life. Why would I help you give it away? I'm not going to lift a finger for you."

"Good point," he said briskly, then pushed another official document toward her. "Would this convince you?"

She picked up the attached papers, frowning. "Another résumé will hardly—"

But, as she read the first words on the page, her jaw fell open and she collapsed back against the hard wooden chair.

"It's a custody agreement," she gasped when she could speak.

"Yes," he said pleasantly.

She fumbled through the pages, but her hands were shaking and the paper clip fell to the floor. Bending to pick it up, she looked up at him. "You're going to give me joint custody?"

"Call it incentive."

"What do you want in return?" she said guardedly.

"I'll sign the custody agreement if you help me find a good executive assistant within ten days."

She stared at him. "That's all? I just have to help you find a new secretary and you'll give me joint custody of Misha? You'll let me leave?"

He gave a graceful shrug. "I'm a desperate man. I need this settled by the time I leave for Singapore."

She could hardly believe her ears. It was way too good to be true. "I thought you said you were going to make me suffer for betraying you?"

"As I said yesterday, I've come to appreciate your love and care for my son."

Yeah, right. "There's something you're not telling me."

"So suspicious," he said, then closed his laptop with a sigh. "You will, of course, agree never to see Victor Sinistyn again."

She nearly laughed aloud. At last it made sense. Perhaps he did want her help finding a new secretary, but it was Victor that really worried him. Her plan had worked better than she'd ever dared dream.

She opened her mouth to tell him she'd be perfectly happy to cross Victor's name permanently off her Christmas card list, but closed it as another thought occurred to her.

What if Nikos changed his mind before she found him a new assistant and he signed the custody agreement? If she agreed to stop seeing Victor she'd lose her only hold on Nikos. She couldn't play out her hand so easily.

"I'm not sure I can do that." She tilted her head, as if considering his offer. "Victor is a hard man to forget."

She saw a glint of something hard and flinty in Nikos's eyes, then it was veiled beneath a studiously careless expression. "It's your choice, of course."

"Whether I'm friends with Victor?"

"Whether you want joint custody of our son."

Hardly able to believe her own daring, she said, "Of course I do. But I'll need more than your signature on a custody agreement to give up a man who might be the love of my life."

His eyes were decidedly hard now, glittering like coal turning to diamonds under pressure. "What do you want?"

"You want a new secretary to replace me. Understandable. I want a new boss to replace *you*. Give me a glowing reference so I can find a good job in New York."

"I never agreed you could take our son to New York."

"What do you care? You'll be in Singapore—"

"And you'll never need to work again," he interrupted, not listening. "I will supply you with all the money you could possibly need to raise our child in comfort. Do not insult me."

"It's hardly an insult to wish to work."

"Your job now is to take care of our son."

"That's your job too, since you're his parent as well, but I haven't noticed you putting Stavrakis Resorts up for sale."

"The company is my son's legacy," he said. "I have no choice but to work."

"Neither do I."

"I will always support Michael. And you as well, for the rest of your life. I protect what is mine. You need never fear for money again."

"And my family, too? Will you support my mother and sister for all their lives as well?"

"A reasonable amount…" he started, then his gaze sharpened. "Why do you ask? Is your family in some kind of trouble?"

She really didn't want to discuss this. Backtracking furiously, she said, "I appreciate your offer of support, Nikos, I really do, but I don't want to be beholden to you for the rest of my life."

He drummed his fingers impatiently on the table. "So let me get this straight. You want our son to be raised by a nanny just so you can work as a secretary?"

"Are you implying my job is less important than yours?" she countered.

"No, I'm flat-out saying it. Stavrakis Resorts has thousands of employees around the world, all depending on the company for their salary. It's not even close to the same. In your case, I think the world can survive with one less typist."

"You know perfectly well there's more to what I do!" she said, outraged.

"Nothing in your job description could possibly be as important as—" He visibly restrained himself. He sat back in his leather chair and gave her a smile that didn't reach his eyes. "Anna, there's no reason we have to discuss this now. Until you help me find your replacement, it's all a moot point."

"I want to discuss it now," she said mutinously.

He sat in stillness, then gave a sigh. "Fine. Find me a new secretary—a good one—and I'll give you your job reference, if that's really what you want. God knows you deserve it."

"Even though I was *just a typist*?"

"You know I didn't mean that." He scowled. "Let me explain."

That surprised her. Nikos never explained, he just gave orders. "I'm listening."

Raking back his hair, he looked through the window. Outside, a gardener was riding a lawn mower across the expansive heavily watered lawn, a slash of green against barren brown mountains and harsh blue sky. "I barely saw my mother growing up. She was always working three jobs to keep a roof over our heads. By the time I was old enough to help support us she'd died. I never knew her except as a pale ghost with a broken heart."

He looked at Anna. "I never want my son, or you, to endure that kind of wretched life. I know I've given you no reason to accept anything from me, but please let me do this one thing. Let me give Michael the happy childhood I never had."

Anna swallowed. It was hard to ignore a plea like that. And harder still to ignore the pleas of her own heart. She didn't want to leave her baby all day long so she could go to work, but what choice did she have? It was either work or beg money from Nikos for the rest of her life.

But maybe it wouldn't be like that.

Stupid to even consider it. She'd trusted Nikos once before and she'd just been abandoned, fired, cheated on…

He never cheated on me, a voice whispered. *And, no matter how misguided and Neanderthal his attempts were, he was only trying to keep us both comfortable and safe.*

She stomped on the thought. She wouldn't let herself weaken now and start going soft again. She wouldn't let Nikos get under her skin, no matter how vulnerable he looked asking for her help, or how warm his eyes had glowed when he'd laughed with their son. She wouldn't let herself fall back in love, no matter how wonderful he seemed to be at this moment.

She snatched the résumé back out of his hands, eager

for distraction from her thoughts. "This is the job candidate you plan to interview first?"

"Yes, I thought—"

Skimming the page, she nearly jumped out of her chair. "Have you totally lost your mind? She has no secretarial experience. Her references are a strip club and—" she squinted her eyes "—a place called the Hot Mustang Ranch."

"I was trying to keep an open mind," he said defensively. "Your reference was Victor Sinistyn, but you were still the best damn secretary I've ever had."

"But there are three typos on her *résumé*. Even Lindsey wasn't this bad." She crumpled up the paper in her hands. "There's no point even doing an interview—not unless you need an erotic dancer with bordello experience."

"Fine," he said gruffly. "I'll have her sent away. Maybe your friend Victor will hire her at one of his clubs."

He held out his hand for the paper. As their fingers touched their eyes met, and an electric shock went through her. He looked at her so hungrily. She waited for him to take her in his arms, to kiss her senseless. To reach across the mahogany desk and take what she'd been aching for him to take.

She heard him take a long, slow breath. His fingers slowly moved up her bare arm as they both leaned forward over the table.

There was a hard knock at the door, the sound of it swinging open. "Excuse me, sir, miss?"

Anna whirled around in her chair, blushing when she saw a maid standing in the doorway.

"I have standing orders not to be interrupted in my office," Nikos said in a controlled voice.

"Yes, sir. But, begging your pardon, it's Miss Rost-off who's wanted. Your sister's here, miss. She's quite agitated and said if we didn't get you she'd be calling the police and telling them you were being kept here against your will."

"Let me go!" Anna heard her sister's voice, shrill and frantic down the hall. "Get out of my way. Anna? Anna!"

Natalie pushed past the maid, nearly knocking the girl aside. Her linen shift dress was rumpled and dirty, as if it had been slept in.

She stopped abruptly when she saw Anna in her T-shirt and shorts, sitting casually on the desk near Nikos. Natalie's jaw dropped, then her eyes blazed through her thick glasses.

"You've got some nerve," she said to Anna. "Do you have any idea what's going on? I've been calling and calling, but you never called back. I thought you were in trouble. I thought he was keeping you prisoner again. And instead I find you lazing in luxury with the man you called your deadliest enemy!"

"Excuse us," Anna said hastily, and grabbed her sister's wrist, pulling her out of the office before she could repeat any of the insulting things Anna had once said about Nikos. She couldn't risk alienating him now—not when they'd finally made a fragile peace and he was actually considering joint custody.

She dragged Natalie into her bedroom and closed the door behind her.

"You've gone back to him, haven't you?" her sister said bitterly, rubbing her wrist. "Even after all the stuff he did. Ruining Father's company! Abandoning you! Cheating on you! Firing you because you were pregnant—with his baby! That's blatant sex discrimination. You should sue."

"Natalie, I'm not going to sue the father of my child."

"Why, when he's such a monster?"

Anna took a deep breath. "I blew things out of proportion. And I just found out that what I told you about Father's company…wasn't true."

"What?"

Anna looked at her young, idealistic sister and just couldn't bear to disillusion her by telling her about their father's embezzlement. "There were complications and problems that I didn't know about. Nikos didn't ruin the company. He was trying to save it when Father made some…bad choices."

Natalie looked at her keenly. "So if Nikos suddenly isn't so bad, why are you marrying Victor and moving to Russia?"

"What?"

"You don't know?" Staring at her in amazement, her younger sister, usually so trusting and sweet, gave a harsh laugh. "No, of course you don't. I've only left ten messages on your cellphone since yesterday. Victor Sinistyn just bought great-grandmother's palace this morning from Mother. She sold it to him for a fraction of its value—two million off our debt, plus another twenty thousand to her in cash. Which she's already spent on clothes, of course. Victor is going to raze the old palace and build something new in its place. For you."

"For me? What are you talking about?"

"Vitya always seemed so strong, so handsome. Even after he quit his partnership with Father so suddenly I thought he was kind. I flew here last night to ask him to leave the palace alone. I thought he'd listen to me."

She shook her head angrily. "But he just laughed. He said that the air in Las Vegas was getting unhealthy, and that he needed to raze the palace immediately because the two of you would be moving to St. Petersburg as soon as you were married."

"That's not true!" Anna gasped. "We're not getting married. He hasn't even proposed." *At least not lately,* she added silently.

"Well, he obviously thinks proposing is just a formality. Any reason why he'd think that?"

Anna paced across the thick blue carpet. "I've only seen him once since I got here! And even then it was only because…" Glancing right and left, as if she feared Nikos might be listening from the large walk-in closet or beneath the elegant canopied bed, Anna whispered, "Being Victor's friend is my only bargaining chip against Nikos to get joint custody. So I can leave here. So I can be free."

Natalie eyes widened, looking owlish beneath her glasses. "And you asked Vitya for help? When I went to his club I saw the kind of man he really is. He isn't our friend. If he were, he wouldn't have been loaning our parents money at that huge interest rate. I thought he was trying to help us. But now I think he only went into business with Father in the first place to be close to you. After you left to work for Nikos he dissolved the partnership and started loaning Father money instead." She took a deep breath. "I think since you wouldn't agree to marry him he's been drowning our family in debt to force your hand."

"It can't be true," Anna gasped. All right, so Victor had made advances the whole time she'd been his secretary. He'd chased off other suitors. He'd pressured her to marry him. He'd even gotten her father to try to use his influence over her. But Victor would never have deliberately hurt her family just to possess her.

Would he?

"It's the only thing that makes sense," Natalie pressed. "Why else does he keep loaning Mother money? He knows we have no way to repay it."

Anna rubbed her head wearily. "I don't know. But I'll figure it out. I'll handle this, Natalie, don't worry. As soon as I get custody of Misha I'll return to New York and find a job—"

"You still think he'll let you repay the money?" Natalie interrupted, looking at Anna as if seeing her for the first time. "If you think he's gone to all this trouble to let you set up some kind of payment plan, you're as delusional as Mother. Who's happy to take his money, by the way, because she's sure you'll marry him. Which you probably will. You always have to sacrifice yourself, don't you? Even when it does more harm than good. You'll reward him after he's destroyed our family to get his hands on you."

"You don't know that's really true!"

"I don't?" Natalie shook her head. "You need to grow up and see the real world."

Her baby sister was telling *her* to grow up? "I do see the real world—"

"My whole life I've thought you were some kind of saint, you know? Sacrificing your own future to take care of us. When I wanted to study accounting so I could get a good job to help support our family you insisted I major in art instead—"

"I knew art was your passion!" Anna said, stung.

"Maybe." Natalie snorted derisively. "But it's no way to make a living. The truth is, you didn't *want* my help.

You always have to be the one to do everything. God forbid you ever depend on someone else."

"I was trying to do the right thing for you!"

"Then why didn't you stand up to Victor ages ago and tell him to back off? Instead of running away to work for someone else? Why did you get pregnant by Nikos, then run away? Why are you still so desperate to run away from Nikos now? You're keen to stand up for others, but when it comes to yourself you just run away."

Anna stared at her, breathing heavily. "Natalie, please…" she whispered.

Natalie's eyes were hard. "You want to be strong? Fine. You got yourself in your mess. With Victor. With Nikos. Get yourself out of it. Just don't kid yourself that your choices are for us. All you've done is make things worse for *us*. Thanks. Thanks a lot."

Turning on her heel, she went for the door.

"Natalie!" She grabbed her sister's wrist. "Don't leave like this. Please."

"Let me go," Natalie said coldly. Her sister wrenched her arm away, and this time Anna released her.

After she left, Anna slowly sat down on the bed in the cool darkness of her room, still shocked by Natalie's attack. Her sister had always been the one person Anna could count on. She hadn't asked any questions when Anna had appeared on her doorstep in Russia, but had simply taken her in her arms and let her cry on her shoulder. She'd fought Nikos's armed henchmen to try to keep Misha safe.

Heartsick, Anna left her room and realized she'd blindly gone to Nikos's office to seek comfort. But his door was closed. She stared at the door, longing for him to take her in his strong arms and tell her everything would be okay. She would almost believe it if he was the one who said it. No doubt another example of her being *delusional*.

Was Natalie right?

Instead of being the one who'd saved and supported her family, had Anna been the cause of its ruin?

It was true that she'd never really stood up to Victor. He'd made passes at her, and Anna hadn't known how to deal with his flirtations, so she'd simply put up with them. She'd never told him flat-out to leave her alone. When they'd gotten to be too much, she'd run away to work for Nikos.

And as for Nikos... She'd known his faults, but she'd still fallen in love with him. She should have been more careful. Especially about jumping into his bed. What had she been thinking to allow herself to conceive a child with a man who not only wasn't her husband but didn't even love her?

The closed office door stared down at her reproachfully.

Turning away with a heavy heart, she went to the nursery, where Misha was still napping in his crib. She gently picked him up and cuddled him in the rocking chair. Tears filled her eyes as she stared out the window at the pool, where for a brief time that morning she'd felt like she was part of a happy family.

How could she fix everything she'd done wrong?

How could she make things right?

The one thing she couldn't do was ask Nikos—or anyone—for help. Natalie was right. Anna had caused this mess. She was the one who should take care of it. Alone.

Closing her eyes, she held her baby as she rocked back and forth. It was time to face reality.

Misha shouldn't suffer just because Anna had such a

hard time being around his father. No matter how much she wanted to return to New York, she couldn't. She had to live close enough to Nikos that they could raise their son together. Misha deserved that much.

But she wouldn't marry Nikos either. She'd been careless enough to get pregnant, but she wouldn't make it worse by marrying him. She'd be miserable as his wife, committing herself to a man who didn't even love her.

Anna would share parenting with Nikos, but that was it. She needed her own place. Her own life. Her own job.

She sat up straight in her chair as her eyes flew open.

She'd get Nikos to rehire her.

It was the perfect solution. She'd be able to travel with him around the world, so Misha would always see them both. Plus, working as his executive assistant was not only the best job she'd ever had, he'd also paid her a high salary that would be virtually impossible to find anywhere else. Enough so that she could set up a payment plan with Victor, which she'd force him to take.

It might be difficult to see Nikos every day, no doubt watching him date other women, but she'd deal with it. She would take responsibility for the choices she'd made.

Misha gave a little sigh. Opening his dark eyes, so much like his father's, he smiled up at her. Anna smiled back.

All she had to do was convince Nikos to hire her as his secretary—while keeping herself from falling into his arms—and everything else would fall into place.

It wouldn't be easy, but, hey—Nikos *had* asked for her help weeding out unsuitable résumés. She grinned. She'd pretend to go through them while taking over the secretarial job herself. She'd lull Nikos into complacency while she proved she could both work *and* be a good mother to his child. She'd prove to them both that she wasn't a screwup. She'd prove she could do it all.

"What's wrong with this one?" Nikos demanded, exasperated. "Carmen Ortega has thirty years of experience working with CEOs of billion-dollar companies!"

"Those companies had shareholders," Anna said sweetly, tossing the résumé in the trash. "She's accustomed to toeing the line for many bosses instead of sticking to one. Too many cooks, you know."

No, he didn't. He had no idea what she was talking about. Nine days of looking through résumés, and Anna had found fault with every single one. But, since he'd asked specifically for her assistance, he had no choice but to continue this farce until he could get Anna to fall in love with him.

It was proving to be harder than he'd thought.

His plan had been to lure her with romantic dinners, gifts, and family outings. Instead, work had somehow taken over. She'd turned the romantic dinners into working meals, taking notes in shorthand between dainty bites of Cavaleri's pasta *primavera* and *pad thai*. When he'd given her flowers and chocolates, she'd thanked him gravely for remembering Secretaries' Day. Secretaries' Day! As if there was any damn way he'd remember some made-up holiday like that!

The family outings with baby Michael, including splashing in the pool, taking walks along the edge of the desert, and strolling through L'Hermitage, had certainly been enjoyable. Nikos had relished holding his son as they walked across the casino floor, through the Moskva Shopping Complex and into the elegant, soaring lobby of the turn-of-the-century-styled hotel. "This will all be yours someday," he'd whispered into his son's ear, and he'd been filled with pride.

But, though Anna seemed glad that he was learning to be a father, she didn't seem at all inclined to fall at his feet for that alone.

At least the time had made a difference at his home office. The piled-up papers were gone, sorted and filed. His appointments had already been reorganized to better suit his schedule, with no more double-bookings. In nine short days Anna had mended Lindsey's ineptitude with efficiency and poise.

He looked around his office. A man could get used to this, he thought with satisfaction. Then he stopped himself cold. No, he *couldn't* get used to this. He couldn't let himself. After the ten days were over Anna would return to full-time motherhood. Her place was at home, in luxury and comfort, raising their son.

It had been nice working from home for the last week, though, instead of going to his office at the casino as usual. He'd seen a lot of Michael, too, since Anna was still feeding him every three hours. She usually had him in the office with them for much of the afternoon. Right now the baby was in the nursery, taking his afternoon nap, but just a few moments ago he'd been lying on a mat on the floor, batting at the dangling toys of his playgym while he gurgled and laughed. Remembering, a smile formed on Nikos's lips.

He shook himself. What kind of work environment was this? In spite of Anna's organization, his work habits were slipping. His usual sixteen- or eighteen-hour days just weren't possible when he was constantly being distracted by the laughter of his son and the gorgeous vision of Anna in a slim-fitting white shirt and black pencil skirt, crossing her killer legs while she took dictation.

No, he had to stick to his plan. Anna would be free of the burden of work, and he'd find some other secretary. He'd make do for the sake of his son having a happy childhood, and return to his eighteen-hour work days. He'd shown his son the empire that would soon be his; he couldn't slack off on the job now.

But he was leaving tomorrow. He only had tonight to make Anna fall for him before he left for Singapore, and, while he still believed he'd achieve his goal, it might be time to get creative. He'd soon have no choice but to…ugh…talk more about *feelings*. He had no idea how to do that, but he'd improvise. How hard could it be? He'd talk about his childhood. Didn't women swoon over stories of poverty and misery?

"What are you doing?" he asked, suddenly distracted by the vision of Anna's sweet backside in the form-fitting black skirt as she knelt near the trash can and leaned forward on her hands. Wild images went through him.

"This must have bounced off the rim." She picked up the crumpled résumé from the floor, then spotted something behind the can. Nikos groaned inwardly as she saw the pale blue envelope that he'd tossed there early this morning.

Leaning back on her haunches, she picked it up and read the envelope. "It's postmarked from Greece."

Nikos grabbed a new résumé. "Have you looked at this one?"

She refused to be distracted, and held the blue envelope a little higher. "When did you get this letter?"

"Yesterday," he said, grinding his teeth.

She pushed back a long tendril that had escaped from

her sleek chignon. "It hasn't been opened, but it was in the trash."

"And your point is?"

"Aren't you going to read it?"

"I think my actions are self-explanatory."

"But if your father's widow wrote all the way from Greece to try to mend the breach in your family…"

"There is no breach, because there is no family," he said shortly. "My father meant nothing to me, and now he's dead, so why should I care about his widow? She can write me or not. That is her choice. I'm perfectly capable of throwing her letters in the trash without your advice."

He still remembered all too well the first letter he'd received from the Greek woman. She'd broken the news of his father's death, and informed him that he'd left Nikos a share in his shipping business—the same shipping business that Nikos had tried to crush as an adult. Worse, she'd told him that his father had been the secret investor who had helped Nikos create Stavrakis Resorts. His father had been the one to help Nikos build his very first hotel.

Shaken, Nikos had still refused to go to the funeral, or meet his half-siblings. He'd also refused the shares in the company. He hadn't wanted any part of the family who'd been more important to his father than he and his mother had been.

But it was the kindness in her letter that had shocked him the most. She'd been so gentle, when he'd expected only hate. The confusion and pain had driven him to Anna's house. He'd instinctively sought her comfort, her arms, her bed, and they'd conceived Michael…

Anna gave him a piercing turquoise glance, as if she

guessed his thoughts. "But how can you still hate your father now that you know that he helped you?"

"If I'd known he was the investor behind the venture capital firm that financed my first hotel, I would have tossed the money back in his face."

"But—"

"He was a married man when he seduced my mother. He got her pregnant, then sent her packing to New York. The man is nothing to me."

"But your stepmother—"

"Don't ever call her that again."

"Your—your father's widow said he tried to send you money every month of your childhood. Your mother was the one who always sent it back."

Yes, he remembered what the Greek woman had said—that his father had always loved Nikos, that he'd tried to visit and send child support but his proud mother had refused. She'd even said that his father hadn't wanted his mother to go to New York, that he'd been heartbroken when she'd left. She'd said his mother was the one who had refused to let him see his son.

Nikos didn't know who to believe.

His mother, of course, he told himself furiously. She had died taking care of him. She deserved his loyalty.

The last thing Nikos wanted to do was read another of the Greek woman's letters. The past was dead and gone. Better to let it remain buried.

Unfortunately, Anna didn't see it that way. Her lips pressed in a determined line. "I'm going to read the letter."

He grabbed her hand as she reached for the letter opener on his desk. "You're quick to arrange my family affairs. Is it to avoid dealing with your own?"

She hesitated. "What do you mean?"

"Why did your sister come here? You've evaded the question for over a week. I'd like an answer."

She tugged on her hand, but he held her fast. "It's nothing," she mumbled. "A family quarrel."

"Does it have anything to do with Victor Sinistyn?"

She pulled away with a savage force that he hadn't expected. "Just stay out of it! I don't need your pity and I don't need your help. I can handle it on my own—"

She grabbed at the letter opener with a trembling hand, plunging the sharp edge of the blade into the side of the blue envelope with far too much vigor. It sliced her palm, and she squelched a scream, holding out her bleeding hand.

"Let me see your hand," Nikos demanded.

She turned her face away in a fruitless attempt to hide her tears. He was relieved that she didn't resist as he gently took her hand. Blood from the cut smudged against the cuff of his shirt as he narrowly examined the wound.

"I don't think you'll need stitches." He'd been hurt enough times while sparring in his boxing club to be a pretty good judge. "Let's just clean it in case of infection."

He led her into the adjoining bathroom, and she followed him, seemingly in a daze. She winced as he placed her hand under the running water. He dried it off softly with a thick white cotton hand towel.

"This might sting a little," he said, before he applied the antiseptic he kept in the cabinet for any injuries he got working out at the club.

She closed her eyes. His hand tightened over her fingers and he felt a strangely agonizing beat of his heart that he was hurting her, even though it was for her own good.

He placed the small bandage over the cut. "All done."

She opened her eyes. "Thank you." She started to pull away, but he stopped her.

"Anna, tell me what hold Sinistyn has got over you."

"He doesn't."

"You're a terrible liar."

"I don't need your charity, and I don't want your help," she said. "It's my family's private business." But even as she spoke the words he could see the tremor of her swanlike throat, the nervous flutter of her dark lashes.

"Not if it affects my son."

Her eyes went wide. "You think I would endanger Misha?"

He glowered at her silently until he saw her blush. Good. Let her remember her worldwide travels to unheated ramshackle apartments on her own.

"Go to hell," she said, and left him. But she'd barely gone three steps back into his office before he caught her unhurt hand.

"Tell me, or I'll beat it out of Sinistyn. Or maybe I'll just ask Cooper to track down Natalie. I doubt she's gone far."

"Please don't." She lowered her gaze to her clasped hands, then sank slowly into the hard wooden chair by his desk. "All right. I'll tell you. We're in debt."

"How much?"

She took a deep breath, still unable to meet his eyes. "It was six million, but now it's four." She suddenly gave a hysterical laugh and leaned forward, rubbing her temples. "It's at a thirty-five-percent interest rate and compounding daily. That's why we were at my great-grandmother's palace, trying to get it into decent shape to find a buyer. But the palace needs a fortune in renovations to make it livable."

"You should have asked me for the money."

"You think I'd sell myself for a palace?"

"Anna!"

"Thank you for your kind offer, but we found a buyer already."

"For the palace, or for you?" he asked, trying to spur her into energy. Anything to make her eyes look less dead and defeated than they did at this moment. But she didn't even rise to his bait.

"Both, I think," she said dully. "Victor bought the palace from my mother for two million dollars. That's why we only owe him four million instead of six. He's planning to raze the palace and build a new house as a wedding present to me."

"What?" he exploded.

"Victor has wanted me for a long time." Rubbing the back of her neck wearily, she rose from the chair and started to pace. "He's been lending my parents money over the years because he knew that eventually we'd default. I think it was his way to…to back me into a corner."

Rage went through Nikos. Looking at the circles under her eyes, he wanted to rip the other man apart. "I'll kill him."

She shook her head. "No. I can handle him. I'll talk to Victor, make him understand that I don't love him and I'll never be his wife. If you want to help me, there's just one thing you can do. One thing that would really, really help me."

"What's that?" Nikos asked, relieved at her admission that she had no intention of marrying Victor Sinistyn.

She looked at him with a painful expression of hope in her lovely almond-shaped eyes. "Hire me back as your secretary so I can pay back our family's debt."

"I told you. You don't have to worry about the debt. I'll handle it," Nikos said. *And I'll start by destroying Sinistyn,* he vowed privately.

"Please, just hire me back," she begged—Anna the proud, who never begged for anything.

He took her hand. He wanted to cover her with kisses, let her know that she was safe, let her know that he'd never let anyone hurt her again. "I'll keep you safe, and your family, too. I swear to you on my life."

"I just need a job." She licked her lips nervously— full pink lips that were made to be kissed. For a moment he couldn't stop looking at her mouth. Why hadn't he bedded her yet? Why hadn't he kissed her every hour, every moment? He tried to remember as she continued desperately, "I'll work from home so I can still take good care of the baby. And you'll be glad to have me back in your office, I promise. I'll make you so glad—"

"No," he said harshly, furious at how tempted he was to give in to her. Hell, he'd love to have her as his secretary again. His life was so much easier with Anna by his side. And it was hard for him to deny her anything when he wanted to kiss her so badly. But he couldn't be selfish. Not now. "I don't want you as my secretary. I want you as my wife."

"Nikos, please," she whispered, with those full pink lips. She crossed her arms over her chest, pushing her breasts upwards beneath her slim white shirt. "I need this so badly—"

So did he.

Taking her in his arms, he kissed her.

CHAPTER SEVEN

ANNA COULD NOT even try to stop him. His kiss was hot, demanding. She felt his fingers run down her neck and along her back, and her whole body seemed to relax like a sigh. For a brief moment she thought she could put all her cares and worries aside. She was safe in his arms. Maybe Nikos could protect her, care for her. Love her...

His tongue brushed against hers as he deepened the kiss, caressing her in an erotic dance that left her breathless. She leaned against him with a sigh.

"Anna," he whispered, so softly that the words were a mere breath against her skin. "You belong with me. Always."

He pressed her against the desk, kissing the vulnerable spot between her neck and shoulder until prickles of longing spread across her body. He ran his hands through her hair, causing bobby pins to scatter to the floor and her hair to tumble out of its chignon around her shoulders. She braced herself with an unsteady hand against his muscled shoulder. His fingers played with the waistband of her black pencil skirt, then moved beneath her fitted white shirt. A gasp escaped her as she felt his wide fingers splay lightly against the skin of her belly.

Without warning he lifted her up on the desk, crushing papers beneath her weight, cradling her to his body. He spread her legs to wrap them around him. Through his finely cut trousers, she could feel how badly he wanted her.

She wanted him too. But she was afraid. Afraid to trust too much, to give too much. What if she let herself depend on him and he crushed her?

She couldn't let herself give in to her desire. If she agreed to be his wife it would mean disaster. She couldn't give herself away to a man who didn't love her!

He drew away. "You're trembling."

Grasping at straws, she indicated the résumés, their laptops, the appointment calendars spread across his large mahogany desk. "We can't do this," she panted. "There's too much at stake—"

With an angry growl, he swept everything on the desk to the floor. Not even seeming to notice the crash of the laptops as they hit the carpet, he pushed her backward against the glossy wood of the desk. "Here. Now."

"Nikos—"

He leaned forward, pressing his body against hers. His face inches from hers, his dark eyes pierced hers as he looked into her own searchingly. "Tell me that you don't want this. Tell me you don't want *me*."

Licking her lips, she tried to speak the words. But the lies could not form themselves on her mouth when all she wanted to do was kiss him all over and feel his naked skin against her body.

She closed her eyes as she felt him slowly unbuttoning her shirt. He kissed her bare skin with each newly revealed inch until he finally pulled the shirt off her body. Without even knowing what she was doing, she whispered, "Please."

He stopped. "Please what?"

Please hurry.

Please make love to me now.

Please love me...

"Wait," she gasped. To her surprise, he released her, and, bereft of his touch, she opened her eyes.

He pushed himself up on one arm, looking down at her, and the expression on his face was one she'd never seen before. No, that wasn't true. She'd seen it once. The night they'd conceived Misha. Nikos Stavrakis, the ruthless billionaire, was watching her with a vulnerable light in his dark eyes. As if she alone had the power to hurt him. Or save him.

"What is it, *zoe mou*?" he asked softly.

"I'm afraid," she blurted out, then stopped, aghast.

"Of what?"

"I'm afraid you'll hurt me," she whispered.

A smile suddenly curved his lips, softening the hard angles of his handsome face as he gently brushed her cheek with his hand. "I would never hurt you, *agape mou*. Never."

And at that moment she believed him.

"I will be gentle. I swear to you on my life." With two easy movements he pulled off her skirt, murmuring with awe, "You are so beautiful."

She reached up for him, unbuttoning his crisp linen shirt. Unlike his easy removal of her clothes, her fingers felt clumsy. They trembled in excitement, until finally she gave up on the last button and ripped off the shirt in her impatience.

"That was my favorite shirt," he said, amused.

"Stupid of you to wear it today," she murmured.

Growling under his breath, he braced himself with his knees on the desk over her and slowly stroked down her full breasts, beneath the lacy fabric of her bra, until the only sound she could make was a moan.

He unhooked the front clasp of her bra and pulled the fabric off her body, tossing it to the floor. "Beautiful," he breathed again, cupping them in his hands, and she arched her back against the desk, straining to bring him closer to her. He lowered his head to taste her breasts. Then abruptly stopped.

Wondering why, she looked down and saw that a small trickle of milk had escaped her left breast. She felt a squirm of embarrassment, then defiance. She was a nursing mother. She wouldn't, couldn't, be ashamed of it. But still...

He raised a dark eyebrow at her, then lowered his head and slowly licked the other breast with his rough tongue. She sighed with pleasure. She gasped as he lowered his head between her legs.

He worked his tongue with agonizing slowness, spreading her wide to taste the very heart of her. The full thickness of his tongue seemed to touch every nerve-ending of her body, leaving her quivering and taut with longing.

Gripping his hair with her hands, she stared up at the ceiling, knowing she should make him stop, that she should pull away, but she couldn't. She was naked in his office, her thighs spread wide on his mahogany desk, and her boss—the playboy desired by women far more beautiful than she—was lapping her with his tongue until she thought she would explode.

And then she did. She heard a loud cry and realized it had come from her own mouth. For a few seconds afterward all she could do was breathe, and Nikos took her in his arms, holding her close as he whispered endearments. Anna realized that he wasn't even all the way naked. But he was all the way hard. She could feel that through his tailored pants, pressing against her. And yet he wasn't trying to make love to her.

Why not?

She started to stroke him through the fabric, but he caught her hands. His eyes, looking down at her, were vulnerable. "Marry me, Anna. Be my wife."

Yes.

Yes.

God, yes.

"I can't." It felt horrible to say. Ungenerous and so, so wrong. And it wasn't what she wanted. Especially when it made him abruptly pull away. "We can raise our son together, but I can't marry you, Nikos. It would never work."

"So you say." He pulled away from her and without even looking in her direction started to put on his shirt.

She sat up, still naked, feeling dizzy. "Don't you understand? We'd never be happy together."

"No, I don't understand. I see only a spoiled woman who is determined to toss away happiness with both hands."

"You don't love me—" she started, praying he would argue.

Instead, he cut her off with, "And you don't love me." His face, so warm and loving just moments before, now expressed icy contempt. "But we both love our son. I am trying to do what's best for him. I wish you would do the same."

"I am!" she said, stung.

"Right." He rapidly buttoned up his shirt. "What have I done to make you hate me, Anna? What did I do that was so horrible? What have I ever done except try to take care of all of us? One of us has to take responsibility for the family we've created. Especially since you obviously don't give a damn."

"Wait—that's not true—you know it's not true!"

His lip curled as he turned to go. "I'm going to go find Sinistyn and handle him once and for all. Before he talks his way into becoming Michael's stepfather. Because apparently you have a problem telling him no. Unlike me."

"I'm not trying to hurt you. I just don't want you to get involved."

"Too late."

"It's not your problem, it's mine. I should be the one to—"

"My God, you really don't trust me at all, do you? No matter what I do or say, you won't accept my help. You'd rather fight me. You'd rather put both yourself and our son in danger." He stopped in the doorway. "I always admired you, Anna. A pity the good sense you have as a secretary is lacking in you as a woman."

His words struck her to the bone. His face was in shadow as he added quietly, "Look through the résumés, Anna. Find me a new secretary. When I come back, give me a name. I'm done fighting with you."

Nikos was grim as he rode in the back of his limo, poring through documents about the last-minute details of the Singapore land lease bid as his chauffeur drove him back to the casino.

He'd lost his temper.

He never lost his temper.

Damn it, Anna was really starting to get to him. He'd accused her of letting her emotions run her reason, but he had just done the same.

The way he'd shouted at her. It made him wince now.

It had not gone according to plan. Yelling at her was no way to make her fall in love. Even he knew that.

He sighed, leaning his head against the darkened glass and staring out at the empty, barren landscape as the Nevada desert flew by. He'd felt so close. His soul had soared when he'd felt her tremble beneath his tongue. He'd felt sure that she would say yes to his proposal. Why else had he restrained himself, when he could think of nothing but having her in his bed? He'd said that he wanted to make love to her only as his wife, and that was still true.

He ground his teeth. Forget those stupid scruples. He only had twenty-four hours to close the deal. Next time he wouldn't hesitate. He wouldn't relent. He'd seduce her, and he'd get both his satisfaction and her agreement to his proposal. And before she had a chance to change her mind he'd take her straight to one of the all-night wedding chapels and get it all nailed down.

He glanced at the document still in his briefcase. His lawyers had already drawn up the standard prenuptial agreement: if the marriage should end, both parties would end up with what they'd started with. Leaving Anna virtually penniless.

He didn't intend for her to suffer. On the contrary, he meant for her to live in luxury. He'd even keep her snooty mother in Hermès handbags. Anything to make Anna happy. The prenup was for one reason only—to make sure that Anna would never have any incentive to walk away from their marriage.

He twisted his neck, cracking the joints to relieve the stress, and revised his tattered game plan. Tonight was his last night to close the deal. After he'd finished with Sinistyn he'd go straight home, make love to Anna until she couldn't see straight, and then she'd sign the prenup. Then they'd go to the courthouse for a license and, from there, a drive-thru chapel.

He flexed his hands, trying to make himself relax. Anna was getting under his skin—probably because they were spending so much time together, blending home and work. It had been wonderful, in a way, having her back in the office. Best damn secretary he'd ever had. Together they were the perfect team. Unbeatable.

No. He pushed the thought away. He'd already made up his mind, and tonight it would be done. He'd get a new secretary, take Anna as his wife, and keep his home and work life separate—the way they were supposed to be. He'd enjoy Anna at night, see his son every day, and go back to putting in eighteen-hour days at the office. That was the life that made sense to him. That was a life he could control.

But Anna *had* to marry him. Without that everything else fell apart.

Rubbing his hand against his forehead, he sighed. It was time for him to play his last card. He had no choice. He was leaving for Singapore tomorrow, to meet with government officials and make sure Stavrakis Resorts' land lease bid was successful. The new casino resort would be an important asset in his son's fortune.

But first he had to close the deal with Anna.

He would tell her he loved her.

He'd never said the words before—to anyone. And even tonight it would be a lie. He would lie to make her capitulate, to make her love him in return. He'd told himself that he'd never say those three words to anyone, but he'd give up that tiny slice of honor now. He'd do far more than that to protect his family.

He'd tell her he loved her, and make her believe it. He had to convince her he meant it. Convince her he'd make a good husband. Convince her he was worthy of her love, even if it all was a lie…

He had a sudden memory of Anna in his bed, naked, with tousled hair and a sweetly seductive smile, looking up at him with honest, trusting eyes.

He shook the disturbing image away. As his chauffeur pulled up to the private garage on the third level parking deck of L'Hermitage, he focused instead on his meeting with Victor Sinistyn, whom he'd called on the drive into town.

He couldn't blame the man for wanting Anna for himself. Nikos ground his teeth as he strode into his private elevator. Any man would want Anna. But Sinistyn had gone too far, trying to force her into a marriage against her will. Trying to *buy* her through trickery and putting pressure on her family.

Images of Anna went through his mind: laughing in the pool last week, splashing with their child, smiling up at Nikos in the bright sunlight. She was so beautiful, so vibrant, so warm and alive. How *dare* Sinistyn try to imprison her? How dare he try to seize by manipulation and force something he had no right to call his own?

"It's time you picked on someone your own size," Nikos muttered under his breath as he entered his private office.

"What was that, sir?" Margaret, the senior administrative assistant for the casino, was filling in on some rudimentary duties as his executive secretary. She temporarily sat in Anna's old desk outside his office.

"Please let me know when Victor Sinistyn arrives." Closing the door behind him, he went to the outside windows and stared down at Las Vegas Boulevard, watching the hectic traffic below. He went to the crystal decanter and started to pour himself a small bourbon, then stopped.

Was it possible that he was doing the same thing as Sinistyn? Trying to possess Anna when he had no right?

No, he told himself fiercely. It wasn't the same at all. Sinistyn was trying to force Anna to marry him to satisfy his own selfish lust. Nikos just wanted to protect his family. To protect his son.

But still, the voice of conscience, rusty from disuse, whispered in his mind, *you're going to make her fall in love with you on false pretenses, to bind her to you forever. Isn't that just as bad?*

He tried to shake the thought out of his mind, but it wouldn't go away. He paced back and forth through his office, trying to concentrate on Sinistyn, the Singapore deal—anything but his plans for Anna. In the end he gave up, and pummeled the boxing bag in the corner of his office with his bare hands to clear his mind. The pain helped him forget. Helped him focus.

There was blood on two knuckles when he went over to the wall of one-sided windows that overlooked the main casino floor. He glanced down, impatiently looking at his watch. Sinistyn was two minutes late.

Then his eyes sharpened.

Sinistyn wasn't late. He was already in the casino downstairs, beneath the high crystal chandeliers, in between the gilded nineteenth-century columns and wealthy, attractive gamblers at the roulette tables and slot machines.

He wasn't alone, either. He'd brought two hulking bodyguards from his club. But he wasn't talking to them.

He was talking to Anna.

Anna. Still wearing the slim white shirt and black

skirt, but sexier than ever, with her long, long legs and glossy black pumps. Her dark hair, which he'd mussed so thoroughly nearly making love to her on his desk, cascaded down her shoulders. Her lips were full, pink and bruised, as if she'd just come from bed.

She was too enticing—innocence and sin wrapped up into one luscious package.

Nikos cursed under his breath. She'd defied his direct orders and come down here to intercept Sinistyn. He clenched his jaw. From this distance he couldn't read the expressions on their faces. What was she saying to him? What was he saying to her? His hands clenched into fists as he strode out of his office to the elevator.

When he reached the casino floor he signaled Cooper, his head of security, to follow with two bodyguards. Trailing bodyguards in his wake, he stalked through the noise of slot machines and gamblers toward Anna and Sinistyn, barely able to keep his fury in check.

Why couldn't she trust him to handle things? Not even once? Why did she always have to make everything *so damned hard*?

"Sinistyn," he said coldly, grabbing the man's shoulder. "Let's go upstairs to talk." He gave Anna a look. "Leave."

"I'm staying," she said, raising her chin.

He heard Sinistyn snicker under his breath. Nikos ground his teeth. "Let me handle this."

"This isn't your fight. It's mine." To Nikos's shock, she turned to Victor Sinistyn and put her hand on his hairy arm, looking deep and soulfully into his eyes. "Victor, I'm sorry this has gone so far. It's my fault."

"About time you came to your senses, *loobemaya*. I've waited long enough for you to be my wife." Looking up from her cleavage with a triumphant half-smile, he locked eyes with Nikos. "About time you chose the better man."

Nikos felt a strange lurch in his chest. A sick feeling spread through his body. She'd chosen Sinistyn over him? She trusted that man over him?

"No." Anna was shaking her head at Sinistyn. "That's what I'm trying to tell you. I'm sorry, but I don't love you, Victor. I never have. I should have made it clear from the first time you flirted with me, ten years ago. I will never be with you. No matter how much money you loan my parents. Never."

The smug expression disappeared from Sinistyn's face. He looked dangerous and hard. "You don't know what you're saying."

"You bought the palace for nothing. I'll pay you back the money we owe. But I don't want you."

His eyes became hooded, his face flushed with anger. "At the club last week you made me think differently."

She took a deep breath and looked him straight in the eye. "I was going to ask for your help to get custody of my son. It was wrong of me. But then you were wrong to loan my parents millions of dollars at a thirty-five percent interest rate while claiming to be our friend."

"Your father promised that you would be mine. When we were in business together he said he'd convince you—"

"He tried, but I refused. We've known each other for a long time, Victor. It is time for us to be honest. I will never be your wife, but I will pay back every dime we owe you. Can we at least part as friends?"

She held out her hand.

But Victor's expression was hard as he looked from her outstretched hand to her face. He grabbed her arm roughly, causing her to cry out.

"I waited for you," he said softly. "I've tried to be nice. But it seems there's only one language you'll understand. You're mine, Anna. Mine."

He drew back a fist. Sucking in her breath, she winced in anticipation.

Quick as a flash, Nikos stepped between them, grabbing the other man's hand. He knocked him off balance with a hard right hook and shoved him to the ground.

"Don't touch her," Nikos shouted. "Not now. Not ever."

His body was crying out for the man's blood. He wanted to bash Victor Sinistyn into a pulp for threatening her. He wanted to kill the man for trying to hurt her.

Then he heard Anna's soft moan.

Nikos realized that his own bodyguards were barely keeping Sinistyn's men in check, and that at any moment a full brawl would break out in his own casino. They were already being watched by gamblers, gawkers and slack-jawed tourists, a couple of whom were holding cameras in anticipation of the coming action.

Breathing hard, Nikos jerked away from Sinistyn. "Get him out of here," he ordered Cooper. Cooper nodded, and with a single gesture a phalanx of security guards appeared.

"Follow me, gentlemen," Cooper said, holding out his arm in an ironic gesture.

One of Sinistyn's bodyguards tried to help his boss to his feet, but the Russian jerked his arm away and rose slowly on his own.

"You'll regret this, Stavrakis," Sinistyn said, and then his eyes shifted to Anna. "You'll both regret this."

He stormed out, followed closely by his shamefaced bodyguards.

"I'll make sure he doesn't get back in," Cooper said

quietly. "And post extra guards on the night watch."
He said loudly to the crowd, "Show's over, folks. The
waitresses will be out to make sure everyone's getting
their drinks."

Nikos felt Anna in his arms as she threw herself
against his chest. "Oh, Nikos, I'm so sorry. It's all my
fault."

At her touch, he slowly came back to himself. He
looked down at her, stroking her hair.

"Everything you said was right," she said tearfully.
"Everything. I should have trusted you. I've been a fool.
A selfish, cowardly fool." She pressed her face against
his shirt with a sob, then looked up at him, tears stream-
ing down her pale cheeks. "I ran away when you were
only trying to protect us. Can you ever forgive me?"

Nikos had been right about Victor.

Anna's stomach hurt. She'd known Victor was bad,
but she'd never thought he'd actually want to hurt her.
Natalie had also tried to tell her, but she wouldn't listen.

Nikos had been right about everything. Maybe he'd
been bossy and controlling, but at least his motives had
been good. Strong and loyal and true, he'd put their new
little family first in his life. Why hadn't she done the
same? Why hadn't she been brave enough to stay and
fight, rather than believe the worst of him?

"Forgive me," she said again.

His dark eyes were unreadable as he softly touched
her lips with his finger. "There is nothing to forgive."

She was suddenly aware of the curious stares of on-
lookers and the noise of the slot machines. "Before you
leave for Asia, I need to talk to you."

"Let's go upstairs." He hugged her close to his body,
guiding her gently toward the private elevator. His body

felt warm against hers. She wrapped her hand around his muscular waist, enveloped in the scent of him— clean, but with a hint of something dangerous, as searing as the desert sun.

She knew the risk of reaching for the sun. Its heat and fire could consume her.

But she was suddenly so tired of feeling frozen inside.

Nikos had made it clear that he was done fighting with her. She'd been praying that she would have changed his mind by now, that she'd have proved she could both be a good mother and a good employee. But it was too late. He didn't want her as his secretary. He wanted her to fulfill their deal.

She'd blown it.

Once they were upstairs he'd demand the name of his new secretary. She'd give it to him, and tomorrow he would fly off for Singapore. There would be nothing left for her to do but pack for a new life in New York.

A new life that, for all its freedoms, would be missing one thing she wanted desperately. The man she loved.

She loved him. There. She'd admitted it—if only to herself. But he didn't want to hire her, and without his love she didn't want to marry him. There was nothing left to say.

Except that if their relationship had to end she wanted one last night to remember. One night to laugh with him again. To be daring. To be bold. One night where she allowed herself to love him with her whole heart.

One night to prove how much she trusted him.

But, as much as she knew he wanted her, he'd already refused her too many times, holding out for marriage. She licked her lips, glancing at him from beneath her lashes. Before he left, could she make him change his mind—just for one night?

She'd never seduced a man in her life, but maybe it was time to try.

Marveling at her own boldness as she crossed the casino floor with his arm around her, she ran her fingers surreptitiously along his waistband, stroking his flat belly through his shirt. "You changed your shirt."

She heard his intake of breath, but his voice was even as he replied, "You ripped up the last one."

"Sorry." She rubbed her breast against his side as they walked. She heard a slight growl from his throat.

"What are you doing?"

"What do you mean?" she asked innocently.

He picked up his pace toward the elevator, and the moment the doors were closed behind them he was on her. Pressing her against the cool metal wall, he kissed her savagely, running his hands up and down her body.

"God, you drive me crazy," he whispered against her skin. "I want you, Anna. It's killing me."

"Good." She reached for his shirt and saw his expression as she untucked the fabric and ran her hands underneath, exploring his flat belly and the muscular chest covered with dark hair. "This time you're not going to refuse me," she said, using a tone she'd heard him use many times—the tone no one could refuse. She unbuttoned his shirt, her fingers somehow moving deftly, as if she'd been seducing men all her life. "You're not going to make me wait. You're not going to demand that I marry you."

"Anna." His breathing was coming harder. "We both know—"

"Later." She already knew what he was going to say, and she didn't want to hear a word of it. She didn't want to think about the résumés in her purse, or the fact that Nikos had finally decided to let her go. Tomorrow she'd face those cold, hard facts. But tonight she'd stop time. She'd have one perfect night with him that could be crystallized in her memory forever—something to remember during all the cold and lonely nights.

Tonight she would give herself to him completely.

I love you, Nikos. I love you.

"Did you say something?" he murmured.

Oh, my God, had she whispered those words aloud? She had to distract him.

"I said *no talking.*" She reached for his waist. Unbuckling his belt, she pulled it out of the loops and tossed it to the floor of the elevator. She slowly stroked his bare belly beneath his shirt, swaying her body against his.

With a taunting smile, she undid the top button of his pants.

He gave an audible gasp and grabbed her wrists, yanking them tight above her head. "Is this what you want?" he choked out. "Hard and fast? Here in the elevator?"

She struggled against the shackles of his hands, wanting to touch him, to feel his naked skin against her own. Her whole body ached for him.

The elevator dinged as it reached their floor, and the doors slid open. She felt drunk, drugged with desire, as with a throaty growl Nikos picked her up, carrying her roughly into the penthouse.

Against a backdrop of two-story-high windows, the only color was a minimalist red sofa against white walls and white carpet. He took her swiftly into his enormous bedroom. He pressed a button on the wall and the room suddenly glowed with firelight. She'd wondered what this room would be like. It was spartan, empty, and ghostly white. The floor was white tile, covered by a white fur rug in front of a white adobe fireplace. Surrounded by oceans of unused space, the king-sized bed sat, pristine and untouched, in the center of the room.

Nikos started to kiss her again, and she closed her eyes. She forgot where she was, forgot everything. He lowered her gently to the enormous mattress, caressing her long hair. He stroked her cheek, down her neck, then placed his hand softly between her breasts, over her heart.

"Last chance to leave," he growled.

Deliberately, she leaned back against his bed.

Unblinking as a wolf, he stared at her. Her eyes devoured his bare chest. Dark hair covered his torso, tightening to a vertical line that disappeared beneath the waistband of his exquisitely tailored pants.

His clothes were elegant and fine. The uniform of a wealthy, civilized man. But his body was something else, something more. As he discarded his clothes, tossing them on the white tile floor, he revealed the savage warrior beneath.

He stood in front of her, naked and unselfconscious. His muscles were hard, wide. She saw the old scars, almost faded, brought into stark relief by new white lines across his ribs and collarbone. She saw how much he wanted her. Most of all she saw his dark eyes, hungry with need. She sat up, reaching for him, holding out her arms.

He was on her in an instant, pressing her back roughly against the luxuriant softness of the bed.

"Agape mou," he whispered. "I have waited so long. Wanted you for so long…"

Reaching his broad hands beneath her back, he unzipped her skirt. He pulled his shirt over her head and tossed them both to the floor. The stroke of the fabric, the sheen of his breath, sent prickles of longing up and down her skin. As he kissed slowly down her body, between her breasts and down her belly, it was all she could do not to blurt out the three forbidden words.

Kissing her, he pushed her back against the soft goose-down comforter, spreading his hands wide as he caressed her body, making her shiver as he ran his fingers over her white panties and bra.

He covered her with his naked body, pressing her into the soft folds of the thick comforter. She felt as if she was drowning. She clutched at him like a life preserver, gasping as he unhooked her bra and freed her breasts. He slowly moved his body up against hers, rubbing his chest against her, pressing his naked hardness between her legs as he sucked on her neck, her shoulder, her earlobes. Holding her tightly, he ran his tongue around the tender edge of her ear, slowly moving inward until he made her gasp as he penetrated the center with his tongue. She turned her face to him, grabbing the back of his head as she kissed him hungrily.

Then she pulled away, looking into his eyes.

She had to say the words. She couldn't keep them inside anymore.

"Nikos, I love you."

CHAPTER EIGHT

NIKOS FROZE. "WHAT?"

"I love you." Anna's face looked bare, vulnerable, as she repeated the words.

Nikos had tried for the last hour to speak those same three words—the simple lie that would close the deal and give him the upper hand. But he'd been unable to force the words out of his mouth. He hadn't wanted to say them, hadn't wanted to lie to her. He'd let himself hope that making love to her would be enough.

Tsou. No. It was now or never. He had to act now, or it was all over.

He pictured his son with a man like Sinistyn as his stepfather. He imagined Anna in another man's arms, and his lips pressed into a line. To protect his family he'd do anything, say anything, sacrifice anything.

Even his honor.

Watching his face with a troubled expression, Anna rushed to say, "I know you don't love me back, and it's okay—"

"I love you, too." He spoke the words quickly, spitting them out as if they were a live grenade in his mouth.

"You love me?" Anna stared at him in amazement, as if she couldn't believe what she'd heard.

"Yes." His voice was low, strained.

Her whole face started to light up from within, like a thousand Christmas candles glowing at once. "You love me?" she repeated in a whisper, her eyes filling with tears. If he'd truly loved her, the joy on her face would have been enough to keep him warm through a thousand cold, dark winters. "I never expected—I never dreamed— Oh, Nikos…"

She kissed him then with a passion so pure and sweet it was unlike anything he'd ever known. He returned her kiss with fervor, desperate to forget the lie he'd told, to wipe his sin clean through the fire of his longing for her. He wanted her. He wanted every part of her. Her beauty and innocence and goodness. He kissed her back with all the hard, brutal honesty in his soul.

He ran his hands down the length of her soft skin, kissing her lips, her breasts, sucking the tips of her fingers as she reached for him, trying to pull him closer. The way she moved, the sway and tremble of her body beneath him, brought him perilously close to exploding. Only the thin barrier of fabric kept him from seizing her hips and plunging himself into her. The image had barely crossed his mind before he kissed down her belly, running his hands beneath the fabric, gently nudging her panties down as his kisses went lower. He pulled the cotton down with his teeth even as he ran his fingers between her splayed legs, lightly tracing upwards from the sensitive area behind her knees to her inner thighs. He reached his hands beneath her panties and pulled them down. His tongue descended on her, spreading and licking her wide. As he ran his tongue over her hot nub, swirling in a circular motion, she writhed and moaned beneath him.

"No—" she gasped, trying to push him away. "I want you inside me—"

But he was merciless. Instead of stopping, he reached a thick finger inside her, then another finger. He pushed into her as his tongue licked and lapped her. She arched violently, her body snapping back against the bed, and he felt her shake and tremble as she came.

Feeling like he was going to explode, he lifted up on his arms and positioned himself between her legs. He found her wet core, pressing right into her, then hesitated, panting from the effort of restraint. He didn't want to hurt her. He would have to go slowly…

But Anna, more merciful than he, took things into her own hands. As he gritted his teeth, aching as he pushed himself slowly inside her, she reached behind him and yanked his naked buttocks towards her, forcing him through the tight sheath, impaling her. He heard her gasp, and he tried to pull back, but the pleasure of being buried deep inside her after all the months of longing was too much. He moaned her name softly, moving inside her, and took her in his arms, kissing her.

He'd never known it could be like this.

It hurt when he pushed into her. Had he always been this big?

Then he kissed her. His tongue twined around hers, caressing her deeply, and as her body relaxed the pleasure returned, built, intensified.

He loves me, she thought in amazement. Her eyes fluttered open and she saw the expression on his face as he was kissing her. It was worshipful. Devout. Intent. *He loves me.*

Her body relaxed. She didn't have to leave him, ever. Her heart was flooded with joy such as she'd never known before. He'd never said *I love you* before.

With those three words her whole world had changed.

Somehow everything would work out. Why not? What problem was insurmountable, what miracles were impossible, when Nikos loved her?

Running his hands along her breasts, he slowly pushed into her again. Her nerves grew taut. She wanted him, wanted more. She lifted her hips to meet his thrust, holding on to his shoulders. But the bed was far too soft, swallowing her into the comforter under his weight.

With a growl of frustration he lifted her up from the bed, careful not to pull out as he wrapped her naked body around him. In five long steps he crossed the fire-lit room to the nearest wall—the thick windows that overlooked the Las Vegas Strip, twenty floors below. Thick, unbreakable windows that she herself had discussed with the architects—but she'd never dreamed she would put them to use like this.

Anna moaned as he pressed her naked body against the windows. She glanced down at his tanned skin, at the ripple of his hard muscles in the flickering firelight. She tightened her legs around his rock-hard buttocks as he pushed into her. A groan came from his lips as he thrust into her again and again, causing her full breasts to move with each force of his thrust. Leaning forward, he bit her neck as the pleasure began to spiral within her, even deeper and harder than she'd felt before. Her whole body began to shake, so tense that she could hardly breathe for want of him. She felt him explode inside her with a shout, and she screamed, rocked hard against the windows behind her, as she was devoured by the most intense pleasure she'd ever known.

She fell forward onto him, weak and spent. He lifted her in his arms and lowered her to the white bearskin rug in front of the fire. Murmuring her name tenderly, kissing her face, he held her close.

It took Anna several minutes to open her eyes, but when she did Nikos was looking down at her. His dark eyes were fierce, guarded.

"Anna—" he said, then stopped.

She licked her lips uncertainly. Was he already thinking that he'd made a mistake telling her he loved her? Or maybe she'd imagined the whole thing? Suddenly she felt afraid. For a long moment she heard only the low roar of the fire.

He reached down to caress her cheek. "I don't want to be like Sinistyn. Answer me this one last time, and I promise you I will never ask again." He took a deep breath. "Will you marry me?"

A rush of relief and joy went through her.

"Yes," she said.

He visibly exhaled. "Tonight? Right now?"

She snickered, playfully tugging on his ear. "We'll have to get a license, won't we? The courthouse closed hours ago."

"I'll call the judge at home—"

"No. Let's do this right. Please."

"Tomorrow, then?" he growled. "First thing in the morning?"

"All right," she said, kissing his cheek and smiling.

"You're really going to marry me?"

"Yes!"

"Say it again," he ordered, holding her close.

She laughed out of pure happiness. "Nikos, I'll marry you."

As Nikos held Anna in his arms through the long, interminable night, he stared up at the moonlight creeping slowly across the ceiling above the wide bed. He held her close, listening to her sighs of sleep against his bare shoulder. She was so sweet. So trusting.

And he'd deceived her.

I did what I had to do, he told himself fiercely. Anna would be his forever. Michael would have a permanent family. He'd saved his family. He'd matched his wits against hers, laying siege against her heart until it fell, like a golden city overrun by a savage army.

But he'd never thought winning would feel like this.

He'd lied to her. Now, even holding her in his arms, so warm and soft against him, he felt cold. He stared down at her lovely face in the shadows and moonlight. She was smiling in her sleep, pressing her body against his. She was radiating warmth and contentment. She believed that he finally loved her. She believed in happy endings—even for a man like him.

His whole body was racked with tension. But even as he tried to justify what he'd done the thought that she would learn soon enough about his lie pounded through him. She wouldn't be satisfied with an unlimited bank account in lieu of his love. She would demand things of him—emotion, energy, vulnerability—that he simply couldn't give. Not even if he tried. He just wasn't made that way.

And as soon as she found out how she'd been deceived, her joy would be snuffed out like a candle. It would cause the bright new light in her to go out, perhaps forever.

Shortly before dawn he heard snuffling moans from the next room, where Mrs. Burbridge had brought their baby to spend the night. At their son's cries, Anna stirred in his arms.

She gently pushed out of his embrace and crept into

the baby's room to nurse, before returning back into his bed.

"Nikos?" Anna whispered.

He kept his breathing even, feigning sleep.

"Thank you," she said, so quietly it was barely audible. "I have the home I dreamed of, the family I dreamed of. I don't know what I did to deserve this. Thank you for loving me."

God, this was intolerable. He turned on his side, pulling away from her, every nerve taut. As soon as he was sure she was really asleep, he sat up in bed. Feeling bone-weary, he raked his hands through his hair and rose slowly from the bed.

Glancing at Anna, slumbering peacefully beneath the white goose-down comforter, he came to a decision. He looked at the clock. It was almost six. He'd intended to have her sign the prenuptial agreement as soon as she woke, then drive straight to the courthouse for a license. He'd planned for them to be married at a drive-thru chapel before breakfast.

But, no matter how pure his motives, now that he held her fate in the palm of his hands he just couldn't do it. He couldn't take her honesty and trust and love and use them as weapons against her. He couldn't break her heart and destroy her life, no matter how good his motives might be.

Anna Rostoff deserved a man who could love her with his whole heart.

If he wasn't that man, he had to let her go.

A fine time to grow a conscience, Nikos thought bleakly. Apparently he did have one last bit of honor left.

He gave Anna one final, lingering glance. Her dark hair was sprawled across his pillow, her creamy skin like ivory against the white thousand-count sheets. Her cheeks still glowed pink, a remnant of their lovemaking, and her lips curved into a soft smile as she sighed in her sleep.

It was an image he knew he'd never see again.

Anna woke in a flood of early morning light with one bright thought: today was her wedding day!

She stretched her limbs against the luxurious sheets with a contented yawn. Her body felt sore. A good kind of sore. She smiled to herself, almost blushing as she remembered everything Nikos had done to her last night. She'd woken up twice for the baby, but, as worn out as she'd been from their lovemaking, with Nikos's hard body curled protectively around hers she'd still had an amazing night's sleep.

She glanced over to the wall of windows, revealing the wide blue Nevada sky from the twentieth-floor penthouse. She'd never felt happy like this before. Safe. Optimistic. Secure. For the first time in her whole life she not only had a home, she had someone who would actually watch over and protect her, instead of just looking out for their own interests. And she had someone she could protect and love in return not because she had to, but because she wanted to.

She and Nikos would be partners, in work as in life. Together they'd be as unbreakable as tempered steel.

It was an exquisitely heady feeling. She wanted to do cartwheels across the penthouse.

She wanted to kiss Nikos *right now*.

Where was he? In the kitchen, making her breakfast? Humming to herself, she rose from the bed and threw on a satin robe, barely stopping long enough to loosely tie the belt to cover her naked body. She paused briefly outside the door of the second bedroom, where Misha was sleeping. She heard only blessed silence.

She smiled to herself. With any luck she and Nikos would have time for more than a kiss before their child woke up demanding breakfast.

She went down the hall and found the kitchen, but it was empty. The immaculate white counters looked as if they'd never even been touched. Nikos was probably already working in his office. Wouldn't he be surprised and happy if she made him coffee, eggs and toast?

Looking in the bare cupboards and refrigerator, she made a face. Even she couldn't manage to manufacture breakfast out of sugar cubes, Greek olives and ice. She turned away when she heard voices down the hall. She followed the sound, stopping outside the door at the other end of the hall.

Muffled through the door, she heard a man's voice say, "Sir, in my opinion you're making an enormous mistake. As your attorney, I must advise—"

"Since I'm paying you five hundred dollars an hour, I won't waste more time discussing it. I've heard your complaints. Thank you for your assistance. There's the door."

Anna's ear was pressed against the wood; she jumped as the door was flung open and an older man in a dark gray suit came through it.

He gave her a sharp glance, then a scowl. "Congratulations, miss." He put on his hat and stomped out of the apartment with his briefcase.

"Anna. You're awake," Nikos said. "Come in."

His face was dark, half hidden in the shadows of morning where he sat behind a black lacquer desk. The furniture here was as sleek and soulless as everything else in this penthouse. Anna suddenly felt uneasy.

"I thought you were going to wake me up," she said. "Early morning wedding and all that." She glanced behind her. "Why was your lawyer here? Oh. He brought the prenup?"

His eyes flicked at her in surprise. "You knew I wanted you to sign a prenuptial agreement?"

"I assumed you would. I mean, of course you'd want me to sign one. You're a wealthy man," she said lamely, even as disappointment surged through her. He didn't trust her. He honestly thought she cared about his money, that she'd try to take it. He thought they were at risk of getting a divorce. It cast a pall over her happiness.

Then she realized what he'd said. "Wait a minute. You *wanted* for me to sign a prenup? But not anymore?"

"No," he said quietly. "Not anymore."

She blinked as the joy came back through her. He'd realized he could trust her!

"Nikos," she breathed. She crossed the room in five steps and, pulling back his chair, climbed in his lap and threw her arms around him. "You won't regret it," she murmured against the warm skin of his neck. "I'll never let you down. I'll be true to you until the day I die. We're going to be so happy…"

She kissed him then, a long, lingering kiss that held her whole heart in every breath.

"Stop, Anna. Just stop." Pushing her off his lap, he stood up, rubbing his temples. His whole body was tense. He didn't seem like a man who was about to get married. He seemed miserable. And furious. Like a wounded lion with a thorn in his paw. He seemed both hurt and dangerous.

"What is it?" she asked warily. "What's wrong?"

He picked up a file from his desk and held it out to

her without a word, careful not to let their hands touch. Pulling the papers out of the file, she looked down at the first page and her knees felt weak.

She looked up at him slowly, her mouth dry. "I don't...I don't understand."

"There's nothing to understand. I'm giving you joint custody. You can live wherever you like, and I'll provide you with a generous allowance. Enough to clear your family's debt. Enough to support your mother and sister. My brownstone in the Upper East Side will be transferred to your name. My son will have every support, the best schools, vacations abroad—whatever you think best. All I ask is that I have visitation at will, as well as some arrangement to be made for holidays."

Her head was spinning. "But I don't need custody papers. Once we're married we—"

He was shaking his head grimly. "That was a fairy tale, Anna, nothing more. I wanted you in my bed, that's all."

"No." She frowned at him, feeling like she'd fallen into some strange nightmare. "You could have had me in your bed long ago. You were the one who insisted we wait. You've done everything under the sun to convince me to marry you. Why would you change your mind now? It doesn't make sense."

He gave her a careless smile. "I guess I'm just not marriage material."

"But you are!" she gasped. "I know you are. You've changed over the last weeks. You've become the husband I've always wanted, the father I dreamed of for Misha. Kind, brave, strong." She closed her eyes, a thousand images going through her of all the time they'd spent together over the last weeks. Working together.

Laughing. Nikos playing with their child. "All the time we've spent together—"

"It was a trick, Anna. God, don't you get it? It was all an act. I wanted you. I would have pretended anything to win you. It was pride, I suppose. I couldn't stand the thought of you leaving me. But now—" he shrugged. "The charade's already growing old. I don't want the burden of a wife or the full-time care of a child. I want my freedom."

"It's not true! You're lying!"

He grabbed her wrist, searing her with his hot, dark gaze. "You know me," he said cruelly. "You know how I am. So many beautiful women, so little time. Did you really think I could ever settle down with one woman? With you?"

She felt like she'd just gotten punched. She looked up into his face as tears filled her eyes. "Why are you saying this?"

For an instant something like regret and pain washed over his handsome face. "It's better for you to be free," he said finally. "Forget about me, Anna. You deserve a man who will truly love you."

"But *you* love me. You said so," she whispered.

He shook his head, and now his eyes were only cold. "I lied. I don't love anyone. I don't know how."

At those words, all the hope she'd been holding in her chest disappeared.

Nikos didn't love her. He'd chased her out of pride, out of his determination to possess her, to beat his rival. But now that she'd given him her heart he was already bored with her.

For the first time she believed him, and she felt sick. She turned away.

"Fine." She was relieved that her voice didn't tremble. She tried to remember the plan she'd once had—the plan that had sounded so wonderful before she'd fallen back in love with Nikos. "I guess I'll…I'll go back to New York and get a job."

"No." His voice was dark, inexorable. "I told you. You'll never need to work again."

She looked up at him, pressing her fingernails into her palms to fight back tears. She had her pride too— too much pride to ever cry in front of him again.

"I won't take a penny from a man who doesn't love me. I'm going to find a job. Whether you give me a recommendation or not."

He blinked at her, then turned away, clenching his jaw. "I didn't want it to end like this."

"How did you expect it to end?"

He didn't answer the question. His dark eyes looked haunted as he gazed down at her. "You're right. If you truly want to work, I can't stop you. I have no right to stop you," he said in a low voice. "All I can do is ask that you make the decision carefully. And I know you will. I see now that you'll always look out for Misha. I just have one favor to ask. When you marry again, choose well. Choose carefully for our son."

"I thought I had," she said softly. Her feelings were rushing through her, almost uncontrollable. He'd finally agreed that she could work, but even that didn't matter anymore. She wanted to wrap her arms around him, to weep, to beg him not to leave her.

But she was the great-granddaughter of a princess. She was Misha's mother and she had to be strong. Anna clung to her dignity and pride. They were all she had left.

Reaching into her purse, she quietly handed him two pieces of paper. "Here."

"What are these?" he said, sounding shaken.

"The two best résumés for an executive secretary. I lied when I said they weren't any good because I hoped you'd hire me instead. But now that I'm leaving I don't want the company to suffer. I care too much about the company. I care too much about you. I love you."

"Anna—"

She stepped away from him, looking into his eyes. "Goodbye, Nikos. Good luck."

She turned to go, still praying he'd stop her.

He didn't.

Going into the next room, she found the overnight bag Mrs. Burbridge had packed for her the previous night and put on a T-shirt and jeans. She carefully placed the custody agreement into her old diaper bag. She fed and changed Misha and cuddled him close.

Taking a deep breath, she glanced down the hall, hoping against hope that Nikos would appear, put his strong arms around her, and tell her this had all been a horrible mistake.

But Nikos's office door remained closed.

He didn't even care enough to say goodbye. He was probably already phoning the employment agency about the résumés. Or maybe he was calling some sexy show-girl to ask for a date.

Apparently she was easy to replace. In every way.

Straightening, she held on to the frayed edges of her dignity and walked out of the penthouse where, just an hour ago, she'd thought she found love and se-curity at last. She wouldn't let herself cry. Not in his casino, where his men and his security cameras were everywhere.

She managed to hold back her sobs until she reached the sidewalk on Las Vegas Boulevard. Where to now?

There was a taxi stand at the hotel across the street. She could barely see through her tears as she stepped off the curb. Just in time she saw the van barreling toward her in the sparse early morning traffic. She jumped back on the sidewalk in a cold sweat, frightened at how close she'd come to walking into traffic with her son.

"Just who I was looking for," a cold voice said. She looked up with a gasp to see Victor sitting inside the van's open door with several of his men. "What? No snappy comeback? Not so brave when you're alone, are you? Grab the kid," he ordered.

Anna started to fight and scream, trying to run away, but it was hopeless. When Misha was ripped from her arms she immediately surrendered. Ten seconds later she was tied up in the back of the van, on her way to hell. Victor faced her with cold eyes and an oily smile.

"You have a choice to make, *loobemaya*. What happens next is up to you."

Nikos had a sick feeling in his gut.

Pacing around his L'Hermitage penthouse, he poured himself a bourbon, then put it down untasted. He went to his home office, started to check his email, then closed the laptop without reading a single message. He finally went to the window overlooking Las Vegas. Twenty floors above the city, he had a clear view. He could see the wide desert beyond the city to the far mountains. It seemed to stretch forever. The emptiness was everywhere.

Especially here.

I did the right thing letting her go, he told himself. But the sick feeling only got worse. His knees felt weak, as if he'd just run twenty miles without stopping, or gone twenty rounds with a heavyweight champ; he sank into the sleek red-upholstered chair by the edge of the window. He put his head in his hands.

It was the silence that was killing him.

The absolute silence of his beautifully decorated apartment. No baby laughter. No lullabies from Anna. No voices at all. Just dead silence.

He could call one of his trusted employees, like Cooper. He could call acquaintances from the club. He could call any of a dozen women he'd dated. They would be here in less than ten minutes to fill his home with noise.

But he didn't want them.

He wanted his family.

He wanted *her*. His secretary. His lover. His friend.

"*I had to give her up*," he repeated to himself, raking his hand through his hair. I didn't love her.

"Are you sure about that, sir?" a Scottish voice said from behind him.

Nikos jumped when he realized he'd spoken his last words aloud. Mrs. Burbridge was standing in the doorway, her hands folded in front of her. A sharp reply rose to his lips, but her plump face looked so gentle and understanding he bit back the words. Instead, he muttered, "Of course I'm sure."

"You told me to pick up the baby early this morning, as you'd be going to a wedding, but I've arrived to find an open door, no wee babe, and no bride. Am I to understand the wedding's off?"

"They're both gone," he said wearily. He went to his desk, sat down and opened his checkbook. "Your job here is done, Mrs. Burbridge. I'm sorry to bring you so far for just a few weeks. I'll compensate you—"

She reached over and shut the checkbook with a bang. "Where are they, sir? Anna and your child?"

"I let them go," he said, resting his head in his hands. "My son deserved a mother."

"But the bairn was happy enough. So was his mother, I thought. Why send them away?"

"Because Anna deserves better," he exploded. "She deserves a man who can love her. She's been through enough. From her family. From me. I just want her to be happy."

"And you? You don't look terribly happy."

He gave a bitter laugh. "I'll get by. But Anna..." He rubbed the back of his head wearily. "I couldn't let her down. She loved me. Marrying me would have ruined her life."

"Her happiness means more to you than your own?"

"She's the mother of my son. The best damn partner I ever had at work. My friend. My lover. Of course I want her to be happy. It's all I want."

The Scotswoman raised her head and looked at him. Her eyes were kind, but sad. "Sir, what do you think love *is*?"

For a second he just stared at her. Then his heart started to pound in his chest.

"Oh, my God," he whispered.

Was it possible that she was right? That he *loved* Anna?

He didn't just want her in his bed, that was true. He didn't just enjoy her company, appreciate her skills as a mother or respect her perfect secretarial work.

He wanted her face to be the first he woke up to and the last he saw before he slept.

He wanted to see her face light up when she had a business idea, or when she was splashing around in the pool with their son.

He wanted her to be happy. To work as his secretary

if that was what it took to make her glow from the inside out. Her happiness was everything.

That was love?

Oh, my God. *He loved her.* He didn't deserve her, but what if he could spend the rest of his life striving to make her happy?

Because without Anna he now realized that his life was empty. His fortune, his business empire—meant nothing. Without her this penthouse was no better than his childhood tenement, and his life was just as lonely and hungry.

Money didn't matter.

Love mattered.

Family mattered.

Oh, my God. Anna.

"Bless you," he said to Mrs. Burbridge. He raced down the hall to the door. He had to find Anna—now, at once.

He stopped short when he saw Cooper standing outside his door. The burly bodyguard's face was white and drawn.

"Boss—"

But at that moment Nikos saw the bundle in Cooper's arms. His baby son, wrapped in a blanket. Michael's little face was red and miserable as he cried.

"We found him at the front entrance to the casino," Cooper said. "Alone."

Nikos's heart stopped in his throat as he took his son in his arms. "Alone?"

The burly man nodded grimly. "A valet said a van stopped beneath the marquee, left the baby on the ground, and drove away."

Nikos held his son close, crooning to him softly, rocking him back and forth against his chest, just like Anna had taught him. The baby's tears subsided. Michael was comforted, but Nikos was not. "Anna wouldn't let herself be separated from Misha."

Looking miserable, Cooper handed him a letter. Nikos scanned it quickly.

Nikos
I've realized that sharing custody will never work. I'm in love with Victor Sinistyn and leaving with him for South America. You once said I was no kind of mother, and I guess you were right. Trying to keep our baby safe and warm would be too much effort where we're going. Please don't bother trying to find me. Raise our son well.
Anna

"Boss?" Cooper repeated unhappily. His voice echoed in the private outside hallway against the steel of the elevator doors. "What do you want me to do?"

Nikos's heart was pounding. She'd left him. The moment he'd realized he loved her with all his heart, she'd left him. His worst fear had come true.

But something nagged at him, overriding the pain, and he read the letter again. A mere hour after she'd left Nikos she'd decided to leave both him and Misha behind for a life with Victor Sinistyn?

Maybe it *was* her handwriting, but he didn't believe a word of it.

"She's in trouble," Nikos said slowly. "Someone forced her to write this letter."

"You think she's been kidnapped?"

"Sinistyn," he breathed. The man had made it clear he wanted Anna, and when Nikos had shoved her out of L'Hermitage without bodyguards he'd handed her to him on a silver plate. He cursed himself under his breath. "Get the plane ready."

"It's ready now—for your trip to Asia."

"Screw Singapore. Let Haverstock take the bid," he said, throwing away the billion-dollar deal to his chief rival without a thought.

"Where are we going to look for her? South America?"

Nikos shook his head. "Sinistyn put that in to throw us off the track. No. He's going someplace else. Somewhere private. Somewhere my power does not easily reach." He glanced down at the letter, forcing himself to read it again slowly.

You once said I was no kind of mother...
Trying to keep our baby safe and warm would be
too much effort where we're going...

He sucked in his breath. She was trying to tell him where they were going. Folding the letter, he shoved it at Cooper. "They're going to Russia."

"Let me guess, boss," Cooper said sourly. "You want to handle this alone."

Nikos gently handed the baby to Mrs. Burbridge. Kissing his son goodbye, he turned to face Cooper with rage surging through his veins. "Hell, no. I want every man we've got on the plane within the hour. And get Yuri Andropov on the phone. It's time to call in a favor."

CHAPTER NINE

ANNA SHIFTED SLIGHTLY in her chair, trying to shift the cords that bound her wrists without attracting the attention of Victor or his goons. Her hands felt hot and sweaty with the effort, but the rest of her felt like ice as she worked the broken tines of her great-grandmother's ring against the rope.

On the car ride from St. Petersburg she'd briefly felt the spring sun on her face, but the backroom of the Rostov Palace felt cold as ever. Especially as she'd listened to Victor's men ransack the princess's china in the kitchen. Biting her lip, she watched as Victor and one of his men set up an old black-and-white television near the fire.

"It's not working. We'll miss the game," the bodyguard complained in Russian, trying to position the antenna.

"It'll be fine," Victor snapped in the same language. He took the antenna then, realizing that there was no electricity, dropped it in disgust. "Go help with dinner."

"Why can't *she* make us dinner?" the man grumbled, nodding at Anna. "Make the woman useful for once."

Victor glanced back at her, and she froze.

"Oh, she will be useful. But only to me. Get out, I said. I want some time with my future bride."

As Victor approached she pressed her wrists against her T-shirt, hoping he wouldn't notice that one of the cords binding her to the chair was finally starting to fray.

She'd been praying that customs officials would discover her when they arrived in St. Petersburg, but Victor's connections, along with a well-placed bribe, had allowed his private plane to arrive unmolested.

At least her baby was safe, thousands of miles away with Nikos. She'd bought her child's safety with that horrible letter Victor had forced her to write. Would Nikos see her clues?

Maybe he won't even care, she thought hollowly. He'd made it clear that he wanted her permanently out of his life, and this was about as permanent as it could get.

Victor pulled off her gag. "Here," he said, sounding amused. "Scream all you want. No one will hear you."

But she didn't scream. She just pulled away from his touch, glaring at him.

He laughed, folding his arms as he looked around them. "I can see I need to renovate my so-called palace. No heat. No electricity. And all they've found in the kitchen so far are potatoes and tea bags."

"I hope you starve," she replied pleasantly.

"That's not a very kind thing to say to your future husband, is it? You and I both need to keep up our strength. I'll send one of the boys to the grocery store. And as for heat…we can supply that on our own, later." He gave her a sly smile. "Any requests? You've been refusing food and drink for hours." He ran his hand down her arm, making her shudder with revulsion. "You must eat something."

"So you can drug me? No, thanks."

"Ah, *loobemaya*," Victor said softly, brushing back

a tendril of her hair. "I wouldn't go to so much trouble if I didn't love you so much."

"You call this love?"

"Until Stavrakis's spell wears off, and you understand it's really me you want, I need to keep you close. You will realize how much you want me." His voice sounded threatening as, massaging her shoulder hard enough to leave a bruise, he added softly, "Very soon."

Ignoring the loud sounds of crashing china and slamming cabinet doors in the kitchen, Anna pulled her shoulder away from his hand. "I love Nikos, and I always will."

He yanked back her hair, causing her head to jerk back. Anna dimly heard men shouting from the kitchen, but all she could see was Victor's sadistic face, inches away from her own. "Forget him. Forget his baby. I will give you others. I will fill you with my child tonight. You belong to me now. You will learn to obey my will. You will learn to crave my touch—"

He forced his lips on hers in a painful ravishment that was meant to teach fear. And it worked. For the first time Anna began to feel truly scared of what he would do to her.

When he pulled away, Victor smiled at the expression on her face. He ran a hand up the inner thigh of her jeans.

"You have no right," she whispered, shaking.

"This is my country. I have half the police in my pocket. Here, you are my slave." He reached to fondle a breast, and without thinking she brought up her bound wrists to block him. His smile stretched to a grin. "Yes," he breathed. "Fight me. That's what I want. Stavrakis isn't here to save you. You'll never see him or your precious son again. You're mine. You're totally in my power—"

"Let her go."

Victor looked up with a gasp. Anna saw Nikos standing in the kitchen doorway and almost sobbed aloud.

Nikos's face had an expression she'd never seen before—as cold and deadly as the gun he was pointing at Sinistyn.

Victor looked up with an intake of breath which he quickly masked with a sneer. "You're as good as dead, Stavrakis. My men will—"

"Your men will do nothing. They barely tried. When they saw they were outnumbered, most of them gave up without a fight." He cocked the gun, assessing his aim at Victor's head. "Some loyalty you inspire, Sinistyn."

With a single smooth movement Victor twisted behind Anna, using her body to block his own. "Come closer and I'll kill her."

He put his beefy hands around her neck. Anna flinched, then struggled, unable to breathe. As he slowly tightened his grip, the room around her seemed to shimmer and fade.

Nikos uncocked the gun, pointing it at the ceiling. "You really are a coward."

"It's easy to throw insults when you have a gun."

"Let her go, damn you!" Nikos threw the gun on the floor, then straightened with a scornful expression. "Even now I'm unarmed, I know you won't fight me. I'm stronger, faster, smarter than you—"

"Shut up!" Victor screamed, releasing Anna's throat. She took a long, shuddering gasp of air and felt the world right itself around her.

Victor stormed toward Nikos, lunging for the gun. Nikos kicked it into the roaring fireplace and threw himself at the other man's midsection. The two men fought while Anna watched in terror, desperately struggling with the cords that bound her to the chair. Victor lashed out wildly, hitting Nikos's jaw with his knee. Nikos's head snapped back, but he fought grimly, as if he were in the battle he'd trained for all his life. With a crunching uppercut to the chin, Nikos knocked Victor to the floor.

Gasping for air, Victor slid back, scuttling like a crab. Reaching into the fireplace, he picked up the gun with his sleeve and pushed himself up against the wall, panting.

"Now you're going to die." Victor shot a crazed look from Nikos to Anna. "And you're going to watch. After this, only his ghost will haunt us." He cocked the gun, pointing it at Nikos with triumph.

"No!" Anna screamed, desperately struggling with the cord. By some miracle it snapped open against her wrist. She threw herself from the chair, flinging her body in front of Nikos as Victor squeezed the trigger.

She closed her eyes, waiting to feel the bullet tear through her body.

Instead, she just heard a soft *click*.

The gun was empty!

Victor shook the gun with impotent fury.

Nikos turned to one side, tucking her protectively behind him as he faced Victor. "Guess I forgot the bullets. Sorry."

With a scream of frustration Victor threw the gun at him, but Nikos dodged it easily. It clattered to the floor.

Nikos glanced at it with a derisive snort. He raised an eyebrow, giving Victor the darkly arrogant look that Anna had once despised. But she appreciated it now.

She knew he used all his arrogance, all his strength and power, to protect the people he loved.

"Fight me, Sinistyn," Nikos demanded coldly. "Just you and me."

Victor swore in Russian, shaking his head. He looked straight at Anna, muttering all the sadistic things he'd do to her if Nikos wasn't there to protect her.

Anna felt her cheeks grow hot with horror. Nikos didn't speak Russian, but when he saw the effect the man's words were having on her he strode forward grimly.

With a yelp, Victor turned and ran in the other direction. But Nikos caught up with him, grabbing his shoulder and whirling him around.

"Like scaring women, do you?" He punched Victor in the face—once, twice. "Too much of a coward to fight someone your own size? Fight me, damn you! Or are you going to just let me kill you?" Nikos's eyes narrowed and he looked dangerous indeed. "Don't think I won't."

Victor started fighting dirty. He tried to knee Nikos in the groin, to trip him. When Nikos blocked him, he stumbled back to the fireplace and grabbed a sharp iron poker.

"I'll stab you like a pig, you Greek bastard," he panted, swinging the poker at Nikos's face.

He blocked it with his right arm, but Anna heard the crunch of bone and saw the way Nikos's right hand hung at a strange angle.

Victor had broken his wrist. She trembled with fury. She started to run at Victor, to fight him two to one, but Nikos stopped her with a hard glance.

With his left hand he wrenched the poker away and threw Victor to the floor. He held him to the ground with one hand against his neck. Anna watched in horror as he tightened his grip.

"How does it feel to be vulnerable?" Nikos demanded.

"Nikos, let him go," Anna sobbed.

"Why? Do you think he would have let *you* go?" he demanded, not looking at her. "Did he ever show mercy to anyone weaker? Why should I let him live after what he's done to you?"

Slowly she put her hands against his shoulders, feeling the hard tension of his muscles. "Do it for us. Please, my love, let him go so we can go back to our son."

Abruptly, he released his choke hold on the other man and rose to his feet. She had one brief vision of his face, and she thought she saw tears in his eyes as, without a word, he took her in his arms and held her tightly.

Nikos looked down at her as he held her tenderly to his chest. His dark eyes were shining.

"Thank you, *agape mou*," he whispered, brushing her cheek softly with his hand. "Thank you for trying to take that bullet. There weren't any bullets, but you didn't know that. You...you saved me. In so many ways."

"And you started early," a man said from the doorway in heavily accented English. Anna looked up to see a man in a Russian police uniform, with half a dozen policemen behind him. "We missed it."

"I couldn't wait, Yuri." Nikos jerked his head toward Victor, still stretched out on the floor. "There he is."

The man called Yuri smiled. "You said you were calling in a favor. I wish I had to pay more favors like this. We've wanted Sinistyn a long time, but he was untouchable. Now, with your testimony and influence, he won't see the sun again for a long time." The policeman looked with concern at Nikos's wrist. "My friend, you are hurt."

"It's nothing—"

"It's his wrist. I think it's broken. We need a doctor right away," Anna said, then looked up anxiously at the face of the man she loved. "Please, Nikos. I need you to be well."

"All right," he muttered. "Get the doctor."

Turning away from the policeman, he sank into a nearby chair and pulled her into his lap. "Anna, before the doctor starts filling me with drugs, I have to tell you something. I should have told you this a long time ago, but I was too stupid to see it and too stubborn to admit it—even to myself. I really do love you."

"Nikos, I love—"

"Please let me finish, while I can still get this out." He took a deep breath. "You saved me. From a life that was empty. I was stupid to prevent you from working, or doing anything else that brings you joy. If it makes you happy, I want you to work. As my secretary, as vice-president, as any damn thing you want."

Tears filled her eyes even as she gave him a mischievous smile. "I think I'd make a good CEO."

"Cocky." He returned her grin. "You always were the only one who could stand up to me. I need that in my life. Someone to keep me in my place."

As she looked into his handsome face she barely heard the noises of the swarming police, or Victor's whining complaints as they took him away.

"Your place is with me." She cupped his jaw, rough with dark stubble, in her hands. "As long as we're together, anyplace in the world is my home. But there's something that I have to ask you. Something I've never said before to anyone." He'd called her cocky, but what she wanted to ask him now terrified her. She took a deep breath. "Nikos, will you marry me?"

For his answer, his smile lit his face from within, his dark eyes shining at her with hope and love. "I thought you'd never ask."

"I told you we should have gotten married at the drive-thru chapel in Vegas," Anna whispered when she reached the end of the aisle.

"And miss all this? Never," he whispered back with a wink.

As the priest began to speak the words that would bind them together for all time Nikos knew he should pay attention, but all he could do was look at his bride. Beneath the hot Greek sun, on the edge of a rocky cliff overlooking the Aegean Sea, they were surrounded by flowers and a small audience of people who loved them. It was a simple wedding, plain by some standards, but he knew in his heart it was what Anna wanted.

And, looking at her now, he knew he'd never be able to deny her anything. Her turquoise eyes, a mixture of sea and sky, smiled at him as he lifted her veil. She wore a white shift that made her look like a medieval maiden.

Her engagement ring, a four-carat diamond in an antique gold setting, sparkled from her finger. He'd given it to her two nights ago. She'd tried to refuse it until she'd realized that he'd found the original stone from her great-grandmother's wedding ring. Now it was one of her greatest treasures.

The way she'd thanked him had made him forget all about the cast on his wrist. Remembering that night, and every night since they'd returned from Russia, still made his body feel hot from the inside out. He could hardly wait to give Anna her honeymoon present—Rostov Palace, which he'd bought from Sinistyn's confiscated estates. Sinistyn didn't need it anymore, as he'd be living out his days in a Russian prison.

Nikos glanced around him at family and friends and the sea and the bright blue sky. *Justice.* Another thing he'd thought existed only in fairy tales, along with love and happy endings.

He'd not only held his wedding in his parents' hometown, but, at Anna's urging, he'd invited his father's family—Eudocia Dounas and her three daughters—to the wedding. To his surprise they'd all come, bringing their husbands and children. He now had a family. Siblings, nieces, nephews. He didn't know them yet, but he would.

Near his family sat Anna's mother who, in another wedding-day miracle, was not only on her best behavior, but had pinched his cheek and declared it was "about time" the two were married. Anna had spent last night talking to her sister, barring Nikos from her bedroom because it was "bad luck" for him to see her. Now, Natalie was bouncing Misha on her knee while she watched the wedding, smiling through her tears. And he could see his son's two new top teeth in his smile as he watched his parents wed.

It was a day for families to join together.

All right, he'd admit it. It wasn't just Anna who'd wanted this kind of wedding. He had wanted it as well. In some way he'd wanted this all his life.

Family.

Home.

Love.

As Anna said the words that made her his wife her voice was sweet and true. He barely remembered repeating the words himself, but he must have done so since before he knew it the priest was speaking in accented English, declaring them husband and wife, and he was kissing the bride. Over the sound of the crashing surf he heard their family and friends behind them burst into applause, and a noisy cheer from Cooper. But as he kissed her, holding her tightly in his arms, all he could feel was the pounding of his heart against hers.

She pulled back, caressing his face as she grinned up at him through tears. "See?" she whispered. "Wasn't that better than having Elvis marry us?"

Hiding a grin, he looked down at her solemnly. "I'm yours to command now, Mrs. Stavrakis."

"Mine to command?" She paused, pretending to consider her options, and then leaned forward to whisper in his ear. "In that case, my first order is that you take me to bed."

"Leaving our guests to start the reception?"

She gave him a wicked smile. "They won't miss us."

"They won't even notice," he agreed with a grin. He picked her up in his arms and, to the delighted gasps of the crowd, he turned to carry her back to his villa.

"Ah, Anna. I can tell I'm going to have a hard life with you," he observed with a sigh, and he kissed her with all his heart.

* * * * *

COMING NEXT MONTH from Harlequin Presents®
AVAILABLE MARCH 19, 2013

#3129 MASTER OF HER VIRTUE
Miranda Lee

Shy, cautious Violet has had enough of living life in the shadows. She resolves to experience all that life has to offer, starting with internationally renowned film director Leo Wolfe. But is Violet ready for where he wants to take her?

#3130 A TASTE OF THE FORBIDDEN
Buenos Aires Nights
Carole Mortimer

Argentinian tycoon Cesar Navarro has his sexy little chef, Grace Blake, right where he wants her—in his penthouse, at his command! She should be off-limits, but Grace has tantalized his jaded palette, and Cesar finds himself ordering something new from the menu!

#3131 THE MERCILESS TRAVIS WILDE
The Wilde Brothers
Sandra Marton

Travis Wilde would never turn down a willing woman in a king-size bed! Normally innocence like Jennie Cooper's would have the same effect as a cold shower, yet her determination and mouth-watering curves have him burning up all over!

#3132 A GAME WITH ONE WINNER
Scandal in the Spotlight
Lynn Raye Harris

Paparazzi darling Caroline Sullivan hides a secret behind her dazzling smile. Her ex-flame, Russian businessman Roman Kazarov, is back on the scene—is he seeking revenge for her humiliating rejection or wanting to take possession of her troubled business?

You can find more information on upcoming Harlequin® titles, free excerpts and more at www.Harlequin.com.

HPCNM0313RA

#3133 HEIR TO A DESERT LEGACY
Secret Heirs of Powerful Men
Maisey Yates

When recently and reluctantly crowned Sheikh Sayid discovers his country's true heir, he'll do anything to protect him—even marry the child's aunt. It may appease his kingdom, but will it release the blistering chemistry between them...?

#3134 THE COST OF HER INNOCENCE
Jacqueline Baird

Newly free Beth Lazenby has closed the door on her past, until she encounters lawyer Dante Cannavaro who is still convinced of her guilt. But when anger boils over into passion, will the consequences forever bind her to her enemy?

#3135 COUNT VALIERI'S PRISONER
Sara Craven

Kidnapped and held for ransom... His price? Her innocence! Things like this just don't happen to Maddie Lang, but held under lock and key, the only deal Count Valieri will strike is one with an *unconventional* method of payment!

#3136 THE SINFUL ART OF REVENGE
Maya Blake

Reiko has two things art dealer Damion Fortier wants; a priceless Fortier heirloom and her seriously off-limits body! And she has no intention of giving him access to either. So Damion turns up lethal charm to ensure he gets *exactly* he wants....

You can find more information on upcoming Harlequin® titles, free excerpts and more at www.Harlequin.com.

HPCNM0313RB

REQUEST YOUR
FREE BOOKS!

2 FREE NOVELS PLUS
2 FREE GIFTS!

YES! Please send me 2 FREE Harlequin Presents® novels and my 2 FREE gifts (gifts are worth about $10). After receiving them, if I don't wish to receive any more books, I can return the shipping statement marked "cancel." If I don't cancel, I will receive 6 brand-new novels every month and be billed just $4.30 per book in the U.S. or $4.99 per book in Canada. That's a saving of at least 14% off the cover price! It's quite a bargain! Shipping and handling is just 50¢ per book in the U.S. and 75¢ per book in Canada.* I understand that accepting the 2 free books and gifts places me under no obligation to buy anything. I can always return a shipment and cancel at any time. Even if I never buy another book, the two free books and gifts are mine to keep forever.

106/306 HDN FVRK

Name _____ (PLEASE PRINT) _____

Address _____ Apt. # _____

City _____ State/Prov. _____ Zip/Postal Code _____

Signature (if under 18, a parent or guardian must sign)

Mail to the Harlequin® Reader Service:
IN U.S.A.: P.O. Box 1867, Buffalo, NY 14240-1867
IN CANADA: P.O. Box 609, Fort Erie, Ontario L2A 5X3

**Are you a current subscriber to Harlequin Presents books
and want to receive the larger-print edition?
Call 1-800-873-8635 or visit www.ReaderService.com.**

* Terms and prices subject to change without notice. Prices do not include applicable taxes. Sales tax applicable in N.Y. Canadian residents will be charged applicable taxes. Offer not valid in Quebec. This offer is limited to one order per household. Not valid for current subscribers to Harlequin Presents books. All orders subject to credit approval. Credit or debit balances in a customer's account(s) may be offset by any other outstanding balance owed by or to the customer. Please allow 4 to 6 weeks for delivery. Offer available while quantities last.

Your Privacy—The Harlequin® Reader Service is committed to protecting your privacy. Our Privacy Policy is available online at www.ReaderService.com or upon request from the Harlequin Reader Service.

We make a portion of our mailing list available to reputable third parties that offer products we believe may interest you. If you prefer that we not exchange your name with third parties, or if you wish to clarify or modify your communication preferences, please visit us at www.ReaderService.com/consumerschoice or write to us at Harlequin Reader Service Preference Service, P.O. Box 9062, Buffalo, NY 14269. Include your complete name and address.

SPECIAL EXCERPT FROM

HARLEQUIN®

Presents

*These two men have fought battles, waged wars and won.
But when their command—their legacy—is challenged by
the very women they desire the most...who will win?*

*Enjoy a sneak peek from HEIR TO A DESERT LEGACY,
the first tale in the potent new duet,*
SECRET HEIRS OF POWERFUL MEN,
by USA TODAY bestselling author Maisey Yates.

* * *

CHLOE stood up quickly, her chair tilting and knocking into the chair next to it, the sound loud in the cavernous room. "Sorry, sorry." She tried to straighten them, her cheeks burning, her heart pounding. "I have to go."

Sayid was faster than she was, his movements smoother. He crossed to her side of the table and caught her arm, drawing her to him, his expression dark. "Why are you running from me?" he asked, dipping his face lower, his expression fierce. "It's because you know, isn't it? You feel it?"

"Feel what?" she asked.

"This...need between us. How everything in me is demanding that I reach out and pull you hard against me. And how everything in you is begging me to."

"I don't know what you're talking about," she said.

"I think you do." He lowered his hand and traced her collarbone with his fingertip, sliding it slowly up the side of her neck, along her jawbone.

She shook her head, pulling away from him, from his touch. "No," she lied, "I don't."

She didn't understand what was happening with her body, why it was betraying her like this. She'd never felt this kind of wild, overpowering attraction for anyone in her life. But if she was going to, it would have been for a nice scientist who had a large collection of dry-erase pens and looked good in a lab coat.

It would not be for this rough, uncivilized man who believed he could move people around at his whim. This man who sought to control everything and everyone around him.

Unfortunately, her body hadn't asked her opinion on who she should find attractive. Because that was most definitely what this was. Scientific, irrefutable evidence of arousal.

* * *

Will Chloe give in to temptation? And will she ever be able to tame the wild warrior?

Find out in HEIR TO A DESERT LEGACY,
available March 19, 2013.

Copyright © 2013 by Maisey Yates

HPEXP0213-2

SPECIAL EXCERPT FROM

H) HARLEQUIN

~Presents~

*Paparazzi darling Caroline Sullivan is hiding a secret
behind her dazzling-yet-inscrutable smile, and no wonder
with ex-flame Russian businessman Roman Kazarov
back on the scene!*

*Read on for an excerpt from
A GAME WITH ONE WINNER by USA TODAY
bestselling author Lynn Raye Harris.*

* * *

"IT won't work," she said, her voice fiercer than she'd
thought she could manage at that moment.

Roman cocked an eyebrow. "What won't work, darling?"

A shiver chased down her spine. Once, he'd meant the
endearment, and she'd loved the way his Russian accent
slid across the words as he spoke. It was a caress before the
caress. Now, however, he did it to torment her. The words
were not a caress so much as a threat.

She turned and faced him head-on, tilting her head
back to look him in the eye. He stood with his hands in his
pockets, one corner of his beautiful mouth slanted up in a
mocking grin.

Evil, heartless. That was what he was now. He wasn't
here to do her any favors. He would not be merciful.

Especially if he discovered her secret.

"I know what you want and I plan to fight you," she said.

He laughed. "I welcome it. Because you will not win.

Not this time." His eyes narrowed as he studied her. "Funny, I would have never thought your father would step down and leave you in charge. I always thought they would carry him from his office someday."

A shard of cold fear dug into her belly, as it always did when someone mentioned her father these days. "People change," she said coolly.

"In my experience, they don't." His gaze slid over her again, and her skin prickled.

"Then you must not know many people," she said. "We all change. No one stays the same."

"No, we don't. But whatever the essence was, that remains. If one is heartless, for instance, one doesn't suddenly grow a heart."

Caroline's skin glowed with heat. She knew he was speaking of her, speaking of that night when she'd thrown his love back in his face. She wanted to deny it, wanted to tell him the truth, but what good would it do? None whatsoever.

* * *

Find out if Roman is seeking revenge or seduction in
A GAME WITH ONE WINNER, available March 19, 2013.

Copyright © 2013 by Lynn Raye Harris

Discover the first book in a red-hot
new duet from *USA TODAY*
bestselling author Carole Mortimer.

Buenos Aires Nights

*After dark with Argentina's most
infamous billionaires!*

World-renowned Argentinean Cesar Navarro has
sexy chef Grace Blake right where he wants her—in
his penthouse, at his command! She should be
off-limits, but Grace has tantalized his jaded palate,
and Cesar finds himself craving…

A TASTE OF THE
FORBIDDEN

Pick up a copy March 19, 2013,
wherever books are sold!

www.Harlequin.com

HP13136